The Secrets of the Immortal
Nicholas Flamel

BOOK 2

THE MAGICIAN

www.thealchemyst.co.uk

Josh Newman

Josh Newman was born on December 21st 1991, just seconds
after his twin sister, Sophie, with whom he has a very strong bond,
as is often the case with twins. Tall, athletic, with blond hair and
blue eyes, Josh is quite impulsive, hates snakes, rats, spiders and
scorpions and sometimes suffers from claustrophobia. Only a
few days ago, he survived a devastating battle of magic between
powerful immortals and escaped in the nick of time with two vital
pages of the ancient book of Abraham, the Codex. He is not at
all sure that he trusts Nicholas Flamel and he really dislikes what's
happened to Sophie since she's had her magical powers awakened.

Sophie Newman

Also blonde with blue eyes, Sophie Newman tends to be more
trusting and less quick to judge than her twin brother, Josh. She is
still learning how to control her new power of the Magic of the Air.
She has also been given the memories of the Witch of Endor, which
sometimes appear to be taking over. In amongst the confusion, she
is also aware that Josh seems strangely jealous of her magical powers.
Her magical aura is silver, with a scent of vanilla.

Nicholas Flamel

Nicholas Flamel was born in France in 1330 and is a powerful
alchemyst. With his wife, Perenelle, he discovered the secret of
immortality contained within the Book of Abraham, the Codex,
which also contains the spell which would allow the Dark Elders
to regain control of our world. The Flamels have spent centuries
protecting the Codex while searching for the twins of prophecy,
whose magical powers, once fully awakened, could banish the

Dark Elders forever. Flamel believes that Josh and Sophie are those twins and has escaped with them to Paris. His magical aura is green with a scent of peppermint.

Perenelle Flamel

Tall, elegant, with black hair and green eyes, the seventh daughter of a seventh daughter and over 600 years old, Perenelle Flamel is a powerful alchemyst and sorceress. Like her husband, Perry uses the spells in the Codex to become immortal. Without the book, which was stolen a few days previously by Dr John Dee, neither of the Flamels can renew their immortality and will soon begin to age rapidly. Imprisoned by Dee on the island of Alcatraz, Perry knows that she will need to use all her ingenuity to escape and rejoin Nicholas and the twins. Perry's aura is white, without a specific scent.

Dr. John Dee

Originally magician and advisor to the Tudor queen, Elizabeth I, Dr John Dee is an immortal, bound to serve the Dark Elders. Having once served as an apprentice to Nicholas Flamel, from whom he learned alchemy and other arcane secrets, Dee now has an abiding hatred for his former teacher. Over the centuries, he has tried several times to slay the Flamels and regain the Codex as commanded by his master. Now he has at last stolen the book but he knows it is useless without the final two pages which Josh tore out in the last seconds of the battle in San Francisco. His Dark Elder master is getting increasingly impatient. Dee's magical aura is yellow with a scent of brimstone.

Scatach

Also known as Scatty, The Warrior Maid or The Shadow, this slight,
athletic girl with spiky red hair appears to be about 17 years old but
has been in this world for millennia. She is both a Next Generation
Elder and a vampire. She has trained generations of warriors and
heroes of legend, she has sung in a punk rock band, she has defeated
monsters and servants of the Dark Elders time and time again.
She is an implacable foe while being capable of strong love and
friendship. Her magical aura is grey of unknown scent.

More information about the characters
in these books can be found at
http://j.mp/flamelcharacters

The Secrets of the Immortal
Nicholas Flamel

BOOK 2

THE MAGICIAN

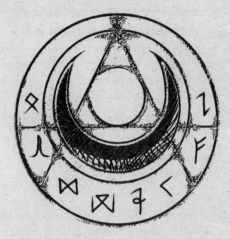

MICHAEL SCOTT

CORGI

THE MAGICIAN
A CORGI BOOK 978 0552 56253 9

Published in the US by Delacorte Press,
an imprint of Random House Children's Books
a division of Random House, Inc

First published in Great Britain by Doubleday,
an imprint of Random House Children's Books

This Corgi edition published 2010

1 3 5 7 9 10 8 6 4 2

Copyright © Michael Scott, 2008
Cover artwork © Michael Wagner

The Random House Group Limited supports the Forest Stewardship Council (FSC®),
the leading international forest certification organization. Our books carrying the FSC label
are printed on FSC®-certified paper. FSC is the only forest certification scheme endorsed
by the leading environmental organizations, including Greenpeace. Our paper procurement
policy can be found at www.randomhouse.co.uk/environment.

MIX
Paper from
responsible sources
FSC
www.fsc.org
FSC® C016897

Set in Galliard

Corgi Books are published by Random House Children's Books,
61–63 Uxbridge Road, London W5 5SA

www.kidsatrandomhouse.co.uk
www.randomhouse.co.uk

Addresses for companies within The Random House Group Limited can be found
at: www.randomhouse.co.uk/offices.htm

THE RANDOM HOUSE GROUP Limited Reg. No. 954009
A CIP catalogue record for this book is available from the British Library.

Printed and bound by CPI Group (UK) Ltd, Croydon, CR0 4YY

For Courtney and Piers
Hoc opus, hic labor est

I am dying.

Perenelle, too, is dying.

The spell that has kept us alive these six hundred years is fading, and now we age a year for every day that passes. I need the Codex, the Book of Abraham the Mage, to re-create the immortality spell; without it, we have less than a month to live.

But much can be achieved in a month.

Dee and his dark masters have my dear Perenelle prisoner, they have finally secured the Book, and they know that Perenelle and I cannot survive for much longer.

But they cannot be resting easy.

They do not have the complete Book yet. We still have the final two pages, and by now they must know that Sophie and Josh Newman are the twins described in that ancient text: twins with auras of silver and gold, a brother and sister with the power to either save the world . . . or destroy it. The girl's powers have been Awakened and her training begun in the elemental magics, though, sadly, the boy's have not.

We are now in Paris, the city of my birth, the city where I first discovered the Codex and began the long quest to translate it. That journey ultimately led me to discover the existence of the Elder Race and revealed the mystery of the philosopher's stone and finally the secret of immortality. I love this city. It holds many secrets and is home to more than one human immortal and ancient Elder. Here, I will find a way to Awaken Josh's powers and continue Sophie's education.

I must.

For their sakes—and for the continuance of the human race.

From the Day Booke of Nicholas Flamel, Alchemyst
Writ this day, Saturday, 2nd June,
in Paris, the city of my youth

CHAPTER ONE

$\mathcal{T}$he charity auction hadn't started until well after midnight, when the gala dinner had ended. It was almost four in the morning and the auction was only now drawing to a close. A digital display behind the celebrity auctioneer—an actor who had played James Bond on-screen for many years—showed the running total at more than one million euro.

"Lot number two hundred and ten: a pair of early-nineteenth-century Japanese Kabuki masks."

A ripple of excitement ran through the crowded room. Inlaid with chips of solid jade, the Kabuki masks were the highlight of the auction and were expected to fetch in excess of half a million euro.

At the back of the room the tall, thin man with the fuzz of close-cropped snow white hair was prepared to pay twice that.

Niccolò Machiavelli stood apart from the rest of the

crowd, arms lightly folded across his chest, careful not to wrinkle his Savile Row–tailored black silk tuxedo. Stone gray eyes swept over the other bidders, analyzing and assessing them. There were really only five others he needed to look out for: two private collectors like himself, a minor European royal, a once-famous American movie actor and a Canadian antiques dealer. The remainder of the audience were tired, had spent their budget or were unwilling to bid on the vaguely disturbing-looking masks.

Machiavelli loved all types of masks. He had been collecting them for a very long time, and he wanted this particular pair to complete his collection of Japanese theater costumes. These masks had last come up for sale in 1898 in Vienna, and he had then been outbid by a Romanov prince. Machiavelli had patiently bided his time; the masks would come back on the market again when the Prince and his descendents died. Machiavelli knew he would still be around to buy them; it was one of the many advantages of being immortal.

"Shall we start the bidding at one hundred thousand euro?"

Machiavelli looked up, caught the auctioneer's attention and nodded.

The auctioneer had been expecting his bid and nodded in return. "I am bid one hundred thousand euro by Monsieur Machiavelli. Always one of this charity's most generous supporters and sponsors."

A smattering of applause ran around the room, and several people turned to look at him and raise their glasses. Niccolò acknowledged them with a polite smile.

"Do I have one hundred and ten?" the auctioneer asked.

One of the private collectors raised his hand slightly.

"One-twenty?" The auctioneer looked back to Machiavelli, who immediately nodded.

Within the next three minutes, a flurry of bids brought the price up to two hundred and fifty thousand euro. There were only three serious bidders left: Machiavelli, the American actor and the Canadian.

Machiavelli's thin lips twisted into a rare smile; his patience was about to be rewarded, and finally the masks would be his. Then the smile faded as he felt the cell phone in his back pocket buzz silently. For an instant he was tempted to ignore it; he'd given his staff strict instructions that he was not to be disturbed unless it was absolutely critical. He also knew they were so terrified of him that they would not phone unless it was an emergency. Reaching into his pocket, he pulled out the ultraslim phone and glanced down.

A picture of a sword pulsed gently on the large LCD screen.

Machiavelli's smile vanished. In that second he knew he was not going to be able to buy the Kabuki masks this century. Turning on his heel, he strode out of the room and pressed the phone to his ear. Behind him, he could hear the auctioneer's hammer hit the lectern "Sold. For two hundred and sixty thousand euro . . ."

"I'm here," Machiavelli said, reverting to the Italian of his youth.

The line crackled and an English-accented voice responded in the same language, using a dialect that had not been heard in Europe for more than four hundred years. "I need your help."

The man on the other end of the line didn't identify himself, nor did he need to; Machiavelli knew it was the immortal magician and necromancer Dr. John Dee, one of the most powerful and dangerous men in the world.

Niccolò Machiavelli strode out of the small hotel into the broad cobbled square of the Place du Tertre and stopped to breathe in the chill night air. "What can I do for you?" he asked cautiously. He detested Dee and knew the feeling was mutual, but they both served the Dark Elders, and that meant they had been forced to work together down through the centuries. Machiavelli was also slightly envious that Dee was younger than he—and looked it. Machiavelli had been born in Florence in 1469, which made him fifty-eight years older than the English Magician. History recorded that he had *died* in the same year that Dee had been born, 1527.

"Flamel is back in Paris."

Machiavelli straightened. "When?"

"Just now. He got there through a leygate. I've no idea where it comes out. He's got Scathach with him. . . ."

Machiavelli's lips curled into an ugly grimace. The last time he'd encountered the Warrior, she'd pushed him through a door. It had been closed at the time, and he'd spent weeks picking splinters from his chest and shoulders.

"There are two humani children with him. Americans," Dee said, his voice echoing and fading on the transatlantic line. "Twins," he added.

"Say again?" Machiavelli asked.

"Twins," Dee added, "with pure gold and silver auras. You know what that means," he snapped.

"Yes," Machiavelli muttered. It meant trouble. Then the tiniest of smiles curled his thin lips. It could also mean opportunity.

Static crackled and then Dee's voice continued. "The girl's powers were Awakened by Hekate before the Goddess and her Shadowrealm were destroyed."

"Untrained, the girl is no threat," Machiavelli murmured, quickly assessing the situation. He took a breath and added, "Except perhaps to herself and those around her."

"Flamel took the girl to Ojai. There, the Witch of Endor instructed her in the Magic of Air."

"No doubt you tried to stop them?" There was a hint of amusement in Machiavelli's voice.

"Tried. And failed," Dee admitted bitterly. "The girl has some knowledge but is without skill."

"What do you want me to do?" Machiavelli asked carefully, although he already had a very good idea.

"Find Flamel and the twins," Dee demanded. "Capture them. Kill Scathach if you can. I'm just leaving Ojai. But it's going to take me fourteen or fifteen hours to get to Paris."

"What happened to the leygate?" Machiavelli wondered aloud. If a leygate connected Ojai and Paris, then why didn't Dee . . . ?

"Destroyed by the Witch of Endor," Dee raged, "and she nearly killed me, too. I was lucky to escape with a few cuts and scratches," he added, and then ended the call without saying good-bye.

Niccolò Machiavelli closed his phone carefully and tapped it against his bottom lip. Somehow he doubted that Dee had been lucky—if the Witch of Endor had wanted him dead, then even the legendary Dr. Dee would not have escaped. Machiavelli turned and walked across the square to where his driver was patiently waiting with the car. If Flamel, Scathach and the American twins had come to Paris via a leygate, then there were only a few places in the city where they could have emerged. It should be relatively easy to find and capture them.

And if he could capture them tonight, then he would have plenty of time to work on them before Dee arrived.

Machiavelli smiled; he'd only need a few hours, and in that time they would tell him everything they knew. Half a millennium on this earth had taught him how to be very persuasive indeed.

CHAPTER TWO

*J*osh Newman reached out and pressed the palm of his right hand against the cold stone wall to steady himself.

What had just happened?

One moment he'd been standing in the Witch of Endor's shop in Ojai, California. His sister, Sophie, Scathach and the man he now knew to be Nicholas Flamel had been *in* the mirror looking out at him. And the next thing he knew, Sophie had stepped out of the glass, taken his hand and pulled him *through* it. He'd squeezed his eyes shut and felt something icy touch his skin and raise the small hairs on the back of his neck. When he'd opened his eyes again, he was standing in what looked like a tiny storage room. Pots of paint, stacked ladders, broken pieces of pottery and bundled paint-spattered cloths were piled around a large, rather ordinary-looking grimy mirror fixed to the stone wall. A single low-wattage lightbulb shed a dim yellow glow over the room. "What happened?" he asked, his voice cracking. He swallowed hard and tried again. "What happened? Where are we?"

"We're in Paris," Nicholas Flamel said delightedly, rubbing his dusty hands against his black jeans. "The city of my birth."

"Paris?" Josh whispered. He was going to say "Impossible," but he was beginning to understand that that word had no meaning anymore. "How?" he asked aloud. "Sophie?" He looked to his twin sister, but she had pressed her ear against the room's only door and was listening intently. She waved him away. He turned to Scathach, but the red-haired warrior just shook her head, both hands covering her mouth. She looked as if she was about to throw up. Josh finally turned to the legendary Alchemyst, Nicholas Flamel. "How did we get here?" he asked.

"This planet is crisscrossed with invisible lines of power sometimes called ley lines or cursus," Flamel explained. He crossed his index fingers. "Where two or more lines intersect a gateway exists. Gates are incredibly rare now, but in ancient times the Elder Race used them to travel from one side of the world to the other in an instant—just as we did. The Witch opened the leygate in Ojai and we ended up here, in Paris." He made it sound so matter-of-fact.

"Leygates: I hate them," Scatty mumbled. In the gloomy light, her pale, freckled skin looked green. "You ever been seasick?" she asked.

Josh shook his head. "Never."

Sophie looked up from her spot leaning against the door.

"Liar! He gets seasick in a swimming pool." She grinned, then pressed the side of her face back against the cool wood.

"Seasick," Scatty mumbled. "That's exactly what it feels like. Only worse."

Sophie turned her head again to look at the Alchemyst. "Do you have any idea where we are in Paris?"

"Someplace old, I'm guessing," Flamel said, joining her at the door. He put the side of his head back against the door and listened.

Sophie stepped back. "I'm not so sure," she said hesitantly.

"Why not?" Josh asked. He glanced around the small untidy room. It certainly looked as though it was part of an old building.

Sophie shook her head. "I don't know . . . it just doesn't feel that old." She reached out and touched the wall with the palm of her hand, then immediately jerked it back again.

"What's wrong?" Josh whispered.

Sophie placed her hand against the wall again. "I can hear voices, songs and what sounds like organ music."

Josh shrugged. "I can't hear anything." He stopped, abruptly conscious of the huge difference between himself and his twin. Sophie's magical potential had been Awakened by Hekate, and she was now hypersensitive to sights and sounds, smells, touch and taste.

"I can." Sophie lifted her hand from the stone wall and the sounds in her head faded.

"You're hearing ghost sounds," Flamel explained. "They're

11

just noises absorbed by the building, recorded into the very structure itself."

"This is a church," Sophie said decisively, then frowned. "It's a new church . . . modern, late nineteenth century, early twentieth. But it's built on a much, much older site."

Flamel paused at the wooden door and looked over his shoulder. In the dim overhead light, his features were suddenly sharp and angular, disturbingly skull-like, his eyes completely in shadow. "There are many churches in Paris," he said, "though there is only one, I believe, which matches that description." He reached for the door handle.

"Hang on a second," Josh said quickly. "Don't you think there'll be some sort of alarm?"

"Oh, I doubt it," Nicholas said confidently. "Who would put an alarm on a storeroom in a church?" he asked, jerking the door open.

Immediately an alarm pealed through the air, the sound echoing and reechoing off the flagstones and walls. Red security lights strobed and flashed.

Scatty sighed and muttered something in an ancient Celtic language. "Didn't you tell me once to wait before moving, to look before stepping and to observe everything?" she demanded.

Nicholas shook his head and sighed at the stupid mistake. "Getting old, I guess," he said in the same language. But there was no time for apologies. "Let's go!" he shouted over the shrieking alarm, and darted down the corridor. Sophie and Josh followed close behind, while Scatty took up the rear, moving slowly and grumbling with every step.

The door opened onto a short narrow stone corridor that led to another wooden door. Without pausing, Flamel pushed through the second door—and immediately a new alarm began to shriek. He turned left into a huge open space that smelled of old incense, floor polish and wax. Banks of lit candles shed a golden yellow light over walls and floor and, combined with the security lights, revealed a pair of enormous doors with the word EXIT above them. Flamel raced toward it, his footsteps echoing.

"Don't touch—" Josh began, but Nicholas Flamel grasped the door handles and pulled hard.

A third alarm—much louder than the others—went off, and a red light above the door began to wink on and off.

"Told you not to touch," Josh muttered.

"I can't understand it—why is it not open?" Flamel asked, shouting to be heard above the din. "This church is always open." He turned and looked around. "Where is everyone? What time is it?" he asked, as a thought struck him.

"How long does it take to travel from one place to another through the leygate?" Sophie asked.

"It's instantaneous."

"And you're sure we're in Paris, France?"

"Positive."

Sophie looked at her watch and did a quick calculation. "Paris is nine hours ahead of Ojai?" she asked.

Flamel nodded, suddenly understanding.

"It's about four o'clock in the morning; that's why the church is closed," Sophie said.

"The police will be on their way," Scatty said glumly. She

13

reached for her nunchaku. "I hate fighting when I'm not feeling well," she muttered.

"What do we do now?" Josh demanded, panic rising in his voice.

"I could try and blast the doors apart with wind," Sophie suggested hesitantly. She wasn't sure she had the energy to raise the wind again so soon. She had used her new magical powers to battle the undead in Ojai, but the effort had completely exhausted her.

"I forbid it," Flamel shouted, his face painted in shades of crimson and shadow. He turned and pointed across rows of wooden pews toward an ornate altar picked out in a tracery of white marble. Candlelight hinted at an intricate mosaic in glittering blues and golds in the dome over the altar. "This is a national monument; I'll not let you destroy it."

"Where are we?" the twins asked together, looking around the building. Now that their eyes had adjusted to the gloom, they realized that the building was huge. They could distinguish columns soaring high into the shadows overhead and were able to make out the shapes of small side altars, statues in nooks and countless banks of candles.

"This," Flamel announced proudly, "is the church of Sacré-Coeur."

Sitting in the back of his limousine, Niccolò Machiavelli tapped coordinates into his laptop and watched a high-resolution map of Paris wink into existence on the screen. Paris was an incredibly ancient city. The first settlement went

14

back more than two thousand years, though there had been humans living on the island in the Seine for generations before that. And like many of the earth's oldest cities, it had been sited where groups of ley lines met.

Machiavelli hit a keystroke, which laid down a complicated pattern of ley lines over the map of the city. He was looking for a line that connected with the United States. He finally managed to reduce the number of possibilities to six. With a perfectly manicured fingernail, he traced two lines that directly linked the West Coast of America to Paris. One finished at the great cathedral of Notre Dame, the other in the more modern but equally famous Sacré-Coeur basilica in Montmartre.

But which one?

Suddenly, the Parisian night was broken by a series of howling alarms. Machiavelli hit the control for the electric window and the darkened glass whispered down. Cool night air swirled into the car. In the distance, rising high above the rooftops on the opposite side of the Place du Tertre, was Sacré-Coeur. The imposing domed building was always lit up at night in stark white light. Tonight, however, red alarm lights pulsed around the building

That one. Machiavelli's smile was terrifying. He called up a program on the laptop and waited while the hard drive spun.

Enter password.

His fingers flew over the keyboard as he typed: *Discorsi sopra la prima deca di Tito Livio*. No one was going to break that password. It wasn't one of his better-known books.

A rather ordinary-looking text document appeared, written in a combination of Latin, Greek and Italian. Once, magicians had had to keep their spells and incantations in handwritten books called grimoires, but Machiavelli had always used the latest technology. He preferred to keep his spells on his hard drive. Now he just needed a little something to keep Flamel and his friends busy while he gathered his forces.

Josh's head snapped up. "I hear police sirens."

"There are twelve police cars headed this way," Sophie said, her head tilted to one side, eyes closed as she listened intently.

"Twelve? How can you tell?"

Sophie looked at her twin. "I can distinguish the different locations of the sirens."

"You can tell them apart?" he asked. He found himself wondering, yet again, at the full extent of his sister's senses.

"Each one," she said.

"We must not be captured by the police," Flamel interjected sharply. "We've neither passports nor alibis. We've got to get out of here!"

"How?" the twins asked simultaneously.

Flamel shook his head. "There has to be another entrance . . . ," he began, and then stopped, nostrils flaring.

Josh watched uneasily as both Sophie and Scatty suddenly reacted to something he could not smell. "What . . . what is it?" he demanded, and then he suddenly caught the faintest whiff of something musky and rank. It was the sort of smell he'd come to associate with a zoo.

"Trouble," Scathach said grimly, putting away her nunchaku and drawing her swords. "Big trouble."

CHAPTER THREE

"*W*hat?" Josh demanded, looking around. The smell was stronger now, stale and bitter, and almost familiar. . . .

"Snake," Sophie said, breathing deeply. "It's a snake."

Josh felt his stomach lurch. Snake. Why did it have to be snakes? He was terrified of snakes—though he'd never admit it to anyone, especially not his sister. "Snakes . . . ," he began, but his voice sounded high-pitched and strangled. He coughed and tried again. "Where?" he asked, looking around desperately, imagining them everywhere, sliding out from under the pews, curling down the pillars, dropping down from the light fixtures.

Sophie shook her head and frowned. "I don't hear any. . . . I'm just . . . smelling them." Her nostrils flared as she drew a deep breath. "No, there's just one. . . ."

"Oh, you're smelling a snake, all right . . . but one that

18

walks on two legs," Scatty snapped. "You're smelling the rank odor of Niccolò Machiavelli."

Flamel knelt on the floor in front of the massive main doors and ran his hands over the locks. Wisps of green smoke curled from his fingers. "Machiavelli!" he spat. "Dee didn't waste any time contacting his allies, I see."

"You can tell who it is from the smell?" Josh asked, still surprised and a little confused.

"Every person has a distinctive magical odor," Scatty explained, standing with her back to the Alchemyst, protecting him. "You two smell of vanilla ice cream and oranges, Nicholas smells of mint . . ."

"And Dee smelled of rotten eggs . . . ," Sophie added.

"Sulfur," Josh said.

"Which was once known as brimstone," Scatty said. "Very appropriate for Dr. Dee." Her head was moving from side to side as she paid particular attention to the deep shadows behind the statues. "Well, Machiavelli smells of snakes. Appropriate too."

"Who is he?" Josh asked. He felt as if he should know the name, almost as if he'd heard it before. "A friends of Dee's?"

"Machiavelli is an immortal allied to the Dark Elders," Scatty explained, "and no friend to Dee, though they are on the same side. Machiavelli is older than the Magician, infinitely more dangerous and certainly more cunning. I should have killed him when I had the chance," she said bitterly. "For the past five hundred years he has been at the heart of European politics, the puppet master working in the shadows. The last

19

I heard, he had been appointed the head of the DGSE, the Direction Générale de la Sécurité Extérieure."

"Is that like a bank?" Josh asked.

Scatty's lips curled in a tiny smile that exposed her over-long vampire incisors. "It means the General Board of External Security. It is the French secret service."

"The secret service! Oh, that's just great," Josh said sarcastically.

"The smell is getting stronger," Sophie said, her Awakened senses acutely aware of the odor. Concentrating hard, she allowed a little of her power to trickle into her aura, which bloomed into a ghostly shadow around her. Crackles of lustrous silver threads sparkled in her blond hair, and her eyes turned to reflective silver coins.

Almost unconsciously, Josh stepped away from his sister. He'd seen her like this before, and she'd scared him.

"That means he's close by. He's working some magic," Scatty said. "Nicholas . . . ?"

"I just need another minute." Flamel's fingertips glowed emerald green, smoking as they traced a pattern around the lock. A solid click sounded from within, but when the Alchemyst tried the handle, the door didn't move. "Maybe more than a minute."

"Too late," Josh whispered, raising an arm and pointing. "Something's here."

At the opposite end of the great basilica, the banks of candles had gone out. It was as if an unfelt breeze was sweeping down the aisles, snuffing out the flickering circular night-lights and thicker candles as it passed, leaving curls of gray-white smoke hanging on the air. Abruptly, the smell of candle wax grew stronger, much, much stronger, almost obliterating the odor of serpent.

"I can't see anything . . . ," Josh began.

"It's here!" Sophie shouted.

The creature that flowed up off the cold flagstones was only marginally human. Standing taller than a man, broad and grotesque, it was a gelatinous white shape with only the vaguest hint of a head set directly onto broad shoulders. There were no visible features. As they watched, two huge arms separated from the trunk of the body with a squelch and grew handlike shapes.

"Golem!" Sophie shouted in horror. "A wax Golem!" She flung out her hand and her aura blazed. Ice-cold wind surged from her fingertips to batter the creature, but the white waxy skin simply rippled and flowed beneath the breeze.

"Protect Nicholas!" Scathach commanded, darting forward, her matched swords flickering out, biting into the creature, but without any effect. The soft wax trapped her swords, and it took all her strength to pull them free. She struck again and chips of wax sprayed into the air. The creature struck at her, and she had to abandon her grip on her swords as she danced backward to avoid the crushing blow. A bulbous fist thundered into the floor at her feet, spattering globules of white wax in every direction.

Josh grabbed one of the folding wooden chairs stacked outside the gift shop at the back of the church. Holding it by two legs, he slammed it into the creature's chest . . . where it stuck fast. As the wax shape turned toward Josh, the chair was wrenched from his hands. He grabbed another chair, darted around behind the creature and slammed the chair down. It shattered across the creature's shoulders, leaving scores of splinters protruding like bizarre porcupine spines.

Sophie froze. She desperately tried to recall some of the secrets of Air magic that the Witch of Endor had taught her only a few hours ago. The Witch said it was the most powerful of all magics—and Sophie had seen what it had done to the undead army of long-deceased humans and beasts Dee had raised in Ojai. But she had no idea what would work against the wax monster before her. She knew how to raise a miniature tornado, but she couldn't risk calling it up in the confined space of the basilica.

"Nicholas!" Scatty called. With her swords stuck in the creature, the Warrior was using her nunchaku—two lengths of wood attached by a short chain—to batter at the Golem. They left deep indentations in its skin but otherwise seemed to have no effect. She delivered one particularly fierce blow that embedded the polished wood in the creature's side. Wax flowed around the nunchaku, trapping them. When the creature twisted toward Josh, the weapon was ripped from the Warrior's hands, sending her spinning across the room.

A hand that was only thumb and fused fingers, like a giant mitten, caught Josh's shoulder and squeezed. The pain was incredible and drove the boy to his knees.

"Josh!" Sophie screamed, the sound echoing in the huge church.

Josh tried to pull the hand away, but the wax was too slippery and his fingers sank into the white goo. Warm wax began to flow off the creature's hand, then curl and wrap around his shoulder and roll down onto his chest, constricting his breathing.

"Josh, duck!"

Sophie grabbed a wooden chair and swung it through the air. It whistled over her brother's head, the wind ruffling his hair, and she brought it down hard—edge-first—on the thick wax arm where the elbow should have been. The chair stuck halfway through, but the movement distracted the creature and it abandoned Josh, leaving him bruised and coated in a layer of candle wax. From his place kneeling on the ground, Josh watched in horror as two gelatinous hands reached for his twin's throat.

Terrified, Sophie screamed.

Josh watched as his sister's eyes flickered, the blue replaced with silver, and then her aura blazed incandescent the moment the Golem's paws came close to her skin. Immediately, its waxy hands began to run liquid and spatter to the floor. Sophie stretched out her own hand, fingers splayed, and pressed it against the Golem's chest, where it sank, sizzling and hissing, into the mass of wax.

Josh crouched on the ground, close to Flamel, his hands thrown up to protect his eyes from the brilliant silver light. He saw his sister step closer to the creature, her aura now painfully bright, arms spread wide, an invisible unfelt heat melting the creature, reducing the wax to liquid. Scathach's swords and nunchaku clattered to the stone floor, followed, seconds later, by the remains of the wooden chair.

Sophie's aura flickered and Josh was on his feet and by her

side to catch her as she swayed. "I feel dizzy," she said thickly as she slumped into his arms. She was barely conscious, and she felt ice cold, the usually sweet vanilla scent of her aura now sour and bitter.

Scatty swooped in to gather up her weapons from the pile of semiliquid wax that now resembled a half-melted snowman. She fastidiously wiped her blades clean before she slipped them back into the sheaths she wore on her back. Picking curls of white wax off her nunchaku, she slipped them back into their holster on her belt; then she turned to Sophie. "You saved us," she said gravely. "That's a debt I'll not forget."

"Got it," Flamel said suddenly. He stood back, and Sophie, Josh and Scathach watched as curls of green smoke seeped from the lock. The Alchemyst pushed the door and it clicked open, cool night air rushing in, dispelling the cloying odor of melted wax.

"We could have done with a little help, you know," Scatty grumbled.

Flamel grinned and wiped his fingers on his jeans, leaving traces of green light on the cloth. "I knew you had it well under control," he said, stepping out of the basilica. Scathach and the twins followed.

The sounds of police sirens were louder now, but the area directly in front of the church was empty. Sacré-Coeur was set on a hill, one of the highest points in Paris, and from where they stood, they had a view of the entire city. Nicholas Flamel's face lit up with delight. "Home!"

"What is it with European magicians and Golems?" Scatty

asked, following him. "First Dee and now Machiavelli. Have they no imaginations?"

Flamel looked surprised. "That wasn't a Golem. Golems need to have a spell on their body to animate them."

Scatty nodded. She knew that, of course. "What, then—?"

"That was a tulpa."

Scatty's bright green eyes widened in surprise. "A tulpa! Is Machiavelli that powerful, then?"

"Obviously."

"What's a tulpa?" Josh asked Flamel, but it was his sister who answered, and Josh was once again reminded of the huge gulf that had opened up between them the moment her powers had been Awakened.

"A creature created and animated entirely by the power of the imagination," Sophie explained casually.

"Precisely," Nicholas Flamel said, breathing deeply. "Machiavelli knew there would be wax in the church. So he brought it to life."

"But surely he knew it would not be able to stop us?" Scatty asked.

Nicholas walked out from under the central arch that framed the front of the basilica and stood at the edge of the first of the two hundred and twenty-one steps that led down to the street far below. "Oh, he knew it wouldn't stop us," he said patiently. "He just wanted to slow us down, to keep us here until he arrived." He pointed.

Far below, the narrow streets of Montmartre had come alive with the sounds and lights of a fleet of French police cars. Dozens of uniformed gendarmes had gathered at the

25

bottom of the steps, with more arriving from the narrow side streets to form a cordon around the building. Surprisingly, none of them had started climbing.

Flamel, Scatty and the twins ignored the police. They were watching the tall thin white-haired man in the elegant tuxedo slowly make his way up the steps toward them. He stopped when he saw them emerge from the basilica, leaned on a low metal railing and raised his right hand in a lazy salute.

"Let me guess," Josh said, "that must be Niccolò Machiavelli."

"The most dangerous immortal in Europe," the Alchemyst said grimly. "Trust me: this man makes Dee look like an amateur."

CHAPTER FOUR

"*W*elcome back to Paris, Alchemyst."

Sophie and Josh jumped. Machiavelli was still far away to be heard so clearly. Strangely, his voice seemed to be coming from somewhere behind them, and both turned to look, but there were only two stained green metal statues over the three arches in front of the church: a woman on a horse to their right, her raised arm holding a sword, and a man holding a scepter on their left.

"I've been waiting for you." The voice seemed to be coming from the statue of the man.

"It's a cheap trick," Scatty said dismissively, picking strips of wax off the front of her steel-toed combat boots. "It's nothing more than ventriloquism."

Sophie smiled sheepishly. "I thought the statue was talking," she admitted, embarrassed.

Josh started to laugh at his sister and then immediately reconsidered. "I guess I wouldn't be surprised if it did."

"The good Dr. Dee sends his regards." Machiavelli's voice continued to hang in the air around them.

"So he survived Ojai, then," Nicholas said conversationally, not raising his voice. Standing tall and straight, he casually put both hands behind his back and glanced sidelong at Scatty. Then the fingers of his right hand started dancing against the palm and fingers of his left.

Scatty drew the twins away from Nicholas and slowly retreated under the shadowed arches. Standing between them, she put her arms around their shoulders—both their auras crackling silver and gold with her touch—and drew their heads together.

"Machiavelli. The master of lies." Scatty's whisper was the merest breath against their ears. "He must not hear us."

"I cannot say I am pleased to see you, Signor Machiavelli. Or is it Monsieur Machiavelli in this age?" the Alchemyst said quietly, leaning against the balustrade, looking down the white steps to where Machiavelli was still small in the distance.

"This century, I am French," Machiavelli replied, his voice clearly audible. "I love Paris. It is my favorite city in Europe—after Florence, of course."

While Nicholas talked to Machiavelli, he kept his hands behind his back, out of sight of the other immortal. His fingers were moving in an intricate series of taps and beats.

"Is he working a spell?" Sophie breathed, watching his hands.

28

"No, he's talking to me," Scatty said.

"How?" Josh whispered. "Magic? Telepathy?"

"ASL: American Sign Language."

The twins glanced quickly at one another. "American Sign Language?" Josh asked. "He knows sign language? How?"

"You seem to keep forgetting that he's lived a long time," Scathach said with a grin that showed her vampire teeth. "And he did help create French sign language in the eighteenth century," she added casually.

"What's he saying?" Sophie asked impatiently. Nowhere in the witch's memory could she find the knowledge necessary to translate the older man's gestures.

Scathach frowned, her lips moving as she spelled out a word. "Sophie . . . *brouillard* . . . fog," she translated. She shook her head. "Sophie, he's asking you for fog. That doesn't make sense."

"It does to me," Sophie said as a dozen images of fog, clouds and smoke flashed through her brain.

Niccolò Machiavelli paused on the steps and drew in a deep breath. "My people have the entire area surrounded," he said, moving slowly toward the Alchemyst. He was slightly out of breath and his heart was hammering; he really needed to get back to the gym.

Creating the wax tulpa had exhausted him. He had never made one so big before, and never from the back of a car roaring through Montmartre's narrow and winding streets. It wasn't an elegant solution, but all he had needed to do was to keep Flamel and his companions trapped in the church until he got there, and he had succeeded. Now the church was surrounded, more gendarmes were en route and he had called in all available agents. As the head of the DGSE, his powers were almost limitless, and he'd issued an order to impose a press blackout. He prided himself on having complete control of his emotions, but he had to admit that right now he was feeling quite excited: soon he would have Nicholas Flamel, Scathach and the children in custody. He would have triumphed where Dee had failed.

Later he would have someone in his department leak a story to the press that thieves had been apprehended breaking into the national monument. Close to dawn—just in time for the early-morning news—a second report would be leaked, revealing how the desperate prisoners had overpowered their guards and escaped on their way to the police station. They would never be seen again.

"I have you now, Nicholas Flamel."

Flamel came to stand at the edge of the steps and pushed his hands into the back pockets of his worn black jeans. "I believe the last time you made that statement, you were just about to break into my tomb."

Machiavelli stopped in shock. "How do you know that?"

More than three hundred years ago, in the dead of night, Machiavelli had cracked open Nicholas and Perenelle's tomb, looking for proof that the Alchemyst and his wife were indeed dead and trying to determine whether they had been buried with the Book of Abraham the Mage. The Italian hadn't been entirely surprised to find that both coffins were filled with stones.

"Perry and I were right there behind you, standing in the shadows, close enough to touch you when you lifted the top off our tomb. I knew someone would come . . . I just never imagined it would be you. I'll admit I was disappointed, Niccolò," he added.

The white-haired man continued up the steps to Sacré-Coeur. "You always thought I was a better person than I was, Nicholas."

"I believe there is good in everyone," Flamel whispered, "even you."

"Not me, Alchemyst, not anymore, and not for a very long time." Machiavelli stopped and indicated the police and heavily armed black-clad French special forces gathering at the bottom of the steps. "Come now. Surrender. No harm will come to you."

"I cannot tell you how many people have said that to me," Nicholas said sadly. "And they were always lying," he added.

Machiavelli's voice hardened. "You can deal with me or with Dr. Dee. And you know the English Magician never had any patience."

"There is one other option," Flamel said with a shrug. His thin lips curled in a smile. "I could deal with neither of you." He half turned, but when he looked back at Machiavelli, the expression on the Alchemyst's face made the immortal Italian take a step back in shock. For an instant something ancient and implacable shone through Flamel's pale eyes, which flickered a brilliant emerald green. Now it was Flamel's voice that dropped to a whisper, still clearly audible to Machiavelli. "It would be better if you and I were never to meet again."

Machiavelli attempted a laugh, but it came out sounding shaky. "That sounds like a threat . . . and believe me, you are in no position to issue threats."

"Not a threat," Flamel said, and stepped back from the top steps. "A promise."

The cool damp Parisian night air was abruptly touched with the rich odor of vanilla, and Niccolò Machiavelli knew then that something was very wrong.

Standing straight, eyes closed, arms at her sides, palms facing outward, Sophie Newman took a deep breath, attempting to calm her thundering heart and allow her mind to wander. When the Witch of Endor had wrapped her like a mummy with bandages of solidified air, she had imparted thousands of years of knowledge into the girl in a matter of heartbeats. Sophie had imagined she'd felt her head swelling as her brain filled with the Witch's memories. Since then, her skull had throbbed with a headache, the base of her neck felt stiff and tight and there was a dull ache behind her eyes. Two days ago she had been an ordinary American teenager, her head filled with normal everyday things: homework and school projects, the latest songs and videos, boys she liked, cell phone numbers and Web addresses, blogs and urls.

Now she knew things that no person should ever know.

Sophie Newman possessed the Witch of Endor's memories; she knew all that the Witch had seen, everything she had done over millennia. It was all a jumble: a mixture of thoughts and wishes, observations, fears and desires, a confusing mess of bizarre sights, terrifying images and incomprehensible sounds. It was as if a thousand movies had been mixed up and edited together. And scattered throughout the tangle of memories were countless incidences when the Witch had actually used her special power, the Magic of Air. All Sophie had to do was find a time when the Witch had used fog.

But when and where and how to find it?

Ignoring Flamel's voice calling down to Machiavelli, blanking out the sour smell of her brother's fear and the jingle of Scathach's swords, Sophie concentrated her thoughts on mist and fog.

San Francisco was often wrapped in fog, and she'd seen the Golden Gate Bridge rising out of a thick layer of cloud. And only last fall, when the family had been in St. Paul's Cathedral in Boston, they'd stepped out onto Tremont Street to find that a damp fog had completely obscured the Common. Other memories began to intrude: mist in Glasgow; swirling damp fog in Vienna; thick foul-smelling yellow smog in London.

Sophie frowned; *she* had never been to Glasgow, Vienna or London. But the Witch had . . . and these were the Witch of Endor's memories.

Images, thoughts and memories—like the strands of fog she was seeing in her head—shifted and twisted. And then they suddenly cleared. Sophie clearly remembered standing alongside a figure dressed in the formal clothing of the nineteenth century. She could see him in her mind's eye, a man with a long nose and a high forehead topped with graying curly hair. He was sitting at a high desk, a thick sheaf of cream-colored paper before him, dipping a simple pen into a brimming inkwell. It took her a moment to realize that this was not one of her own memories, nor was it something she had seen on TV or in a movie. She was *remembering* something the Witch of Endor had done and seen. As she turned to look closely at the figure, the Witch's memories flooded her: the man was a famous English writer and was just about to begin work on a new book. The writer glanced up and smiled at her; then his lips moved, but there was no sound. Leaning over his shoulder, she saw him write the words *Fog everywhere. Fog up the river. Fog down the river* in an elegant curling script. Outside the writer's study window, fog, thick and opaque, rolled like smoke against the dirty glass, blotting out the background in an impenetrable blanket.

And beneath the portico of Sacré-Coeur in Paris, the air turned chill and moist, rich with the odor of vanilla ice cream. A trickle of white dribbled from each of Sophie's outstretched fingers. The wispy streams curled down to puddle at her feet. Behind her closed eyes, she watched the writer dip his pen into the inkwell and continue. *Fog creeping . . . fog lying . . . fog drooping . . . fog in the eyes and throats . . .*

Thick white fog spilled from Sophie's fingers and spread across the stones, shifting like heavy smoke, flowing in twisting ropes and gossamer threads. Coiling and shifting, it flowed through Flamel's legs and tumbled down the steps, growing, thickening, darkening.

✧ ✧ ✧

Niccolò watched the fog flow down the steps of Sacré-Coeur like dirty milk, watched it condense and grow as it tumbled, and knew, in that moment, that Flamel was going to elude him. By the time the fog reached him it was chest high, wet and vanilla scented. He breathed deeply, recognizing the odor of magic.

"Remarkable," he said, but the fog flattened his voice, dulling his carefully cultivated French accent, revealing the harsher Italian beneath.

"Leave us alone," Flamel's voice boomed out of the fog.

"That sounds like another threat, Nicholas. Believe me when I tell you that you have no idea of the forces gathered against you now. Your parlor tricks will not save you." Machiavelli pulled out his cell phone and hit a speed dial number. "Attack. Attack now!" He raced up the steps as he spoke, moving silently on expensive leather-soled shoes, while far below, booted feet thumped on stone as the gathered police charged up the steps.

"I've survived for a very long time." Flamel's voice didn't come from where Machiavelli expected it to, and he stopped, turning left and right, trying to make out a shape in the fog.

"The world moved on, Nicholas," Machiavelli said. "You did not. You might have escaped us in America, but here, in Europe, there are too many Elders, too many immortal humans who know you. You will not be able to remain hidden for long. We will find you."

Machiavelli dashed up the final few steps that brought him directly to the entrance of the church. There was no mist here. The unnatural fog started on the top step and flowed downward, leaving the church floating like an island on a cloudy sea. Even before he ran into the church, Machiavelli knew he would not find them in there: Flamel, Scathach and the twins had escaped.

For the moment.

But Paris was no longer Nicholas Flamel's city. The city that had once honored Flamel and his wife as patrons of the sick and poor, the city that named streets after them, was long gone. Paris now belonged to Machiavelli and the Dark Elders he served. Looking out over the ancient city, Niccolò Machiavelli swore that he was going to turn Paris into a trap—and maybe even a tomb—for the legendary Alchemyst.

CHAPTER FIVE

$\mathcal{T}$he ghosts of Alcatraz awoke Perenelle Flamel.

The woman lay unmoving on the narrow cot in the cramped icy cell deep beneath the abandoned prison and listened to them whisper and murmur in the shadows around her. There were a dozen languages she could understand, many more she could identify and a few that were completely incomprehensible.

Keeping her eyes closed, Perenelle concentrated on the languages, trying to make out the individual voices, wondering if there were any she recognized. And then a sudden thought struck her: how was she able to hear the ghosts?

Sitting outside the cell was a sphinx, a monster with a lion's body, an eagle's wings and the head of a beautiful woman. One of its special powers was the ability to absorb the magical energies of another living being. It had drained

Perenelle's, rendering her helpless, trapping her in this terrible prison cell.

A tiny smile curled Perenelle's lips as she realized something: she was the seventh daughter of a seventh daughter; she had been *born* with the ability to hear and see ghosts. She had been doing so long before she had learned how to train and concentrate her aura. Her gift had nothing to do with magic, and therefore the sphinx had no power over it. Throughout the centuries of her long life, she had used her skill with magic to protect herself from ghosts, to coat and shield her aura with colors that rendered her invisible to the apparitions. But as the sphinx had absorbed her energies, those shields had been wiped away, revealing her to the spirit realm.

And now they were coming.

Perenelle Flamel had seen her first ghost—that of her beloved grandmother Mamom—when she was seven years old. Perenelle knew that there was nothing to fear from ghosts; they could be annoying, certainly, were often irritating and sometimes downright rude, but they possessed no physical presence. There were even a few she had learned to call friends. Over the centuries certain spirits had returned to her again and again, drawn to her because they knew she could hear, see or help them—and often, Perenelle thought, simply because they were lonely. Mamom turned up every decade or so just to check up on her.

But even though they had no presence in the real world, ghosts were not powerless.

Opening her eyes, Perenelle concentrated on the chipped

stone wall directly in front of her face. The wall ran with green-tinged water that smelled of rust and salt, the two elements that had ultimately destroyed Alcatraz the prison. Dee had made a mistake, as she had known he would. If Dr. John Dee had one great failing, it was arrogance. He obviously thought that if she was imprisoned deep below Alcatraz and guarded by a sphinx, then she was powerless. He could not be more wrong.

Alcatraz was a place of ghosts.

And Perenelle Flamel would show him just how powerful she was.

Closing her eyes, relaxing, Perenelle listened to the ghosts of Alcatraz, and then slowly, her voice barely above a breathed whisper, she began to talk to them, to call them and to gather them all to her.

CHAPTER SIX

"I'm OK," Sophie murmured sleepily, "really I am."

"You don't look OK," Josh muttered through gritted teeth. For the second time in as many days, Josh was carrying his sister in his arms, one arm under her back, the other beneath her legs. He moved cautiously down the steps of Sacré-Coeur, terrified he was going to drop his twin. "Flamel told us every time you use magic it will steal a little of your energy," he added. "You look exhausted."

"I'm fine . . . ," she muttered. "Let me down." But then her eyes flickered closed once more.

The small group moved silently through the thick vanilla-scented fog, Scathach in the lead with Flamel taking up the rear. All around them they could hear the tramp of boots, the jingle of weapons, and the muted commands of the French police and special forces as they climbed the steps. Some of them came dangerously close, and twice Josh was forced to crouch low as a uniformed figure darted by.

Scathach suddenly loomed up out of the thick fog, a short, stubby finger pressed to her lips. Water droplets frosted her spiky red hair, and her white skin looked even paler than usual. She pointed to the right with her ornately carved nunchaku. The fog swirled and suddenly a gendarme was standing almost directly in front of them, close enough to touch, his dark uniform sparkling with beads of liquid. Behind him, Josh was able to make out a group of French police clustered around what looked like an old-fashioned merry-go-round. They were all staring upward, and Josh heard the word *brouillard* murmured again and again. He knew that they were talking about the strange fog that had suddenly descended over the church. The gendarme was holding his service pistol in his hand, the barrel pointed skyward, but his finger was lightly curled over the trigger and Josh was once again reminded just how much danger they were in—not only from Flamel's nonhuman and inhuman enemies, but from his all-too-human foes as well.

They walked perhaps another dozen steps . . . and suddenly the fog stopped. One moment Josh was carrying his sister through the thick mist; then, as if he had stepped through a curtain, he was standing in front of a tiny art gallery, a café and a souvenir shop. He turned to look behind him and found that he was facing a solid wall of mist. The police were little more than indistinct shapes in the yellow-white fog.

Scathach and Flamel stepped out of the murk. "Allow

me," Scathach said, catching hold of Sophie and lifting her from Josh's arms. He tried to protest—Sophie was his twin, his responsibility—but he was exhausted. The backs of his calves were cramping, and the muscles in his arms burned with the effort of carrying his sister down what had felt like countless steps.

Josh looked into Scathach's bright green eyes. "She's going to be OK?"

The ancient Celtic warrior opened her mouth to reply, but Nicholas Flamel shook his head, silencing her. He rested his left hand on Josh's shoulder, but the boy shrugged it off. If Flamel noticed the gesture, he ignored it. "She just needs to sleep. The effort of raising the fog so soon after melting the tulpa has completely drained the last of her physical strength," Flamel said.

"You asked her to create fog," Josh said quickly, accusingly.

Nicholas spread his arms. "What else could I do?"

"I . . . I don't know," Josh admitted. "There must have been something you could do. I've seen you throw spears of green energy."

"The fog allowed us to escape without harming anyone," Flamel said.

"Except Sophie," Josh replied bitterly.

Flamel looked at him for a long moment and then turned away. "Let's go." He nodded toward a side street that sloped sharply downward, and they hurried into the night, Scathach effortlessly carrying Sophie, Josh struggling to keep up. He was not going to leave his sister's side.

"Where to?" Scathach asked.

"We need to get off the streets," Flamel murmured. "It looks like every gendarme in the city has descended on Sacré-Coeur. I also saw special forces and plainclothes police that I guess are secret service. Once they realize we're not in the church, they'll probably cordon off the area and do a street-by-street search."

Scathach smiled quickly, her long incisors briefly visible against her lips. "And let's face it: we're not exactly inconspicuous."

"We need to find a place to—" Nicholas Flamel began.

The police officer who came racing around the corner looked to be no more than nineteen—tall, thin and gangly—with bright red cheeks and the fuzzy beginnings of a mustache on his upper lip. One hand was on his holster; the other was holding on to his hat. He skidded to a halt directly in front of them and managed a quick yelp of surprise as he fumbled for the gun in its holster. "Hey! *Arrêtez!*"

Nicholas lunged forward and Josh actually saw the green mist flow from the Alchemyst's hand before his fingers brushed against the gendarme's chest. Emerald light flared around the police officer's body, outlining it in brilliant green, and then the man simply folded to the ground.

"What did you do?" Josh asked in a horrified whisper. He looked at the young police officer lying still, and was suddenly chilled and sickened. "You didn't . . . you didn't . . . kill him?"

"No," Flamel said tiredly. "Just overloaded his aura. Bit like an electric shock. He'll awaken shortly with a headache."

He pressed his fingertips to his forehead, massaging just over his left eye. "I hope it'll not be as bad as mine," he added.

"You do know," Scathach said grimly, "that your little display will have alerted Machiavelli to our position." Her nostrils flared and Josh breathed deeply; the air around them stank of peppermint: the distinctive odor of Nicholas Flamel's power.

"What else could I do?" Nicholas protested. "You had your hands full."

Scatty curled her lips in disgust. "I could have taken him. Remember, who got you out of Lubyanka Prison with both hands manacled behind my back?"

"What are you talking about? Where's Lubyanka?" Josh asked, confused.

"Moscow." Nicholas glanced sidelong at Josh. "Don't ask; it's a long story," he murmured.

"He was going to be shot as a spy," Scathach said gleefully.

"A *very* long story," Flamel repeated.

Following Scathach and Flamel through the winding streets of Montmartre, Josh thought back to how John Dee had described Nicholas Flamel to him only the day before.

"He has been many things in his time: a physician and a cook, a bookseller, a soldier, a teacher of languages and chemistry, both an officer of the law and a thief. But he is now, and has always been, a liar, a charlatan and a crook."

And a spy, Josh added. He wondered if Dee knew that. He peered at the rather ordinary-looking man: with his close-cropped hair and his pale eyes, in his black jeans and T-shirt under a battered black leather jacket, he would have passed unnoticed on any street in any city in the world. And yet he was anything but ordinary: born in the year 1330, he claimed to be working for the good of humanity, by keeping the Codex away from Dee and the shadowy and terrifying creatures he served, the Dark Elders.

But whom did Flamel serve? Josh wondered. Just who was the immortal Nicholas Flamel?

CHAPTER SEVEN

Keeping a tight rein on his temper, Niccolò Machiavelli strode down the steps of Sacré-Coeur, the fog curling and swirling behind him like a cloak. Although the air was beginning to clear, it was still touched with the odor of vanilla. Machiavelli threw his head back and breathed deeply, drawing the smell into his nostrils. He would remember this scent; it was as distinctive as a fingerprint. Everyone on the planet possessed an aura—the electrical field that surrounded the human body—and when that electrical field was focused and directed, it interacted with the user's endorphin system and adrenal glands to produce a distinctive odor unique to that person: a signature scent. Machiavelli took a final breath. He could almost taste the vanilla on the air, crisp, clear and pure: the scent of raw untrained power.

And in that moment, Machiavelli knew beyond a doubt

that Dee was correct: this was the odor of one of the legendary twins.

"I want the entire area sealed off," Machiavelli snapped to the semicircle of high-ranking police who had gathered at the bottom of the steps in the Square Willette. "Cordon off every street, alleyway and lane from the Rue Custine to the Rue Caulaincourt, from the Boulevard de Clichy to the Boulevard de Rochechouart and the Rue de Clignancourt. I want these people found!"

"You are suggesting closing down Montmartre," a deeply tanned police officer said in the silence that followed. He looked to his colleagues for support, but none of them would meet his eye. "It's the height of the tourist season," he protested, turning back to Machiavelli.

Machiavelli rounded on the captain, his face as impassive as the masks he collected. His cold gray eyes bored into the man, but when he spoke his voice was even and controlled, barely above a whisper. "You know who I am?" he asked mildly.

The captain, a decorated veteran of the French Foreign Legion, felt something cold and sour at the back of his throat as he looked into the man's stony eyes. Licking suddenly dry lips, he said, "You are Monsieur Machiavelli, the new head of the Direction Générale de la Sécurité Extérieure. But this is a police matter, sir, not an external security matter. You have no authority—"

"I am making this a DGSE matter," Machiavelli interrupted softly. "My powers come directly from the president.

47

I will shut down this entire city if necessary. I want these people found. Tonight, a catastrophe was averted." He waved his hand vaguely in the direction of Sacré-Coeur, now beginning to appear out of the thinning mist. "Who knows what other terrors they have planned? I want a progress report on the hour, every hour," he finished, and without waiting for a response turned and marched over to his car, where his dark-suited driver waited, arms folded across his massive chest. The driver, face half hidden behind wraparound mirrored sunglasses, opened the door and then closed it gently behind Machiavelli. After he had climbed into the car, the driver sat patiently, black gloved hands resting lightly on the leather steering wheel, and awaited instructions. The sheet of privacy glass that separated the driver's section from the back of the car buzzed down.

"Flamel is in Paris. Where would he go?" Machiavelli asked without preamble.

The creature known as Dagon had served Machiavelli for close to four hundred years. It was the name by which he had been known for millennia, and despite his appearance, he had never been even remotely human. Turning in the seat, he pulled off his mirrored sunglasses. In the dim car interior, his eyes were bulbous and fishlike, huge and liquid behind a clear, glassy film: he had no eyelids. When he spoke, two rows of tiny ragged teeth were visible behind his thin lips. "Who are his allies?" Dagon asked, shifting from deplorable French to appalling Italian before dropping back to the bubbling, liquid language of his long-lost youth.

"Flamel and his wife have always been loners," Machiavelli said. "That is why they have survived for so long. To the best of my knowledge, they have not lived in this city since the end of the eighteenth century." He pulled out his slender black laptop and ran his index finger over the integrated fingerprint reader. The machine blipped and the screen blinked to life.

"If they came through a leygate, then they came unprepared," Dagon said wetly. "No money, no passports, no clothes other than those they were wearing."

"Exactly," Machiavelli whispered. "So they're going to need to find themselves an ally."

"Humani or immortal?" Dagon asked.

Machiavelli took a moment to consider. "An immortal," he said finally. "I'm not sure they know many humani in this city."

"So which immortals are currently living in Paris?" Dagon asked.

The Italian's fingers hit a complicated series of keystrokes and the screen scrolled to reveal a directory called Temp. There were dozens of .jpg, .bmp and .tmp files in the directory. Machiavelli highlighted one and hit Enter. A box appeared in the center of the screen.

Enter Password.

His slender fingers clicked across the keyboard as he typed in the password *Del modo di trattare i sudditi della Val di Chiana ribellati*, and a database encoded with unbreakable 256-bit AES encryption, the same encryption used by most governments for their top-secret files, blinked open. Over the course of his long life, Niccolò Machiavelli had amassed a huge fortune, but he considered this single file to be his most valuable treasure. It was a complete dossier on every immortal human still living in the twenty-first century, compiled by his network of spies across the globe—most of whom didn't even know they were working for him. He scrolled through the names. Not even his own Dark Elder masters knew he possessed this list, and he was sure some would be very unhappy if they were to discover that he also knew the locations and attributes of almost all the Elders and Dark Elders still walking the earth or in the Shadowrealms that bordered this world.

Knowledge, as Machiavelli well knew, was power.

Although there were three screens devoted to Nicholas and Perenelle Flamel, hard information was scarce. There were hundreds of entries, each one a reported sighting of the Flamels since their supposed deaths in 1418. They had been seen on just about every continent in the world—except Australia. For the past 150 years, they had lived on the North American continent, with the first confirmed and verified sighting of the last century taking place in Buffalo, New York, in September 1901. He skipped to the section marked *Known Immortal Associates*. It was blank.

"Nothing. I have no records of the Flamels' associating with other immortals."

"But now he is back in Paris," Dagon said, bubbles of liquid forming on his lips as he spoke. "He will seek out old friends. People behave differently at home," he added; "their guard comes down. And no matter how long Flamel has lived away from this city, he will still consider it his home."

Niccolò Machiavelli looked over the top of the computer screen. He was reminded yet again of how little he knew about his faithful employee. "And where is your home, Dagon?" he asked.

"Gone. Long gone." A translucent skin flickered across the huge globes of his eyes.

"Why have you remained with me?" Machiavelli wondered aloud. "Why have you not sought out others of your kind?"

"They too are gone. I am the last of my kind, and besides, you are not that dissimilar to me."

"But you are not human," Machiavelli said softly.

"Are you?" Dagon asked, eyes wide and unblinking.

Machiavelli took a long moment before finally nodding and returning to the screen. "So we're looking for someone the Flamels would have known when they were still living here. And we know they haven't been in the city since the eighteenth century, so let us limit our search to immortals who were around then." His fingers tapped the keys, filtering the results. "Seven only. Five are loyal to us."

"And the other two?"

"Catherine de Medici is living off the Rue du Dragon."

"She's not French," Dagon mumbled stickily.

"Well, she was the mother of three French kings," Machiavelli said with a rare smile. "But she is loyal only to herself. . . ." His voice trailed away and he straightened. "But what do we have here?"

51

Dagon remained unmoving.

Niccolò Machiavelli swiveled the computer screen so that his servant could see the photograph of a man staring directly at the camera in what was obviously a posed publicity shot. Thick curling black hair tumbled to his shoulders, framing a round face. His eyes were startlingly blue.

"I do not know this man," Dagon said.

"Oh, but I do. I know him very well. This is the immortal human once known as the Comte de Saint-Germain. He was a magician, an inventor, a musician . . . and an alchemist." Machiavelli closed the program and shut down the computer. "Saint-Germain was also the student of Nicholas Flamel. And he's currently living in Paris," he finished triumphantly.

Dagon smiled, his mouth a perfect O filled with razor teeth. "Does Flamel know that Saint-Germain is here?"

"I have no idea. No one knows the extent of Nicholas Flamel's knowledge."

Dagon pushed his sunglasses back in place. "And I thought you knew everything."

CHAPTER EIGHT

"We need to rest," Josh said finally. "I can't go any farther." He stopped and leaned against a building, bent over and wheezing. Every breath was an effort, and he was beginning to see black spots dancing in front of his eyes. Any moment now he was going to throw up. He felt this way sometimes after football practice, and he knew from experience that he needed to sit and get some liquids into his system.

"He's right." Scatty turned to Flamel. "We need to rest, even if only briefly. She was still carrying Sophie in her arms, and with gray glimmers of light illuminating the Parisian rooftops toward the east, the first of the early-morning workers had begun to appear. The fugitives had kept to the dark side streets, and so far no one had paid any attention to the strange group, but that would quickly change as the street filled first with Parisians, then with tourists.

Nicholas stood outlined at the mouth of the narrow street. He glanced up and down before turning to look over his shoulder. "We have to push on," he protested. "Every second we delay brings Machiavelli closer to us."

"We can't," Scatty said. She looked at Flamel, and for a single instant, her bright green eyes glowed. "The twins need to rest," she said, and then added softly, "And so do you, Nicholas. You're exhausted."

The Alchemyst considered her and then he nodded and his shoulders slumped. "You're right, of course. I'll do as you say."

"Maybe we could check into a hotel?" Josh suggested. He was achingly tired, his eyes and throat gritty, head throbbing.

Scatty shook her head. "They would ask for our passports. . . ." Sophie stirred in her arms, and Scathach gently eased her to the ground and leaned her up against the wall.

Josh was immediately by her side. "You're awake," he said, relief in his voice.

"I wasn't really asleep," Sophie answered, her tongue feeling too big for her mouth. "I knew what was going on, but it was as if I was looking at it from the outside. Like watching something on TV." She pressed her hands into the small of her back and pushed hard as she rotated her neck. "Ouch. That hurt."

"What hurts?" Josh asked immediately.

"Everything." She attempted to straighten, but aching muscles protested and a sick headache pulsed behind her eyes.

"Is there anyone here you can call for help?" Josh looked

from Nicholas to Scathach. "Are there any more immortals or Elders?"

"There are immortals and Elders everywhere," Scatty said. "Few are as friendly as we are, though," she added with a humorless smile.

"There will be immortals in Paris," Flamel agreed slowly, "but I've no idea where to find one, and even if I did, I would have no idea where their allegiances lay. Perenelle would know," he added, a hint of sadness in his voice.

"Would your grandmother know?" Josh asked Scatty.

The Warrior glanced at him. "I'm sure she would." She turned to look at Sophie. "Amongst all of your new memories, can you recall anything about immortals or Elders living in Paris?"

Sophie closed her eyes and tried to concentrate, but the scenes and images that flashed by—fire raining from a blood-red sky, a huge flat-topped pyramid about to be overwhelmed by a gigantic wave—were chaotic and terrifying. She started to shake her head, then stopped. Even the simplest of movements hurt. "I can't think," she sighed. "My head is so full, it feels like it's going to burst."

"The Witch might know," Flamel said, "but we have no way of getting in touch with her. She has no phone."

"What about her neighbors, friends?" Josh asked. He turned back to his sister. "I know you don't want to think about this, but you have to. It's important."

"I can't think . . . ," Sophie began, looking away and shaking her head.

"Don't think. Just answer," Josh snapped. He took a

quick breath and lowered his voice, speaking slowly. "Sis, who is the Witch of Endor's closest friend in Ojai?"

Sophie's bright blue eyes closed again and she swayed as if she was about to faint. When her eyes opened, she shook her head. "She has no friends there. But everyone knows her. Maybe we could call the store next to hers . . . ," she suggested. Then she shook her head. "It's too late there."

Flamel nodded. "Sophie's right; it'll be closed at this time of night."

"It'll be closed, all right," Josh agreed, a touch of excitement entering his voice, "but when we left Ojai, the place was in chaos. And don't forget, I drove a Hummer into the fountain in Libbey Park; that had to have caught someone's attention. I'll bet the police and the press are there right now. And the press might answer some questions if we ask the right ones. I mean, if the Witch's shop was damaged they're sure to be looking for a story."

"It might work . . . ," Flamel began. "I just need to know the name of the newspaper."

"*Ojai Valley News,* 646-1476," Sophie said immediately. "I remember that much . . . or the Witch does," she added, and then shuddered. There were so many memories in her head, so many thoughts and ideas . . . and not just the terrifying and fantastic images of people and places that should never have existed, but also ordinary mundane thoughts: phone numbers and recipes, names and addresses of people she'd never heard of, pictures from old TV shows, posters from movies. She even knew the name of every single Elvis Presley song.

But all of these were the Witch's memories. And right now, she had to struggle to remember her own cell phone number. What would happen if the Witch's memories grew so strong that they overwhelmed her own? She tried to focus on the faces of her parents, Richard and Sara. Hundreds of faces flickered past, images of figures carved in stone, the heads of giant statues, paintings daubed onto the sides of buildings, tiny shapes etched in shards of pottery. Sophie started to get frantic. Why couldn't she remember her parents' faces? Closing her eyes, she concentrated hard on the last time she had seen her mother and father. It would have been about three weeks ago, just before they had left for the dig in Utah. More faces tumbled behind Sophie's closed eyes: images on scraps of parchment, fragments of manuscripts or cracked oil paintings; faces in faded sepia photographs, in blurred newspapers . . .

"Sophie?"

And then, in a flash of color, the faces of her parents popped into her head, and Sophie felt the Witch's memories fade away and her own come back to the surface. She suddenly knew her own phone number.

"Sis?"

She opened her eyes and blinked at her brother. He was standing directly in front of her, his face close to hers, his eyes pinched with concern.

"I'm OK," she whispered. "I was just trying to remember something."

"What?"

She attempted a smile. "My phone number."

"Your phone number? Why?" He stopped, and then added, "No one ever remembers their own phone number. When was the last time you called yourself?"

Hands wrapped around steaming mugs of bittersweet hot chocolate, Sophie and Josh sat opposite one another in an otherwise empty all-night café close to the Gare du Nord Metro station. There was only one staff member behind the counter, a surly shaven-headed assistant wearing an upside-down name tag that said ROUX.

"I need a shower," Sophie said grimly. "I need to wash my hair and brush my teeth, and I need to change my clothes. It feels like days since my last shower."

"I think it is days. You look terrible," Josh agreed. He reached over and pulled loose a strand of blond hair that had stuck to his sister's cheek.

"I feel terrible," Sophie whispered. "Remember that time last summer when we were in Long Beach and I had all that ice cream, then ate the chili dog and the curly fries and had the extra-large root beer?"

Josh grinned. "And you finished off my buffalo wings. *And* my ice cream!"

Sophie smiled at the memory, but her grin quickly faded. Although the temperature that day had risen into the hundreds, she'd started shivering, icy beads of sweat running down her back as a ball of iron settled into the pit of her stomach. Luckily, she hadn't fastened her seat belt before she'd thrown up, but the results had still been spectacularly messy, and the car had been unusable for at least a week afterward. "That's how I feel right now: cold, shivery, aching all over."

"Well, try not to throw up in here," Josh murmured. "I don't think Roux, our cheerful server, would be too impressed."

Roux had worked in the café for four years, and in that time he had been robbed twice and threatened often but never hurt. The all-night café saw all sorts of strange and often dangerous characters come through the doors, and Roux decided that this unusual quartet certainly qualified as the first sort and maybe even both. The two teenagers were dirty and smelly and looked terrified and exhausted. The older man—maybe the kids' grandfather, Roux thought—was not in much better shape. Only the fourth member of the group—the red-haired, green-eyed young woman wearing a black top, black trousers and chunky combat boots—looked bright and alert. He wondered what her relationship was to the others; she certainly didn't look as if she was related to any of them, but the boy and girl were alike enough to be twins.

Roux had hesitated when the old man had produced a credit card to pay for the two hot chocolates. People usually paid cash for something so small, and he wondered if the card was stolen. "I've run out of euros," the old man said with a smile. "Could you ring up twenty and give me some cash?" Roux thought he spoke French with a peculiar, old-fashioned, almost formal lilt.

59

"It is strictly against our policy . . . ," Roux began, but another look at the hard-eyed red-haired girl made him reconsider. He attempted a smile at her as he said, "Sure, I think I can do that." If the card had been reported stolen, it wouldn't scan in the machine anyway.

"I would be very grateful." The man smiled. "And could you give me some coins?"

Roux rang up eight euro for the two hot chocolates and swiped the Visa for twenty euro. He was surprised that it was an American credit card; he would have sworn by his accent that the man was French. There was a delay and then the card went through, and he deducted the cost of the two drinks and handed over the change in one- and two-euro coins. Roux went back to the math textbook hidden under the counter. He'd been wrong about the group. It wasn't the first time and wouldn't be the last. They were probably visitors just off one of the early-morning trains; they were nothing out of the ordinary.

Well, maybe not all of them. Keeping his head down, he raised his eyes to look at the red-haired young woman. She was standing with her back to him, talking to the old man. And then she slowly and deliberately turned to look at him. She smiled, the merest curl of her lips, and Roux suddenly found his textbook very interesting.

Flamel stood at the café counter and looked at Scathach. "I want you to stay here," he said softly, slipping from French into Latin. His eyes flickered to where the twins sat drinking their hot chocolate. "Watch over them. I'll go find a phone."

The Shadow nodded. "Be careful. If anything happens and we get separated, let's meet back in Montmartre. Machiavelli will never expect us to double back. We'll wait outside one of the restaurants—maybe La Maison Rose—for five minutes at the top of every hour."

"Agreed. But if I'm not back by noon," he continued very softly, "I want you to take the twins and leave."

"I will not abandon you," Scathach said evenly.

"If I don't come back, it's because Machiavelli has me," the Alchemyst said seriously. "Scathach, even you would not be able to rescue me from his army."

"I've faced down armies before."

Flamel reached out and laid his hand on the Warrior's shoulder. "The twins are our priority now. They must be protected at all cost. Continue Sophie's training; find someone to Awaken Josh and train him. And rescue my dear Perenelle, if you can. And if I die, tell her my ghost will find her," he added. Then, before she could say anything else, he turned and strode out into the chilly predawn air.

"Hurry back . . . ," Scatty whispered, but Flamel had gone. If he was captured, she decided, no matter what he said, she was going to tear this city apart until she found him. Taking a deep breath, she looked over her shoulder and found the shaven-headed assistant staring at her. There was a spiderweb tattooed onto the side of his neck, and the entire length of both of his ears was pierced with at least a dozen little studs. She wondered how painful that had been. She'd always wanted pierced ears, but her flesh simply healed too quickly, and she'd no sooner had the piercing done than the hole closed up.

"Something to drink?" Roux asked, smiling nervously, a metal ball visible in his tongue.

"Water," Scatty said.

"Sure. Perrier?"

"Tap. No ice," she added, and turned away to join the twins at the table. She spun a chair around and straddled it, leaning her forearms across the top of the chair and resting her chin on her arms.

"Nicholas has gone to try and get in touch with my grandmother to see if she knows anyone here. I'm not sure what we're going to do if he cannot get through."

"Why?" Sophie asked.

Scatty shook her head. "We've got to get off the streets. We were lucky to get away from Sacré-Coeur before the police threw up a cordon around it. No doubt they have found that stunned officer by now, so their search will have moved outward, and the patrols will have our descriptions. It's only a matter of time before we're spotted."

"What will happen then?" Josh wondered aloud.

Scathach's smile was terrifying. "Then they'll see why I am called the Warrior."

"But what happens if we're caught?" Josh persisted. He still found the idea of being hunted by the police nearly incomprehensible. It was almost easier to imagine being hunted by mythical creatures or immortal humans. "What would happen to us?"

"You would be turned over to Machiavelli. The Dark Elders would consider you pair quite a prize."

"What . . ." Sophie looked quickly at her brother. "What would they do to us?"

"You really don't want to know," Scathach said sincerely, "but trust me when I tell you that it would not be pleasant."

"And what about you?" Josh asked.

"I have no friends amongst the Dark Elders," Scathach said softly. "I've been their enemy for over two and a half thousand years. I would imagine they have a very special Shadowrealm prison prepared for me. Something cold and wet. They know I hate that." She smiled, the tips of her teeth pressing against her lips. "But they haven't got us yet," she said lightly, "and they'll not get us easily." She turned to squint at Sophie. "You look terrible."

"So I've been told," Sophie said, wrapping both hands around the steaming mug of chocolate and bringing it to her lips. She breathed deeply. She could smell every subtlety in the rich aroma of cocoa and felt her stomach rumble, reminding her that it had been a long time since they had eaten. The hot chocolate tasted bitter on her tongue, eye-wateringly strong, and she remembered reading somewhere that European chocolate had a greater cocoa content than the American chocolate she had grown up with.

Scatty leaned forward and dropped her voice. "You need to give yourselves time to recuperate from all the stresses you've been through. Traveling from one side of the world to the other via a leygate takes its toll—it feels like massive jet lag, I'm told."

"And I guess you don't get jet lag?" Josh muttered. There was a joke in the family that he could get jet lag on a car trip from one state to the next.

Scatty shook her head. "No, I don't get jet lag. I don't fly," she explained. "You'd never get me up in one of those things. Only creatures with flapping wings are meant to be in the skies. Though I did ride a lung once."

"A lung?" Josh asked, confused.

"Ying lung, a Chinese dragon," Sophie said.

Scathach turned to look at the girl. "Calling up the fog must have burned through a lot of your aura's energy. It's important that you not use your power again for as long as possible."

The trio sat back as Roux came out from behind the counter with a tall glass of water. He placed it on the edge of the table, attempted a nervous smile at Scatty and then backed away.

"I think he likes you," Sophie said with a weak grin.

Scatty turned to glare at the assistant again, but the twins saw her lips twist in a smile. "He's got piercings," she said, loud enough for him to hear. "I don't like boys with piercings."

Both girls smiled as the back of Roux's neck flared bright red.

"Why is it important that Sophie not use her powers?" Josh asked, bringing the conversation back to Scatty's earlier comment. An alarm had gone off at the back of his mind.

Scathach leaned forward across the table, and both Sophie and Josh moved in to hear her. "Once a person uses all their natural auric energy, then the power starts to feed off their flesh for its fuel."

"What happens then?" Sophie asked.

"Have you ever heard of spontaneous human combustion?"

Sophie's expression was blank, but Josh nodded. "I have. People just bursting into flames for no reason: it's an urban legend."

Scatty shook her head. "It's no legend. Many cases have been recorded throughout history," she said evenly. "I've even witnessed a couple myself. It can happen in a heartbeat, and the fire, which usually starts in the stomach and lungs, burns so fiercely that it leaves little more than ash behind. You have to be careful now, Sophie: in fact, I'd like you to promise me not to use your power again today, no matter what happens."

"And Flamel knew this," Josh said quickly, unable to keep the anger from his voice.

"Of course," Scatty said evenly.

"And he didn't think it was worth telling us?" Josh snapped. Roux looked over at the raised voice, and Josh took a deep breath and continued in a hoarse whisper. "What else isn't he telling us?" he demanded. "What else comes with this *gift?*" He almost spat out the last word.

"Everything has happened so fast, Josh," Scatty said.

"There simply hasn't been time to train or instruct you properly. But I want you to remember that Nicholas has your best interests at heart. He is trying to keep you safe."

"We were safe until we met him," Josh said.

The skin tightened across Scatty's cheekbones and the muscles in her neck and shoulders twitched. Something dark and ugly flickered behind her green eyes.

Sophie reached out and put a hand on both Scatty's and Josh's arms. "Enough," she said tiredly. "We shouldn't fight with each other."

Josh was about to respond, but the look on his sister's exhausted face scared him, and he nodded. "OK. For now," he added.

Scatty nodded too. "Sophie is correct." She turned to look at Josh. "It is unfortunate that everything has fallen on Sophie at the moment. It's a pity your powers weren't Awakened."

"You're not half as sorry as I am," he said, unable to keep the note of bitterness from his voice. Despite all that he had seen, and even knowing the dangers, he wanted the powers his twin had. "It's not too late, though, is it?" he asked quickly.

Scatty shook her head. "You can be Awakened at any time, but I don't know who would have the power to Awaken you. It needs to be done by an Elder, and there are only a handful with that particular skill."

"Like who?" he demanded, looking at Scathach, but it was his sister who answered, dreamily.

"In America, Black Annis or Persephone could do it."

Josh and Scatty turned to look at her.

Sophie blinked in surprise. "I know the names, but I don't even know who they are." Suddenly, her eyes filled with tears. "I have all these memories . . . that aren't even mine."

Josh took his sister's hand and squeezed it gently.

"They are all the Witch of Endor's memories," Scathach said softly. "And be glad you don't know who Black Annis or Persephone is. Especially Black Annis," she added grimly. "I'm surprised that if my grandmother knew where she was, she let her live."

"She's in the Catskills," Sophie began, but Scathach reached over and pinched the back of her hand. "Ouch!"

"I just wanted to distract you," Scathach explained. "Don't even *think* about Black Annis. There are some names that should never be spoken aloud."

"That's like saying don't think of elephants," Josh said, "and then all you can think of are elephants."

"Then let me give you something else to think about," Scathach said softly. "There are two police officers in the window staring at us. Don't look," she added urgently.

Too late. Josh turned to look, and whatever expression crossed his face—shock, horror, guilt or fear—brought both officers racing into the café, one pulling his automatic from its holster, the other speaking urgently into his radio as he drew his baton.

CHAPTER NINE

*W*ith hands pushed deep in the pockets of his leather jacket, still wearing his none-too-clean black jeans and scuffed cowboy boots, Nicholas Flamel didn't look out of place with either the early-morning workers or the homeless beginning to appear on the streets of Paris. The gendarmes gathered in small groups on the corners were talking urgently together or listening to their radios and didn't even give him a second glance.

This wasn't the first time he had been hunted in these streets, but it was the first time without allies and friends to help him. He and Perenelle had returned to their home city at the end of the Seven Years' War in 1763. An old friend needed their help, and the Flamels never refused a friend. Unfortunately, however, Dee had discovered their where-abouts and had chased them through the streets with an army of black-clad assassins, none of whom was entirely human.

They had escaped then. Escaping now might not be so easy. Paris had changed utterly. When Baron Haussmann had redesigned Paris in the nineteenth century, he had destroyed a huge portion of the medieval section of the city, the city Flamel was so familiar with. All the Alchemyst's hiding places and safe houses, the secret vaults and hidden attics, were gone. He had once known every street and alley, each twisting lane and hidden courtyard of Paris; now he knew as much as the average tourist.

And at that moment, not only did he have Machiavelli chasing them, the entire French police force was also on the lookout for them. And Dee was on his way. Dee, as Flamel well knew, was capable of just about anything.

Nicholas breathed in the cool predawn Parisian air and glanced at the cheap digital watch he wore on his left wrist. It was still set to Pacific time, where it was now twenty minutes past eight in the evening, which meant—he did a quick calculation in his head—that it was five-twenty a.m. in Paris. He thought briefly about resetting the watch to Greenwich Mean Time, but quickly decided against it. A couple of months ago, when he'd tried resetting the watch for daylight savings, it had started madly blipping and flashing. He'd worked on it for over an hour without any success; it had taken Perenelle thirty seconds to fix it. He only wore it because it came with a countdown timer. Every month, when he and Perenelle created a new batch of the immortality potion, he reset the counter to 720 hours and allowed it to count down to zero. With the passing of years, they had discovered that the potion was timed to a lunar cycle and lasted roughly thirty days.

Over the course of the month, they would age slowly, almost imperceptibly, but once they drank the potion, the effects of the aging process would quickly reverse—hair would darken, wrinkles soften and disappear, aching joints and stiff muscles become supple again, eyesight and hearing sharpen.

Unfortunately, it was not a recipe that could be copied down; each month the formula was unique, and each recipe only worked once. The Book of Abraham the Mage was written in a language that predated humanity, and in an ever-changing, always-moving script, so that entire libraries of knowledge were held within the slender volume. But every month, on page seven of the copper-bound manuscript, the secret of Life Eternal appeared. The crawling script remained static for less then an hour before it shifted, twisted and trickled away.

The one and only time the Flamels had tried using the same recipe twice, it had actually sped up the aging process. Luckily, Nicholas had taken only a sip of the colorless, rather ordinary-looking potion when Perenelle noticed that lines were appearing around his eyes and on his forehead and that the hair from his full beard was falling away from his face. She'd knocked the cup from his hand before he'd taken another mouthful. However, the lines remained etched on his face, and the thick beard he had been so proud of had never grown again.

Nicholas and Perenelle had brewed the most recent batch of the potion at midnight the past Sunday, just under a week ago. He pressed the left-hand button on the watch and called up the stopwatch function: 116 hours and 21 minutes had passed. Another press of the button brought up the time remaining: 603 hours, 39 minutes, or about 25 days. As he watched, another minute ticked away: 38 minutes. He and Perenelle would age and weaken, and of course, every time either of them used their powers, that would only quicken the onset of old age. If he did not retrieve the Book before the end of the month and create a new batch of the potion, then they would both rapidly age and die.

And the world would die with them.

Unless . . .

A police car roared past, siren howling. It was followed by a second and a third. Like everyone else on the street, Flamel turned to follow their progress. The last thing he needed to do was to attract attention to himself by standing out from the crowd.

He had to retrieve the Codex. The *rest* of the Codex, he reminded himself, his hand absently touching his chest. Hidden beneath his T-shirt, dangling on a leather cord, he wore a simple square cotton bag that Perenelle had stitched for him half a millennium ago, when he had first found the Book. She had created it to hold the ancient volume; now all it contained were two pages Josh had managed to tear out. The book was still incredibly dangerous in the hands of Dee, but it was the last two pages, which contained the spell known as the Final Summoning, that Dee needed to bring his Dark Elder masters back to this world.

And Flamel would not—could not—allow that.

Two police officers turned a corner and strolled down the center of the street. They stared hard at some of the pedestrians

71

and peered into the shop windows, but they walked past Nicholas without even looking at him.

Nicholas knew that his priority now was to find a safe haven for the twins. And that meant he had to find an immortal living in Paris. Every city in the world had its share of humans with life spans that extended into centuries or even millennia, and Paris was no exception. He knew that immortals liked the big anonymous cities, where it was easier to disappear amongst an ever-changing population.

Long ago, Nicholas and Perenelle had come to realize that at the heart of every myth and legend was a grain of truth. And every race told stories of people who lived exceptionally long lives: the immortals.

Over the centuries, the Flamels had come into contact with three entirely different types of immortal humans. There were the Ancients—of whom there were now perhaps no more than a handful still alive—who hailed from earth's very distant past. Some had witnessed the entire span of human history, and it had made them more, and less, than human.

Then there were a few others who, like Nicholas and Perenelle, had discovered for themselves how to become immortal. Down through the millennia, the secrets of alchemy had been discovered, lost and rediscovered countless times. One of the greatest secrets of alchemy was the formula for immortality. And all alchemy—and possibly even modern science—had one single source: the Book of Abraham the Mage.

Then there were those who had been given the gift of immortality. These were humans who had, either accidentally or deliberately, come to the attention of one or other of the

Elders who had remained in this world after the Fall of Danu Talis. The Elders were always on the lookout for people of exceptional or unusual ability to recruit to their cause. And in return for their service, the Elders granted their followers extended life. It was a gift very few humans could refuse. It was also a gift that ensured absolute, unswerving loyalty . . . because it could be withdrawn as quickly as it had been given. Nicholas knew that if he encountered immortals in Paris— even if he had known them in the past—there would now be a very real danger that they were in the service of the Dark Elders.

He was passing an all-night video store that advertised high-speed Internet when he noticed the sign in the window, written in ten languages: NATIONAL & INTERNATIONAL CALLS. CHEAPEST RATES. Pushing open the door, he suddenly breathed in the sour odor of unwashed bodies, stale perfume, greasy food and the ozone of too many computers packed tightly together. The store was surprisingly busy: a group of students who looked like they'd been up all night clustered around three computers displaying the World of Warcraft logo, while most of the other machines were taken up by serious-faced young men and women staring intently at the screens. As he made his way to the counter at the back of the shop, Nicholas could see that most of the young people were e-mailing and instant-messaging. He smiled briefly; only a few days ago, on Monday afternoon, when the bookshop was quiet, Josh had spent an hour explaining to him the difference between the two methods of communication. Josh had even set him up with his own e-mail account—which Nicholas doubted he

73

would ever use—though he could see a use for the instant-messaging programs.

The Chinese girl behind the counter was dressed in ragged and torn clothes that Nicholas thought looked fit only for the trash but that he guessed had probably cost a fortune. She was in full goth makeup and was busy painting her nails when Nicholas stepped up to the desk.

"Three euro for fifteen minutes, five for thirty, seven for forty-five, ten for an hour," she rattled off in atrocious French without looking up.

"I want to make an international call."

"Cash or credit card?" She still hadn't raised her head, and Nicholas noticed that she was blackening her nails not with polish but with a felt-tip marker.

"Credit card." He wanted to conserve the little cash he had to buy some food. Although he rarely ate, and Scathach never ate, he would need to feed the children.

"Use booth number one. Instructions are on the wall."

Nicholas slipped into the glass-fronted booth and pulled the door closed behind him. The shouts of the students faded, but the booth smelled strongly of stale food. He quickly read the instructions as he fished the credit card he'd used to buy hot chocolate for the twins from the back of his wallet. It was in the name of Nick Fleming, the name he'd been using for the past ten years, and he briefly wondered whether Dee or Machiavelli had the resources to track him through it. He knew that of course they did, but a quick smile curled Flamel's thin lips; what did it matter? All it would tell them was that he was in Paris, and they already knew that.

Following the instructions on the wall, he dialed the international access code and then the number Sophie had recalled from the Witch of Endor's memories.

The line crackled and clicked with transatlantic static, and then, more than five and a half thousand miles away, the phone started ringing. It was answered on the second ring. "*Ojai Valley News;* how can I help?" The young woman's voice was surprisingly clear.

Nicholas deliberately affected a thick French accent. "Good morning . . . or rather, good evening to you. I'm delighted to find you still at the office. This is Monsieur Montmorency, phoning you from Paris, France. I'm a reporter with *Le Monde* newspaper. I've just seen online that you've had quite an exciting evening there."

"Gosh—news does travel fast, Mr. . . ."

"Montmorency."

"Montmorency. Yes, we've had quite an evening. How can we help?"

"We would like to include a piece in this evening's paper—I was wondering if you had a reporter on the scene?"

"Actually, all our reporters are downtown at the moment."

"Would it be possible to put me through, do you think? I can get a quick on-the-spot description of the scene and a comment." When there was no immediate response, he added quickly, "There would be a proper credit for your newspaper, of course."

"Let me see if I can patch you through to one of our reporters on the street, Mr. Montmorency."

"*Merci*. I am very grateful."

The line clicked again, and there was a long pause. Nicholas guessed that the receptionist was talking to the reporter before transferring the call. There was another click, and the girl said, "Putting you through. . . ." He was saying thank you when the phone was answered.

"Michael Carroll, *Ojai Valley News*. I understand you're calling from Paris, France?" There was a note of incredulity in the man's voice.

"Indeed I am, Monsieur Carroll."

"News travels fast," the reporter said, echoing the receptionist.

"The Internet," Flamel said vaguely, adding, "There's a video on YouTube." He had absolutely no doubt that there were videos of the scene in Ojai online. He turned to stare out into the Internet café. From where he was standing he could see half a dozen screens; each one displayed a Web page in a different language. "I've been asked to get a quote for our arts and culture page. One of our editors has visited your beautiful city often and bought several amazing glass pieces from an antiques shop on Ojai Avenue. I'm not sure if you know it: the shop sells only mirrors and glassware," Flamel added.

"Witcherly Antiques," Michael Carroll said immediately. "I know it well. I'm afraid it was completely destroyed in an explosion."

Flamel felt suddenly breathless. Hekate had died because he had brought the twins into her Shadowrealm; had the

76

Witch of Endor shared Hekate's fate? He cleared his throat and swallowed hard. "And the owner, Mrs. Witcherly? Is she . . . ?"

"She's fine," the reporter said, and Flamel felt a wave of relief wash over him. "I've just taken a statement from her. She's in remarkably good spirits for someone whose shop has just blown up." He laughed and added, "She said that when you've lived as long as she has, nothing much surprises you."

"Is she still there?" Flamel asked, trying to contain the eagerness is his voice. "Would she like to make a statement for the French press? Tell her it's Nicholas Montmorency. We spoke once before; I'm sure she'll remember me," he added.

"I'll ask. . . ."

The voice faded away and Flamel heard the reporter calling out for Dora Witcherly. In the background, he also heard the sound of countless police, fire and ambulance sirens and the fainter shouts and cries of distressed people.

And it was all his fault.

He shook his head quickly. No, it was *not* his fault. This was Dee's doing. Dee knew no sense of proportion; he had almost burned London to the ground in 1666, had devastated Ireland with the Great Famine in the 1840s, had destroyed most of San Francisco in 1906—and now he'd emptied the graveyards around Ojai. No doubt the streets were littered with bones and bodies. Nicholas heard the reporter's muted voice and then the sound of the cell phone being handed over.

"Monsieur Montmorency?" Dora said politely in perfect French.

"Madame. You are unharmed?"

Dora's voice fell to a whisper and she slipped into an archaic form of the French language that would be incomprehensible to any modern eavesdropper. "It's not that easy to kill me," she said quickly. "Dee has escaped, cut, bruised, battered and very, very upset. You are all safe? Scathach too?"

"Scatty is safe. However, we've had an encounter with Niccolò Machiavelli."

"So he's still around. Dee must have warned him. Be careful, Nicholas. Machiavelli is more dangerous than you can imagine. He is even more cunning than Dee. Now I must hurry," she added urgently. "This reporter is getting suspicious. He probably thinks I'm giving you a better story than I gave him. What do you want?"

"I need your help, Dora. I need to know who I can trust in Paris. I need to get the children off the streets. They're exhausted."

"Hmmm." The line crackled with the sound of rustling paper. "I don't know who is in Paris at the moment. But I'll find out," she said decisively. "What time is it there?"

He glanced at his watch and did the math. "Five-thirty in the morning."

"Get to the Eiffel Tower. Be there by seven a.m. and wait for ten minutes. If I can find someone trustworthy, I'll have them meet you there. If no one you recognize arrives, go back at eight and then at nine. If no one is there by nine, then you'll know there is no one in Paris you can trust, and you will have to make your own arrangements."

"Thank you, Madame Dora," he said quietly. "I'll not forget this debt."

"There are no debts between friends," she said. "Oh, and Nicholas, try and keep my granddaughter out of trouble."

"I'll do my best," Flamel said. "But you know what she's like: she seems to attract trouble. Though right now, she's watching over the twins in a café not far from here. At least she can't get into any trouble there."

CHAPTER TEN

Scathach brought her leg up, pressed the sole of her foot against the seat of a chair and shoved hard. The wooden chair skipped across the floor and slammed into the two police officers as they pushed through the door. They crashed to the ground, a radio flying from the hand of one, a baton from the hand of the other. The squawking radio skidded to a halt at Josh's feet. He leaned over and poured his hot chocolate on it. It died in a fizz of sparks.

Scathach surged to her feet. Without turning her head, she raised an arm and pointed at Roux. "You. Stay right where you are. And don't even think about phoning for the police."

Heart hammering, Josh grabbed Sophie and pulled her away from the table, toward the back of the shop, shielding her with his body from the police at the door.

One of the officers raised a gun. And Scatty's nunchaku

80

struck it in the barrel with enough force to bend the metal and send the weapon spinning from the man's hand.

The second officer scrambled to his feet, pulling out a long black baton. Scathach's right shoulder dipped and the nunchaku reversed direction in midair, the twelve-inch length of hardened wood striking the police baton just above its short handle. The baton shattered into ragged splinters. Scathach flipped the nunchaku back and it dropped into her outstretched hand.

"I'm in a really bad mood," she said in perfect French. "Believe me when I tell you that you really do not want to fight me."

"Scatty . . . ," Josh hissed in alarm.

"Not now," the Warrior snapped in English. "Can't you see I'm busy?"

"Yeah, well, you're about to get busier," Josh shouted. "A lot busier. Look outside."

A police riot squad, in black body armor, full-face helmets and shields, armed with batons and assault rifles, were racing down the street, straight for the café.

"RAID," the shop assistant whispered in horror.

"Just like SWAT," Scathach said in English, "only tougher." She sounded almost pleased. Glancing sidelong at Roux, she snapped in French, "Is there a back door?"

The shop assistant was shocked into immobility, staring at the approaching squad, and didn't react until Scathach whipped out the nunchaku and the rounded end whistled past his face, the breeze making him blink.

"Is there a back door?" she demanded again, but in English.

"Yes, yes, of course."

"Then get my friends out."

"No . . . ," Josh began.

"Let me do something," Sophie said, a dozen wind spells flickering into her consciousness. "I can help. . . ."

"No," Josh protested, and reached for his twin just as her blond hair crackled, sparkling silver.

"Out!" Scatty shouted, and suddenly it was as if the planes and angles of her face had altered, cheekbones and chin becoming prominent, green eyes turned to reflective glass. For an instant, there was something ancient and primeval—and totally alien—in her face. "I can take care of this." She started spinning the nunchaku, creating an impenetrable shield between her and the two policemen. One officer picked up a chair and flung it at her, but the nunchaku turned it to matchwood.

"Roux—get them out *now*!" Scatty snarled.

"This way," the terrified clerk said in American-accented English. He pushed past the twins and led them down a narrow chilly corridor and out into a small foul-smelling yard piled high with trash cans, bits of broken restaurant furniture and the skeleton of a long-abandoned Christmas tree. Behind them came the sound of breaking wood.

Roux pointed to a red gate and continued in English. His face was the color of chalk. "That leads to the alleyway. Turn left for the Rue de Dunkerque; right will bring you down to the Gare du Nord Metro station." Behind them there was a

82

tremendous smash, followed by the sound of breaking glass. "Your friend, she is in so much trouble," he moaned miserably. "And RAID will wreck the shop. How am I going to explain that to the owner?"

There was another crash from inside. A slate tile slid off the roof and crashed into the yard.

"Go, go now." He spun the combination lock and tugged the gate open.

Sophie and Josh ignored him. "What do we do?" Josh asked his twin. "Go or stay?"

Sophie shook her head. She glanced at Roux and lowered her voice to a whisper. "We have nowhere to go—we don't know anyone in the city except Scatty and Nicholas. We don't have any money and we have no passports."

"We could go to the American embassy." Josh turned to Roux. "Is there an American embassy in Paris?"

"Yes, of course, on the Avenue Gabriel, beside the Hôtel de Crillon." The shaven-headed youth cringed as a colossal thump shook the whole building, filling the air with minute particles of dust. The glass in the window beside them cracked from top to bottom and more tiles slid off the roof, to rain down into the yard.

"And what do we tell the embassy?" Sophie demanded. "They'll want to know how we got here."

"Kidnapped?" Josh suggested. And then a sudden thought struck him and he felt sick. "And what do we tell Mom and Dad? How are we going to explain it to them?"

Crockery tinkled and shattered, and then there was a tremendous crack.

83

Sophie cocked her head to one side and brushed her hair off her ear. "That was the main window." She took a step back toward the door. "I should help her." Wisps of mist curled off her fingers as she reached for the handle.

"No!" Josh snatched her hand, and static crackled between them. "You can't use your powers," he whispered urgently. "You're too exhausted; remember what Scatty said. You could burst into flames."

"She's our friend—we can't abandon her," Sophie snapped. "*I* won't, anyway." Her brother was a loner and had never been good at making or keeping friends in school, whereas she was intensely loyal to hers, and she had started to think of Scatty as more than just a friend. Although she loved her brother deeply, she had always wanted a sister.

Josh caught Sophie's shoulders and turned her to face him. He was already a head taller than she was and had to look down into the blue eyes that mirrored his own. "She's *not* our friend, Sophie," his voice low and serious. "She's never going to be our friend. She's a two-and-a-half-thousand-year-old . . . *something*. She admitted to us that she's a vampire. You saw the way her face changed in there: she's not even human. And . . . and I'm not sure she's all Flamel makes her out to be. I know *he* isn't!"

"What do you mean?" Sophie demanded. "What are you trying to say?"

Josh opened his mouth to reply, but a series of rattling thumps vibrated through the entire building. Whimpering with fear, Roux darted out into the alley. The twins ignored him.

"What do you mean?" Sophie asked again.

"Dee said—"

"*Dee!*"

"I talked to him in Ojai. When you were in the shop with the Witch of Endor."

"But he's our enemy!"

"Only because Flamel *says* he is," Josh said quickly. "Sophie, Dee told me that Flamel is a criminal and Scathach is basically just a hired thug. He said that she was cursed for her crimes to wear the body of a teenager for the rest of her life." He shook his head quickly and hurried on, his voice low and desperate. "Sis, we know next to nothing about these people . . . Flamel, Perenelle and Scathach. The only thing we *do* know is that they've made you different—dangerously different. They've taken us halfway across the world, and look where we are now." Even as he was speaking, the building shook, and then a dozen more tiles slid off the roof and crashed into the yard, sending razor-sharp fragments flying around them. Josh yelped as a chunk stung his arm. "We can't trust them, Soph. We shouldn't."

"Josh, you have no idea what powers they've given me. . . ." Sophie caught her brother's arm, and the air, which was foul with the stink of rotting food, was touched with the odor of vanilla, and then, a moment later, the scent of oranges as Josh's aura flared briefly golden. "Oh, Josh, the things I could tell you. I know everything the Witch of Endor knew. . . ."

"And it's making you sick!" Josh yelled angrily. "And don't forget, if you use your powers one more time, you could literally explode."

The twins' auras flared gold and silver. Sophie squeezed her eyes shut as a flood of impressions, vague thoughts and random ideas slammed into her consciousness. Her blue eyes blinked, momentarily silver, and she suddenly realized that she was experiencing her brother's thoughts. She wrenched her hand away from him and the thoughts and sensations immediately faded.

"You're jealous!" she whispered in amazement. "Jealous of my powers."

Color touched Josh's cheeks, and Sophie saw the truth in his eyes even before he spoke the lie. "I am not!"

Suddenly, a black-clad police officer burst through the door and out into the yard. There was a long crack running down the front of his face visor, and he was missing one of his black boots. Without pausing, he limped past them and ran into the alley. They could hear the pat of his naked foot and the slap of the leather sole fade away.

Then Scatty strolled out into the yard. She was twirling her nunchaku as if she were Charlie Chaplin swinging a cane. There wasn't a hair out of place or a mark on her body, and her green eyes were bright and alert. "Oh, I'm in a much better mood now," she announced.

The twins looked past her into the corridor. Nothing and no one moved in the darkness beyond.

"But there were about ten of them . . . ," Sophie began.

Scathach shrugged. "Twelve, actually."

"Armed . . . ," Josh said. He glanced sidelong at his sister, then back at the Warrior. He swallowed hard. "You didn't . . . didn't kill them, did you?"

86

Wood snapped and something collapsed in the shop

"No, they're just . . . sleeping." Scatty smiled.

"But how did you—" Josh began.

"I am the Warrior," Scatty said simply.

Sophie caught a hint of movement and opened her mouth to scream just as the shape appeared out of the corridor and a long-fingered hand fell on Scathach's shoulder. The Warrior didn't react.

"I can't leave you alone for ten minutes," Nicholas Flamel said, stepping out of the shadows. He nodded at the open gate. "We'd better go," he added, ushering them toward the alleyway.

"You missed the fight," Josh told him. "There were ten of them. . . ."

"Twelve," Scathach corrected him quickly.

"I know," the Alchemyst said with a wry smile, "only twelve: they didn't stand a chance."

CHAPTER ELEVEN

"*E*scaped!" Dr. John Dee snarled into the cell phone. "You had them surrounded. How could you let them escape?"

On the other side of the Atlantic, Niccolò Machiavelli remained calm and controlled, only the tightening of his jaw muscles revealing his anger. "You are remarkably well informed."

"I have my sources," Dee snapped, his thin lips twisting into an ugly smile. He knew it would drive Machiavelli crazy knowing there was a spy in his camp.

"You had them trapped in Ojai, I understand," Machiavelli continued softly, "surrounded by an army of the risen dead. And yet they escaped. How could you let them do that?"

Dee sat back in the soft leather seat of the speeding limousine. His face was lit only by the screen of his cell phone, its glow touching his cheekbones and outlining his sharp goatee in cold light, leaving his eyes in shadow. He hadn't told Machiavelli that he'd used necromancy to raise an army of dead humans and beasts. Was this the Italian's subtle way of letting him know that he had a spy in Dee's camp?

"Where are you now?" Machiavelli asked.

Dee glanced out the window of the limousine, trying to read the road signs flashing past. "Somewhere on the 101, heading down to L.A. My jet is fueled and ready to go, and we're cleared for takeoff as soon as I arrive."

"I would anticipate having them in custody before you land in Paris," Machiavelli said. The line crackled furiously, and he paused before adding, "I believe they will attempt to contact Saint-Germain."

Dee sat bolt upright. "The Comte de Saint-Germain? He's back in Paris? I heard he had died in India looking for the lost city of Ophir."

"Obviously not. He has an apartment off the Champs-Elysées and two homes in the suburbs that we are aware of. They are all under observation. If Flamel contacts him, we'll know."

"Don't let them escape this time," Dee barked. "Our masters would not be pleased." He snapped the phone shut before Machiavelli could respond. Then his teeth flashed in a quick smile. The net was closing tighter and tighter.

"He can be so childish," Machiavelli muttered in Italian. "Always has to have the last word." Standing in the ruins of the coffee shop, he carefully closed his phone and looked around at the devastation. It was as if a tornado had ripped through the café. Every item of furniture was broken, the windows were shattered, and there were even cracks in the ceiling. The powdery remains of cups and saucers mixed with spilled coffee beans, scattered tea leaves and broken pastries on the floor. Machiavelli bent to lift up a fork. It was curled in a perfect S shape. Tossing it aside, he picked his way through the debris. Scathach had single-handedly defeated twelve highly trained and heavily armed RAID officers. He had been vaguely hoping that perhaps she had lost some of her martial arts skills in the years since he had last encountered her, but it seemed that his hope had been in vain. The Shadow was as deadly as ever. Getting close to Flamel and the children would be difficult with the Warrior in the picture. In his long life, Niccolò had encountered her on at least half a dozen occasions, and he'd barely survived each time. They'd last met in the frozen ruins of Stalingrad in the winter of 1942. If it hadn't been for her, his forces would have taken the city. He'd sworn then that he would kill her: maybe now was the time to keep that promise.

But how to kill the unkillable? What could stand against the warrior who had trained all of history's greatest heroes, who had fought in every great conflict and whose fighting style was at the heart of just about every martial art?

Stepping out of the demolished shop, Machiavelli breathed deeply, clearing his lungs of the bitter, acrid odor of spilled coffee and sour milk that hung in the air. Dagon pulled open the car door as he approached, and the Italian saw himself reflected in his driver's dark glasses. He paused before stepping into the car and glanced up at the police closing off the streets, the heavily armed riot squad gathering in small groups and the plain clothes officers in their unmarked cars. The French secret service were his to command, he could order in the police, and he had access to a private army of hundreds of men and women who would do his bidding without question. And yet he knew that none of them could stand against the Warrior. He came to a decision and looked at Dagon before climbing into the car.

"Find the Disir."

Dagon stiffened, showing a rare sign of emotion. "Is that wise?" he asked.

"It is necessary."

CHAPTER TWELVE

"The Witch said we should get to the Eiffel Tower by seven, and to wait there for ten minutes," Nicholas Flamel said as they hurried down the narrow alley. "If no one shows up in that time, we are to return there at eight and again at nine."

"Who'll be there?" Sophie asked, jogging to keep up with Flamel's long stride. She was exhausted, and the few moments sitting in the café had only served to emphasize just how tired she was. Her legs felt leaden and there was a sharp stitch in her left side.

The Alchemyst shrugged. "I don't know. Whoever the Witch can contact."

"That's assuming there is anyone in Paris willing to risk helping you," Scathach said lightly. "You are a dangerous enemy, Nicholas, and probably an even more dangerous friend.

Death and destruction have always followed closely at your heels."

Josh glanced sidelong at his sister, knowing she was listening. She deliberately looked away, but he knew she was uncomfortable with the conversation.

"Well, if no one turns up," Flamel said, "then we'll go to plan B."

Scathach's lips curled into a humorless smile. "I didn't even know we had a plan A. What's plan B?"

"I haven't gotten that far yet." He grinned. Then the smile faded. "I just wish Perenelle were here; she'd know what to do."

"We should split up," Josh said suddenly.

Flamel, who was in the lead, glanced over his shoulder. "I don't think so."

"We have to," Josh said firmly. "It makes sense." But as he said it, he wondered why the Alchemyst didn't want them to split up.

"Josh is right," Sophie said. "The police are looking for the four of us. I'm sure they have a description by now: two teenagers, a red-haired girl and an old man. It's not really a common group."

"Old!" Nicholas sounded vaguely insulted, his French accent pronounced. "Scatty is two thousand years older than I!"

"Yes. But the difference is that I don't look it," the Warrior teased with a grin. "Splitting up is a good idea."

Josh stopped at the mouth of the narrow alley and looked

up and down. Police sirens wailed and warbled all around them.

Sophie stood beside her brother, and while the similarity in their features was obvious, he suddenly noticed that there were now lines on her forehead, and her bright blue eyes had become cloudy, the irises flecked with silver. "Roux said we should turn left for the Rue de Dunkerque or right for the Metro station."

"I'm not sure that splitting up . . ." Flamel hesitated.

Josh spun around. "We have to," he said decisively. "Sophie and I will—" he began, but Nicholas shook his head, interrupting him.

"OK. I agree that we should split up. But the police may be looking for twins. . . ."

"We don't look too much like twins," Sophie said quickly. "Josh is taller than me."

"And you both have blond hair and bright blue eyes, and neither of you speaks French," Scatty added. "Sophie, you come with me. Two girls together will not attract too much attention. Josh and Nicholas can go together."

"I'm not leaving Sophie . . . ," Josh protested, suddenly panicked at even the thought of being separated from his sister in this strange city.

"I'll be safe with Scatty," Sophie said with a smile. "You worry too much. And I know Nicholas will look after you."

Josh didn't look too sure. "I'd rather stay with my sister," Josh said firmly.

"Let the girls go together; it's better this way," Flamel said. "Safer."

"Safer?" Josh said incredulously. "Nothing about this is safe."

"Josh!" Sophie snapped, in the exact tone that their mother sometimes used. "Enough." She turned back to the Warrior. "You'll need to do something with your hair. If the police have a description of a red-haired girl in black combats . . ."

"You're right." Scathach's left hand moved in a quick twisting gesture and suddenly she was holding a short-bladed knife between her fingers. She turned to Flamel. "I'm going to need some cloth." Without waiting for an answer, she spun him around and lifted his battered leather jacket. With neat precise moves, she cut a square from the back of Flamel's loose black T-shirt. Then she dropped his leather jacket back in place and twisted the square of fabric into a bandana, knotting it at the back of her head, covering her distinctive hair.

"This was my favorite T-shirt," Flamel muttered. "It's vintage." He shifted his shoulder uncomfortably. "And now my back is cold."

"Don't be such a baby. I'll buy you a new one," Scatty said. She caught Sophie's hand. "Come on. Let's go. See you at the Tower."

"Do you know the way?" Nicholas called after her.

Scatty laughed. "I lived here for nearly sixty years, remember? I was here when the tower was built."

Flamel nodded. "Well, try not to draw attention to yourself."

"I'll try."

"Sophie . . . ," Josh began.

"I know," his sister answered, "be careful." She turned back and hugged her brother quickly, their auras crackling. "Everything's going to be all right," she said softly, reading the fear in his eyes.

Josh forced himself to smile, and he nodded. "How do you know? Magic?"

"I just know," she said simply. Her eyes blinked briefly silver. "This is all happening for a reason—remember the prophecy. Everything's going to work out fine."

"I believe you," he said, even though he didn't. "Be careful, and remember," he added, "no wind."

Sophie hugged him quickly again. "No wind," she whispered in his ear, and then spun away.

Nicholas and Josh watched Scatty and Sophie disappear down the street, heading toward the Metro station; then they turned in the opposite direction. Just before they rounded a corner, Josh glanced back over his shoulder and saw that his sister had done the same. They both raised their hands and waved good-bye.

Josh waited until she had turned away and then lowered his hand. Now he was truly alone, in a strange city, thousands of miles from home, with a man he didn't trust, a man he had started to fear.

"I thought you said you knew the way," Sophie said.

"It's been a while since I was here," the Warrior admitted, "and the streets have changed quite a bit."

"But you said you were here when the Eiffel Tower was

built." She stopped, abruptly realizing what she had just said. "And when was that exactly?" she asked.

"In 1889. I left a couple of months later."

Scathach stopped outside the Metro station and asked directions from a newspaper and magazine seller. The tiny Chinese woman spoke very little French so Scathach quickly switched to another language. Sophie abruptly realized that she recognized it—it was Mandarin. The smiling clerk came out from behind the counter and pointed down the street, speaking so quickly that Sophie was unable to pick up individual words, despite the Witch's knowledge of the language. It sounded as if she were singing. Scathach thanked her, then bowed, and the woman matched the bow.

Sophie caught the Warrior's arm and dragged her away. "So much for not attracting attention to yourself," she murmured. "People were starting to stare."

"What were they staring at?" Scathach asked, genuinely puzzled.

"Oh, probably just the sight of a white girl speaking fluent Chinese and then bowing," Sophie said with a grin. "It was quite a performance."

"One day everyone will speak Mandarin, and bowing is just good manners," Scathach said, setting off down the street, following the directions the woman had given.

Sophie fell into step beside her. "Where did you learn Chinese?" she asked.

"In China. Actually, I was speaking Mandarin to the woman, but I also speak Wu and Cantonese. I've spent a lot of time in the Far East over the centuries. I used to love it there."

They walked in silence, and then Sophie said, "So how many languages do you speak?"

Scathach frowned, eyes briefly closing as she considered. "Six or seven . . ."

Sophie nodded. "Six or seven; that's impressive. My mom and dad want us to learn Spanish, and Dad is teaching us Greek and Latin. But I'd really like to learn Japanese. I really want to visit Japan," she added.

". . . six or seven hundred," Scathach continued, then laughed aloud at the stunned expression on Sophie's face. She slipped her arm through Sophie's. "Well, I suppose a few of those would be dead languages, so I'm not sure they count, but remember, I've been around for a very long time."

"Have you really lived for two and a half thousand years?" Sophie asked, glancing sidelong at the girl who looked no older than seventeen. She suddenly grinned: never once had she imagined herself asking a question like that. It was just another example of how her life had changed.

"Two thousand, five hundred and seventeen humani years." Scathach smiled a tight-lipped smile that hid her vampire teeth. "Hekate once abandoned me in a particularly nasty Underworld Shadowrealm. It took me centuries to find my way out. And when I was younger I spent a lot of time in the Shadowrealms of Lyonesse, Hy-Brasil and Tir na nOg, where time moves at a different pace. Shadowrealm time is not the same as humani time, so I really only count my time on this earth. And who knows, you may get to find out for yourself. You and Josh are unique and powerful and will grow even more powerful as you master the elemental magics. If you don't discover the secret of immortality yourselves, someone may offer it to you as a gift. Come on, let's cross." Catching hold of Sophie's hand, she pulled her across a narrow road.

Although it had only just turned six in the morning, traffic was starting to build. Vans were making deliveries to restaurants, and the chill morning air was beginning to fill with the mouth-watering odors of fresh-baked bread and pastries and percolating coffee. Sophie breathed in the familiar fragrances: croissants and coffee reminded her that only two days ago she had been serving those in The Coffee Cup. She blinked away the sting of sudden tears. So much had happened, so much had changed in the past two days. "What's it like to live so long?" she wondered aloud.

"Lonely," Scatty said quietly.

"How long . . . how long will you live?" she asked the Warrior cautiously.

Scatty shrugged and smiled. "Who knows? If I'm careful, exercise regularly and watch my diet, I could live another couple of thousand years." Then her smile faded. "But I'm not invulnerable, nor am I invincible. I can be killed." She saw the stricken look on Sophie's face and squeezed her arm. "But that's not going to happen. Do you know how many humani, immortals, Elders, were-creatures and assorted monsters have tried to kill me?"

The girl shook her head.

"Well, nor do I, actually. But there have been thousands. Maybe even tens of thousands. And I'm still here; what does that tell you?"

"That you're good?"

"Hah! I'm better than good. I am the best. I am the Warrior." Scathach stopped and looked into a bookshop window, but Sophie noticed that when she turned to talk, her bright green eyes were darting everywhere, taking in their surroundings.

Resisting the temptation to turn around, Sophie lowered her voice to a whisper. "Are we being followed?" She was surprised to discover that she wasn't the least bit afraid; she knew, instinctively, that nothing could harm her when she was with Scatty.

"No, I don't think so. Just old habits." Scathach smiled. "The same habits that have kept me alive through the centuries." She moved away from the shop and Sophie linked her arm with Scatty's.

"Nicholas called you other names when we met you. . . ." Sophie frowned, trying to remember how he'd first introduced Scathach back in San Francisco only two days ago. "He called you the Warrior Maid, the Shadow, the Daemon Slayer, the King Maker."

"Those are just names," Scathach muttered, sounding embarrassed.

"They sound like more than names," Sophie pressed. "They sound like titles . . . titles you've earned?" she persisted.

"Well, I've had lots of names," Scathach said, "names my

friends gave me, names my foes called me. I was the Warrior Maid first, and then I became the Shadow, because of my skills at concealment. I perfected the first camouflage clothing."

"You sound like a ninja," Sophie laughed. Listening to the Warrior talk, images from the Witch's memories flickered through her head, and she knew that Scatty was telling the truth.

"I tried teaching ninjas, but they were never that good, believe me. I became the Daemon Slayer when I killed Raktabija. And I was called the King Maker when I helped put Arthur on the throne," she added, her voice turning grim. She shook her head quickly. "That was a mistake. And not my first either." She laughed, but it came out shaky and sounding forced. "I've made a lot of mistakes."

"My dad says you can learn from your mistakes."

Scatty barked a laugh. "Not me." She was unable to keep the note of bitterness from her voice.

"It sounds like you've had a tough life," Sophie said quietly.

"It's been tough," the Warrior admitted.

"Has there ever been a . . ." Sophie paused, hunting for the word. "Have you ever had a . . . a boyfriend?"

Scathach looked at her sharply, then turned her face away to stare into a shop window. For a moment Sophie thought she was examining the display of shoes, but then she realized that the Warrior was looking at her own reflection in the glass. The girl wondered what she saw.

"No," Scatty finally admitted. "There's never been

anyone close, anyone special." She smiled tightly. "The Elders fear and avoid me. And I try not to get too close to humani. It's too hard watching them age and die. That is the curse of immortality: to watch the world change, to see everything you know wither. Remember that, Sophie, if someone offers you the gift of immortality." She made the last word sound like a profanity.

"It sounds so lonely," Sophie said carefully. She never thought about what it must be like to be immortal before—to live on while everything familiar changed and everyone you knew left you. They walked a dozen steps in silence before Scatty spoke again.

"Yes, it's been lonely," she admitted, "very lonely."

"I know about lonely," Sophie said thoughtfully. "With Mom and Dad away so much or moving us from city to city, it's hard to make friends. It's almost impossible to keep them. I suppose that's why Josh and I have always been so close; we've had no one else. My best friend, Elle, is in New York. We talk on the phone all the time, and e-mail and chat on IM, but I haven't seen her since Christmas. She sends me photos off her cell every time she changes her hair color, so I know what she looks like," she added with a smile. "Josh doesn't even try to make friends, though."

"Friends are important," Scathach agreed, squeezing Sophie's arm lightly. "But while friends come and go, you will always have family."

"What about your family? The Witch of Endor mentioned your mother and brother." Even as she was speaking,

102

images from the Witch's memories popped into her mind: a sharp-faced older woman with bloodred eyes and an ashen-skinned young man with blazing red hair.

The Warrior shrugged uncomfortably. "We don't talk much these days. My parents were Elders, born and raised on the isle of Danu Talis. When my grandmother Dora left the island to teach the first humani, they never forgave her. Like many Elders, they considered the humani to be little better than beasts. 'Curiosities,' my father called them." A flicker of disgust crossed her face. "Prejudice has always been with us. My mother and father were even more shocked when I announced that I too was going to work with the humani, to fight for them, to protect them when I could."

"Why?" Sophie asked.

Scatty's voice grew soft. "It was obvious to me, even then, that the humani were the future and that the days of the Elder Races were drawing to a close." She glanced sidelong at Sophie, who was surprised to find Scathach's eyes bright and glittering, almost as if there were tears in them. "My parents warned me that if I left home, I would bring shame on the family name and they would disown me." Scatty's voice trailed into silence.

"But you still left," Sophie guessed.

The Warrior nodded. "I left. We didn't speak for a millennium . . . until they were in trouble and needed my help," she added with a grim smile. "We talk occasionally now, but I'm afraid they still consider me an embarrassment."

Sophie squeezed her hand gently. She felt uncomfortable

with what the Warrior had just told her, but she also realized that Scatty had shared something incredibly personal, something that Sophie doubted the ancient warrior had ever shared with anyone else. "I'm sorry. I didn't mean to upset you."

Scathach squeezed back. "You didn't upset me. They upset me—more than two thousand years ago, in fact—and I can still remember it as if it were yesterday. It's been a long time since anyone took the trouble to ask about my life. And believe me, it's not been all bad. I've had some wonderful adventures," she said brightly. "Did I tell you about the time I was the lead singer in an all-girl band? Sort of goth-punk Spice Girls, but we only did Tori Amos covers. We were very big in Germany." She lowered her voice. "The problem was, we were all vampires. . . ."

Nicholas and Josh turned onto the Rue de Dunkerque and discovered there were police everywhere. "Keep walking," Nicholas said urgently as Josh slowed. "And act natural."

"Natural," Josh muttered. "I don't even know what that means anymore."

"Walk quickly, but don't run," Nicholas said patiently. "You're completely innocent, a student on the way to class or heading to a summer job. Look at the police, but don't stare. And if one looks at you, don't turn away quickly, just let your eyes drift on to the next character. That's what an ordinary citizen would do. If we're stopped, I'll do the talking. We'll be fine." He saw the skeptical look on the boy's face and his smile widened. "Trust me, I've been doing this for a very long time. The trick is to move as if you have every right in the world to be here. The police are trained to look for people who look and act suspicious."

"Don't you think we fall into both categories?" Josh asked.

"We look like we belong—and that makes us invisible."

A group of three policemen didn't even look in their direction as they walked past. Josh noticed that each was wearing a different type of uniform, and the men seemed to be arguing.

"Good," Nicholas said when they were out of earshot.

"What's good?"

Nicholas inclined his head in the direction they had just come. "You saw the different uniforms?"

The boy nodded.

"France has a complicated police system; Paris even more so. There is the Police Nationale, the Gendarmerie Nationale and the Préfecture de Police. Machiavelli has obviously pulled out all the stops to find us, but his great failing has always been that he assumes that other people are as coldly logical as he is. He obviously thinks that if he puts all these police resources on the streets, they will do nothing but search for us. But there is a great deal of rivalry between the various units, and no doubt everyone wants the credit for capturing the dangerous criminals."

"Is that what you've made us into now?" Josh asked, unable to disguise the sudden bitterness in his voice. "Two days ago, Sophie and I were happy, normal people. And now look at us: I barely know my own sister. We've been hunted, attacked by monsters and now we're on a police most-wanted list. You've made us criminals, Mr. Flamel. But this isn't the first time you've been a criminal, is it?" he snapped. He shoved his hands deep into his pockets and closed them into fists to prevent them from shaking. He was scared and angry, and the fear was making him reckless. He'd never talked to an adult like that before.

"No," Nicholas said mildly, his pale eyes starting to glitter dangerously. "I've been called a criminal. But only by my enemies. It seems to me," he added after a long pause, "that you've been talking to Dr. Dee. And the only place you could have encountered him was in Ojai, since that was the only time you were out of my sight."

Josh didn't even think about denying it. "I met Dee when the three of you were busy with the Witch," he admitted defiantly. "He told me a lot about you."

"I'm quite sure he did," Flamel murmured. He waited by the curb as a dozen students on bicycles and mopeds sped past; then he strolled across the street. Josh hurried after him.

"He said that you never tell anyone everything."

"True," Flamel agreed. "If you tell people everything, you take away their opportunity to learn."

"He said you stole the Book of Abraham from the Louvre."

Nicholas walked for half a dozen steps before nodding. "Well, I suppose that is true too," he said, "though it's not quite so straightforward as he would like to paint it. Certainly, in the seventeenth century, the book briefly fell into the hands of Cardinal Richelieu."

Josh shook his head. "Who's that?"

"Have you never read *The Three Musketeers*?" Flamel asked in astonishment.

"Nope. Didn't even see the movie."

Flamel shook his head. "I've got a copy in the shop . . . ," he began, and then stopped. When he'd walked away from the bookshop on Thursday, it had been a trashed ruin. "Richelieu appears in the books—and the movies, too. He was a real person and was known as the l'Eminence Rouge—the Red Eminence—so named after his cardinal's red robes," he explained. "He was King Louis XIII's chief minister, but in reality he ruled the country. In 1632, Dee managed to trap Perenelle and me in a part of the old city. His inhuman agents had surrounded us; there were ghouls in the earth beneath our feet, Dire-Crows in the air, and Baobhan Sith were tracking us through the streets." Nicholas shrugged uncomfortably at the memory and looked up and around, almost as if he expected to see the creatures appear again. "I was beginning to think that I was going to have to destroy the Codex rather than see it fall into Dee's hands. Then Perenelle suggested one last option: we could hide the book in plain sight. It was simple and brilliant!"

"What did you do?" Josh asked, curious now.

Flamel's teeth flashed in a quick smile. "I sought an audience with Cardinal Richelieu and presented him with the book."

"You *gave* it to him? Did he know what it was?"

"Of course he did. The Book of Abraham is famous, Josh—or maybe *infamous* might be a better word. Next time you go online, look it up."

"Did the cardinal know who you were?" he asked. Listening to Flamel talk, it was easy—so easy—to believe everything he said. And then he remembered how believable Dee had been back in Ojai.

Flamel smiled, remembering. "Cardinal Richelieu believed I was one of the descendants of Nicholas Flamel. So we presented him with the Book of Abraham and he put it in his library." Nicholas laughed softly as he shook his head. "The safest place in all of France."

Josh frowned. "But surely when he looked at it, he saw that the text moved?"

"Perenelle put a glamour over the book. It's a particular type of spell—astonishingly simple, apparently, though I could never master it—so when the cardinal looked at the book, he saw what he expected to see: pages of ornate Greek and Aramaic writing."

"Did Dee catch you?"

"Almost. We escaped down the Seine on a barge. Dee himself stood on the Pont Neuf with a dozen musketeers and fired scores of shots at us. They all missed; despite the musketeers' reputation, they were terrible shots," he added. "And then, a couple of weeks later, Perenelle and I returned to Paris, broke into the library and stole our book back. So I suppose you could say that Dee is right," he concluded. "I am a thief."

Josh walked on in silence; he had no idea what to believe.

He *wanted* to believe Flamel; working in the bookshop alongside the man, he'd grown to like and respect him. He *wanted* to trust him . . . and yet he could never forgive him for putting Sophie in danger.

Flamel glanced up and down the street; then, putting his hand on Josh's shoulder, he guided him through the stalled traffic and across the Rue de Dunkerque. "Just in case we're being followed," he said softly, his lips barely moving as they darted through the early-morning traffic.

Once they were across the road, Josh shrugged off Nicholas's hand. "What Dee said made a lot of sense," he continued.

"I'm sure it did," Flamel said with a laugh. "Dr. John Dee has been many things in his long and colorful life, a magus and a mathematician, an alchemist and spy. But let me tell you, Josh, he was often a rogue and always a liar. He is a master of lies and half-truths, and he practiced and perfected his craft in that most dangerous of times, the Elizabethan Age. He knows that the best lie is one that is wrapped around a core of truth." He paused, his eyes flickering over the crowd streaming past them. "What else did he tell you?"

Josh hesitated for a moment before replying. He was tempted not to reveal all of his conversation with Dee but then realized that he'd probably said too much already. "Dee said that you only used the spells in the Codex for your own good."

Nicholas nodded. "It's a fair point. I use the immortality spell to keep Perenelle and myself alive, that is true. And I use the philosopher's stone formulation to turn ordinary metal into gold and coal into diamonds. There's no money in book-selling, let me tell you. But we only make as much wealth as we need—we're not greedy."

Josh hurried ahead of Flamel, then turned around to face him. "This isn't about the money," he snapped. "There is so much else you could be doing with what's in that book. Dee said it could be used to turn this world into a paradise, that it could cure all disease, even repair the environment." He found it incomprehensible that someone would *not* want to do that.

Flamel stopped in front of Josh. His eyes were almost on a level with the boy's. "Yes, there are spells in the Book which would do all that and much, much more," he said seriously. "I've glimpsed spells in the Book that could reduce this world to a cinder, others that would make the deserts bloom. But Josh, even if I could work those spells—which I cannot—the material in the Book is not mine to use." Flamel's pale eyes bored into Josh's, and Josh had no doubt now that the Alchemyst was telling the truth. "Perenelle and I are only the Guardians of the Book. We are simply holding it in trust until we can pass it on to its rightful owners. They will know how to use it."

"But who are the rightful owners? Where are they?"

Nicholas Flamel put both hands on Josh's shoulders and stared into his bright blue eyes. "Well, I was hoping," he said very softly, "that it might be you and Sophie. In fact, I'm gambling everything—my life, Perenelle's life, the survival of the entire human race—that you are."

Standing on the Rue de Dunkerque, looking into the

110

Alchemyst's eyes, reading the truth in them, Josh felt the people fade away until it was as if they were standing alone on the street. He swallowed hard. "And you believe that?"

"With all my heart," Flamel said simply. "And everything I have done, I've done to protect you and Sophie and to prepare you for what is to come. You have to believe me, Josh. You must. I know you're angry because of what has happened with Sophie, but I would never let her come to harm."

"She could have died or fallen into a coma," Josh muttered.

Flamel shook his head. "If she were an ordinary human, then yes, that could have happened. But I know she isn't ordinary. Nor are you," he added.

"Because of our auras?" Josh asked, digging for as much information as he could get.

"Because you are the twins of legend."

"And if you're wrong? Have you thought about that: what happens if you're wrong?"

"Then the Dark Elders return."

"Would that be so bad?" Josh wondered aloud.

Nicholas opened his mouth to reply and quickly pressed his lips tightly together, biting back whatever he had been about to say, but not before Josh saw the quick flash of anger that darted across his face. Finally, Nicholas forced his lips into a smile. Gently, he turned Josh around so that he was facing the street. "What do you see?" he asked.

Josh shook his head and shrugged. "Nothing . . . just a bunch of people heading off to work. And the police looking for us," he added.

Nicholas caught Josh's shoulder and urged him down the street. "Don't think of them as a bunch of people," Flamel admonished sharply. "That's how Dee and his kind see humankind: what they call the humani. I see individuals, with worries and cares, with family and loved ones, with friends and colleagues. I see people."

Josh shook his head. "I don't understand."

"Dee and the Elders he serves look at these people and see only slaves." He paused, then quietly added, "Or food."

CHAPTER THIRTEEN

Lying flat on her back, Perenelle Flamel stared at the stained stone ceiling directly above her head and wondered how many other prisoners incarcerated on Alcatraz had done the same. How many others had traced the lines and cracks in the stonework, seen shapes in the black water marks, imagined pictures in the brown damp? Almost all of them, she guessed.

And how many had heard voices? she wondered. She was sure that many of the prisoners had imagined they heard sounds in the dark—whispered words, hushed phrases—but unless they possessed Perenelle's special gift, what they were hearing did not exist outside their imaginations.

Perenelle heard the voices of the ghosts of Alcatraz.

Listening intently, she could distinguish hundreds of voices, maybe even thousands. Men and women—children, too—clamoring and shouting, muttering and crying, calling out for lost loved ones, repeating their own names again and again, proclaiming their innocence, cursing their jailers. She frowned; they weren't what she was looking for.

Allowing the voices to wash over her, she sorted through the sounds until she picked up one voice louder than all the rest: strong and confident, it cut through the babble, and Perenelle found herself concentrating on it, focusing on the words, identifying the language.

"This is my island."

It was a man, speaking Spanish in an old, very formal accent. Concentrating on the ceiling, Perenelle tuned out the other voices. "Who are you?" In the chill damp of the cell, her words puffed from her mouth like smoke and the myriad ghosts fell silent.

There was a long pause, as if the ghost was surprised to be spoken to; then he said proudly, *"I was the first European to sail into this bay, the first to see this island."*

A shape began to form on the roof directly over her head, the crude outline of a face appearing in the cracks and spiderwebs, the black damp and the green moss lending it shape and definition.

"I called this place la Isla de los Alcatraces."

"The Isle of the Pelicans," Perenelle said, her words the merest whispered breath.

The face in the ceiling solidified briefly. It was that of a handsome man with a long, narrow face and dark eyes. Water droplets formed and the eyes blinked tears.

"Who are you?" Perenelle asked again.

"I am Juan Manuel de Ayala. I discovered Alcatraz."

114

Claws click-clacked on the stones outside the cell, and the smell of snake and rancid meat wafted down the corridor. Perenelle remained silent until the scent and the footsteps retreated, and when she looked at the ceiling again, the face had taken on more detail, the cracks in the stonework creating the deep wrinkles on the man's forehead and around his eyes. A sailor's face, she realized, the wrinkles caused by squinting toward distant horizons.

"Why are you here?" she wondered aloud. "Did you die here?"

"No. Not here." Narrow lips curled in a smile. *"I returned because I fell in love with this place from the very first moment I set eyes on it. It was in the year of Our Lord 1775, and I was on the good ship* San Carlos. *I even remember the month, August, and the date, the fifth."*

Perenelle nodded. She had come across ghosts like de Ayala's before. Men and women who had been so influenced or affected by a place that they returned to it again and again in their dreams, and eventually, when they died, their spirit returned to the same location to become a Guardian ghost.

"I have watched over this island for generations. I will always watch over it."

Perenelle stared up at the face. "It must have saddened you to see your beautiful island become a place of pain and suffering," she probed.

Something twisted in the shape's mouth, and a single drop of water fell from its eye to spatter on Perenelle's cheek.

"Dark days, sad days, but gone now . . . thankfully, gone." The ghost's lips moved and the words whispered in Perenelle's

115

head. *"There has not been a human prisoner on Alcatraz since 1963, and the island has been peaceful since 1971."*

"But now there is a new prisoner on your beloved island," Perenelle said evenly. "A prisoner guarded by a warden more terrible than any this island has ever seen before."

The face in the ceiling altered, watery eyes narrowing, blinking. *"Who? You?"*

"I am held here against my will," Perenelle said. "I am Alcatraz's last prisoner, and I am guarded by no human jailor, but by a sphinx."

"No!"

"See for yourself!"

The plaster crackled and damp dust rained down on Perenelle's face. When she opened her eyes again, the face in the ceiling had gone, leaving nothing more than a stain in its wake.

Perenelle allowed herself a smile.

"What amuses you, humani?" The voice was a slithering hiss, and the language predated the human race.

Swinging herself into a sitting position, Perenelle focused on the creature standing in the corridor less than six feet from her.

Generations of ancient humans had tried to capture the image of this creature on cave walls and pots, etching her shape in stone, capturing her likeness on parchments. And none of them had even come close to the true horror of the sphinx.

The body was that of a hugely muscled lion, the fur scarred and cut with the evidence of old wounds. A pair of eagle's wings curled out of its shoulders and lay flat against its back, the feathers ragged and filthy. And the small, almost delicate-looking head was that of a beautiful young woman.

The sphinx stepped up to the bars of the cell, and a black forked tongue wavered in the air in front of Perenelle. "You have no reason to smile, humani. I have learned that your husband and the Warrior are trapped in Paris. Soon they will be prisoners, and this time Dr. Dee will ensure that they never escape again. I understand the Elders have given the doctor permission to finally slay the legendary Alchemyst."

Perenelle felt something twist in the pit of her stomach. For generations the Dark Elders had been intent on capturing Nicholas and Perenelle alive. If she was to believe the sphinx and they were prepared to kill Nicholas, then everything had changed. "Nicholas will escape," she said confidently.

"Not this time." The lion's tail of the sphinx whipped excitedly back and forth, raising plumes of dust. "Paris belongs to the Italian, Machiavelli, and soon he will be joined by the English Magician. The Alchemyst cannot evade them both."

"And the children?" Perenelle asked, eyes narrowing dangerously. If anything had happened to Nicholas or the children . . .

The sphinx's feathers ruffled, raising a musty sour smell. "Dee believes the humani children are powerful, that they may indeed be the twins of prophecy and legend. He also believes they can be convinced that they should serve us, rather than following the ramblings of a mad old bookseller." The sphinx took a deep shuddering breath. "But if they do not do as they are told, then they too will perish."

"And what about me?"

The sphinx's pretty mouth opened to reveal a maw of savage, needle-pointed teeth. Her long black tongue thrashed wildly in the air. "You are mine, Sorceress," she hissed. "The Elders have given you to me as a gift for my millennia of service to them. When your husband has been captured and slain, then I will be given permission to eat your memories. What a feast it will be. I intend to savor every last morsel. When I am finished with you, you will remember nothing, not even your own name." The sphinx started to laugh, the sound hissing and mocking, bouncing off the bare stone walls.

And then a cell door slammed.

The sudden sound shocked the sphinx into silence. Her small head turned, her tongue flickering, tasting the air.

Another door boomed shut.

And then another.

And another.

The sphinx spun away, claws striking sparks off the floor. "Who's there?" Her voice screeched off the damp stones.

Abruptly, all the cell doors in the upper gallery rattled open and closed in quick succession, the sound a rumbling detonation that vibrated deep into the heart of the prison, causing dust to rain from the ceiling.

Snarling and hissing, the sphinx bounded away, looking for the source of the noise.

With an icy smile, Perenelle swung her feet back up on the bench, lay back and rested her head on her laced fingers.

The island of Alcatraz belonged to Juan Manuel de Ayala, and it looked as though he was announcing his presence. Perenelle heard cell doors clang, wood thump and walls rattle and knew what de Ayala had become: a poltergeist.

A noisy ghost.

She also knew what de Ayala was doing. The sphinx fed off Perenelle's magical energies; all the poltergeist had to do was to keep the creature away from the cell for a little time and Perenelle's powers could begin to regenerate. Raising her left hand, the woman concentrated hard. The tiniest ice white spark danced between her fingers, then fizzled away.

Soon.

Soon.

The Sorceress closed her hand into a fist. When her powers had recovered, she would bring Alcatraz tumbling down around the sphinx's ears.

CHAPTER FOURTEEN

*T*he beautifully intricate Eiffel Tower loomed more than nine hundred feet over Josh's head. There was a time when he'd compiled a list for a school project of the Ten Wonders of the Modern World. The metal tower had been number two on that list, and he'd always promised himself that someday he'd get to see it.

And now that he was finally in Paris, he didn't even look up.

Standing almost directly beneath the center of the tower, he rose on his toes, turning his head left and right, searching for his twin among the surprisingly large number of early-morning tourists. Where was she?

Josh was scared.

No, more than scared—he was terrified.

The last couple of days had taught him the true meaning of fear. Prior to the events of Thursday, Josh had only ever really been afraid of failing a test or being publicly humiliated in class. He had other fears too, those vague, shivery thoughts that came in the dead of night, when he found himself lying awake wondering what would happen if his parents had an accident. Sara and Richard Newman both held PhD's in archaeology and paleontology, and while that wasn't the most dangerous line of work, their research sometimes took them into countries in the midst of religious or political turmoil, or they conducted their digs in areas of the world ravaged by hurricanes or in earthquake zones or close to active volcanoes. The sudden movements of the earth's crust often threw up extraordinary archaeological finds.

But his deepest, darkest fear was that something would happen to his sister. Although Sophie was twenty-eight seconds older, he always thought of her as his baby sister. He was bigger and stronger, and it was his job to protect her.

And now, in a way, something terrible *had* happened to his twin.

She had changed in ways he could not even begin to comprehend. She had become more like Flamel and Scathach and their kind than like him: she had become more than human.

For the first time in his life, he felt alone. He was losing his sister. But there was one way to be her equal again: he had to have his own powers Awakened.

Josh turned—just as Sophie and Scathach appeared, hurrying across a broad bridge that led directly to the tower. Relief washed over him. "They're here," he said to Flamel, who was facing the opposite direction.

"I know," Nicholas said, his French accent sounding stronger than usual. "And they're not alone."

121

Josh tore his gaze away from his approaching sister and Scathach. "What do you mean?"

Nicholas inclined his head slightly and Josh turned. Two tourist buses had just arrived at the Place Joffre and were disgorging their passengers. The tourists—Americans, Josh guessed by their clothing—milled around, chatting and laughing, cameras and videos already whirring while their guides tried to gather them together. A third bus, bright yellow, pulled up, spilling dozens of excited Japanese tourists out on the pavement. Confused, Josh looked at Nicholas: did he mean the buses?

"In black," Flamel said enigmatically, pointing by lifting his chin.

Josh turned and spotted the man in black striding toward them, moving swiftly through the holiday crowd. None of the tourists even glanced at the stranger weaving his way among them, twisting and turning like a dancer, taking care to not so much as brush against them. Josh guessed the man was probably about his own height, but it was impossible to make out his body shape because he was wearing a three-quarter-length black leather coat that flapped about him as he walked. The collar was turned up, and his hands were pushed deep into the pockets. Josh felt his heart sink: now what?

Sophie raced up and punched her brother in the arm. "You got here," she said breathlessly. "Any trouble?"

Josh tilted his head toward the approaching man in the leather coat. "I'm not sure."

Scathach appeared beside the twins. She wasn't even breathing hard, Josh noted. In fact, she wasn't breathing at all.

"Trouble?" Sophie asked, looking at Scathach.

The Warrior smiled, tight-lipped. "Depends how you define trouble," she murmured.

"On the contrary," Nicholas said, smiling broadly. He heaved a sigh of relief. "It's a friend. An old friend. A good friend."

The man in the black coat was closer now, and the twins could see that he had a small, almost round face, deeply tanned skin and piercing blue eyes. Thick shoulder-length black hair was swept back off his high forehead. Mounting the steps, he pulled both hands out of his pockets and spread his arms wide, silver rings winking on every finger and on his thumbs, matching the silver studs in both ears. A broad smile revealed misshapen, slightly yellowed teeth.

"Master," he said, wrapping both arms around Nicholas and kissing him quickly on both cheeks. "You have returned." The man blinked, eyes moist, and for an instant the pupils winked red. There was a sudden hint of burnt leaves in the air.

"And you never left," Nicholas said warmly, holding the man at arm's length and examining him critically. "You look well, Francis. Better than the last time I saw you." He turned, putting his arm around the man's shoulder. "Scathach you know, of course."

"Who could forget the Shadow?" The blue-eyed man stepped forward, caught the Warrior's pale hand in his and brought it to his lips in an old-fashioned courtly gesture.

Scathach leaned forward and pinched the man's cheek hard enough to leave a red mark. "I told you last time; don't do that to me."

"Admit it—you love it." He grinned. "And this must be Sophie and Josh. The Witch told me about them," he added. The man's bright blue eyes remained wide and unblinking as he regarded the two in turn. "The twins of legend," he murmured, frowning a bit as he stared hard at them. "You're sure?"

"I'm sure," Nicholas said firmly.

The stranger nodded and bowed slightly. "The twins of legend," he repeated. "I am honored to make your acquaintance. Allow me to introduce myself. I am le Comte de Saint-Germain," he announced dramatically, and then paused, almost as if he expected them to know the name.

The twins looked at him blankly, identical expressions on their faces.

"But you must call me Francis; all my friends do."

"My favorite student," Nicholas added fondly. "Certainly my best student. We've known one another a long time."

"How long?" Sophie asked automatically, although even as she was asking the question, the answer popped into her head.

"For about three hundred years or so," Nicholas said. "Francis trained to be an alchemist with me. He quickly surpassed me," he added. "He specialized in creating jewels."

"I learned everything I know about alchemy from the master: Nicholas Flamel," Saint-Germain said quickly.

"In the eighteenth century, Francis was also an accomplished singer and musician. And what are you this century?" Nicholas asked.

"Well, I have to say I am disappointed you've not heard of

me," the man said in accentless English. "You've obviously not been keeping up with the charts. I've had five number-one hits in the States and three in Germany, and I won an MTV Europe Best Newcomer award."

"Best *New*comer?" Nicholas grinned, emphasizing the word *new*. "You!"

"You know that I have always been a musician, but in this century, Nicholas, I'm a rock star!" he said proudly. "I am Germain!" He looked at the twins as he spoke, eyebrows raised, nodding, waiting for them to react to the announcement.

They shook their heads simultaneously. "Never heard of you," Josh said bluntly.

Saint-Germain shrugged and looked disappointed. He brought the collar of his coat up around his ears. "Five number-one hits," he muttered.

"What type of music?" Sophie asked, biting the inside of her cheek to keep herself from smiling at the crestfallen expression on the man's face.

"Dance . . . electro . . . techno . . . that sort of thing."

Sophie and Josh shook their heads again. "Don't listen to it," Josh answered, but Saint-Germain was no longer looking at the twins. His head had swiveled toward the Avenue Gustave Eiffel, to where a long sleek black Mercedes had pulled up to the curb. Three plain black vans drew up behind it.

"Machiavelli!" Flamel snapped angrily. "Francis, you were followed."

"But how . . . ," the count began.

"Remember, it's Niccolò we're dealing with." Flamel looked around quickly, assessing the situation. "Scathach,

125

take the twins, go with Saint-Germain. Protect them with your lives."

"We can stay, I can fight," Scathach said.

Nicholas shook his head. He waved at the gathered tourists. "Too many people. Someone would be killed. But Machiavelli is not Dee; he's subtle. He'll not use magic—not if he can help it. We can use that to our advantage. If we split up, he will follow me; I'm the one he wants. And not just me." Reaching under his shirt, he pulled out a small square cloth bag.

"What's that?" Saint-Germain asked.

Nicholas answered Saint-Germain but looked at the twins as he spoke. "Once it held the entire Codex, but now Dee has that. Josh managed to tear two pages from the back of the book. They're in here. The pages contain the Final Summoning," he added significantly. "Dee and his Elders need these pages." He smoothed the cloth and then suddenly handed the bag over to Josh. "Keep these safe," he said.

"Me?" Josh looked from the bag to Flamel's face but made no move to take it from the man's hand.

"Yes, you. Take it," Flamel commanded.

Reluctantly, the boy reached for the bag, the cloth crackling and sparking as he shoved it under his T-shirt. "Why me?" he asked. He looked quickly at his sister. "I mean, Scathach or Saint-Germain would be better. . . ."

"You rescued the pages, Josh. It's only right that you should guard them." Flamel gripped Josh's shoulders and looked into the boy's eyes. "I know I can trust you to take care of them."

Josh pressed his hand against his stomach, feeling the

126

cloth against his skin. When Josh and Sophie had started working in the bookshop and the coffee shop respectively, their father had used an almost identical phrase when talking about Sophie. "I know I can trust you to take care of her." In that moment, he'd felt both proud and a little bit frightened. Right now, he just felt frightened.

The Mercedes driver's door opened and a man in a black suit climbed out, mirrored shades reflecting the early-morning sky, making it look as if he had two holes in his face.

"Dagon," Scathach snarled, sharp teeth suddenly visible, and reached for a weapon in her bag, but Nicholas caught her arm and squeezed it.

"This is not the time."

Dagon opened the rear door and Niccolò Machiavelli emerged. Although he was at least a hundred yards away, they could clearly see the look of triumph on his face.

Behind the Mercedes, the vans' doors slid open simultaneously and heavily armed and armored police jumped out and started jogging toward the tower. A tourist screamed, and the dozens of people standing around the base of the Eiffel Tower immediately swiveled their cameras in that direction.

"Time to go," Flamel said quickly. "You head across the river, I'll lead them in the other direction. Saint-Germain, my friend," Nicholas whispered softly, "we're going to need a distraction to help us escape. Something spectacular."

"Where will you go?" Saint-Germain demanded.

Flamel smiled. "This was my city long before Machiavelli came here. Perhaps some of my old haunts still remain."

"It has changed a lot since you were last here," Saint-Germain warned. As he was speaking, he took Flamel's left hand in both of his, turned it over and pressed the ball of his right thumb into the center of the Alchemyst's palm. Sophie and Josh were close enough to see that when he took his hand away, there was the impression of a tiny black-winged butterfly on Flamel's skin. "It will lead you back to me," Saint-Germain said mysteriously. "Now, you wanted something spectacular." He grinned and pushed back the sleeves of his leather coat to reveal bare arms. His skin was covered in dozens of tiny tattooed butterflies that wrapped around his wrists like bracelets, then coiled up around his arm to the crook of his elbow. Lacing the fingers of his hands together, he twisted his wrists and bent them outward with an audible crack, like a pianist preparing to play. "Did you ever see what Paris did to celebrate the millennium?"

"The millennium?" The twins looked at him blankly.

"The millennium. The year 2000. Although the millennium should have been celebrated in 2001," he added.

"Oh, that millennium," Sophie said. She looked at her brother, confused. What did the millennium have to do with anything?

"Our parents took us to Times Square," Josh said. "Why?"

"Then you missed something truly spectacular here in Paris. Next time you're online, check out the pictures." Saint-Germain rubbed his arms briskly and then, standing below the huge metal tower, he raised his hands high and suddenly the scent of burnt leaves filled the air.

Both Sophie and Josh watched the butterfly tattoos

spasm, then shiver and pulse on Saint-Germain's arms. Gossamer wings trembled and vibrated, antennas twitched . . . and then the tattoos lifted away from the man's flesh.

An endless stream of tiny red and white butterflies peeled off Saint-Germain's pale skin and curled into the cool Parisian air. They circled upward, spinning away from the small man, a seemingly never-ending spiral of crimson and ashen dots. The butterflies curled around the struts and spars, the rivets and bolts of the metal tower, covering it in an iridescent, shimmering skin.

"*Ignis,*" Saint-Germain whispered, throwing back his head and clapping his hands together.

And the Tower exploded into a cracking, sparking fountain of light.

He laughed delightedly at the twins' expressions and said, "Know me: I am le Comte de Saint-Germain. I am the Master of Fire!"

CHAPTER FIFTEEN

"*F*ireworks," Sophie breathed in awe.

The Eiffel Tower lit up with a spectacular fireworks display. Blue and gold traceries of light raced almost one thousand feet to the mast at the very top of the tower, where they blossomed into fountains of blue globes. Sparking, hissing, fizzing rainbow-colored threads wove through the struts, bursting and snapping. The tower's thick rivets popped with white fire, while the arching spars rained cool ice blue droplets into the street far below.

The effect was dramatic, but it became truly spectacular when Saint-Germain snapped the fingers of both hands and the entire Eiffel Tower turned bronze, then gold, then green and finally blue in the morning sun. Rattling traceries of light darted up and down the metal. Catherine wheels and rockets, fountains and Roman candles, flying spinners and snakes spun off from every floor. The mast at the very tip of the tower fountained red, white and blue sparks that cascaded like bubbling liquid down through the heart of the tower.

The crowd was entranced.

People gathered at the base, oohing and aahing, applauding at each new explosion, their cameras clicking furiously. Motorists stopped on the roads and climbed out of their cars, holding camera phones to snap the stunning and beautiful images. Within moments, the dozens of people around the tower had grown to a hundred and then, within a matter of minutes, had doubled and then doubled again as people came running from shops and homes to observe the extraordinary display.

And Nicholas Flamel and his companions were swallowed up by the crowd.

In a rare display of emotion, Machiavelli hit the side of the car so hard it hurt his hand. He watched the growing crowd of people and knew his men would not be able to get through in time to prevent Flamel and the others from escaping.

The air sizzled and spat with fireworks; rockets went whizzing high into the air, where they exploded into spheres and streamers of light. Firecrackers and sparklers rattled around each of the tower's four giant metal legs.

"Sir!" A young police captain stopped before Machiavelli and saluted. "What are your orders? We can push through the crowd, but there may be injuries."

Machiavelli shook his head. "No, do not do that." Dee would do it, he knew. Dee would not hesitate to level the entire tower, killing hundreds just to capture Flamel. Drawing himself up to his full height, Niccolò could just about make out the shape of the leather-clad Saint-Germain and the lethal Scathach herding the young man and woman away. They melted into the now-huge crowd and disappeared. But surprisingly, shockingly, when he looked back, Nicholas Flamel remained where he had first seen him, standing almost directly beneath the center of the tower.

Flamel raised his right hand in a mocking salute, the silver-link bracelet he wore reflecting the light.

Machiavelli caught the police captain's shoulder, spun him around with surprising strength and pointed with his long narrow fingers. "That one! If you do nothing else today, get me that one. And I want him alive and unharmed!"

As they both watched, Flamel turned and hurried toward the west leg of the Eiffel Tower, toward the Pont d'Iéna, but whereas the others had run across the bridge, Flamel turned to the right, onto the Quai Branly.

"Yes, sir!" The captain struck out at an angle, determined to cut off Flamel. "Follow me," he shouted, and his troops spread out in a line behind him.

Dagon stepped up to Machiavelli. "Do you want me to track Saint-Germain and the Shadow?" His head turned, nostrils flaring with a wet sticky sound. "I can follow their scent."

Niccolò Machiavelli shook his head slightly as he climbed back into the car. "Get us out of here before the press turns up. Saint-Germain is nothing if not predictable. He's undoubtedly heading to one of his homes, and we have them all under observation. All we can do is hope we capture Flamel."

Dagon's face was impassive as he slammed the car door closed behind his master. He turned in the direction Flamel had run and saw him disappear amongst the crowd. The police were close behind, moving fast even though they were weighed down by their body armor and weapons. But Dagon knew that over the centuries Flamel had escaped both human and inhuman hunters, had slipped past creatures that had been myth before the evolution of the apes and had outwitted monsters that had no right to exist outside of nightmares. Dagon doubted that the police would catch the Alchemyst.

Then he cocked his head, nostrils flaring again, catching the scent of Scathach. The Shadow had returned!

The enmity between Dagon and the Shadow went back millennia. He was the last of his kind . . . because she had destroyed his entire race one terrible night two thousand years ago. Behind his wraparound mirrored sunglasses, the creature's eyes filled with sticky colorless tears, and he swore that, no matter what happened between Machiavelli and Flamel, this time he would have his revenge on the Shadow.

"Walk, don't run," Scathach commanded. "Saint-Germain, take the lead, Sophie and Josh in the middle, I'll take up the rear." Scatty's tone left no room for argument.

They darted across the bridge and turned right onto the

Avenue de New York. A series of lefts and rights brought them to a narrow side street. It was still early, and the street was entirely in shadow. The temperature dropped dramatically, and the twins immediately noticed that the fingers of Saint-Germain's left hand, which were gently brushing against the dirty wall, left tiny sparks in their wake.

Sophie frowned, sorting through her memories—the Witch of Endor's memories, she reminded herself—of the Comte de Saint-Germain. She caught her brother looking sidelong at her and raised her eyebrows in a silent question.

"Your eyes turned silver. Just for a second," he said.

Sophie glanced over her shoulder to where Scathach was trailing behind and then looked at the man in the leather coat. They were both out of earshot, she thought. "I was trying to remember what I knew. . . ." She shook her head. "What *the Witch* knew about Saint-Germain."

"What about him?" Josh said. "I've never heard of him."

"He is a famous French alchemist," she whispered, "and along with Flamel, probably one of the most mysterious men in history."

"Is he human?" Josh wondered aloud, but Sophie pressed on.

"He's not an Elder or Next Generation. He's human. Even the Witch of Endor didn't know a lot about him. She met him for the first time in London in 1740. She knew immediately that he was an immortal human, and he claimed he'd discovered the secret of immortality when he was studying with Nicholas Flamel." She shook her head quickly. "But

I don't think the Witch quite believed that. He told her that while traveling in Tibet he had perfected a formula for immortality that didn't need to be renewed each month. But when she asked him for a copy, he told her he'd lost it. Apparently, he spoke every language in the world fluently, was a brilliant musician and had a reputation as a jewel maker." Her eyes blinked silver again as the memories faded. "And the Witch didn't like or trust him."

"Then neither should we," Josh whispered urgently.

Sophie nodded, agreeing. "But Nicholas likes him, and obviously trusts him," she said slowly. "Why is that?"

Josh's expression was grim. "I've told you before: I don't think we should be trusting Nicholas Flamel, either. Something's not right about him—I'm convinced."

Sophie bit back her response and looked away. She knew why Josh was angry with the Alchemyst; her brother was envious of her Awakened powers, and she knew he blamed Flamel for putting her in danger. But that didn't mean he was wrong.

The narrow side street led onto a broad tree-lined avenue. Although it was still too early for rush-hour, the spectacular light and fireworks display around the Eiffel Tower had brought any traffic in the area to a standstill. The air was filled with the blare of car horns and the whooping of police sirens. A fire truck was caught in the traffic jam, its wails rising and falling, though there was nowhere for it to go. Saint-Germain strode across the road, looking neither left nor right

135

as he dug in his pocket for a slender black cell phone. He flipped it open and hit speed dial. Then he spoke in rapid-fire French.

"Are you calling for help?" Sophie asked when he had closed the phone.

Saint-Germain shook his head. "Ordering breakfast. I'm famished." He jerked his thumb back in the direction of the Eiffel Tower, which was still erupting fireworks. "Creating something like that—if you'll pardon the pun—burns a lot of calories."

Sophie nodded, understanding now why her stomach had been rumbling with hunger since she'd created the fog.

Scathach caught up with the twins and fell into step alongside Sophie as they hurried past the American Cathedral. "I don't think we're being followed," she said, sounding surprised. "I would have expected Machiavelli to send someone after us." She rubbed the edge of her thumb against her bottom lip, chewing on her ragged nails.

Sophie automatically brushed Scatty's hand away from her mouth. "Don't bite your nails."

Scathach blinked at her in surprise, then self-consciously put her hand down. "An old habit," she muttered. "A very old habit."

"What happens now?" Josh asked.

"We get off the streets and rest," Scathach said grimly. "Have we much farther to go?" she called out to Saint-Germain, who was still in the lead.

"A few minutes," he said, without turning around. "One of my smaller town houses is nearby."

Scathach nodded. "Once we get there, we'll lie low until Nicholas returns, get some rest and a change of clothes." She wrinkled her nose in Josh's direction. "And a shower, too," she added significantly.

Color touched the young man's cheeks. "Are you saying I smell?" he asked, both embarrassed and angry.

Sophie laid her hand on her brother's arm before the Warrior could answer. "Just a little," she said. "We probably all do."

Josh looked away, clearly upset, then glanced back at Scathach. "I don't suppose you smell," he snapped.

"No," she said. "No sweat glands. The Vampire are a much more evolved species than the humani."

They continued in silence until the Rue Pierre Charron opened out onto the broad Champs-Elysées, Paris's main thoroughfare. To their left they could see the Arc de Triomphe. Traffic on both sides of the street was stopped, with drivers standing alongside their cars chatting animatedly, gesticulating wildly. All eyes were turned to the rippling fireworks still exploding over the Eiffel Tower.

"How do you think this will be reported on the news?" Josh said. "The Eiffel Tower suddenly erupting with fireworks."

Saint-Germain glanced over his shoulder. "Truth is, it's not that out of the ordinary. The tower is often lit up with fireworks—on New Year's Eve and Bastille Day, for example. I would imagine it will be reported that next month's Bastille Day fireworks went off prematurely." He stopped and looked around, hearing someone call out his name.

"Don't look . . . ," Scatty began, but it was too late: the twins and Saint-Germain had turned in the direction of the shouts.

"Germain . . ."

"Hey, Germain . . ."

Two young men who were standing next to their unmoving car were pointing at Saint-Germain and shouting his name.

Both men were dressed in jeans and T-shirts and looked alike, with slicked-backed hair and overlarge sunglasses. Abandoning their car in the middle of the road, they wove through the stalled traffic, both holding what Josh thought looked like long, narrow blades in their hands.

"Francis," Scatty warned urgently, her hands locking into fists. She moved forward just as the first man reached Saint-Germain, "let me. . . ."

"Gentlemen." Saint-Germain turned toward the two men, smiling widely, though the twins, who were behind him, saw yellow-blue flames dance across his fingertips.

"Great concert last night," the first man said breathlessly, speaking English with a strong German accent. He pushed back his sunglasses and held out his right hand, and Josh realized that what he'd first imagined was a knife was nothing more than a fat pen. "Any chance I could get an autograph?"

The flames on Saint-Germain's fingers winked out. "Of course," he said, smiling delightedly, reaching for the pen and pulling a spiral-bound notebook from an inner pocket. "Did you get the new CD?" he asked, flipping open the notebook.

The second man, wearing identical glasses, plucked a

black and red iPod from the back pocket of his jeans. "Got it on iTunes yesterday," he answered in the same distinctive accent.

"And don't forget to check out the DVD of the show when it comes out in a month's time. Got some great extras, a couple of remixes and a great mashup," Saint-Germain added as he signed his name with an elaborate flourish and pulled the pages from the notebook. "I'd love to chat, guys, but I'm in a rush. Thanks for stopping, I appreciate it."

They shook hands quickly and the two men hurried back to their car, high-fiving one another as they compared their autographs.

Smiling broadly, Saint-Germain took a deep breath and turned to look at the twins. "Told you I was famous."

"And you'll soon be dead famous if we don't get off this street," Scathach reminded him. "Or maybe just dead."

"We're just here," Saint-Germain muttered. He led them across the Champs-Elysées and down a side street, then ducked into a narrow, high-walled cobbled lane that snaked around the backs of the buildings. Stopping halfway down the alley, he slid a key into an anonymous-looking door set flush with the wall. The wooden door was chipped and scarred, foul green paint peeling in long strips to reveal blistered wood beneath; the bottom was splintered and cracked from rubbing the ground.

"May I suggest a new gate?" Scathach said.

"This *is* the new gate." Saint-Germain smiled quickly. "The wood is just a disguise. Beneath it is a slab of solid steel with a five-point dead bolt." He stepped back and allowed the twins to precede him through the entrance. "Enter freely and of your own will," he said formally.

The twins stepped forward and were vaguely disappointed with what they found. Behind the gate was a small courtyard and a four-story building. To the left and right, tall spike-tipped walls separated the house from its neighbors. Sophie and Josh had been expecting something exotic or even dramatic, but all they saw was an unkempt leaf-strewn rear garden. A huge and hideous stone birdbath was set in the center of the courtyard, but instead of water, the bowl was filled with dead leaves and the remains of a bird's nest. All the plants in the pots and baskets surrounding the fountain at its center were dead or dying.

"The gardener's away," Saint-Germain said without a trace of embarrassment, "and I'm really not very good with plants." He held up his right hand and spread his fingers. Each one popped alight with a different-colored flame. He grinned and the colored flames painted his face in flickering shadows. "Not my specialty."

Scathach paused by the gate, looking up and down the alleyway, head tilted to one side, listening. When she was satisfied that they were not being followed, she closed the door and turned the key in the lock. The dead bolts slid into place with a satisfying thunk.

"How will Flamel find us?" Josh asked. Even though he was wary and fearful of the Alchemyst, he felt even more nervous around Saint-Germain.

"I gave him a little guide," Saint-Germain explained.

"Will he be all right?" Sophie asked Scathach.

"I'm sure he will be," she said, though the tone of her voice and the look in her eyes betrayed her fears. She was turning away from the gate when she stiffened, jaw unhinging, vampire teeth suddenly—terrifyingly—visible.

The door to the rear of the house had opened suddenly, and a figure stepped out into the courtyard. Abruptly, Sophie's aura blazed silver-white, the shock sending her spinning back into her brother, bringing his aura to crackling life as well, outlining his body in gold and bronze. And as the twins held on to one another, blinded by the silver and gold light of their own auras, they heard Scathach scream. It was the most terrifying sound they had ever heard.

CHAPTER SIXTEEN

"Stop!"

Nicholas Flamel kept running, turning to the right, racing down the Quai Branly.

"Stop or I shoot!"

Flamel knew the police wouldn't shoot—they couldn't. Machiavelli would not want him harmed.

The slap of leather on concrete and the jingle of weapons were close now, and he could hear his pursuer's even breathing. Nicholas's own breathing was beginning to come in great heaving gasps, and there was a stitch in his side just below his ribs. The recipe in the Codex kept him alive and healthy, but there was no way he could outrun this highly trained and obviously fit police officer.

Nicholas Flamel stopped so suddenly that the police captain almost ran right into him. Standing still, the Alchemyst turned his head to look back over his left shoulder. The policeman had drawn an ugly black pistol and was holding it in a steady two-handed grip.

"Don't move. Raise your hands."

Nicholas turned slowly to face the police officer. "Well, make your mind up, what's it to be?" he asked mildly.

Behind his protective goggles, the man blinked at him in surprise.

"Do I not move? Or do I raise my hands?"

The police officer gestured with the barrel of the gun and Flamel raised his hands. Five more RAID officers came running up. They trained a variety of weapons on the Alchemyst as they spread out in a line alongside their captain. With his hands still in the air, Nicholas turned his head slowly to look at each of them in turn. In their black uniforms, helmets, balaclavas and goggles, they looked like insects.

"Get down on the ground. Do it, do it now!" the captain commanded. "Keep your hands in the air."

Nicholas slowly folded to his knees.

"Now lie down! Facedown!"

The Alchemyst lay flat on the Parisian street, his cheek against the cool, gritty pavement.

"Stretch your arms wide."

Nicholas stretched out his arms. The police officers shifted position, quickly encircling him, but they still kept their distance.

"We have him." The police captain spoke into the microphone positioned in front of his lips. "No, sir. We've not touched him. Yes, sir. Immediately."

Nicholas wished Perenelle were with him now; she would

know what to do. But if the Sorceress had been with him, then he would not be in this mess in the first place. Perenelle was a fighter. How often had she urged him to stop running, to use half a millennium of his alchemical knowledge and her sorcery and magic and take the fight to the Dark Elders? She'd wanted him to gather the immortals, the Elders and the Next Generation who supported the humani and wage a war against the Dark Elders, Dee and his kind. But he couldn't; he'd been waiting all his life for the twins foretold in the Codex.

"The two that are one, the one that is all."

There had never been any doubt in his mind that he would discover the twins. The prophecies in the Codex were never wrong, but like everything else in the book, the words of Abraham were never clear and were written in a variety of archaic or forgotten languages.

> *The two that are one, the one that is all.*
> *There will come a time when the Book is taken*
> *And the Queen's man is allied with the Crow.*
> *Then the Elder will step out of the Shadows*
> *And the immortal must train the mortal. The two*
> *that are one must become the one that is all.*

And Nicholas knew—beyond a shadow of a doubt—that he was the immortal mentioned in the prophecy: the hook-handed man had told him.

Half a millennium ago, Nicholas and Perenelle Flamel had traveled throughout Europe in an attempt to understand the enigmatic metal-bound book. Finally, in Spain, they had met a mysterious one-handed man who had helped translate portions of the ever-changing text. The one-handed man had revealed that the secret of Life Eternal always appeared on page seven of the Codex at the full moon, while the recipe for transmutation, for changing the composition of any material, appeared only on page fourteen. When the one-handed man had translated the first prophecy, he had looked at Nicholas with coal black eyes and reached over to tap the Frenchman's chest with the hook that took the place of his left hand.

"Alchemyst, here is your destiny," he had whispered.

The mysterious words suggested that Flamel would one day find the twins . . . the prophecy hadn't revealed that he'd end up lying spread-eagled on a dirty Parisian street surrounded by armed and very nervous police officers.

Flamel closed his eyes and breathed deeply. Pressing his outspread fingers against the stones, he reluctantly drew upon his aura. The merest gossamer thread of green-gold energy seeped off his fingertips and soaked into the stones. Nicholas felt the tendril of his auric energy curl through the pavement, then into the earth beneath. The hair-thin thread snaked through the soil, looking . . . searching . . . and then, finally, finding what he was looking for: a seething mass of teeming life. Then it was a simple matter of using transmutation, the basic principal of alchemy, to create glucose and fructose and bind them together with a glycosidic bond to create sucrose. The life stirred, shifted, flowed toward the sweetness.

The police captain raised his voice. "Cuff him. Search him."

Nicholas heard the shuffling approach of two police officers, one on either side. Directly in front of his face, he saw highly polished thick-soled black leather boots.

And then, magnified because of its closeness to his face, Nicholas spotted the ant. It popped up out of a crack in the pavement, antennae waving. It was followed by a second, and a third.

The Alchemyst pressed his thumbs against the third finger of each hand and snapped his fingers. Minuscule sparkles of mint-smelling green-gold spun into the air, coating the six police officers in infinitesimal particles of power.

Then he transmuted the particles into sugar.

Abruptly, the pavement around Flamel turned black. A mass of tiny ants erupted from below the street, surging up out of the cracks in the stone. Like a thick glutinous syrup, they spread across the pavement, flowing over boots before suddenly curling up around the legs of the police officers, coating them in a heaving swarm of insects. For a moment the men were shocked into immobility. Their suits and gloves protected them for another instant, and then one man twitched, and another and another as the ants found the tiniest of openings in the men's suits and darted inside, legs tickling, jaws nipping. The men began jerking, twisting, turning, slapping at themselves, throwing down their weapons, pulling off their gloves, tugging at their helmets, tossing aside their goggles and balaclavas as thousands of ants crawled over their bodies.

The police captain watched as their prisoner—who was completely untouched by the heaving blanket of ants—sat up and fastidiously dusted himself off before rising to his feet. The captain tried to point his gun at the man, but ants were clawing at his wrists, tickling the palms of his hands, nipping his flesh, and he couldn't hold the weapon steady. He wanted to order the man to sit down, but there were ants crawling across his lips, and he knew if he opened his mouth they would dart inside. Reaching up, brushing his helmet off his head, he jerked off his balaclava and flung it to the ground, arching his back as insects crawled along his spine. He ran his hand across his head and felt it dislodge at least a dozen ants. They fell across his face and he squeezed his eyes shut. When he opened them again, the prisoner was strolling towards the Pont de l'Alma train station, hands in his pockets, looking as if he hadn't a care in the world.

CHAPTER SEVENTEEN

Josh forced his eyes open. Black spots danced in front of them, and when he raised his hand to his face, he could see the ghost of his own golden aura still visible around his flesh. Reaching out, he found his sister's hand and caught it. She squeezed gently, and he turned to find her blinking her eyes open.

"What happened?" he mumbled, too shocked and numb to even be scared.

Sophie shook her head. "It was like an explosion. . . ."

"I heard Scathach scream," he added.

"And I thought I saw someone coming out of the house . . . ," she added.

They both turned back to the town house. Scathach was at the door, her arms wrapped around a young woman, holding her tightly, swinging her around in a circle. Both women were laughing and squealing with delight, shouting at one another in rapid-fire French. "I guess they know each other," Josh said as he helped his sister to her feet.

The twins turned to look at the Comte de Saint-Germain, who was standing to one side, arms folded across his chest, smiling delightedly. "They're old friends," he explained. "They've not met in a long time . . . a very long time." Saint-Germain coughed. "Joan," he said politely.

The two women broke apart and the woman he'd called Joan turned to look at Saint-Germain, her head tilted at a quizzical angle. It was impossible to guess her age. Dressed in jeans and a white T-shirt, she was Sophie's height, almost un-naturally slender, and her deeply tanned and flawless skin emphasized huge gray eyes. Her auburn hair was cut in a short boyish style. There were tears on her cheeks that she brushed away with a quick movement of her palm. "Francis?" she asked.

"And these are our visitors."

Holding Scathach's hand, the young woman stepped closer to Sophie. As the woman approached, Sophie felt a sudden pressure in the air between them, as if some invisible force was pushing her back, and then, abruptly, her aura flared silver around her and the air was filled with the sweet aroma of vanilla. Josh grabbed his sister's arm and his own aura crackled alight, adding the scent of oranges to the air.

"Sophie . . . Josh . . . ," Saint-Germain began. The rich, sweet aroma of lavender filled the courtyard as a hissing silver aura grew around the short-haired young woman. It hard-ened and solidified, becoming metallic and reflective, mold-ing itself into a breastplate and greaves, gloves and boots, before finally solidifying into a complete medieval suit of armor. "I would like to introduce my wife, Joan . . ."

"Your wife!" Scatty squealed, shocked.

". . . whom you—and history—know as Joan of Arc."

Breakfast had been laid out on a long polished wooden table in the kitchen. The air was rich with the odor of newly baked bread and brewing coffee. Plates were piled high with fresh fruit, pancakes and scones, while sausages and eggs sizzled in a pan on the old-fashioned iron range.

Josh's stomach started rumbling the moment he stepped into the room and saw the food. His mouth filled with saliva, reminding him just how long it had been since he'd last eaten. He'd only managed a couple of sips of the hot chocolate at the café earlier before the police arrived.

"Eat, eat," Saint-Germain said, grabbing a plate in one hand and a thick croissant in the other. He bit into the pastry, spilling wafer-thin flakes onto the tiled floor. "You must be famished."

Sophie leaned in close to her brother. "Could you get me something to eat? I want to talk to Joan. I need to ask her something."

Josh glanced quickly at the young-looking woman who was pulling cups from the dishwasher. Her short haircut made it impossible to guess her age. "Do you really think she's Joan of Arc?"

Sophie squeezed her brother's arm. "After all we've seen, what do you think?" She nodded toward the table. "I just want fruit and cereal."

"No sausage, no eggs?" he asked, surprised. His sister was the only person he knew who could eat more sausages than he could.

"No." She frowned, blue eyes clouding. "It's funny, but even the thought of eating meat is making me feel sick." She grabbed a scone and turned away before he could comment, and approached Joan, who was pouring coffee into a tall glass cup. Sophie's nostrils flared. "Hawaiian Kona coffee?" she asked.

Joan's gray eyes blinked in surprise and she inclined her head. "I'm impressed."

Sophie grinned and shrugged. "I worked in a coffee shop. I'd know the smell of Kona anywhere."

"I fell in love with it when we were in Hawaii," Joan said. She spoke English with the merest hint of an American accent. "I keep it for a special treat."

"I love the smell; hate the taste. Too bitter."

Joan sipped a little more coffee. "I'll bet you didn't come here to talk about coffee?"

Sophie shook her head. "No, I didn't. I just . . ." She stopped. She had just met this woman, yet she was about to ask her an incredibly personal question. "Can I ask you something?" she said quickly.

"Anything," Joan said sincerely, and Sophie believed her. She took a deep breath and her words tumbled out in a rush.

"Scathach once told me you were the last person to have a pure silver aura."

"That's why yours reacted to mine," Joan said, wrapping both hands around the cup and staring at the girl over the rim. "I do apologize. My aura overloaded yours. I can teach you how to prevent that from happening." She smiled, revealing straight white teeth. "Though the chances of meeting another pure silver aura in your lifetime are incredibly slim."

Sophie nibbled nervously on the blueberry scone. "Please excuse me for asking, but are you really . . . really Joan of Arc, *the* Joan of Arc?"

"Yes, I really am Jeanne d'Arc." The woman gave a short bow. "La Pucelle, the Maid of Orléans, at your service."

"But I thought . . . I mean, I always read that you died. . . ."

Joan dipped her head and smiled. "Scathach rescued me." She reached out and touched Sophie's arm, and immediately, flickering images of Scathach on a huge black horse, wearing white and jet armor and wielding two blazing swords, danced behind her eyes.

"The Shadow single-handedly fought her way through the huge crowd who had gathered to watch my execution. No one could stand against her. In the panic, chaos and confusion, she snatched me right out from under the noses of my executioners."

The images flashed in Sophie's head: Joan, wearing ragged and scorched clothing, clinging to Scathach as the Warrior maneuvered her armored black horse through the panicking crowd, the blazing swords in either hand clearing their path.

"Of course, everyone had to say they saw Joan die," Scatty said, joining them, carefully slicing a pineapple into neat chunks with a curved knife. "No one—neither English nor French—was going to admit that the Maid of Orléans

152

had been snatched out from under the noses of perhaps five hundred heavily armed knights, rescued by a single female warrior."

Joan reached out and took a cube of pineapple from Scathach's fingers and popped it into her mouth. "Scatty took me to Nicholas and Perenelle," she continued. "They gave me shelter, looked after me. I'd been injured in the escape and was weakened from months of captivity. But despite Nicholas's best attention, I would have died if it had not been for Scatty." She reached over and squeezed her friend's hand again, not seeming to notice the tears on her cheeks.

"Joan had lost a lot of blood," Scathach said. "No matter what Nicholas or Perenelle did, she was not getting any better. So Nicholas performed one of the first-ever blood transfusions."

"Whose blood—" Sophie started to ask, until she suddenly realized she knew the answer. "Your blood?"

"Scathach's vampire blood saved me. And kept me alive, too—made me immortal." Joan grinned. Sophie noted that her teeth were normal, not pointed like Scatty's. "Luckily, it has none of the vampire side effects. Though I am vegetarian," she added. "Have been for the last few centuries."

"And you're married," Scathach said accusingly. "When did that happen, and how, and why wasn't I invited?" she demanded, all in one breath.

"We got married four years ago on Sunset Beach in Hawaii, at sunset, of course. We looked everywhere for you when we decided," Joan said quickly. "I really wanted you there; I wanted you to be my maid of honor."

Scathach's green eyes narrowed, remembering. "Four years ago . . . I think I was in Nepal chasing down a rogue Nee-gued. An abominable snowman," she added, seeing Sophie's and Joan's blank looks.

"We'd no way of contacting you. Your cell wasn't working, and e-mails bounced back saying your mailbox was full." Joan caught Scathach's hand. "Come, I have photos I can show you." The woman turned back to Sophie. "You should eat now. You need to replace the energy you've burned up. Drink plenty of liquids. Water, fruit juices, but no caffeine—no tea and no coffee, nothing that's going to keep you awake. Once you've eaten, Francis will show you to your rooms, where you can shower and rest." She slowly looked Sophie up and down. "I'll get you some clothes. You're about my size. And then later we'll talk about your aura." Joan held up her left hand and spread her fingers. An articulated metal glove sparkled into existence over her flesh. "I'll show you how to control it, how to shape it, make it into anything you wish." The glove turned into a metal raptor's claw complete with curved talons before it faded back to Joan's tanned flesh. Only her fingernails remained silver. She leaned in and kissed Sophie quickly on each cheek. "But first you must rest. Now," she said, looking at Scathach, "let me show you the photos."

The two women hurried from the kitchen, and Sophie made her way back down the long room to where Saint-Germain was talking earnestly to her brother. Josh handed her a plate piled high with fruit and bread. His own plate was heaped with eggs and sausages. Sophie felt her stomach

154

object at the sight and she forced herself to look away. She nibbled on the fruit, listening to the conversation.

"No, I'm human, I cannot Awaken your powers," Saint-Germain was saying as she joined them. "For that you need an Elder or one of the handful of Next Generation who could do it." He smiled, showing his misshapen teeth. "Don't worry, Nicholas will find someone to Awaken you."

"Is there anyone here, in Paris, who could do it?"

Saint-Germain took a moment to consider. "Machiavelli would know someone, I'm sure. He knows everything. But I don't." He turned to Sophie, bowing slightly. "I understand you were lucky enough to be Awakened by the legendary Hekate and then trained in the Magic of Air by my old teacher, the Witch of Endor." He shook his head. "How is the old witch? She never liked me," he added.

"Still doesn't," Sophie said quickly, then blushed. "I'm sorry. I don't know why I said that."

The Count laughed. "Oh, Sophie, you didn't say it . . . well, not really. The Witch did. It's going to take some time for you to sort through her memories. I got a call from her this morning. She told me how she imbued you not only with the Magic of Air, but with her entire body of knowledge. The mummy technique hasn't been used in living memory; it is incredibly dangerous."

Sophie glanced quickly at her brother. He was watching Saint-Germain carefully, listening to every word. She noted the tension in his neck and jaw from how he was squeezing his mouth shut.

"You should have rested for at least twenty-four hours to

allow your conscious and subconscious time to sort through the sudden influx of alien memories, thoughts and ideas."

"There wasn't time," Sophie muttered.

"Well, there is now. Eat up; then I'll show you to your rooms. Sleep as long as you like. You're completely safe. No one even knows you're here."

CHAPTER EIGHTEEN

"They're in Saint-Germain's town house off the Champs-Elysées." Machiavelli pressed the phone to his ear and leaned back in the black leather chair, swiveling to look through the tall window. In the distance, across the slanted tile rooftops, he could make out the tip of the Eiffel Tower. The fireworks had finally stopped, but a pall of rainbow-colored clouds still hung in the air. "Don't worry, Doctor, we have the house under observation. Saint-Germain, Scathach and the twins are inside. There are no other occupants."

Machiavelli held the phone away from his ear as static rippled and crackled. Dee's jet was just taking off from a small private airfield north of L.A. It would stop in New York to refuel, then fly transatlantic to Shannon in Ireland and refuel again before continuing on to Paris. The crackling faded and Dee's voice, strong and clear, came through the phone.

"And the Alchemyst?"

"Lost in Paris. My men had him on the ground at gunpoint, but he somehow coated them in sugar and then unleashed every ant in the city onto them. They panicked; he escaped."

"Transmutation," Dee remarked. "Water is composed of two parts hydrogen and one part oxygen: sucrose has the same ratio. He changed the water into sugar; it's a parlor trick—I would have expected more of him."

Machiavelli ran his hand across his short snow white hair. "I though it was rather clever myself," he said mildly. "He hospitalized six police officers."

"He will return to the twins," Dee snapped. "He needs them. He's been waiting all his life to find them."

"We've all been waiting," Machiavelli reminded the Magician quietly. "And right now, we know where they are, which means we know where Flamel will go."

"Do nothing until I get there," Dee commanded.

"And have you any idea when that might—" Machiavelli began, but the line was dead. He was unsure whether Dee had hung up or the call had dropped. Knowing Dee, he guessed he'd hung up; that was his usual style. The tall, elegant man tapped the phone against his thin lips before replacing the handset. He had no intention of following Dee's orders; he was going to capture Flamel and the twins before Dee's plane touched down in Paris. He would do what Dee had failed to do for centuries, and in return, the Elders would grant him anything he desired.

Machiavelli's cell phone buzzed in his pocket. He pulled

it out and looked at the screen. An unusually long string of numbers scrolled across it, looking like no other number he'd ever seen before. The head of the DGSE frowned. Only the president of France, a few highly placed cabinet ministers and his own personal staff had this number. He hit Answer but didn't speak.

"The English Magician believes you will try and capture Flamel and the twins before he arrives." The voice on the other end spoke Greek in a dialect that had not been used in millennia.

Niccolò Machiavelli sat bolt upright in his chair. "Master?" he said.

"Give Dee your full support. Do not move against Flamel until he arrives." The line went dead.

Machiavelli carefully placed his cell phone on the bare desk and sat back. Holding both hands up before his face, he was unsurprised to find that they were shaking slightly. The last time he'd spoken to the Elder he called Master had been more than a century and a half ago. This was the Elder who had granted him immortality at the beginning of the sixteenth century. Had Dee somehow contacted him? Machiavelli shook his head. Highly unlikely; probably Dee had contacted his own master and asked him to make the request. But Machiavelli's master was one of the most powerful of the Dark Elders. . . . That brought him back to a question that had troubled him down through the centuries: who was Dee's master?

Every human granted immortality by an Elder was bound

to that Elder. An Elder who bestowed immortality could just as easily revoke it. Machiavelli had even seen it happen: he'd watched a healthy-looking young man wither and age in a matter of heartbeats, eventually collapsing into a pile of crackling bones and dusty skin.

Machiavelli's dossier of immortal humans was cross-linked to the Elder or Dark Elder they served. There were only a very few humani—like Flamel, Perenelle and Saint-Germain—who owed no loyalty to an Elder, because they had become immortal by their own efforts.

No one knew whom Dee served. But it was obviously someone more powerful than Machiavelli's own Dark Elder master. And that made Dee all the more dangerous.

Leaning forward, Machiavelli pressed a button on his desk phone. The door immediately opened and Dagon stepped into the room, his mirrored sunglasses reflecting the bare walls.

"Any reports on the Alchemyst?"

"Nothing. We've accessed the video from the security cameras in the Pont de l'Alma station and every station it connects with and we're analyzing it now, but it's going to take time."

Machiavelli nodded. Time was something he did not have. He waved a long-fingered hand in the air. "Well, we might not know where he is now, but we know where he's going: to Saint-Germain's house."

Dagon's lips parted stickily. "The house is under observation. All entrances and exits are secured; there are even men in the sewers beneath the building. No one can get in or out without us observing them. There are two RAID units in vans in nearby side streets and a third unit in the house next to Saint-Germain's property. They can be over the wall in moments."

Machiavelli stood up and stepped out from behind the desk. With his hands behind his back, he walked around the tiny anonymous office. Although it was his official address, he rarely used this room, and it held nothing but the desk, two chairs, and the telephone. "But is it enough, I wonder? Flamel has escaped from six highly trained officers who were holding him at gunpoint, facedown on the pavement. And we know Saint-Germain—the Master of Fire—is inside this property. We had a little example of his abilities this morning."

"The fireworks were harmless," Dagon said.

"I'm sure he could have just as easily turned the tower to liquid. Remember, he makes diamonds from coal."

Dagon nodded.

Machiavelli continued. "We also know that the American girl's powers have been Awakened, and we've seen a little of what she can do. The fog at Sacré-Coeur was an impressive feat for someone untrained and so young."

"And then there is the Shadow," Dagon added.

Niccolò Machiavelli's face turned into an ugly mask. "And then there is the Shadow," he agreed.

"She took out twelve heavily armed officers in the coffee shop this morning," Dagon said emotionlessly. "I've watched her face down entire armies, and she survived for centuries in an Underworld Shadowrealm. Flamel is obviously using her to protect the twins. She must be destroyed before we move against any of the others."

"Indeed."

"You will need an army."

"Perhaps not. Remember, *'Cunning and deceit will every time serve a man better than force,'*" he quoted.

"Who said that?" Dagon asked.

"I did, in a book, a long time ago. It was true in the court of the Medicis, and it is true now." He looked up. "Did you send for the Disir?"

"They're on their way." Dagon's voice turned sticky. "I don't trust them."

"No one trusts the Disir." There was no humor in Machiavelli's smile. "Did you ever hear the story of how Hekate trapped Scathach in that Underworld?"

Dagon remained unmoving.

"Hekate used the Disir. Their feud with the Shadow goes back to the time just after the sinking of Danu Talis." Putting his hands on the creature's shoulders, Machiavelli stepped close to Dagon, taking care to breathe through his mouth. Dagon exuded a fishy odor; it coated his pale skin like oily, rancid sweat. "I know you hate the Shadow, and I have never asked you why, though I have my suspicions. It is obvious that she has caused you much pain. However, I want you to put aside your feelings; hate is the most useless of all emotions. Success is the best revenge. I need you focused and by my side. We are close now, so close to victory, close to returning the Elder Race to this world. Leave Scathach to the Disir. But if they fail, then she is yours. I promise you."

Dagon opened his mouth to reveal the circle of needle-pointed teeth. "They will not fail. The Disir intend to bring Nidhogg."

Niccolò Machiavelli blinked in surprise. "Nidhogg . . . it's free? How?"

"The World Tree was destroyed."

"If they loose Nidhogg on Scathach, then you are right. They will not fail. They cannot."

Dagon reached up and pulled off his sunglasses. His huge bulbous fish eyes were wide and staring. "And if they lose control of Nidhogg, it could devour the entire city."

Machiavelli took a moment to consider. Then he nodded. "It would be a small price to pay to destroy the Shadow."

"You sound just like Dee."

"Oh, I am nothing like the English Magician," Machi-avelli said feelingly. "Dee is a dangerous fanatic."

"And you're not?" Dagon asked.

"I'm only dangerous."

Dr. John Dee sat back into the soft leather seat and watched the sparkling grid of L.A.'s lights fall away beneath him. Checking an ornate pocket watch, he wondered if Machiavelli had received the phone call from his master yet. He imagined he had. Dee grinned, wondering what the Italian would make of that. If nothing else, it would at least show Machiavelli who was in charge.

It didn't take a genius to realize that the Italian would go after Flamel and the children himself. But Dee had spent too long chasing the Alchemyst to lose him at the very end . . . especially to someone like Niccolò Machiavelli.

He closed his eyes as the plane rose and his stomach twitched. He automatically reached for the paper bag on the seat beside him: he loved flying, but his stomach always protested. If everything went as planned, then he would soon be the ruler of the entire planet and he'd never need to fly again. Everyone would come to him.

The jet climbed at a steep angle and he swallowed hard; he'd had a chicken wrap in the airport and was regretting it now. The fizzy drink had been a definite mistake.

Dee was looking forward to the time when the Elders returned. Perhaps they could reestablish the network of ley-gates across the world and make flying unnecessary. Closing his eyes, Dee concentrated on the Elders and the many benefits they would bring to the planet. In the distant past, he knew the Elders had created a paradise on earth. All the ancient books and scrolls, the myths and legends of every race, spoke about that glorious time. His master had promised him that the Elders would use their powerful magic to return the planet to that paradise. They would reverse the effects of global warming, repair the hole in the ozone layer and bring the deserts to life. The Sahara would bloom; the polar ice caps would melt away, revealing the rich land beneath. Dee thought he would found his capital city in Antarctica on the shores of Lake Vanda. The Elders could reestablish their ancient kingdoms in Sumer, Egypt, Central America and Angkor, and with the knowledge contained in the Book of Abraham, it would be possible to raise Danu Talis again.

Of course, Dee knew that the human population would become slaves, and some would become food for those Elders who still needed to eat, but that was a small price to pay for the many other benefits.

The jet leveled and he felt his stomach settle. Opening his eyes, he breathed deeply and checked his watch again. He found it hard to believe that he was hours—literally hours—away from finally capturing the Alchemyst, Scathach and, now, the twins. They were an added bonus. Once he had Flamel and the pages from the Codex, the world would change.

He would never understand why Flamel and his wife had worked so hard to prevent the Elders from bringing civilization back to earth. But he'd be sure to ask him . . . just before he killed him.

CHAPTER NINETEEN

*N*icholas Flamel paused on the Rue Beaubourg and turned slowly, pale eyes scanning the street. He didn't think he was being followed, but he needed to be certain. He'd taken the train to the Saint-Michel Notre-Dame station and crossed the Seine on the Pont d'Arcole, heading in the direction of the glass-and-steel monstrosity that was the Pompidou Center. Taking his time, stopping often, darting from one side of the road to the other, pausing at a newsstand to buy the morning paper, stopping again for some foul coffee in a cardboard cup, he kept checking for anyone paying close attention to his movements. But as far as he could determine, there was no one following him.

Paris had changed since he'd last been in the city, and though he now called San Francisco home, this was the city of his birth and would always be *his* city. Only a couple of weeks ago, Josh had loaded Google Earth onto the computer in the bookshop's back room and shown him how to use it. Nicholas had spent hours looking down on the streets he'd once walked, finding buildings he'd known in his youth, even discovering the location of the Church of the Holy Innocents, where he'd supposedly been buried.

He had been particularly interested in one street. He'd found it on the map program and *virtually* walked down it, never realizing that he would soon do so in reality.

Nicholas Flamel turned left off the Rue Beaubourg onto the Rue de Montmorency—and stopped as suddenly as if he had walked into a wall.

He drew a deep shuddering breath, conscious that his heart was pounding. The wash of emotions was extraordinarily powerful. The street was so narrow that the morning sunlight didn't reach it, leaving it in shadow. It was lined on both sides with tall, mostly white-and-cream-colored buildings, many of them with hanging baskets spilling flowers and greenery across the walls. Round-topped black metal poles had been inserted into the sidewalk on both sides of the street to prevent cars from stopping.

Nicholas walked slowly down the street, seeing it as it had once been. Remembering.

More than six hundred years ago, he and Perenelle had lived on this street. Images of medieval Paris flickered behind his eyes, a jumbled mismatched mess of wooden and stone houses; narrow winding lanes; rotten bridges; tumbled listing buildings and streets that were little better than open sewers. The noise, the incredible, incessant noise, and the foul miasma that hung over the city—a mixture of unwashed disease-ridden humans and filthy animals—were things he would never forget.

At the bottom of the Rue de Montmorency, he found the building he had been looking for.

It hadn't changed much. The stone had once been cream; now it was ancient, chipped and weathered, stained black with soot. The three wooden windows and doors were new, but the building itself was one of the oldest in Paris. Directly above the middle door was a number in blue metal—51—and above that was a tired-looking stone sign announcing that this had once been the MAISON DE NICOLAS FLAMEL ET DE PERENELLE, SA FEMME. A red sign in the shape of a shield announced that this was the AUBERGE NICOLAS FLAMEL. Now it was a restaurant.

Once it had been his home.

Stepping up to the window, he pretended to read the menu as he peered inside. The interior had been completely remodeled, of course, countless times probably, but the dark beams that stretched across the white ceiling appeared to be the same beams he'd so often looked up at more than six hundred years ago.

He and Perenelle had been happy here, he realized.

And safe.

Their lives had been simpler then: they hadn't known about the Elders or the Dark Elders; they'd known nothing of the Codex, or of the immortals who guarded and fought over it.

And both he and Perenelle had still been fully human.

The ancient stones of the house had been carved with an

assortment of images, symbols and letters that he knew had puzzled and intrigued scholars down through the ages. Most were meaningless, little more than the shop signs of their day, but there were one or two that had special significance. Quickly glancing left and right and finding the narrow street empty, he reached up with his right hand and traced the outline of the letter N, which was cut into the stone to the left of the middle window. Green power curled around the letter. Then he traced the ornate *F* on the opposite side of the window, leaving a shimmering outline of the letter in the air. Catching hold of the window frame with his left hand, he hauled himself up onto the ledge and reached over his head with his right hand, his fingers finding the shapes of letters in the ancient stone. Allowing the tiniest trickle of his aura to flow through his fingers, he pressed a sequence of letters . . . and the stone beneath his flesh turned warm and soft. He pushed . . . and his fingers sank *into* the stone. They wrapped around the object he had secreted within the solid block of granite back in the fifteenth century. Pulling it free, he stepped off the window ledge and dropped lightly to the ground, quickly wrapping his copy of *Le Monde* around the object. Then he turned and headed down the street without so much as a backward glance.

Before he stepped out onto the Rue Beaubourg, Nicholas turned over his left hand. Nestled in the center of his palm was the perfect impression of the black butterfly Saint-Germain had pressed into his skin. "It will lead you back to me," he'd said.

Nicholas Flamel brushed his right forefinger over the

tattoo. "Take me back to Saint-Germain," he murmured. "Bring me to him."

The tattoo shivered on his skin, black wings rippling. Then it suddenly peeled away from his flesh and hung flapping in the air before him. A moment later, it danced and wove down the street. "Clever," Nicholas muttered, "very clever." And he set off after it.

CHAPTER TWENTY

$\mathcal{P}$erenelle Flamel stepped out of the prison cell.

The door had never been locked. There was no need: nothing could get past the sphinx. But now the sphinx was gone. Perenelle breathed deeply: the sour odor of the creature, the musty combination of snake, lion and bird, had lessened, allowing the usual smells of Alcatraz—salt and rusting metal, seaweed and crumbling stone—to take over. She turned to the left, moving swiftly down a long cell-lined corridor. She was on the Rock, but she had no idea where she was within the huge crumbling complex. Although she and Nicholas had lived in San Francisco for years, she had never been tempted to visit the ghost-haunted island. All she knew was that she was deep below the surface of the earth. The only light came from an irregular scattering of low-wattage bulbs set behind wire cages. Perenelle's lips twisted in a wry smile; the light was not for her benefit. The sphinx was afraid of the dark; the creature came from a time and place where there really were monsters in the shadows.

The sphinx had been lured away by the ghost of Juan Manuel de Ayala. She had gone in search of the mysterious noises, the rattling bars and slamming doors that had suddenly filled the building. Every moment the sphinx was away from her cell, Perenelle's aura recharged. She wasn't back up to full strength—she would need to sleep and eat first—but at least she was no longer defenseless. All she had to do was to keep out of the creature's way.

A door slammed somewhere high above her, and Perenelle froze as claws click-clacked. Then a bell began to toll, slow and solemn, lonely and distant. There was a sudden clatter of iron-hard nails on stone as the sphinx raced off to investigate.

Perenelle folded her arms across her body and ran her hands up and down them, shivering slightly. She was wearing a sleeveless summer dress, and normally she'd be able to regulate her temperature by adjusting her aura, but she had very little power left and she was reluctant to use it in any way. One of the sphinx's special talents was her ability to sense and then feed off magical energy.

Perenelle's flat sandals made no sound on the damp stones as she moved down the corridor. She was wary, but not frightened. Perenelle Flamel had lived for more than six hundred years, and while Nicholas had been fascinated with alchemy, she had concentrated on sorcery. Her research had taken her into some very dark and dangerous places, not only on this earth, but also in some of the adjoining Shadow-realms.

Somewhere in the distance, glass shattered and tinkled to the ground. She heard the sphinx hiss and howl in frustration, but that sound too was far away. Perenelle smiled: de Ayala was keeping the sphinx busy, and no matter how hard she looked, she would never find him. Even a creature as powerful as a sphinx had no power over a ghost or a poltergeist.

Perenelle knew that she needed to get to an upper level and out into the sunshine, where her aura would recharge more quickly. Once she was in the open air, she could use any of a dozen simple spells, cantrips and incantations she knew that would make the sphinx's existence a misery. A Scythian mage, who'd claimed to have helped build the pyramids for the survivors of Danu Talis who had settled in Egypt, had taught her a very useful spell for melting stone. Perenelle would not hesitate to use it to bring the entire building down on top of the sphinx. It would probably survive—sphinxes were practically impossible to kill—but it would certainly be slowed down.

Perenelle spotted rusting metal stairs and darted toward them. She was just about to put her foot on the bottom step when she noticed the gray thread spilling across the metal. Perenelle froze, foot raised in the air . . . and then she slowly and carefully stepped back. Crouching down, she looked at the metal steps. From this angle, she could see the threads of spiderwebs crisscrossing and weaving through the stairs.

Anyone who stepped onto the metal staircase would be caught. She backed away, staring hard into the gloomy shadows. The threads were too thick to have been made by any normal spider and were dotted with tiny globules of liquid silver. Perenelle knew a dozen creatures that could have spun the webs, and she didn't want to meet any of them, not here and now, while she was so drained of her power.

Turning, she darted down a long corridor lit only by a single bulb at either end. Now that she knew what she was looking for, she could see the silver webs everywhere, stretched across the ceiling, spreading across the walls, and there were huge nests knotted in corners, growing in the deepest shadows. The webs' presence might explain why she had encountered no vermin in the prison—no ants, flies, mosquitoes or rats. Once the nests hatched, the building would come alive with spiders . . . if indeed that's what the spinners were. Over the centuries, Perenelle had encountered Elders who were associated with spiders, including Arachne and the mysterious and terrifying Spider Woman, but as far as she knew, none of them was aligned with Dee and the Dark Elders.

Perenelle was hurrying past an open door, a perfect spiderweb framed in the opening, when she caught the hint of a sour bitter stench. She slowed, then stopped. The smell was new; it wasn't the smell of the sphinx. Turning back to the door, she went as close as she could to the web without touching it and peered inside. It took her eyes a moment to adjust to the darkness and a moment longer to make sense of what she was seeing.

Vetala.

Perenelle's heart began to beat so strongly in her chest that she could actually feel her flesh vibrating. Hanging upside down from the ceiling were a dozen creatures. Talons that were a cross between human feet and birds' claws bit deep into the soft stone, while leathery bats' wings wrapped around skeletal human bodies. The upside-down heads were beautiful, with the faces of young men and women not yet in their teens.

Vetala.

Perenelle mouthed the word silently. Vampires from the Indian subcontinent. And unlike Scathach, this clan drank blood and ate flesh. But what were they doing here, and more importantly, how had they gotten here? Vetala were always linked to a region or tribe: Perenelle had never known one to leave its homeland.

The Sorceress turned slowly to look at the other open doorways lining the gloomy corridor. What else lay hidden in the cells beneath Alcatraz?

What was Dr. John Dee planning?

SUNDAY, *3rd June*

CHAPTER TWENTY-ONE

Sophie's ragged scream pulled Josh from a deep and dreamless sleep and rolled him out of bed, leaving him swaying on his feet, trying to get his bearings in complete darkness.

Sophie screamed again, the sound raw and terrifying.

Josh blundered across the bedroom, banging his knees on a chair before he discovered the door, visible only because of the thin strip of light beneath it. His sister was in the room directly across the corridor.

Earlier, Saint-Germain had escorted them upstairs and given them their choice of rooms on the top floor of the town house. Sophie had immediately picked the one overlooking the Champs-Elysées—from the bedroom window, she could actually see the Arc de Triomphe over the rooftops—while Josh had taken the room across the hall, which looked over the dried-up rear garden. The rooms were small, with low ceilings and uneven, slightly sloping walls, but each had its own bathroom with a minuscule shower cubicle that had only two settings—scalding and freezing. When Sophie had run the water in her room, Josh's shower stopped working altogether. And although he'd promised his sister that he would come talk to her after he'd showered and changed, he'd sat on the edge of his bed and almost immediately fallen into an exhausted sleep.

Sophie screamed for a third time, a shuddering sob that brought tears to his eyes.

Josh jerked open his door and ran across the narrow corridor. He pushed open the door to his sister's room . . . and stopped.

Joan of Arc was sitting on the edge of his sister's bed, holding Sophie's hand in both of hers. There were no lights in the room, but it was not in total darkness. Joan's hand was glowing with cool silvery light and it looked like she was wearing a soft gray glove. As he watched, his sister's hand took on the same texture and color. The air smelled of vanilla and lavender.

Joan turned to look at Josh, and he was startled to discover that her eyes were glowing silver coins. He took a step toward the bed, but she raised a finger to her lips and shook her head slightly, warning him not to say anything. The glow faded from her eyes. "Your sister is dreaming," Joan said, though he wasn't sure whether she had spoken aloud or if he was hearing her voice in his head. "The nightmare is already passing. It will not return," she said, making the sentence into a promise.

Wood creaked behind Josh and he whirled to see the

Comte de Saint-Germain coming down a narrow staircase at the end of the hall. Francis gestured to Josh from the bottom of the stairs, and although his lips didn't move, the boy clearly heard his voice: "My wife will take care of your sister. Come away."

Josh shook his head. "I should stay." He didn't want to leave Sophie alone with the strange woman, but he also knew instinctively that Joan would never harm his sister.

"There is nothing you can do for her," Saint-Germain said aloud. "Get dressed and come up to the attic. I have my office there." He turned away and disappeared back up the stairs.

Josh took a last look at Sophie. She was resting quietly, her breathing had slowed and he noticed that the dark rings had disappeared from beneath her eyes.

"Go now," Joan said. "There are some things I have to say to your sister. Private things."

"She's asleep . . . ," Josh began.

"But I will still say them," the woman murmured. "And she will still hear me."

In his room, Josh dressed quickly. A bundle of clothes had been laid on a chair beneath the window: underwear, jeans, T-shirts and socks. He guessed the clothes belonged to Saint-Germain: they were about the count's size. Josh dressed quickly in a pair of black designer jeans and a black silk T-shirt before slipping into his own shoes and taking a quick look in the mirror. He was unable to resist a smile; he'd never imagined himself wearing such expensive clothes. In the bathroom, he cracked open a new toothbrush from its packaging, brushed his teeth, splashed cold water on his face and ran his fingers through his overlong blond hair, pulling it back off his forehead. Strapping on his watch, he was shocked to discover that it was a little after midnight on Sunday morning. He'd slept the entire day and most of the night.

When he left the bedroom, he stopped at the door to his sister's room and looked inside. The smell of lavender was so strong it made his eyes water. Sophie lay unmoving on the bed, her breathing regular and even. Joan remained beside her, holding her hand, murmuring softly, but not in any language he could understand. The woman turned her head slowly to look at him, and he discovered that her eyes were once again flat silver discs, without any hint of white or pupil. She turned back to Sophie.

Josh stared at them for a moment before turning away. When the Witch of Endor had instructed Sophie in the Magic of Air, he had been dismissed; now he'd been dismissed again. He was quickly realizing that in this new magical world, there was no place for someone like him, someone without power.

Josh slowly climbed the narrow winding stairs that led up to Saint-Germain's office. Whatever Josh had been expecting to find in the attic, it was not the huge brightly lit white wood and chrome room. The attic ran the length of the entire house and had been remodeled into one vast open space, with an arched window looking over the Champs-Elysées at one end. The enormous room was filled with electronics and musical instruments, but there was no sign of Saint-Germain.

Against the right wall, a long table stretched from one end of the space to the other. It was piled high with computers, both desktops and laptops, screens of all shapes and sizes, synthesizers, a mixing desk, keyboards and electronic drum kits.

On the opposite side of the room a trio of electric guitars were perched on stands, while an assortment of keyboards were arranged around an enormous LCD screen.

"How do you feel?" Saint-Germain asked.

It took Josh a second to identify where the voice was coming from. The musician was lying flat on his back under the table, a bundle of USB cables in his hands. "Good," Josh said, and was surprised to find that it was true. He felt better than he had in a long time. "I don't even remember lying down. . . ."

"You were both exhausted, physically and mentally. And I understand the leygates suck every last drop of energy from you. Not that I've ever traveled through one," he added. "To be truthful, I was surprised you were still on your feet," Saint-Germain muttered as he dropped the cables. "You've slept for about fourteen hours."

Josh knelt alongside Saint-Germain. "What are you trying to do?"

"I moved a monitor and the cable fell out; I'm not sure which one it is."

"You should color code them with tape," Josh said. "That's what I do." Straightening, he caught the end of the cable that was attached to the wide-screen monitor and jerked it up and down. "It's this one." The cable twitched in Saint-Germain's hands.

"Thanks!"

The monitor suddenly flickered to life, displaying a screen filled with sliders and knobs.

Saint-Germain climbed to his feet and dusted himself off. He was wearing clothes identical to Josh's. "They fit." He nodded. "And they look good on you. You should wear black more often."

"Thanks for the clothes. . . ." He stopped. "I don't know how we're going to be able to pay you back, though."

Francis laughed quickly. "They weren't a loan, they were a gift. I don't want them back."

Before Josh could thank him again, Saint-Germain hit the keyboard and Josh jumped as a series of heavy piano chords thumped out from hidden speakers. "Don't worry, the attic is soundproofed," Saint-Germain said. "It'll not wake Sophie."

Josh nodded at the screen. "Do you write all your music on computer?"

"Just about." Saint-Germain looked around the room. "Anyone can make music now; you don't need much more than a computer, some software, patience and a lot of imagination. If I need some real instruments for a final mix, I'll hire musicians. But I can do most things here."

"I downloaded some beat-detection software once," Josh admitted. "But I could never get it right."

"What do you compose?"

"Well, I'm not sure you'd call it composing. . . . I put together some ambient mixes."

"I'd love to listen to anything you have."

"It's all gone. I lost my computer, my cell phone and my

iPod when Yggdrasill was destroyed." Even saying it aloud made him feel sick. And the worst part was that he really had no idea exactly what he'd lost. "I lost my summer project and all my music, and that was about ninety gigs. I had some great bootlegs. I'll never be able to replace them." He sighed. "I also lost hundreds of photos; all the places Mom and Dad took us. Our parents are scientists—they're archaeologists and paleontologists," he added, "so we've seen some amazing places."

"Lost everything! That's got to be tough," Saint-Germain sympathized. "What about backups?"

The stricken look on Josh's face was all the answer the count needed.

"Were you a Mac or a PC user?"

"Both, actually. Dad uses PCs at home, but most of the schools Sophie and I have gone to use Macs. Sophie loves her Macs, but I prefer a PC," he said. "If anything goes wrong, I can usually pull it apart and fix it myself."

Saint-Germain walked to the end of the table and rummaged around underneath it. He pulled out three laptops, different brands and screen sizes, and lined them up on the floor. He gestured dramatically. "Take one."

Josh blinked at him in surprise. "Take one?"

"They're all PCs," Saint-Germain continued, "and they're no use to me. I've completely switched over to Macs now."

Josh looked from Saint-Germain to the laptops and back to the musician again. He'd just met this man, didn't know him, and here he was offering Josh a choice of three expensive laptops. He shook his head. "Thanks, but I couldn't."

"Why not?" Saint-Germain demanded.

And Josh had no answer for that.

"You need a computer. I'm offering you one of these. I would be pleased if you took it." Saint-Germain smiled. "I grew up in an age when gift giving was an art. I have found that people in this century really do not know how to accept a gift gracefully."

"I don't know what to say."

"How about thank you?" Saint-Germain suggested.

Josh grinned. "Yes. Well . . . thank you," he said hesitantly. "Thank you very much." Even as he was speaking, he knew which machine he wanted: the tiny one-inch-thick laptop with an eleven-inch screen.

Saint-Germain dug around under the table and extracted three power cords that he dropped onto the floor alongside the machines. "I'm not using them. They'll probably never be used again. I'll end up reformatting the hard drives and giving the machines to the local schools. Take whichever one you like. You'll find a backpack under the table too." He paused, blue eyes twinkling, and tapped the back of the machine Josh was looking at, then added with a grin, "I've a spare long-life battery for this one. That was my favorite."

"Well, if you're really not using them . . ."

Saint-Germain ran a finger across the back of the small laptop, tracing a line in the dust, holding it up so that Josh could see the black mark on his fingertip. "Trust me: I'm not using them."

"OK . . . thanks. I mean, thank you. No one's ever given me a present like this before," he said, picking up the small computer and turning it over in his hands. "I'll take this one . . . if you're really sure. . . ."

"I'm sure. It's fully loaded; got wireless, too, and it'll autoconvert the power for European and American current. Plus, it's got all my albums on it," Saint-Germain said, "so you can start your music collection again. You'll also find an mpeg of the last concert. Check it out; it's really good."

"I'll do that," Josh said, plugging in the laptop to charge the battery.

"Let me know what you think. And you can be honest with me," Saint-Germain added.

"Really?"

The count took a moment to consider, and then he shook his head. "No, not really. Only tell me if you think I'm good. I don't like negative reviews, though you'd think that after nearly three hundred years, I'd be used to them."

Josh opened the laptop and turned it on. The machine whined and flickered to life. Leaning forward, he gently blew dust off the keyboard. When the laptop booted, the screen flickered and showed an image of Saint-Germain onstage, surrounded by a dozen instruments. "You have a picture of yourself for your wallpaper?" Josh asked incredulously.

"It's one of my favorites," the musician said.

Josh nodded toward the screen and then looked around the room. "Can you play all these?"

"Every one. I started on the violin a long time ago, then moved on to harpsichord and flute. But I've kept up with the times, always learning new instruments. In the eighteenth century, I was using the latest technology—the new violins, the latest keyboards—and here I am, nearly three hundred years later, still doing that. This is a great time to be a musician. And with technology, I can finally play all the sounds I hear in my head." His fingers brushed a keyboard and a full choir sang from the speakers.

Josh jumped. The voices were so clear that he actually looked over his shoulder.

"I load up the computer with sound samples, so I can use anything in my work." Saint-Germain turned back to the screen and his fingers danced on the keys. "Don't you think those fireworks yesterday morning made some great sounds? Crackling. Snapping. Maybe it's time for another Fireworks Suite."

Josh walked around the room, looking at the framed gold records, the signed posters and CD sleeves. "I didn't know there was one already," he said.

"George Frideric Handel, 1749, *Music for the Royal Fireworks*. What a night that was! What music!" Saint-Germain's fingers moved across a keyboard, filling the room with a tune Josh thought sounded vaguely familiar. Maybe he'd heard it on a TV ad. "Good old George," Saint-Germain said. "I never liked him."

"The Witch of Endor doesn't like you," Josh said hesitantly. "Why?"

Saint-Germain grinned. "The Witch doesn't like anyone. She especially doesn't like me because I became immortal through my own efforts and, unlike Nicholas and Perry, I don't need any recipe from a book to remain undying."

Josh frowned. "You mean there are different types of immortality?"

"Many different types, and as many different types of immortals. The most dangerous are those who became immortal because of their loyalty to an Elder. If they fall from favor with the Elder, the gift is rescinded, of course." He snapped his fingers and Josh jumped. "The result is instant old age. Ancient age. It's a great way of ensuring loyalty." He turned back to the keyboard and his fingers drew a haunting breathy sound from the speakers. He looked up as Josh joined him in front of the screen. "But the real reason the Witch of Endor doesn't like me is because I—an ordinary mortal—became the Master of Fire." He held up his left hand and a different-colored flame danced at the tip of each finger. The attic studio suddenly smelled of burnt leaves.

"And why would that bother her?" Josh asked, staring entranced at the dancing flames. He wanted—desperately wanted—to be able to do something like that.

"Maybe because I learned the secret of fire from her brother." The music changed, becoming discordant and harsh. "Well, when I say *learned*, I should really say *stole*."

"You stole the secret of fire!" Josh said.

The Comte de Saint-Germain nodded happily. "From Prometheus."

"And one of these days my uncle will want it back." Scathach's voice made them both jump. Neither had heard her enter the room. "Nicholas is here," she said, and turned away.

CHAPTER TWENTY-TWO

*N*icholas Flamel was sitting at the head of the kitchen table, both hands wrapped around a steaming mug of soup. In front of him was a half-empty bottle of Perrier, a tall glass and a plate piled high with thick-crust bread and cheese. He looked up, nodded and smiled as Josh and Saint-Germain followed Scathach into the room.

Sophie was sitting on one side of the table, facing Joan of Arc, and Josh quickly slid into the seat beside his sister while Saint-Germain took the seat alongside his wife. Only Scathach remained standing, leaning against the sink behind the Alchemyst, staring out into the night. Josh noted that she was still wearing the bandana she had cut from Flamel's loose black T-shirt.

Josh turned his attention to the Alchemyst. The man looked exhausted and old, and there seemed to be a dusting of silver in his close-cropped hair that hadn't been there earlier. His skin was also shockingly pale, emphasizing the bruise-black circles beneath his eyes and the deep lines in his forehead. His clothes were rumpled and speckled with rain, and there was a long muddy streak on the sleeve of the jacket he'd hung off the back of the wooden chair. Water droplets sparkled on the worn leather.

No one spoke while the Alchemyst finished the soup and then broke off chunks of the cheese and bread. He chewed slowly and methodically, then poured water from the green bottle into the glass and drank in short sips. When he was finished, he wiped his lips on a napkin and allowed himself a sigh of satisfaction. "Thank you." He nodded to Joan. "That was perfect."

"There is a larder full of food, Nicholas," she said, her gray eyes huge and concerned. "You really should have more than soup, bread and cheese."

"It was enough," he said gently. "Right now I need to rest, and I didn't want to put a lot of food in my stomach. We shall have a big breakfast in the morning. I'll even cook it myself."

"I didn't know you could cook," Saint-Germain said.

"He can't," Scathach muttered.

"I thought eating cheese late at night gave you nightmares," Josh said. He glanced at his watch. "It's close to one in the morning."

"Oh, I don't need cheese to see nightmares. I've seen them in the flesh." Nicholas smiled, though there was no humor in it. "They're not so scary." He looked from Josh to Sophie. "You're safe and well?"

191

The twins glanced at one another and nodded.

"And rested?"

"They slept all day and most of the night," Joan said.

"Good," Flamel nodded. "You're going to need all your strength. And I like the clothes." While Josh was dressed identically to Saint-Germain, Sophie was wearing a heavy white cotton blouse and blue jeans with the ends turned up to reveal ankle-high boots.

"Joan gave them to me," Sophie explained.

"Almost a perfect fit," the older woman said. "We'll go through my wardrobe shortly, get you some changes for the rest of your journey."

Sophie smiled her thanks.

Nicholas turned to Saint-Germain. "The fireworks on the Eiffel Tower yesterday: inspired, just inspired."

The count bowed. "Thank you, Master," he said, looking tremendously pleased with himself.

Joan's giggle was a low purr. "He's been looking for an excuse to do something like that for months. You should have seen the display he set off in Hawaii when we were married. We waited until the sun went down; then Francis lit up the sky for nearly an hour. It was so beautiful, though the effort exhausted him for a week," she added with a grin.

Two spots of color touched the count's cheeks and he reached over to squeeze his wife's hand. "It was worth it to see the look on your face."

"You hadn't mastered fire the last time we met," Nicholas said slowly. "If I recall, you had some little ability with it, but nothing like the power you demonstrated yesterday. Who trained you?"

"I spent some time in India, in the lost city of Ophir," the count responded, glancing quickly at the Alchemyst. "They still remember you there. Did you know they erected a statue to you and Perenelle in the main square?"

"I didn't. I promised Perenelle I'd take her back there someday," Nicholas said wistfully. "But what has that got to do with your mastery of fire?"

"I met someone there . . . someone who trained me," Saint-Germain said enigmatically. "Showed me how to use all the secret knowledge I'd gleaned from Prometheus . . ."

"Stolen," Scathach corrected.

"Well, he stole it first," Saint-Germain snapped.

Flamel's hand hit the table with enough force to rattle the bottle of water. Only Scathach didn't jump. "Enough!" he barked, and for an instant, the planes and angles of his face altered, cheekbones suddenly prominent, hinting at the skull beneath the flesh. His almost colorless eyes visibly darkened, turning gray, then brown and finally black. Resting his elbows on the table, he rubbed his face with the palms of both hands and took a deep shuddering breath. There was the faintest hint of mint in the air, but it was a sour bitter odor. "I'm sorry. That was inexcusable. I should not have raised my voice," he said quietly into the shocked silence that followed. When he took his hands away from his face, his lips moved into a smile that did not quite reach his eyes. He looked at each of them in turn, his gaze lingering on the twins' stunned faces. "You must forgive me. I'm tired now, so tired; I could sleep for a week. Continue, Francis, please. Who trained you?"

The Comte de Saint-Germain took a breath. "He told me . . . he said that I was never to speak his name aloud," he finished in a rush.

Flamel placed his elbows on the table, wrapped the fingers of both hands together and rested his chin on his knotted fists. He stared at the musician, his face impassive. "Who was it?" he demanded firmly.

"I gave him my word," Saint-Germain said miserably. "It was one of the conditions he imposed when he trained me. He said there was a power in words and that certain names set up vibrations both in this world and the Shadowrealms and attracted unwelcome attention."

Scathach stepped forward and rested her hand lightly on the Alchemyst's shoulder. "Nicholas, you know that is true. There are certain words that should never be spoken, names that should never be used. Old things. Undead things."

Nicholas nodded. "If you gave this person your word, then you should not go back on it, of course. But tell me"—he paused, not looking at the count—"this mysterious person, how many hands did he have?"

Saint-Germain sat back suddenly, and the shocked expression on his face revealed the truth. "How did you know?" he whispered.

The Alchemyst's mouth twisted into an ugly grimace. "In Spain, six hundred years ago, I met a one-handed man who taught me some of the secrets of the Codex. He too refused to speak his name aloud." Flamel suddenly looked at Sophie,

194

eyes wide and staring. "You have within you the Witch's memories. If a name comes to you now—it would be better for all of us if you did not say it aloud."

Sophie closed her mouth so quickly she bit the inside of her lip. She knew the name of the person Flamel and Saint-Germain were talking about. She also knew just who—and what—he was. And she *had* been just about to speak the name aloud.

Flamel turned back to Saint-Germain. "You know that Sophie's powers have been Awakened. The Witch taught her the basics of the Magic of Air, and I am determined that both she and Josh be trained in all the elemental magics as quickly as possible. I know where there are masters of Earth and Water magic. Only yesterday, I was thinking we might have to go in search of one of the Elders associated with fire, Maui or Vulcan or even your old nemesis, Prometheus himself. Now I'm hoping that might not be necessary." He paused for a breath. "Do you think you could you teach Sophie the Magic of Fire?"

Saint-Germain blinked in surprise. He folded his arms across his chest and looked from the girl to the Alchemyst and started to shake his head. "I'm not sure I could. I'm not even sure I should. . . ."

Joan reached over and rested her right hand on the back of her husband's arm. He turned to look at her and she nodded, almost imperceptibly. Her lips didn't move, and yet everyone clearly heard her say, "Francis, you must do it."

The count didn't hesitate. "I'll do it . . . but is it wise?" he asked, serious.

"It is necessary," she said simply.

"It'll be a lot for her to take in. . . ." He bowed to Sophie. "Forgive me. I didn't mean to talk about you as if you weren't here." He looked back at Nicholas and added doubtfully, "Sophie is still dealing with the Witch's memories."

"Not anymore. I attended to that." Joan's grip tightened on her husband's arm. She turned her head to look at everyone sitting around the table, finally stopping at Sophie. "While Sophie slept, I spoke to her, helped her sort the memories, categorize them, separate her own thoughts from the Witch's. I do not think they will trouble her so much now."

Sophie was shocked. "You got into my head while I was asleep?"

Joan of Arc shook her head slightly. "I didn't get into your mind . . . I simply talked to you, instructed you what to do and how to do it."

"I saw you talking . . . ," Josh began, and then frowned. "But Sophie was sound asleep. She couldn't hear you."

"She heard me," Joan said. She looked directly at Sophie and placed her left hand flat on the table. A crackling silver haze appeared on her fingertips, tiny speckles of light dancing from her flesh to bounce, like mercury droplets, across the table toward the girl's hands, which were resting on the polished wood. As they approached, Sophie's fingernails began to glow a muted silver, and then suddenly, the points of light wrapped around her fingers.

"You may be twin to Josh, but we are sisters, you and I. We are Silver. I know what it is like to hear voices inside my head; I know what it is like to see the impossible, to know the unknowable." Joan looked first at Josh and then at the Alchemyst. "While Sophie slept, I spoke directly to her unconscious mind. I taught her how to control the Witch's memories, how to ignore the voices, to shut out the images. I taught her how to protect herself."

Sophie raised her head slowly, eyes wide with surprise. "That's what's different!" she said, both shocked and amazed. "I can't hear the voices anymore." She looked at her twin. "They started when the Witch poured her knowledge into me. There were thousands of them, shouting and whispering in languages I almost understood. It's quiet now."

"They're still there," Joan explained. "They will always be there. But now you will be able to call upon them when you need to, to use their knowledge. I also started the process of teaching you how to control your aura."

"But how could you while she was asleep?" Josh pressed. He even found the thought of it incredibly disturbing.

"Only the conscious mind sleeps—the unconscious is always aware."

"What do you mean, control my aura?" Sophie asked, confused. "I thought it was just this silver-colored electrical field around my body."

Joan shrugged, an elegant movement of her shoulders. "Your aura is as powerful as your imagination. You can shape it, meld it, fashion it to your will." She held out her left hand. "That's how I can do this." A metal glove from a suit of armor clicked into existence around her flesh. Each rivet was perfectly formed, and the back of the fingers was even dappled with rust. "Try it," she suggested.

197

Sophie held out her hand and looked hard at it.

"Visualize the glove," Joan suggested. "See it in your imagination."

A tiny silver thimble appeared on Sophie's little finger, then winked out of existence.

"Well, a little more practice, maybe," Joan admitted. She glanced sidelong at Saint-Germain and then looked at the Alchemyst. "Let me work with Sophie for a couple of hours, teach her a little more about controlling and shaping her aura, before Francis starts to teach her the Magic of Fire."

"This Fire magic. Is it dangerous?" Josh demanded, looking around the room. He still vividly remembered what had happened to his sister when Hekate had Awakened her—she could have died. And the more he'd learned about the Witch of Endor, he'd realized Sophie could have died learning Air magic as well. When no one answered him, he turned to look at Saint-Germain. "Is it dangerous?"

"Yes," the musician said simply. "Very."

Josh shook his head. "Then I don't want—"

Sophie reached out to squeeze her brother's arm. He looked down: the hand that gripped his arm was wrapped in a chain-mail glove. "Josh, I have to do this."

"No, you don't."

"I do."

Josh looked into his sister's face. It was set in the stubborn mask he knew so well. Finally, he turned away, saying nothing. He didn't want his sister learning any more magic—not only was it dangerous . . . but it would also distance her even further from him.

Joan turned to Flamel. "And now, Nicholas, you must rest."

The Alchemyst nodded. "I will."

"We were expecting you back a long time ago," Scathach said. "I was thinking I'd have to go out in search of you."

"The butterfly led me here hours ago," Nicholas said tiredly, voice muffled with exhaustion. "Once I knew where you were, I wanted to wait for night to fall before approaching the house, just in case it is under observation."

"Machiavelli doesn't even know this house exists," Saint-Germain said confidently.

"Perenelle taught me a simple cloaking spell a long time ago, but it only works when it's raining—it uses water droplets to refract light around the user," Flamel explained. "I decided to wait until nightfall to increase my chances of remaining unseen."

"What did you do for the day?" Sophie asked.

"I wandered around the city, looking for some of my old haunts."

"Surely most are gone?" Joan said.

"Most. Not all." Flamel reached down and lifted an object wrapped in newspaper from the floor. It made a solid thump when he dropped it on the table. "The house in Montmorency is still there."

"I should have guessed you'd visit Montmorency," Scathach said with a sad smile. She looked at the twins and explained, "It is the house where Nicholas and Perenelle lived in the fifteenth century. We spent some happy times there."

"Very happy," Flamel agreed.

"And it's still there?" Sophie asked, amazed.

"One of the oldest houses in Paris," Flamel said proudly.

"What else did you do?" Saint-Germain asked.

Nicholas shrugged. "Visited the Musée de Cluny. It's not every day you get to see your own gravestone. I guess it's comforting to know that people still remember me—the real me."

Joan smiled. "There is a street named after you, Nicholas: the Rue Flamel. And one named in honor of Perenelle, too. But somehow, I don't think that's the real reason you visited the museum, is it?" She said shrewdly, "You never struck me as a sentimental man."

The Alchemyst smiled. "Well, not the only reason," he admitted. He reached into his jacket pocket and plucked out a narrow cylindrical tube. Everyone around the table leaned forward. Even Scatty stepped in to look at it. Unscrewing both ends, Flamel removed and unrolled a length of rustling parchment. "Nearly six hundred years ago, I hid this within my tombstone, little thinking that I would ever need to use it." He spread the thick yellow parchment on the table. Drawn in red ink faded to the color of rust was an oval with a circle inside it, surrounded by three lines forming a rough triangle.

Josh leaned over. "I've seen something like that before." He frowned. "Isn't there something like that on the dollar bill?"

"Ignore what it looks like," Flamel said. "It's drawn this way to disguise its true meaning."

"What is it?" Josh asked.

"It's a map," Sophie said suddenly.

"Yes, it's a map," Nicholas agreed. "But how did you know? The Witch of Endor never saw this. . . ."

"No, it has nothing to do with the Witch," Sophie smiled. She leaned across the table, her head brushing her brother's. She pointed to the top right-hand corner of the parchment, where a tiny, barely visible cross was etched in red ink. "This definitely looks like an *N*," she said, pointing to the top of the cross, "and this is an *S*."

"North and south." Josh nodded in quick agreement. "Genius, Soph!" He looked at Nicholas. "It's a map."

The Alchemyst nodded. "Very good. It's a map of all the ley lines in Europe. Towns and cities, even borders might change beyond all recognition, but the ley lines remain the same." He held up the square. "This is our passport out of Europe and back to America."

"Let's hope we get a chance to use it," Scatty muttered.

Josh touched the edge of the newspaper-wrapped bundle that sat in the center of the table. "And what's this?"

Nicholas furled the parchment back into the tube and slipped it into his jacket pocket. Then he began to unwrap layers of newspaper from the object on the table. "Perenelle and I were in Spain close to the end of the fourteenth century when the one-handed man revealed the first secret of the Codex," he said, speaking to no one in particular, his French accent now pronounced.

"The first secret?" Josh asked.

"You've seen the text—it changes . . . but it changes in a strict mathematical sequence. It's not random. The changes are linked to the movements of the stars and planets, the phases of the moon."

"Like a calendar?" Josh said.

Flamel nodded. "Just like a calendar. Once we had learned that code sequence, we knew we could finally return to Paris. It would take us a lifetime—several lifetimes—to translate the book, but at least we had learned where to start. So I changed some stones into diamonds, and some flat pieces of shale into gold, and we started out on the long journey back to Paris. By then, of course, we had come to the attention of the Dark Elders, and Bacon, Dee's foul predecessor, was closing in. Rather than take a direct route into France, we kept to the back roads and avoided the usual passes across the mountains, which we knew would be watched. However, winter arrived early that year—I believe the Dark Elders had something to do with it—and we found ourselves cut off in Andorra. And that is where I found this. . . ." He touched the object on the table.

Josh looked at his sister, eyebrows raised in a silent question. *Andorra?* he mouthed; she was much better at geography than he was.

"One of the smallest countries in the world," she explained in a whisper, "in the Pyrenees between Spain and France."

Flamel unwrapped more paper. "Before I 'died,' I hid this object deep within the stone over the lintel of the house on the Rue de Montmorency. I never thought I would need it again."

"Within?" Josh asked, confused. "Did you say you hid it *within?"*

"Within. I changed the molecular structure of the granite, pushed this into the block of stone and then returned the lintel to its original solid state. Simple transmutation: like pushing a nut into a tub of ice cream." The final sheet of newspaper tore as he pulled it away.

"It's a sword," Josh whispered in awe, looking at the short narrow weapon nestled on the paper-strewn table. He guessed it was about twenty inches long, its simple cross hilt wrapped in strips of stained dark leather. The blade seemed to be made of a sparkling gray metal. No, not metal. "A stone sword," he said aloud, frowning. It reminded him of something—almost as if he had seen it before.

But even as he was speaking, Joan and Saint-Germain scrambled away from the table, the woman's chair falling over in her eagerness to get away from the blade. Behind Flamel, Scathach hissed like a cat, vampire teeth appearing as she opened her mouth, and when she spoke, her voice was shaking, her accent thick and barbaric. She sounded almost angry . . . or afraid. "Nicholas," she said very slowly, "what are you doing with that filthy thing?"

The Alchemyst ignored her. He looked at Josh and Sophie, who had remained sitting at the table, shocked motionless by the reaction of the others, unsure what was happening. "There are four great swords of power," Flamel said urgently, "each one linked to the elements: Earth, Air, Fire and Water. It is said that they predate even the oldest of the

Elder Races. The swords have had many names through the ages: Excalibur and Joyeuse, Mistelteinn and Curtana, Durendal and Tyrfing. The last time one was used as a weapon in the world of men was when Charlemagne, the Holy Roman Emperor, carried Joyeuse into battle."

"This is Joyeuse?" Josh whispered. His sister might be good at geography, but he knew history, and Charlemagne had always fascinated him.

Scathach's laugh was a bitter snarl. "Joyeuse is a thing of beauty. This . . . this is an abomination."

Flamel touched the sword's hilt and the tiny crystals in the stone sparkled with green light. "This is not Joyeuse, though it is true that it once belonged to Charlemagne. I also believe the emperor himself hid this blade in Andorra sometime in the ninth century."

"It's just like Excalibur," Josh said, suddenly realizing why the stone sword was so familiar. He looked at his sister. "Dee had Excalibur; he used it to destroy the World Tree."

"Excalibur is the Sword of Ice," Flamel continued. "This is its twin blade: Clarent, the Sword of Fire. It is the only weapon that can stand against Excalibur."

"It is a cursed blade," Scathach said firmly. "I'll not touch it."

"Nor I," Joan said quickly, and Saint-Germain nodded in agreement.

"I'm not asking any of *you* to carry it or wield it," Nicholas snapped. He spun the weapon on the table until the hilt touched the boy's fingers and then he looked at each of them in turn. "We know Dee and Machiavelli are coming.

Josh is the only one amongst us without the ability to protect himself. Until his powers are Awakened, he is going to need a weapon. I want him to have Clarent."

"Nicholas!" Scathach cried, horrified. "What are you thinking. He's an untrained humani—"

"—with a solid gold aura," Flamel said coldly. "And I am determined to keep him safe." He pushed the sword into Josh's fingers. "This is yours. Take it."

Josh leaned forward and felt the two pages from the Codex press against his skin in their cloth bag. This would be the second gift the Alchemyst had given him in as many days. Part of him wanted to accept the gifts at face value—to trust him and to believe that Flamel liked him and trusted him in turn. And yet, and yet . . . even after the conversation they'd had in the street, somewhere at the back of his mind, Josh couldn't forget what Dee had said by the fountain in Ojai: that half of everything Flamel said was a lie, and the other half wasn't entirely truthful either. He deliberately looked away from the sword and looked into Flamel's pale eyes. The Alchemyst was staring at him, his face an expressionless mask. So what was the Alchemyst up to? Josh wondered. What game was he playing? More of Dee's words popped into his head. "He is now, and has always been, a liar, a charlatan, and a crook."

"Don't you want it?" Nicholas asked. "Take it." He pushed the hilt right into Josh's grip.

Almost against his will, Josh's fingers closed over the smooth leather-wrapped hilt of the stone sword. He lifted it—though it was short, it was surprisingly heavy—and turned it over in his hands. "I've never handled a sword in my life," he said. "I don't know how. . . ."

"Scathach will show you the basics," Flamel said, not looking at the Shadow, but turning the simple statement into a command. "How to carry it, simple thrust and parry. Try and avoid stabbing yourself with it," he added.

Josh suddenly realized that he was grinning widely and tried to wipe away the smile, but it was difficult: the sword felt *amazing* in his hand. He moved his wrist and the sword twitched. Then he looked at Scatty, Francis and Joan and saw how their eyes were fixed on the blade, following its every movement, and his smile faded. "What's wrong with the sword?" he demanded. "Why are you so scared of it?"

Sophie put her hand on her brother's arm, her eyes sparkling silver with the Witch's knowledge. "Clarent," she said, "is an evil, accursed weapon, sometimes called the Coward's Blade. This is the sword Mordred used to kill his uncle, King Arthur."

CHAPTER TWENTY-THREE

*I*n her bedroom at the top of the house, Sophie sat on the deep window ledge and looked down over the Champs-Elysées. The broad tree-lined street was wet with rain and shone amber, red and white in the reflected lights of the cars and buses. She checked her watch: it was almost two a.m. on Sunday morning, yet traffic was still heavy. Anytime after midnight, the streets of San Francisco would be deserted.

The difference emphasized just how far from home she was.

When she'd been younger, she'd gone through a phase when she'd decided that everything about herself was boring. She'd made a conscious effort to be more stylish—more like her friend Elle, who changed her hair color on a weekly basis and had a wardrobe that was always filled with the latest styles. Sophie had collected everything she could find about the exotic European cities she read about in magazines, places where fashion and art were created: London and Paris,

Rome, Milan, Berlin. She was determined that she wasn't going to follow fashion; she was going to create her own. The phase had lasted about a month. Fashion was an expensive business, and the allowance she and her brother got from their parents was strictly limited.

She still wanted to visit the great cities of the world, though. She and Josh had even started talking about taking a year off before college to go backpacking around Europe. And now here they were in one of the most beautiful cities on earth, and she had absolutely no interest in exploring it. The only thing she wanted to do right now was return to San Francisco.

But what would she return to?

The thought stopped her cold.

Though the family had moved around a lot, and traveled even more, two days ago, she'd known what to expect in the coming months. The rest of the year was mapped out in boring detail. In the fall, their parents would resume their teaching positions at the University of San Francisco, and both she and Josh would return to school. In December, the family would take their annual trip to Providence, Rhode Island, where their father had given the Christmas lecture at Brown University for the past two decades. On the twenty-first of December, their birthday, the twins would be taken to New York City to see the shops, admire the lights, look at the tree in Rockefeller Center and then go skating. They would get lunch in the Stage Door Deli: have matzo ball soup and sandwiches as big as their heads and one slice of pumpkin pie between them. On Christmas Eve, they would head out to their aunt Christine's house in Montauk on Long Island, where they'd spend the holiday and then see in the New Year. That had been the tradition for the past ten years.

And now?

Sophie took a deep breath. Now she possessed powers and abilities she could barely comprehend. She had access to memories that were a mixture of truth, myth and fantasy; she knew secrets that could rewrite history books. But she wished, more than anything else, that there were some way she could turn back time, to return to Thursday morning . . . before all this had happened. Before the world had changed.

Sophie rested her forehead against the cool glass. What was going to happen? What was she going to do . . . not just now, but in the years to come? Her brother had no career in mind; every year he announced something different—he was going to be a computer game designer or a programmer, a professional football player, a paramedic or a fireman—but she'd always known what she was going to do. From the time her first-grade teacher had asked her the question—"What do you want to be when you grow up, Sophie?"—she'd known the answer. She wanted to study archaeology and paleontology like her parents, to travel the world and catalog the past, maybe make some discoveries that would help put history in order. But that was never going to happen now. Overnight, she'd realized that the study of archaeology, history, geography and science had been rendered useless . . . or if not useless, then simply wrong.

A sudden wash of emotion caught her by surprise, and she felt a burning at the back of her throat and tears on her cheeks. She pressed the palms of both hands against her face and brushed the tears away.

"Knock-knock . . ." Josh's voice startled her. Sophie turned to look at her twin. Her brother was standing at the door, the stone sword in one hand, a tiny laptop in the other. "Can I come in?"

"You've never asked before." She smiled.

Josh stepped into the room and sat down on the edge of the double bed. He carefully placed Clarent on the floor by his feet and rested the laptop on his knees. "A lot's changed," he said quietly, his blue eyes troubled.

"I was just thinking the same thing," she agreed. "At least *that* hasn't changed." The twins often found they were thinking the same thought at the same moment, and they knew one another so well that they could even finish each other's sentences. "I was just wishing we could go back in time, to before all this happened."

"Why?"

"So I wouldn't have to be like this . . . so we wouldn't be different."

Josh looked into his sister's face and tilted his head slightly. "You'd give it up?" he asked very softly. "The power, the knowledge?"

"In a heartbeat," she said immediately. "I don't like what's happening to me. I never wanted it to happen." Her voice cracked, but she continued. "I want to be ordinary, Josh. I want to be human again. I want to be like you."

Josh looked down. He opened the laptop and concentrated on powering it up.

"But you don't, do you?" she said slowly, interpreting the long silence that followed. "You want the power, you want to be able to shape your aura and control the elements, don't you?"

Josh hesitated. "It would be . . . interesting, I think," he said eventually, staring at the screen. Then he looked up, his eyes bright with the reflected image of the log-on screen. "Yes, I want to be able to do it," he admitted.

Sophie opened her mouth to snap a response, to tell him that he didn't know what he was talking about, to tell him just how sick it made her feel, how scared she was. But she stopped herself; she didn't want to fight, and until Josh had experienced it for himself, he would never understand.

"Where did you get the computer?" she asked, changing the subject when the laptop finally blipped.

"Francis gave it to me," Josh said. "You were out of it when Dee destroyed Yggdrasill. He stabbed the tree with Excalibur and it turned to ice and then shattered like glass. Well, my wallet, cell phone, iPod and laptop were in the tree," he said ruefully. "I lost everything. Including all our photos."

"And the count just *gave* you a laptop?"

Josh nodded. "Gave it to me, insisted I have it. Must be my day for presents." The pale glow from the computer screen lit his face from below, giving his head a vaguely frightening appearance. "He's switched over to Macs; they've got better music software, apparently, and he's not using PCs anymore. He found this one dumped under a table upstairs," he continued, eyes still locked on the small screen. He glanced quickly at his sister. "It's true," he said, recognizing her silence as doubt.

211

Sophie looked away. She knew her brother was telling the truth, and that had nothing to do with the Witch's knowledge. She'd always known when Josh was lying to her, though, strangely, he never knew when she was lying to him . . . which she didn't do too often anyway, and only ever for his own good. "So what are you doing now?" she asked.

"Checking my e-mail." He grinned. "Life goes on . . . ," he began.

". . . e-mail stops for no man," Sophie finished with a smile. It was one of Josh's favorite sayings, and it usually drove her crazy.

"There's loads," he muttered. "Eighty on Gmail, sixty-two on Yahoo, twenty on AOL, three on FastMail . . ."

"I'll never understand why you need so many e-mail accounts," Sophie said. She drew her legs up to her chest, wrapped her arms around her shins and rested her chin on her knees. It felt good to be having an *ordinary* conversation with her brother; it reminded her of how things were supposed to be . . . and had been until Thursday afternoon at two-fifteen precisely. She remembered the time; she'd been talking to her friend Elle in New York when she'd spotted the long black car pulling up outside the bookshop. She'd checked the time just before the man she now knew to be Dr. John Dee had climbed out of the car.

Josh looked up. "We have two e-mails from Mom, one from Dad."

"Read them to me. Start with the oldest."

"OK. Mom sent one on Friday, June first. *Hope you're*

both behaving yourselves. How is Mrs. Fleming? Has she fully recovered?" Josh looked up and frowned, confused.

Sophie sighed. "Remember? We told Mom that the bookshop closed because Perenelle wasn't feeling well." She shook her head. "Try and keep up!"

"It's been a little busy," Josh reminded her. "I can't remember everything. Besides, that's your job."

"Then we said that Nicholas and Perenelle had invited us to spend some time with them in their house in the desert."

"So." Josh looked at his sister, fingers hovering over the keys. "What will I tell Mom?"

"Tell her that everything's OK and Perenelle is feeling a lot better. Remember to call them Nick and Perry, though," she reminded him.

"Thanks," he said, hitting the backspace key, replacing *Perenelle* with *Perry*. His fingers skipped over the keys as he typed. "OK, next one," he continued. "From Mom again, dated yesterday. *'Tried phoning, but my call goes directly to your voice mail. Is everything OK? Got a call from your aunt Agnes. She said you didn't come home to collect any clothes or toiletries. Give me a number where I can call you. We're worried.'*" Josh looked at his sister. "So what do we tell her now?"

Sophie chewed on her bottom lip, thinking aloud. "We should tell her . . ." She hesitated. "Tell her we had the things with us at the shop. She knows we have clothes there. That's not a lie. I hate lying to her."

"Got it," Josh said, typing fast. The twins both kept clothes in his locker in the back room of the bookshop for the occasional evening when they went to the movies or walked down to the Embarcadero.

"Tell her we have no cell service here. Just don't say where *here* is," she added with a smile.

Josh looked disgusted. "You mean we have no cell phones . . ."

"I've still got mine, but the battery is dead. Tell Mom that we'll call as soon as we get a signal."

Josh continued to type. His finger hovered over the Enter key. "Is that it?"

"Send it."

He hit Enter. "Sent!"

"And you said there was an e-mail from Dad?" she asked.

"It's for me." He opened it, read it quickly and smiled broadly. "He's sent a jpeg of some fossil shark teeth he found. They look pretty good. And he's got some new coprolites for my collection."

"Coprolites." Sophie shook her head in mock disgust. "Fossilized poo! Why couldn't you collect stamps or coins like a regular person? It's just too weird."

"Weird?" Josh looked up, suddenly irritated. "Weird! Let me tell you what's weird: we're in a house with a two-thousand-year-old vegetarian vampire, an immortal alchemist, another immortal who's a musician specializing in Fire magic and a French heroine who should have died sometime in the middle of the fifteenth century." He nudged the sword on the floor with his foot. "And let's not forget the sword that was used to kill King Arthur." Josh's voice had been rising as he spoke and he suddenly stopped and drew in a deep shuddering breath, calming himself. He started to smile. "Compared to all that, I think collecting fossil poo is probably the *least* weird thing around here!" His smile turned to a grin and Sophie smiled, and then they were both laughing. Josh laughed so hard he got the hiccups, and that made them laugh even harder, until tears ran down their cheeks and their stomachs hurt.

"Oh, stop," Josh moaned. He hiccupped again, and they both dissolved into near hysteria.

It took a tremendous effort of will to control themselves, but for the first time since Sophie had been Awakened, Josh felt close to her again. Usually, they laughed every day; heading into work on Thursday morning was the last time they'd laughed together as they'd watched a skinny man in roller skates and running shorts being pulled along by a huge Dalmatian. All they needed to do was to keep finding things to laugh at—but unfortunately, there hadn't been too many of those over the past few days.

Sophie sobered up first and turned back to the window. She could see her brother in the glass and waited until he looked down at the screen before she spoke. "I'm surprised you didn't object more when Nicholas suggested that Francis train me in Fire magic," she said.

Josh raised his eyes and looked at his sister's face reflected in the window. "Would it have made any difference if I had?" he asked seriously.

She took a moment to think. "No. I suppose not," she admitted.

"I didn't think so. You'd still have done it."

Sophie turned to look directly at her twin. "I have to. I *need* to."

"I know," he said simply. "I know that now."

Sophie blinked in surprise. "You know?"

Josh closed the laptop and dropped it on the bed. Then he picked up the sword and rested it across his knees, absently rubbing the smooth blade. The stone felt warm. "I was . . . angry, scared—no, more than scared—terrified when Flamel had Hekate Awaken you. He didn't tell us about the dangers. He didn't tell us that you could have died, or fallen into a coma. I'll never forgive him for that."

"He was pretty sure nothing would happen. . . ."

"Pretty sure isn't sure enough."

Sophie nodded, not trusting herself to speak.

"And then, when the Witch of Endor passed her knowledge to you, I was scared again. But not so much scared *for* you . . . I was scared *of* you," he admitted very softly.

"Josh, how can you even say that?" Sophie began, genuinely shocked. "I'm your twin." The look on his face silenced her.

"You haven't seen what I've seen," he said earnestly. "I watched you stand up to the cat-headed woman. I saw your lips move, but when you spoke, the words were out of sync, and when you looked at me, you didn't recognize me. I don't know what you were—but you weren't my twin sister then. You were possessed."

Sophie blinked and huge tears rolled down her cheeks. She had only the vaguest memories, little more than dreamlike fragments, of what her brother was talking about.

216

"Then, in Ojai, I watched you make whirlwinds, and today—*yesterday*—I saw you make fog out of nothing."

"I don't know how I do those things," she murmured.

"I know, Soph, I know." He stood up and crossed to the window, looking out over the rooftops of Paris. "I understand that now. I've been thinking about it a lot. Your powers have been Awakened, but the only way you'll be able to control them, the only way you'll be safe, is by being trained. At the moment they are as much a danger to you as they are to our enemies. Joan of Arc helped you today, didn't she?"

"Yes, she helped a lot. I don't hear the voices anymore. That's a huge help. But there's another reason too, isn't there?" Sophie asked.

Josh turned the sword over in his hand, the blade almost black in the night, tiny flecks of crystal in the stone winking like stars. "We have no idea what sort of trouble we're in," he said slowly. "But we do know that we're in danger . . . real danger. We're fifteen years old—we shouldn't be thinking about being killed . . . or eaten . . . or worse!" He waved vaguely in the direction of the door. "I don't trust them. The only person I can trust is you . . . the real you."

"But Josh," Sophie said very gently, "I do trust them. They are good people. Scatty has fought for humanity for over two thousand years, and Joan is a kind and gentle person. . . ."

"And Flamel has kept the Codex hidden away for centuries," Josh said quickly. He touched his chest and Sophie heard the crackle of the two pages in the bag Flamel had given him. "There are recipes in this book that could make this planet a paradise, could cure every disease." He saw the flicker of doubt in her eyes and pressed on. "And you know that's true."

"The Witch's memories also tell me that there are recipes in the book that could destroy this world."

Josh shook his head quickly. "I think you're seeing what they want you to see."

Sophie pointed to the sword. "But why did Flamel give you the sword and the Codex pages?" she asked triumphantly.

"I think—I *know*—they're using us. I just don't know what for. Not yet, anyway." He saw his twin start to shake her head. "Anyway, we're going to need your powers to keep us both safe."

Sophie reached out and squeezed her brother's hand. "You know I'd never let anything hurt you."

"I know that," Josh said seriously. "At least, not deliberately. But what happens if something uses you, like it did in the Shadowrealm?"

Sophie nodded. "I had no control then," she admitted. "It was like I was in a dream, watching someone who looked like me."

"My football coach says that before you can take control, you have to *be* in control. If you can learn how to control your aura and master the magics," Josh continued, "no one would be able to do that to you ever again. You'd be incredibly powerful. And let's say, for instance, that my power isn't Awakened. I can learn how to use this sword." He twisted it in his hand, attempting to spin the blade, but it slipped sideways and cut a deep gouge in the wall. "Oops."

"Josh!"

"What? You can hardly notice it." He rubbed his sleeve against the cut. Paint and plaster flaked away, exposing the brickwork beneath.

"You're making it worse. And you've probably taken a chunk out of the sword."

But when Josh held the weapon up to the light, there wasn't even a mark on the blade.

Sophie nodded slowly. "I still think—*I know*—you're wrong about Flamel and the others."

"Sophie, you have to trust me."

"I trust you. But remember, the Witch knows these people, and she trusts them."

"Sophie," Josh said in frustration, "we don't know anything about the Witch."

"Oh, Josh, I know *everything* about the Witch," Sophie said feelingly. She tapped her temple with her forefinger. "And I wish I didn't. Her entire life, thousands of years, are in here." Josh opened his mouth to reply, but Sophie held up her hand. "Here's what I'll do: I'll work with Saint-Germain, learn everything he has to teach me."

"And keep an eye on him at the same time; try and find out what he and Flamel are up to."

Sophie ignored him. "Maybe the next time we're attacked, we'll be able to defend ourselves." She looked across the rooftops of Paris. "At least we're safe here."

"But for how long?" her twin asked.

CHAPTER TWENTY-FOUR

Dr. John Dee turned off the light and stepped out of the enormous bedroom onto the balcony, resting his fore-arms on the metal railing and looking out over the city of Paris. It had rained earlier and the air was damp and chill, tainted with the sour smell from the Seine and the hint of ex-haust fumes.

He hated Paris.

It had not always been that way. Once, this had been his favorite city in all of Europe, filled with the most wonderful and extraordinary memories. After all, he had been made im-mortal in this city. In a dungeon deep below the Bastille, the prison fortress, the Crow Goddess had taken him to the Elder who had granted him eternal life in return for unquestioning loyalty.

Dr. John Dee had worked for the Elders, spied for them,

undertaken many dangerous missions through countless Shadowrealms. He had fought armies of the dead and undead, pursued monsters across bitter wastelands, stolen some of the most precious and magical objects sacred to a dozen civilizations. In time he had become the champion of the Dark Elders; nothing was beyond him, no mission was too difficult . . . except when it came to the Flamels. The English Magician had failed, over and over, to capture Nicholas and Perenelle Flamel, several times in this very city.

It remained one of the greatest mysteries of his long existence: how had the Flamels evaded him? He commanded an army of human, inhuman and abhuman agents; he had access to the birds of the air; he could command rats, cats and dogs. He had at his disposal creatures from the darkest edges of mythology. But for more than four hundred years, the Flamels had escaped capture, first here in Paris, then across Europe and into America, always staying one step ahead of him, often leaving town only hours before he arrived. It was almost as if they were being warned. But that, of course, was impossible. The Magician shared his plans with no one.

A door opened and closed in the room behind him. Dee's nostrils flared, smelling a hint of musty serpent. "Good evening, Niccolò," Dee said, without turning around.

"Welcome to Paris." Niccolò Machiavelli spoke Latin with an Italian accent. "I trust you had a good flight and that the room is to your satisfaction?" Machiavelli had arranged for Dee to be met at the airport and given a police escort to his grand town house off the Place du Canada.

"Where are they?" Dee asked rudely, ignoring his host's questions, asserting his authority. He might have been a few years younger than the Italian, but he was in charge.

Machiavelli stepped out of the room and stood beside Dee on the balcony. Unwilling to wrinkle his suit against the metal railing, he stood with his hands clasped behind his back. The tall, elegant, clean-shaven Italian with close-cropped white hair was in great contrast with the small sharp-featured man with his pointed beard and his gray hair pulled back in a tight ponytail. "They are still in Saint-Germain's house. And Flamel has recently joined them."

Dr. Dee glanced sidelong at Machiavelli. "I'm surprised you were not tempted to try and capture them yourself," he said slyly.

Machiavelli looked over the city he controlled. "Oh, I thought I would leave their final capture to you," he said mildly.

"You mean you were instructed to leave them to me," Dee snapped.

Machiavelli said nothing.

"Saint-Germain's house is completely surrounded?"

"Completely."

"And there are only five people in the house? No servants, no guards?"

"The Alchemyst and Saint-Germain, the twins and the Shadow."

"Scathach is the problem," Dee muttered.

"I may have a solution," Machiavelli suggested softly. He waited until the Magician turned to look at him, his stone gray eyes blinking orange in the reflected streetlights. "I sent for the Disir, Scathach's fiercest foes. Three of them have just arrived."

A rare smile curled Dee's thin lips. Then he moved back from Machiavelli and bowed slightly. "The Valkyries—a truly excellent choice."

"We are on the same side," Machiavelli bowed in return. "We serve the same masters."

The Magician was about to step back into the room when he stopped and turned to look at Machiavelli. For a moment, the faintest rotten-egg hint of sulfur hung in the air. "You have no idea whom I serve," he said.

Dagon threw open the tall double doors and stepped back. Niccolò Machiavelli and Dr. John Dee strode into the ornate book-filled library to greet their visitors.

There were three young women in the room.

At first glance they were so alike that they could have been triplets. Tall and thin, with shoulder-length blond hair, they were dressed alike in black tanks under soft leather jackets and blue jeans tucked into knee-high boots. Their faces were all angles: sharp cheekbones, deeply sunken eyes, pointed chins. Only their eyes helped distinguish them. They were different shades of blue, from the palest sapphire to deep, almost purple indigo. All three looked as if they might have been sixteen or seventeen, but in actuality, they were older than most civilizations.

They were the Disir.

Machiavelli stepped into the center of the room and

turned to look at each of the girls in turn, trying to tell them apart. One was sitting at the grand piano, another was lounging on the sofa, while a third leaned against a window, staring out into the night, an unopened leather-bound book in her hands. As he got closer to them, their heads pivoted, and he noticed that their eye colors matched their nail polish. "Thank you for coming," he said, speaking Latin, which, along with Greek, was the one language most of the Elders were familiar with.

The girls looked at him blankly.

Machiavelli glanced at Dagon, who had stepped into the room and closed the door behind him. He pulled off his glasses, revealing his bulbous eyes, and spoke quickly in a language no human throat or tongue could shape.

The women ignored him.

Dr. John Dee sighed dramatically. He dropped into a high-backed leather armchair and clapped his small hands together with a sharp crack. "Enough of this nonsense," he said in English. "You're here for Scathach. Now, do you want her or not?"

The girl sitting at the piano stared at the Magician. If he noticed that her head was now twisted at an impossible angle, he didn't react. "Where is she?" Her English was perfect.

"Close by," Machiavelli said, moving slowly around the room.

The three girls directed their attention to him, heads turning to track him, like owls following a mouse.

"What is she doing?"

"She is protecting the Alchemyst Flamel, Saint-Germain

and two humani," Machiavelli said. "We only want the humani and Flamel. Scathach is yours." He paused and then added, "You can have Saint-Germain, too, if you want him. He's no use to us."

"The Shadow. We just want the Shadow," the woman sitting at the piano said. Her indigo-tipped fingers moved across the keys, the sound delicate and beautiful.

Machiavelli crossed to a side table and poured coffee from a tall silver pot. He looked at Dee and raised his eyebrows and the pot at the same time. The Magician shook his head. "You should know that Scathach is still powerful," Machiavelli continued, speaking now to the woman seated at the piano. The pupils of her indigo eyes were narrow and horizontal. "She knocked out a unit of highly trained police officers yesterday morning."

"Humani," the Disir almost spat. "No humani can stand against the Shadow."

"But we are not humani," the woman standing at the window said.

"We are the Disir," finished the woman sitting across from Dee. "We are the Shieldmaidens, the Choosers of the Dead, the Warriors of—"

"Yes, yes, yes," Dee said impatiently. "We know who you are: Valkyries. Probably the greatest warriors the world has ever seen—according to yourselves, anyway. We want to know if you can defeat the Shadow."

The Disir with indigo eyes swiveled her body away from the piano and flowed smoothly to her feet. She stalked across the carpet to stand before Dee. Her two sisters were suddenly by her side, and the temperature in the room abruptly plummeted.

"It would be a mistake to mock us, Dr. Dee," one said.

Dee sighed. "Can you defeat the Shadow?" he asked again. "Because if you cannot, then I'm sure that there are others who would be only too delighted to try." He held up his cell phone. "I can call upon Amazons, Samurai and Bogatyrs."

The temperature in the room continued to fall as Dee spoke, and his breath plumed white in the air, ice crystals forming on his eyebrows and beard.

"Enough of this trickery!" Dee snapped his fingers and his aura flashed briefly yellow. The room grew warm, then hot, heavy with the stink of rotten eggs.

"There is no need for these lesser warriors. The Disir will slay the Shadow," the girl standing to Dee's right said.

"How?" Dee snapped.

"We have what those other warriors have not."

"You're talking in riddles," Dee said impatiently.

"Tell him," Machiavelli said.

The Disir with the palest eyes turned her head in his direction and then looked back at Dee. Long fingers flickered toward his face. "You destroyed the Yggdrasill and released our pet creature, which had been long trapped in the roots of the World Tree."

Something flickered behind Dee's eyes and a muscle twitched at the corner of his mouth. "Nidhogg?" He looked at Machiavelli. "You knew about this?"

Machiavelli nodded. "Of course."

The Disir with indigo eyes stepped up to Dee and looked down into his face. "Yes, you freed Nidhogg, the Devourer of Corpses." Still leaning toward Dee, she swiveled her head to look at Machiavelli. Her sisters also turned in his direction. "Take us to where the Shadow and the others are hiding, then leave us. Once we have loosed Nidhogg, Scathach is doomed."

"Can you control the creature?" Machiavelli asked curiously.

"Once it feeds off the Shadow, consumes first her memories and then her flesh and bones, it will need to sleep. After a feast like Scathach, it will probably sleep for a couple of centuries. We will recapture it then."

Niccolò Machiavelli nodded. "We didn't discuss your fee."

The three Disir smiled, and even Machiavelli, who had seen horrors, recoiled from the expressions on their faces. "There is no fee," the Disir with indigo eyes said. "This we will do to restore the honor of our clan and avenge our fallen family. Scathach the Shadow destroyed many of our sisters."

Machiavelli nodded. "I understand. When will you attack?"

"At dawn."

"Why not now?" Dee demanded.

"We are creatures of the twilight. In that no-time between night and day, we are at our strongest," one said.

"That is when we are invincible," her sister added.

CHAPTER TWENTY-FIVE

"*I* guess I must still be on American time," Josh said.

"Why?" Scathach asked. They were standing in the fully equipped gym in the basement of Saint-Germain's house. One wall was mirrored, and it reflected the young man and the vampire, surrounded by the latest exercise equipment.

Josh glanced up at the clock on the wall. "It's three a.m. . . . I should be exhausted, but I'm still totally awake. It could be because it's only six at night back home."

Scathach nodded. "That's one of the reasons. Another is because you are around people like Nicholas and Saint-Germain, and especially your sister and Joan. Although your powers have not been Awakened, you are in the company of some of the most powerful auras on the planet. Your own aura is picking up a little of their power, and it is energizing you. But just because you don't feel tired, that doesn't mean you should not rest," she added. "Drink plenty of water too.

Your aura is burning through a lot of liquids. You need to keep hydrated."

A door opened and Joan stepped into the gym. While Scathach was dressed in black, Joan was wearing a long-sleeved white T-shirt over loose white trousers and white sneakers. Like Scathach, however, she was carrying a sword. "I wondered if you needed an assistant," she said, almost shyly.

"I thought you'd gone to bed," Scathach said.

"I don't sleep much these days. And when I do, my dreams are troubled. I dream of fire." She smiled sadly. "Isn't it a wonderful irony: I'm married to a Master of Fire, yet I'm terrified by dreams of fire."

"Where is Francis?"

"In his office, working. He'll be there for hours. I'm not sure if he ever sleeps anymore. Now," she said, looking at Josh and changing the subject, "how are you getting on?"

"I'm still learning how to hold the sword," Josh muttered, sounding vaguely embarrassed. He'd seen movies; he'd thought he knew how people fought with swords. He'd never imagined, though, that just holding one would be so difficult. Scathach had spent the past thirty minutes attempting to teach him how to hold and move Clarent without dropping it. She hadn't had much success; every time he spun the weapon, the weight dragged it from his grip. The highly polished wooden floor was scratched and gouged where the stone blade had struck it. "It's harder than I thought," he finally admitted. "I'm not sure I'll ever learn."

"Scathach can teach you how to fight with a sword," Joan said confidently. "She taught me. She took a simple farm girl

229

and turned her into a warrior." She twisted her wrist, and her sword, which was almost as tall as she was, moved and curled in the air with an almost human-sounding moan. Josh attempted to copy the action and Clarent went spinning from his hand. It buried itself point first in the floor, cracking the wood and swaying to and fro.

"Sorry," Josh muttered.

"Forget everything you think you know about swordplay," Scathach said. She glanced at Joan. "He's watched too much TV. He thinks he can just twirl a sword around like a cheerleader's baton."

Joan grinned. She deftly flipped her longsword and presented it to Josh, hilt first. "Take it."

Josh reached for the sword with his right hand.

"You might think about using both hands," the small Frenchwoman suggested.

Josh ignored her. Wrapping his fingers around the hilt of Joan's sword, he attempted to lift it from her grasp. And failed. It was incredibly heavy.

"You can see why we're still on the basics," Scatty said. She plucked the sword from Josh's grip and tossed it to Joan, who caught it easily.

"Let's start with how to hold a sword." Joan took up a position on Josh's right, while Scathach stood to his left. "Look straight ahead."

Josh looked into the mirror. While he and Scathach were clearly visible in the glass, the faintest silver haze surrounded Joan of Arc. He blinked, squeezing his eyes shut, but when he opened them again, the haze was still there.

"It's my aura," Joan explained, anticipating the question he was just about to ask. "It's usually invisible to the human eyes, but it'll sometimes turn up on photos and in mirrors."

"And your aura is like Sophie's," Josh said.

Joan of Arc shook her head. "Oh no, not like your sister's," she said, surprising him. "Hers is much stronger."

Joan raised the longsword, spinning it around so that the point of the blade was positioned between her feet and both hands rested on the pommel of the hilt. "Now, just do as we do . . . and do it slowly." She stretched out her right arm, holding the long blade steady. On Josh's left, the Shadow extended both arms, holding her two short swords straight out in front of her.

Josh wrapped his fingers around the hilt of the stone sword and raised his right arm. Even before he had it fully extended, it had begun to tremble with the weight of the blade. Gritting his teeth, he attempted to keep his arm steady. "It's too heavy," he gasped as he lowered his arm and rotated his shoulder; his muscles were burning. It felt a bit like the first day of football practice after summer vacation.

"Try it like this. Watch me." Joan showed him how to grip the handle with both hands.

Using both hands, he found that it was easier to hold the sword straight out. He tried it again, this time holding the sword with one hand. For about thirty seconds the weapon remained still; then the tip began to tremble. With a sigh, Josh lowered his arms. "Can't do it with one hand," he muttered.

"In time you will," Scathach snapped, losing patience.

"But in the meantime, I'll teach you how to wield it using both hands, Eastern fashion."

Josh nodded. "That might be easier." He'd spent years studying tae kwon do, and had always wanted to study kendo, Japanese fencing, but his parents had refused, saying it was too dangerous.

"All he needs is practice," Joan said seriously, looking at Scathach's reflection in the mirror, her gray eyes bright and twinkling.

"How much practice?" Josh asked.

"At least three years."

"Three years?" Taking a deep breath, he wiped first one palm and then the other on his pants and gripped the hilt again. Then he looked at himself in the mirror and stretched out both arms. "I hope Sophie is doing better than I am," he muttered.

The Comte de Saint-Germain had brought Sophie up to the house's tiny roof garden. The view of Paris was spectacular, and she leaned on the balustrade to look down onto the Champs-Elysées. Traffic had finally faded to little more than a sparse trickle, and the city was still and silent. She breathed deeply; the air was cool and damp, the slightly sour smell of the river masked by the herbal scents coming from the dozens of overflowing pots and fancy containers scattered across the roof. Sophie wrapped her arms around her body, vigorously rubbed her forearms and shivered.

"Cold?" Saint-Germain asked.

"A little," she said, though she wasn't sure if she was cold or nervous. She knew Saint-Germain had brought her up here to teach her Fire magic.

"After tonight, you will never feel the chill again," Saint-Germain promised. "You could walk across Antarctica wearing shorts and a T-shirt and feel nothing." Brushing his long hair off his forehead, he plucked a leaf from a pot and curled it between the palms of his hands, then rubbed them together. The crisp odor of spearmint filled the air. "Joan loves to cook. She grows all her herbs up here," he explained, breathing deeply. "There are a dozen different types of mint, oregano, thyme, sage and basil. And of course lavender. She loves lavender; it reminds her of her youth."

"Where did you meet Joan? Here, in France?"

"I finally got together with her here, but believe it or not, I first met her in California. It was 1849; I was making a little gold and Joan was working as a missionary, running a soup kitchen and hospital for those who'd gone west in search of gold."

Sophie frowned. "You were making gold during the Gold Rush? Why?"

Saint-Germain shrugged and looked vaguely embarrassed. "Like just about everyone else in America in '48 and '49, I went west in search of gold."

"I thought you could make gold. Nicholas said he can."

"Making gold is a long, laborious process. I thought it would be far easier to dig it up out of the ground. And once an alchemist has a little gold, he can use that to grow more. That's what I thought I'd do. But the land I bought turned out to be useless. So I started planting a few fragments of

gold on the land and then I'd sell the property to those people who had just arrived."

"But that's just wrong," Sophie said, shocked.

"I was young then," Saint-Germain said. "And hungry.
But that's no excuse," he added. "Anyway, Joan was working
in Sacramento, and she kept meeting people who had bought
useless land from me. She thought I was a charlatan—which
I was—and I took her for one of those dreadful do-gooders.
Neither of us knew the other was immortal, of course, and we
hated one another on sight. We kept bumping into one another over the years, and then, during the Second World War,
we met again, here in Paris. She was fighting with the Resistance and I was spying for the Americans. That's when we
realized that we were different. We survived the war, and
we've been inseparable ever since, though Joan keeps very
much to the background. None of my fan blogs or the gossip
magazines even know we're married. We could probably have
sold the wedding pictures for a fortune, but Joan prefers to
keep a very low profile."

"Why?" Sophie knew that celebrities valued their privacy,
but to remain completely invisible seemed just strange.

"Well . . . you have to remember that the last time she was
famous, people tried to burn her at the stake."

Sophie nodded. Suddenly, remaining invisible sounded
perfectly reasonable. "How long have you known Scathach?"
she asked.

"Centuries. When Joan and I got together, we discovered
that we knew a lot of people in common. All immortal, of
course. Joan's known her a lot longer than I have. Though

I'm not sure if anyone really knows the Shadow," he added with a wry smile. "She always seems so . . ." He paused, hunting for the right word.

"Lonely?" she suggested.

"Yes. Lonely." He gazed out across the city and then shook his head sadly and looked back over his shoulder at Sophie. "Do you know how often she has stood alone against the Dark Elders, how many times she has put herself in terrible danger to keep this world safe from them?"

Even as Sophie started to shake her head, a series of images flashed through her consciousness, fragments from the Witch's memories:

Scathach, wearing leather and chain mail, standing alone on a bridge, two blazing swords in her hands, waiting as enormous sluglike monsters gathered at one end.

Scathach in full armor, standing in the door of a great castle, arms folded across her chest, her swords stuck into the ground at her feet. Facing her was an army of huge lizardlike creatures.

Scathach, clad in sealskin and furs, balanced on a shifting ice floe as creatures that looked as if they had been carved out of the ice itself surrounded her.

Sophie licked her lips. "Why . . . why does she do it?"

"Because that is *who* she is. That is *what* she is." The count looked at the girl and smiled sadly. "And because it is all she knows. Now," he said briskly, rubbing his hands together again, sparks and cinders spiraling up into the night air. "Nicholas wants you to learn the Magic of Fire. Nervous?" he asked.

"A little. Have you ever taught anyone else?" Sophie asked hesitantly.

Saint-Germain grinned, showing his uneven teeth. "No one. You will be my first student . . . and probably my last."

She felt her stomach flip-flop, and suddenly this didn't seem like such a good idea anymore. "Why would you say that?"

"Well, the chances of coming across another person whose magical abilities have been Awakened are very slight, and those of finding someone with as pure an aura as yours, next to impossible. A silver aura is incredibly rare. Joan was the last humani to have one, and she was born in 1412. You are very special indeed, Sophie Newman."

Sophie swallowed hard; she wasn't feeling very special.

Saint-Germain sat down on a simple wooden bench set back against the chimney breast. "Sit here beside me, and I'll tell you what I know."

Sophie sat beside the Comte de Saint-Germain and looked across the roof, out over the city. Memories that were not hers flickered at the edge of her consciousness, hinting at a city with a different skyline, a city of low buildings clustered around a massive fortress, thousands of smoke trails rising into the night. She deliberately shied away from the thoughts, realizing she was seeing Paris as the Witch of Endor remembered it, sometime in the past.

Saint-Germain shifted to look at the girl. "Give me your hand," he said softly. Sophie put her right hand in his, and immediately a feeling of warmth coursed through her body, wiping out the chill. "Let me tell you what my own teacher taught me about fire." As he was speaking, the count moved his glowing index finger across the girl's palm, following the lines and ridges in the flesh, tracing a pattern on her skin. "My teacher said that there are those who will say that the Magic of Air or Water or even Earth is the most powerful magic of all. They are wrong. The Magic of Fire surpasses all others."

As he was speaking, the air directly in front of them began to glow, then shimmer. As if through a heat haze, Sophie watched the smoke twist and dance with the count's words, creating images, symbols, pictures. She wanted to reach out and touch them, but she remained still. Then the rooftop faded and Paris vanished; the only sound she could hear was Saint-Germain's softly insistent voice, and all she could see were the burning cinders. But as he spoke, images started to form in the fire.

"Fire consumes air. It can heat water to mist and can crack open the earth."

She watched as a volcano spewed molten rock high into the air. Red-black lava and white-hot cinders rained down on a town of mud and stone. . . .

"Fire destroys, but it also creates. A forest needs fire to thrive. Certain seeds depend on it to germinate."

Flames twisted like leaves and Sophie saw a forest blackened and battered, the trees scarred with the evidence of a terrible fire. But at the base of the trees, brilliant green shoots poked through the cinders. . . .

"In ages past, fire warmed the humani, allowed them to survive in harsh climates."

The fire revealed a desolate landscape, rocky and snow-covered, but she could see that the cave-dotted cliff face was lit up with warm yellow-red flames. . . .

There was a sudden crack and a pencil-thin finger of flame shot up into the night sky. She craned her neck, following it up, up, up, until it disappeared amongst the stars.

"This is the Magic of Fire."

Sophie nodded. Her skin tingled and she looked down to see tiny yellow-green flames curl off Saint-Germain's fingers. They flickered across her skin, coiling around her wrist, feather-soft and cool, leaving faint black traces on her flesh. "I know how important fire is. My mother is an archaeologist," she said dreamily. "She told me once that man didn't begin on the road to civilization until he started cooking his meat."

Saint-Germain flashed a smile. "You have Prometheus and the Witch to thank for that. They brought fire to the first primitive humani. Cooking made it easier for mankind to digest the meat they hunted, allowed them to absorb the nutrients more easily. It kept them warm and safe in their caves, and Prometheus showed them how to use the same fire to harden their tools and weapons." The count gripped Sophie's wrist with his hand, holding it as if he were taking her pulse. "Fire has driven every great civilization, from the ancient world right up to the present day. Without the heat of the sun, this planet would be nothing more than rock and ice."

As he was speaking, images crackled into existence before Sophie's face again, formed from smoke drifting off his hands. They hung undulating in the still air.

. . . A gray-brown planet turning in space, a single moon

spinning around it. There were no white clouds, no blue water, no green continents or golden deserts. Only gray. And the faintest outlines of land masses cut into the solid rock. Sophie abruptly realized that she was looking at the earth, perhaps far, far in the future. She gasped in shock and her breath blew the smoke away, taking the image with it.

"The Magic of Fire is strongest in sunlight." Saint-Germain moved his right hand and traced a symbol with his index finger. It hung glowing in the air, a circle with spikes radiating from it like a sunburst. The count blew on it and it dissolved into sparkles. "Without fire, we are nothing."

Saint-Germain's left hand was now completely wrapped in flame, but he still clutched Sophie's wrist. Red-white ribbons of fire curled around the girl's fingers and puddled in the palm of her hand. Each finger burned like a miniature candle—red, yellow, green, blue and white—yet she felt no pain and no fear.

"Fire can heal; it can seal a wound, can cut out disease," Saint-Germain continued earnestly. Golden cinders of fire burned in his pale blue eyes. "It is unlike any other magic, because it is the only one directly linked to the purity and strength of your aura. Almost anyone can learn the basics of Earth, Air or Water magic. Spells and incantations can be memorized and written down in books, but the power to ignite fire comes from within. The purer the aura, the stronger the fire, and that means, Sophie, that you must be very careful, because your aura is so pure. When you unleash the Magic of Fire, it will be incredibly potent. Has Flamel warned you not to overuse your powers, lest you burst into flame?"

"Scatty told me what might happen," Sophie said.

Saint-Germain nodded. "Never create fire when you are tired or weakened. If you lose control of this element, it will snap back on you and burn you to a crisp in a heartbeat."

A solid ball of flame now burned steadily in Sophie's right hand. She became aware that her left hand was tingling and quickly lifted it off the bench. It left the smoking, blackened impression of a hand burned into the wood. With a dull pop, a puddle of blue flame appeared in her left hand and each finger sparked alight.

"Why can't I feel it?" Sophie wondered aloud.

"You are protected by your aura," Saint-Germain explained. "You can shape the fire, in the same way that Joan showed you how to shape your aura into silver objects. You can create globes and spears of fire." He snapped his fingers and a scattering of thick round sparks bounced across the roof. He then pointed his index finger and a little jagged spearlike flame darted toward the nearest spark, striking it with deadly accuracy. "When you are in full control of your powers, you will be able to draw upon the Magic of Fire at will, but until then you will need a trigger."

"A trigger?"

"Normally it would take hours of meditation to focus your aura to the point at which you could bring it alight. But sometime in the very distant past, someone discovered how to create a trigger. A shortcut. You've seen my butterflies?"

Sophie nodded, remembering the dozens of tiny tattooed

butterflies that wrapped around the count's wrists and coiled up his arm.

"They are my trigger." Saint-Germain lifted the girl's hands. "And now you have yours."

Sophie looked down at her hands. The fire had gone out, leaving black sooty streaks on her flesh and around her wrists. She brushed her hands together, but succeeded only in smearing the dust.

"Allow me." Saint-Germain lifted a watering can and shook it. Liquid sloshed inside. "Hold out your hands." He poured water over her palms—it sizzled as it touched her flesh—washing away the black streaks. The count pulled a spotless white handkerchief from his back pocket, dipped it into the watering can and carefully wiped off the remainder of the soot. But around her right wrist, where Saint-Germain had held it, the soot refused to wash away. A thick black band encircled her wrist like a bracelet.

Saint-Germain snapped his fingers and his index and little finger lit up. He brought the light close to Sophie's hand.

She looked down to discover that a tattoo was burned into her skin.

Silently lifting her arm, she twisted her wrist to examine the ornate band twisted around it. Two strands, gold and silver, entwined and curled around one another to form an intricate, almost Celtic-looking pattern. On the underside of her wrist, where Saint-Germain had pressed his thumb, was a perfect gold circle with a red dot in the center.

"When you wish to trigger the Magic of Fire, press your

241

thumb against the circle and focus your aura," Saint-Germain explained. "That will bring the fire alive instantly."

"And that's it?" Sophie asked, sounding surprised. "That's all?"

Saint-Germain nodded. "That's it. Why, what were you expecting?"

Sophie shook her head. "I don't know, but when the Witch of Endor taught me Air magic, she wrapped me in bandages like a mummy."

Saint-Germain smiled shyly. "Well, I'm not the Witch of Endor, of course. Joan tells me the Witch imbued you with all of her memories and knowledge. I've no idea why she did that; it certainly wasn't necessary. But no doubt she had her reasons. Besides, I don't know how to do that—and I'm not sure I'd want you knowing all my thoughts and memories," he added with a grin. "Some of them are not very nice."

Sophie smiled. "I'm relieved—another batch of memories wouldn't be that great to deal with." Holding up her hand, she pressed the circle on her wrist and her little finger smoked; then the nail glowed dull orange for a moment before it popped alight with a slender, wavering flame. "How did you know what to do?"

"Well, I was first and foremost an alchemist. I suppose you'd call me a scientist today. When Nicholas asked me to train you in the Magic of Fire, I'd no idea how to do it, so I just approached this like any other experiment."

"An experiment?" Sophie blinked. "Could it have gone wrong?"

"The real danger was that it simply would not have worked."

"Thank you," she said finally, and then she grinned. "I was expecting the process to be a lot more dramatic. I'm really glad it was so"—she paused, looking for the right word—"ordinary."

"Well, maybe not that ordinary. It's not every day you learn how to master fire. How about extraordinary?" Saint-Germain suggested.

"Well, that too."

"That's all. Oh, there are tricks I can—and will—teach you. Tomorrow, I'll show you how to create globes, donuts and rings of fire. But once you have the trigger, you can call upon fire at any time."

"But do I need to say anything?" Sophie asked. "Do I need to learn any words?"

"Like what?"

"Well, when you lit up the Eiffel Tower, you said something that sounded like *eggness*."

"*Ignis,*" the count said. "Latin for *fire*. No, you don't need to say anything."

"Why did you do it, then?"

Saint-Germain grinned. "I just thought it sounded cool."

CHAPTER TWENTY-SIX

$\mathcal{P}$erenelle Flamel was puzzled.

Creeping along the dimly lit corridors, she'd discovered that all the lower cells of the island prison were filled with creatures from the darker edges of myth. The Sorceress had encountered a dozen different vampire breeds and various werebeasts, as well as boggarts, trolls and cluricauns. One cell held nothing but a sleeping child minotaur, while in the cell opposite, two cannibal Windigo lay unconscious alongside a trio of oni. An entire corridor of cells was given over to dragon-kin, wyverns and firedrakes.

Perenelle didn't think they were prisoners—none of the cells were locked—yet they were all asleep, and they were secured behind the shining silver spider's web. Still, she wasn't sure whether that was to keep the creatures prisoners or keep them apart. None of the creatures she'd discovered were allies. She passed one cell where the web hung in ragged tatters. The cell was empty, but the web and floor were clogged with bones, none of them even vaguely human.

These were creatures from a dozen lands and as many mythologies. Some—like the Windigo—she had only heard of, but at least they were native to the American continent. Others, as far as she knew, had never traveled to the New World and had remained safe and secure in their homelands or in Shadowrealms that bordered those lands. Japanese oni should not coexist alongside Celtic peists.

There was something terribly wrong here.

Perenelle rounded a corner and felt a breeze ruffle her hair. She turned her face to it, nostrils flaring, smelling salt and seaweed. With a quick glance over her shoulder, she hurried down the corridor.

Dee had to be collecting these creatures, had to be gathering them together, but why? And more importantly, how? Capturing a single vetala was unheard of, but a dozen? And how had they managed to get a baby minotaur away from its mother? Even Scathach, as fearless and deadly as she was, would never face down one of the bull-headed race if she could help it.

Perenelle came to a flight of steps. The smell of salt air was stronger now, the breeze cooler, but she hesitated before putting her foot down and bent to check the stair for silver strands. There were none. She still hadn't spotted whatever had spun the webs that festooned the lower cells, and it was making her incredibly nervous. It suggested that the web creators were probably sleeping . . . which meant that they would wake up sooner or later. When they did, the entire prison would be swarming with spiders—or maybe worse—and she didn't want to be out in the open when that happened.

A little of her power had returned—certainly enough to defend herself, though the moment she used her magic, it would draw the sphinx to her and simultaneously weaken and age her. Perenelle knew she would only get one chance to face down the creature, and she wanted—*needed*—to be as powerful as possible for that encounter. Darting up the creaking metal stairs, she stopped at the rust-eaten door. Pushing back her hair, she placed her ear against the corroded metal. All she could hear was the dull pounding of the sea as it continued to eat away at the island. Gripping the handle in both hands, she gently bore down on it and pushed the door open, gritting her teeth as old hinges squeaked and squalled, the sound echoing through the corridors.

Perenelle stepped out into a broad courtyard surrounded by ruined and tumbled buildings. To the right the sun was sinking in the west, and it painted the stones in a warm orange light. With a sigh of relief, she spread her arms wide, turned her face to the sun, threw her head back and closed her eyes. Static crackled and ran along the length of her black hair, lifting it off her shoulders as her aura immediately began to recharge. The wind whipping in off the bay was cool, and she breathed deeply, ridding her lungs of the stench of rot, mildew and the monsters below.

And then she suddenly realized what all the creatures in the cells had in common: they *were* monsters.

Where were the gentler spirits, the sprites and fey, the huldra and the rusalka, the elves and the inari? Dee had only gathered the hunters, the predators: the Magician was assembling an army of monsters.

A savage howling shriek ripped through the island, vibrating the very stones beneath her feet. *"Sorceress!"*

The sphinx had discovered Perenelle was missing.

"Where are you, Sorceress?" The fresh sea air was suddenly tainted with the stink of the sphinx.

Perenelle was turning back to close the door when she spotted movement in the shadows below. She'd looked into the sun too long, and the golden ball had left burning after-images on her retina. She squeezed her eyes shut for a moment; then she opened them again to peer into the gloom.

The shadows were moving, flowing down the walls, gathering at the bottom of the steps.

Perenelle shook her head. These were no shadows. This was a mass of creatures, thousands, tens of thousands of them. They flowed up the stairs, slowing only as they approached the light.

Perenelle knew what they were then—spiders, deadly and poisonous—and knew why the webs were so different. She glimpsed a seething mass of wolf spiders and tarantulas, black widows and brown recluses, garden spiders and funnel webs. She knew they should not exist together . . . which probably meant that whatever had called them, and now controlled them, probably lurked below.

The Sorceress slammed the metal door shut and wedged a lump of masonry against the base. Then she turned and ran. But she had only taken a dozen steps before the door was ripped off its hinges by the weight of the massed spiders.

CHAPTER TWENTY-SEVEN

*J*osh wearily pushed open the door to the kitchen and stepped into the long low room. Sophie turned away from the sink and watched her brother slump into a chair, drop the stone sword onto the floor, lay his arms on the table and rest his head on them.

"How was it?" Sophie asked.

"I can barely move," he mumbled. "My shoulders ache, my back aches, my arms ache, my head aches, I have blisters on my hands and I can barely close my fingers." He showed her his raw palms. "I never realized just holding a sword would be so hard."

"But did you learn anything?"

"I learned how to hold it."

Sophie slid a plateful of toast across the table and Josh immediately straightened up, grabbed a piece and shoved it in his mouth. "At least you can still eat," she said. Catching hold of his right hand, she turned it over to look at his palm. "Ouch!" she said in sympathy. The skin at the base of his thumb was red, bubbling up in a painful-looking water blister.

"Told you," he said through a mouthful of toast. "I need a Band-Aid."

"Let me try something." Sophie quickly rubbed her hands together, then pressed the thumb of her left hand against her right wrist. Closing her eyes, she concentrated . . . and her little finger popped alight, burning with a cool blue flame.

Josh stopped chewing and stared.

Before he could object, Sophie ran her finger over his blistered flesh. He attempted to pull away, but she held his wrist with surprising strength. When she finally let it go, he jerked his hand back.

"What do you think you're . . . ," he began, looking at his hand. Then he discovered that the blister had vanished, leaving only the faint hint of a circle on his skin.

"Francis told me that fire can heal." Sophie held up her right hand. Wisps of gray smoke curled off her fingers; then they snapped alight. When she closed her hand into a fist, the fire extinguished.

"I thought"—Josh swallowed hard and tried again—"I didn't know you'd even started to learn about fire."

"Started and finished."

"Finished?"

"All done." She brushed her hands together; sparks flew.

Chewing his toast, Josh looked at his sister critically. When she'd first been Awakened and when she'd learned the

Magic of Air, he'd seen the differences in her immediately, especially around her face and eyes. He'd even noted the new subtle shading of her eye color. He couldn't see any changes this time. She looked the same as before . . . but she wasn't. And the Fire magic distanced her even further from him. "You don't seem any different," he said.

"I don't feel any different either. Except warmer," she added. "I don't feel cold."

So this was his sister now, Josh thought. She looked just like any other teenager he knew. And yet . . . she was unlike anyone else on the planet: she could control two of the elemental magics.

Maybe that was the scariest part of all this: the immortal humans—people like Flamel and Perenelle, Joan, flamboyant Saint-Germain and even Dee: they all looked so *ordinary*. They were the type of people you would pass in the street and not give a second glance to. Scathach, with her red hair and grass green eyes, was always going to attract attention. But she wasn't human.

"Did it . . . did it hurt?" he asked, curious.

"Not at all." She smiled. "It was almost disappointing. Francis sort of washed my hands with fire . . . oh, and I got this," she said, holding up her right arm and allowing her sleeve to fall back to reveal the design burned into her flesh.

Josh leaned forward to look closely at Sophie's arm. "It's a tattoo," he said, envy clearly audible in his voice. The twins had always talked about getting tattoos together. "Mom is going to freak when she sees that." Then he added, "Where did you get it? And why?"

"It's not ink, it was burned on with fire," Sophie explained, twisting her wrist to show off the design.

Josh suddenly caught her hand and pointed at the red dot surrounded by the gold circle on the underside of her wrist. "I've seen something like that before," he said slowly, and frowned, trying to remember.

His twin nodded. "It took me a while, but then I remembered that Nicholas has something like it on his wrist," Sophie said. "A circle with a cross through it."

"That's right." Josh closed his eyes. He'd first noted the small tattoo on Flamel's wrist when he'd started working for him in the bookshop, and though he'd wondered why it was in such an unusual place, he'd never asked about it. He opened his eyes again and looked at the tattoo, and he suddenly realized that Sophie was branded by magic, marked as someone who could control the elements. And he didn't like it. "What do you need it for?"

"When I want to use fire, I press on the center of the circle and focus my aura. Saint-Germain called it a shortcut, a trigger for my power."

"I wonder what Flamel needs a trigger for," Josh wondered aloud.

The kettle pinged and Sophie turned back to the sink. She had asked herself the same question. "Maybe we can ask him when he wakes up."

"Any more toast?" Josh asked. "I'm starving."

"You're always starving."

"Yeah, well, the sword training made me hungry."

Sophie stuck a fork through a slice of bread and held it

251

out in front of her. "Watch this," she said. She pressed on the underside of her wrist and her index finger burst into flame. Frowning hard, concentrating, she focused the wavering flame into a thin blue fire and then ran it over the bread, gently toasting it. "Do you want this done on both sides?"

Josh watched with a mixture of fascination and horror. He knew from science class that bread toasted around 310 degrees Fahrenheit.

CHAPTER TWENTY-EIGHT

*M*achiavelli was sitting in the back of his car alongside Dr. John Dee. Facing them were the three Disir. Dagon sat in the driver's seat, eyes invisible behind his wraparound glasses. The car smelled faintly of his sour fishy odor.

A cell phone buzzed, breaking the uncomfortable silence. Machiavelli flipped it open without looking at the screen. He closed it again almost immediately. "All clear. My men have pulled back and there is a security cordon in place around all the connecting streets. No one will accidentally wander into the area."

"Whatever happens, do not enter the house," the Disir with violet eyes said. "Once we free Nidhogg, we shall have very little control until it feeds."

John Dee leaned forward, and for a moment, it looked as if he was about to tap the young woman on the knee. The look on her face prevented him. "Flamel and the children must not be allowed to escape."

"That sounds like a threat, Doctor," the warrior sitting on the left said. "Or an order."

"And we do not like threats," her sister sitting to the right added. "And we don't take orders."

Dee blinked slowly. "It is neither a threat nor an order. Simply a . . . request," he said eventually.

"We are here only for Scathach," the warrior with violet eyes said. "The rest of them are not our concern."

Dagon climbed out of the car and opened the door. Without a backward glance, the Valkyries stepped out into the first glimmers of predawn light, spread out and moved slowly down the back street. They looked like three young women coming home from an all-night party.

Dee shifted position, taking the seat facing Machiavelli. "If they succeed, I will ensure that our masters know that the Disir were your idea," he said pleasantly.

"I'm sure you will." Machiavelli didn't look at the English Magician and continued to follow the progress of the three girls as they walked down the street. "And if they fail, you can tell our masters that the Disir were my idea, and you can absolve yourself of any blame," he added. "Shifting the blame: I believe I originally came up with *that* concept about twenty years before you were born."

"I thought you said they were bringing Nidhogg?" Dee asked, ignoring him.

Niccolò Machiavelli tapped the window with his manicured fingernails. "They did."

As the Disir moved down the narrow, cobbled, high-walled alley, they *changed*.

The transformation occurred as they passed through a patch of shadow. They entered as young women, dressed in soft leather jackets, jeans and boots . . . and a moment later they were Valkyries: warrior maidens. Long coats of ice white chain mail fell to their knees, knee-high metal boots with spiked toes covered their feet, and they wore heavy leather-and-metal gauntlets on their hands. Rounded helmets protected their heads and masked their eyes and noses but left their mouths free. White leather belts around their waists held their sword and knife sheaths. The Valkyries each carried a wide-bladed sword in one hand, but each also had a second weapon strapped to her back: a spear, a double-headed axe and a war hammer.

They stopped before a rotting green gate set into the wall. One of the Valkyries turned to look back at the car and pointed a gloved hand at the gate.

Machiavelli hit a button and the window rolled down. He raised his thumb and nodded. Despite its decrepit appearance, it *was* the back gate to Saint-Germain's house.

Each of the Disir reached into a leather pouch that hung from her belt. Taking out a handful of flat stonelike objects, they tossed them at the base of the door.

"They're Casting the Runes," Machiavelli explained. "They're calling Nidhogg . . . the creature you released, a creature the Elders themselves locked away."

"I didn't know it was trapped by the World Tree," Dee muttered.

"I'm surprised. I thought you knew everything." Machiavelli shifted in the seat to look at Dee. In the gloomy half-light, he could see that the Magician was looking pale and there was the faintest sheen of sweat on his forehead. Centuries of controlling his emotions ensured that Machiavelli didn't smile. "Why did you destroy the Yggdrasill?" he asked.

"It was the source of Hekate's power," Dee said quietly, eyes fixed on the Valkyries, watching them intently. They had stepped back from the stones they'd dropped on the ground and were talking quietly amongst themselves, pointing out individual tiles.

"It was as old as this planet. And yet you destroyed it without a second thought. Why did you do that?" Machiavelli wondered aloud.

"I did what was necessary." Dee's words were ice. "I will always do whatever is necessary to bring the Elders back to this world."

"But you didn't consider the consequences," Niccolò Machiavelli said softly. "Every action has a consequence. The Yggdrasill you destroyed in Hekate's kingdom stretched into several other Shadowrealms. The topmost branches reached the Shadowrealm of Asgard, and the roots stretched deep into Niflheim, the World of Darkness." He saw Dee stiffen. "Not only did you release Nidhogg, but you also destroyed at least three Shadowrealms—maybe more—when you destroyed the World Tree."

"I didn't know. . . ."

"You made a lot of enemies," Machiavelli continued smoothly, ignoring him, "dangerous enemies. I have heard that the Elder Hel escaped the destruction of her kingdom. I understand she is hunting you."

"She does not frighten me," Dee snapped, but there was a quaver in his voice.

"Oh, she should," Machiavelli murmured. "She terrifies me."

"My master will protect me," Dee said confidently.

"He must be a powerful Elder indeed to protect you from Hel; no one has stood against her and survived."

"My master is all-powerful," Dee snapped.

"I look forward to learning the identity of this mysterious Elder."

"When all this is over, maybe I'll introduce you," Dee said. He nodded down the alleyway. "And that could be very soon."

The runestones hissed and sizzled on the ground.

They were irregular pieces of flat black stone, each etched with a series of angular lines, squares and slashes. Now the lines were glowing red, crimson smoke coiling into the still predawn air.

One of the Disir used the tip of her sword to move three of the runestones together. A second nudged a stone out of the way with the steel toe of her boot and then dragged another into place. The third found a single runestone at the edge of the pile and eased it into position at the end of the string of letters with her sword.

"Nidhogg," the Disir whispered, calling the nightmare whose name they had spelled out in the ancient stones.

257

"Nidhogg," Machiavelli said very quietly. He looked over Dee's shoulder to where Dagon sat staring straight ahead, apparently disinterested in what was happening to his left. "I know what the legends say about it, but Dagon, what exactly is it?"

"My people called it the Devourer of Corpses," the driver said, voice sticky and bubbling. "It was already here before my race claimed the seas, and we were amongst the first to arrive on this planet."

Dee quickly swiveled in the seat to look at the driver. "What are you?"

Dagon ignored the question. "Nidhogg was so dangerous that a council of the Elder Race created a terrible Shadowrealm, Niflheim, the World of Darkness, to contain it, and then they used the unbreakable roots of the Yggdrasill to wrap around the creature, chaining it for eternity."

Machiavelli kept his eyes fixed on the red-black smoke coiling from the runestones. He thought he saw the outline of a shape beginning to form. "Why didn't the Elders kill it?"

"Nidhogg was a weapon," Dagon said.

"What did the Elders need a weapon for?" Machiavelli wondered aloud. "Their powers were almost limitless. They had no enemies."

Although he sat with his hands resting lightly on the steering wheel, Dagon's shoulders shifted and his head turned almost completely around so that he was facing Dee and Machiavelli. "The Elders were not the first upon this earth," he said simply. "There were . . . *others*." He pronounced the word slowly and carefully. "The Elders used Nidhogg and some of the other primordial creatures as weapons in the Great War to completely destroy them."

A stunned Machiavelli looked at Dee, who looked equally shocked by the revelation.

Dagon's mouth opened in what might have been a smile, revealing his tooth-filled maw. "You should probably know that the last time a group of Disir used Nidhogg, they lost control of the creature. It ate all of them. In the three days it took to recapture it and chain it in Yggdrasill's roots, it completely destroyed the Anasazi people in what is now New Mexico. It is said that Nidhogg feasted off ten thousand humani and still hungered for more."

"Can these Disir control it?" Dee demanded.

Dagon shrugged. "Thirteen of the finest Disir warriors couldn't control it in New Mexico. . . ."

"Maybe we should—" Dee began.

Machiavelli suddenly stiffened. "Too late," he whispered. "It's here."

CHAPTER TWENTY-NINE

"*I*'m going to bed." Sophie Newman paused by the kitchen door, a glass of water in her hand, and looked back to where Josh was still sitting at the table. "Francis is going to teach me some specific fire spells in the morning. He promised to show me the fireworks trick."

"Great, we'll never have to buy fireworks again for the Fourth of July."

Sophie smiled tiredly. "Don't stay up too long, it's nearly dawn."

Josh shoved another piece of toast into his mouth. "I'm still on Pacific time," he said, his voice muffled. "But I'll be up in a few minutes. Scatty wants to continue my sword training tomorrow. I'm really looking forward to it."

"Liar, liar."

He grunted. "Well, you've got your magic to protect you . . . all I have is a stone sword."

The bitterness was clearly audible in his voice, and Sophie forced herself not to comment. She was getting tired of her brother's constant whining. She had never asked to be Awakened; she hadn't wanted to know the Witch's magic or Saint-Germain's, either. But it had happened and she was dealing with it, and Josh would just have to get over it. "Good night," she said. She closed the door behind her, leaving Josh alone in the kitchen.

When he finished the last of the toast, he gathered up his plate and glass and carried them both to the sink. He ran hot water over the plate, then set it to drip dry in the wire dish rack beside the deep ceramic sink. Refilling his glass from the jug of filtered water, he crossed to the kitchen door, pulled it open and stepped out into the tiny garden. Although it was almost dawn, he didn't feel the least bit tired, but then again, he reminded himself, he had slept for most of the day. Over the high wall, he couldn't see much of the Parisian skyline except for the warm orange glow from the streetlights. He looked up, but there were no stars visible in the heavens. Sitting on the step, he breathed deeply. The air was cool and damp, just like San Francisco's, though it lacked the familiar salt tang that he loved; it was tainted instead with unfamiliar smells, few of which were pleasant. He felt a sneeze gathering at the back of his nose and sniffed hard, eyes watering. There was the stench of overflowing trash cans and rotting fruit, and he detected a nastier, fouler stink that was vaguely familiar. Closing his mouth, he breathed deeply through his nose, trying to identify it: what *was* it? It was something he'd smelled very recently. . . .

Snake.

Josh leapt to his feet. There weren't snakes in Paris, were there? Deep in his chest, Josh felt his heart begin to beat faster. He was terrified of snakes, a bone-chilling fear that he could trace back to when he'd been about ten. He'd been camping with his father in Wupatki National Monument in Arizona when he'd slipped off a trail and slid down an incline, straight into a rattlesnake nest. When the dust had cleared, he'd realized he was lying next to a six-foot-long snake. The creature had raised its wedge-shaped head and stared at him with coal black eyes for what was probably no more than a second—though it felt like a lifetime—before Josh had managed to scramble out, too terrified and breathless even to scream. He'd never been able to work out why the snake hadn't attacked him, though his father told him that rattlesnakes were actually shy and that it had probably just eaten. He'd had nightmares about the incident for weeks afterward, and after every one he would wake up with that smell of serpent musk in his nostrils.

He was smelling it now.

And it was getting stronger.

Josh started backing up the steps. There was a sudden scrabbling sound, like a squirrel running up the side of a tree. Then, directly in front of him, on the other side of the small courtyard, claws, each one the length of his hand, appeared over the top of the nine-foot-high wall. They moved around slowly, almost delicately, questing for a hold, and then abruptly gripped hard enough for the talons to bite deep into the old bricks. Josh froze, all the breath leaving his body in one shocked exhalation.

The arms that followed were covered in thick knobbled hide . . . and then the head of a monster appeared over the wall. It was long and slablike, with two rounded nostrils on the end of a blunt snout directly over its mouth and solid black eyes sunk deep behind circular depressions on either side of its skull. Unable to move, unable to breathe, his heart hammering so hard it was physically shaking his body, Josh watched the huge head swivel lazily from side to side, an immensely long, ghastly white forked tongue flickering in the air. It froze, then slowly, very slowly, shifted its head and looked down at Josh. The merest tip of its tongue tasted the air and then it opened its mouth wide—impossibly wide, enough to swallow him whole—and the boy saw a mouthful of teeth: sharp, ragged curved daggers.

Josh wanted to turn and run screaming, but he couldn't. There was something mesmerizing about the appalling creature clambering over the wall. All his life he'd been fascinated by dinosaurs: he'd collected fossils, eggs, bones and teeth—even dinosaur coprolites. And now he was looking at a living dinosaur. There was even a part of his brain that identified the creature—or at least, what it resembled. It was a Komodo dragon. They didn't grow much longer than ten feet in the wild, but he could already see that this creature was at least three times that.

Stone cracked. An old brick exploded into dust, and then a second, a third.

Then there was a crunching, snapping, ripping sound, and—almost in slow motion—Josh watched as the wall, with the creature draped over the top, swayed, then crashed to the ground. The metal door buckled in two, popped off its hinges and shattered against the water fountain, tearing a huge chunk out of the basin. The monster smashed to the ground, unaffected by the stones raining down around it. The noise jolted Josh free and he staggered back up the steps just as the monster lumbered to its feet and shuffled forward, heading straight for the house. The boy slammed the door closed and rammed home the bolts. He was turning away when through the kitchen window he spotted the figure in white, clutching what looked like a sword, step through the gaping hole that had been the wall.

Josh grabbed the stone sword off the floor and dashed into the hall. "Wake up!" he shouted, his voice so filled with terror even he didn't recognize it. "Sophie! Flamel! Anyone!"

The door behind him shook in its frame. He snapped a quick glance over his shoulder in time to see the monster's white tongue peel off the wood and glass.

"Help!"

Glass shattered and the tongue shot into the kitchen, sweeping plates to the floor, scattering pots and pans, knocking over a chair. Metal hissed where the tongue brushed against it; wood turned black and burned; plastic melted. A drop of the corrosive saliva dripped to the floor and bubbled on the tiles, eating into the stone.

Instinctively, Josh lashed out at the tongue with Clarent. The sword barely touched it, but it suddenly disappeared, darting back into the creature's mouth. There was a single still moment, and then the monster rammed its entire head at the door.

The door crumpled to matchwood; the supporting walls on either side cracked as stones were knocked out. The creature drew its head back and slammed it into the opening again, punching a large hole into the kitchen. The entire house creaked ominously.

A hand fell on Josh's shoulder, almost stopping his heart. "Now look what you've done: you've just gone and made it mad."

Scathach strode into the wrecked kitchen and stood in the gaping hole created by the creature's blows. "Nidhogg," she said, and Josh was unsure whether she was talking to him, "which means the Disir are not far behind." She sounded almost pleased with the news.

Scathach danced backward as Nidhogg's head slammed into the opening again. Its huge nostrils opened wide and its white tongue slapped against the spot where, an instant before, the Shadow had been standing. A glob of spittle burned on the tile, turning it to a liquid sludge. Scathach's twin swords darted out, flickering gray and silver, and two long cuts appeared on the white flesh of the creature's forked tongue.

Without taking her eyes off the creature, Scathach said to Josh, almost calmly, "Get the others out of the house, I'll take care of this. . . ."

And then an enormous claw-tipped arm smashed through the window, wrapped around the Warrior's body in a viselike

265

grip and slammed her back against the wall with enough force to crack the plaster. The Warrior's arms were trapped against her body, her swords useless. Nighogg's huge head appeared in the ruined side of the house, and then its mouth opened wide and its tongue darted out toward Scathach. Once its sticky acid-coated tongue wrapped around the defenseless Warrior, it would drag her into its cavernous maw.

CHAPTER THIRTY

Sophie flew down the stairs, sparks and streamers of blue fire trailing from her outstretched fingers.

She'd been standing in the bathroom brushing her teeth when the entire house had shaken. She'd heard the rumbling crash of bricks, which had been followed a heartbeat later by her brother's scream. It had ripped through the silent house and was the most terrifying sound she had ever heard.

She was running down the corridor past Flamel's room when the door opened. For a single instant she almost didn't recognize the confused-looking old man standing in the doorway. The rings under his eyes were so dark they looked like bruises, and his skin was an unhealthy yellowish hue. "What's happening?" he mumbled, but Sophie hurried past: she had no answers for him. All she knew was that her brother was downstairs.

And then the entire house shook again.

She felt the vibration through the floors and walls. All the pictures on the wall to her left shifted and tilted off center.

Terrified, Sophie raced down the stairs to the first floor just as a bedroom door opened and Joan appeared. One moment the small woman was wearing shiny blue-green satin pajamas—and the next she was clad in full metal armor, a long broad-bladed sword in her gloved hands. "Get back," Joan snapped, her French accent pronounced.

"No," Sophie shouted. "It's Josh—he's in trouble!"

Joan fell into step beside her, armor clinking and rasping. "OK then, but stay behind me and to my right, so I always know where you are," Joan commanded. "Did you see Nicholas?"

"He's awake. But he looked sick."

"Exhaustion. He daren't try any more magic in his condition. It could kill him."

"Where's Francis?"

"Probably in the attic. But the room is soundproofed and he'll have his headphones on and the bass pumped up; I doubt he's heard anything."

"I'm sure he felt the house shake."

"Probably thought it was a good bass line."

"I don't know where Scatty is," Sophie said. She was fighting hard to keep the bubbling panic inside from overwhelming her.

"With any luck, she's downstairs in the kitchen with Josh. If she is, then he's OK," Joan added. "Now follow me." Holding the sword upright in both hands, the woman moved cautiously down the last flight of stairs and stepped into the broad marbled hallway at the front of the house. She stopped so suddenly that Sophie almost walked into her. Joan pointed toward the front door. Sophie spotted the ghostly white shape behind the stained-glass panels, and then there was a crunching snap . . . and the head of an axe appeared through the door. Then, with a crack, the front door was smashed open in a shower of wood and glass fragments.

Two figures stepped into the hallway.

In the light of the ornate crystal chandelier, Sophie saw that they were young women in white chain-mail armor, their faces hidden behind helmets, one wielding a sword and an axe, the other carrying a sword and a spear. She reacted instinctively. Gripping her right wrist with her left hand, she splayed open her fingers, palm outward. Crackling blue-green flames splashed across the floor directly in front of the two girls, shooting upward in a solid sheet of wavering emerald fire.

The women stepped through the flames without even pausing but stopped when they spotted Joan in her armor. They looked at one another, obviously confused. "You're not the silver humani. Who are you?" one demanded.

"This is my house, and I think that's my question," Joan said grimly. She turned sideways, left shoulder toward the women, holding her sword in both hands, the point moving in a slow figure eight between the warriors.

"Stand aside. We have no argument with you," one said.

Joan lifted the sword, bringing the hilt close to her face,

the tip of the longsword pointing straight up. "You come into *my* home and tell me to stand aside," she said incredulously. "Who are you . . . *what* are you?" she demanded.

"We are the Disir," the woman with the sword and spear said softly. "We are here for Scathach. Our argument is only with her. But do not stand in our way or it will become your argument."

"The Shadow is my friend," Joan said.

"Then that makes you our enemy."

Without warning, the Valkyries attacked together, one lunging with sword and spear, the other with sword and axe. Joan's heavy blade shifted, metal clanging, the movement almost too fast to see as she blocked sword thrusts, turned aside the axe and batted down the spear.

The Disir backed away and spread out until they were standing on either side of Joan. She had to keep turning her head to be able to watch them both.

"You fight well."

Joan's lips pulled away from her teeth in a savage smile. "I was taught by the best. Scathach herself trained me."

"I thought I recognized the style," the second Disir said.

Only Joan's gray eyes moved as she tracked the two warriors. "I didn't think I had a style."

"Neither has Scathach."

"Who are you?" the Disir on the right asked. "In my lifetime I've known only a handful who could stand against us. And none of them were humani."

"I am Joan of Arc," she replied simply.

"Never heard of you," the Disir said, and while she was

speaking, her sister, standing to Joan's left, drew back her arm, poised to throw the spear . . .

The weapon burst into white-hot flames.

With a savage howl, the Disir flung the spear to one side; by the time it hit the ground, the wooden shaft was little more than ash and the wickedly pointed metal head was melting into a bubbling puddle.

Standing on the bottom step, Sophie blinked in surprise. She hadn't known she could do that.

The Disir to Joan's right darted forward, sword and axe weaving a deadly humming pattern in the air before her, battering at Joan's sword, driving her back under the vicious onslaught.

The second Disir rounded on Sophie.

Setting the spear shaft alight and melting the head had exhausted her, and she slumped against the banister. But she needed to help Joan; she needed to get to Josh. Pressing hard on the underside of her wrist, Sophie attempted to call upon her Fire magic. Smoke curled from her hand, but there was no fire.

The Disir strode forward until she was standing directly in front of the girl. Sophie was standing on a step, and the girls' faces were almost level. "So, you are the silver humani the English Magician wants so desperately." Behind her metal mask, the Valkyrie's violet eyes were contemptuous.

Drawing in a deep shuddering breath, Sophie straightened. She stretched out both arms, fingers closed into tight fists. Closing her eyes, breathing deeply, trying to calm her thundering heart, she visualized gloves of flame; she saw herself bringing her hands together, shaping a ball of fire in her fists like dough and then flinging it at the figure standing before her. But when she opened her eyes, only the merest hints of gossamer blue flames danced over her flesh. She clapped her hands together and sparks danced harmlessly across the warrior's chain mail.

The Disir tapped her sword against her gloved hand. "Your petty fire tricks do not impress me."

A tremendous crash from the kitchen shook the house again. The ornate chandelier over the center of the hallway started to sway to and fro, tinkling musically as the shadows danced.

"Josh," Sophie whispered. Her fear turned to anger: this creature was preventing her from getting to her brother. And the anger gave her strength. Remembering what Saint-Germain had done on the roof, the girl pointed her index finger at the warrior and unleashed her rage in a single focused beam.

A dirty yellow-black spear of solid fire leapt from Sophie's finger and exploded against the Disir's chain mail. Fire splashed all over the warrior, and the force of the blow drove her to her knees. She shouted an incomprehensible word that sounded like a wolf's howl.

Across the hall, Joan took advantage of the distraction and pressed her attacker hard, pushing her back toward the gaping ruin of a door. The two women were evenly matched, and while Joan's sword was longer and heavier than her opponent's, the Disir had the advantage of wielding two weapons. In addition, it had been a long time since Joan had worn armor and fought with a sword. She could feel the burn in the muscles of her shoulders, and her hips and knees were aching from the weight of the metal she was carrying. She had to finish this.

The fallen Valkyrie climbed to her feet in front of Sophie. The front of her chain mail had taken the full force of the fire bolt, and the links had melted and run like softened wax. The warrior grabbed a handful of the mail and ripped it away from her body, flinging it aside. The plain white robe underneath was scorched and blackened, with sparkling chunks of metal melted into the cloth. "Little girl," the Disir whispered, "I am going to teach you never to play with fire."

CHAPTER THIRTY-ONE

*N*idhogg's sticky tongue unfurled through the air toward Scathach, who was still pinned against the kitchen wall, wrapped tightly in the creature's claws. The Warrior fought in complete silence, struggling in the monster's grip, wrenching herself from side to side, boot heels scrambling for purchase on the slippery tiled floor. With her arms pinned to her sides, she was unable to use her short swords.

Josh knew that if he even paused for thought, he was not going to be able to go through with what he meant to do. The smell of the creature was making him sick to his stomach, and his heart was thumping so hard he could barely catch his breath.

The forked tongue brushed across the table, leaving a deep burn mark on the wood. It punched right through a wooden chair as it headed straight for the Warrior's head.

All he had to do, Josh kept reminding himself, was to

think of his sword as a football. Holding Clarent high above his head in the two-handed grip Joan had shown him earlier, he launched himself forward in a move that the coach at his last school had spent an entire season trying—and failing—to teach him.

But even as he was jumping, he knew he'd miscalculated. The tongue was moving too fast, and he was too far away. With a last desperate effort, he flung the sword from his hand.

The flat of the blade struck the side of Nidhogg's meaty tongue. And stuck fast.

Years of tae kwon do training took over as Josh crashed onto the tiled floor. He hit it hard but still managed to slap it with the palm of his hand, sending his body forward into a neat roll that brought him back to his feet . . . within inches of the meaty acid-dripping tongue. And the sword.

Catching hold of the hilt, he used all his strength to pull it away from the tongue—it came free with a sticky Velcro sound, and the tongue sizzled and hissed as it snapped back into the monster's mouth. Josh knew that if he stopped, both he and Scatty were dead. He plunged Clarent point first into the serpent's arm just above the wrist joint. As the blade sank smoothly into the alligator-like hide, it began to vibrate, a high-pitched keening sound that set Josh's teeth on edge. He felt a rush of warmth flowing up his arm and into his chest. A heartbeat later, a surge of strength and energy wiped away his aches and pains. His aura blossomed bright blinding gold, and there was a tracery of light curling around the gray stone blade when he wrenched it out of the creature.

"The claws, Josh. Cut off a claw," Scathach grunted as Nidhogg shook her hard. The two swords fell from her hands and clattered to the floor.

Josh lashed out at the monster, trying to cut off a claw, but the heavy stone blade turned at the last moment and bounced harmlessly off its foot. He tried again, and this time the sword struck sparks off the creature's armored hide.

"Hey! Be careful," Scathach yelped as the swinging blade came dangerously close to her head. "That's one of the few weapons that really can kill me."

"Sorry," Josh muttered through clenched teeth. "I've never done anything like this before." He slashed out at the claw again. Sparks flew into the Warrior's face. "Why do we want a claw?" he grunted, hacking at the iron-hard skin.

"It can only be killed with one of its own claws," Scathach said, her voice surprisingly calm. "Look out! Get back!"

Josh turned just as the thing's huge head lunged forward, pushing into the side of the ruined house, its white tongue darting forward again. It was coming for him. It was moving too fast; there was nowhere to go—and if he did move, it would just hit Scatty. Planting his feet firmly, both hands wrapped tightly around Clarent's hilt, he held the sword before his face. He closed his eyes at the approaching horror—and immediately opened them again. If he was going to die, he'd do it with his eyes open.

It was like playing a video game, he thought—except that this game was deadly. Almost in slow motion, he saw the two ends of the forked tongue wrap around the blade—as if it was going to wrench it from Josh's hand. He tightened his grip, determined not to let the sword go.

When the flesh of the creature's tongue touched the stone blade, the effect was immediate.

The creature froze, then convulsed and hissed, the sound like escaping steam. The acid from its tongue bubbled on the blade as the sword trembled in Josh's hand, vibrating like a tuning fork, growing warm, then hot, and started to glow with a stark white light. He squeezed his eyes shut . . .

. . . and behind his closed eyes, Josh glimpsed a series of flickering images: a blasted and ruined landscape of black rock, pockmarked with pools of bubbling red lava, while overhead, the sky boiled with filthy clouds that rained ash and cinders. Spread across the sky, dangling from the clouds, were what looked like the roots of a huge tree. The roots were the source of the bitter white ash: they were dissolving, withering, dying. . . .

Nidhogg jerked its blackened tongue free.

Josh gasped and opened his eyes just as his aura flared again, stronger—brighter—this time, blinding him. Panicked, waving the sword before him, he backed up until he felt the kitchen wall against his shoulder blades. He kept blinking furiously, wanting to rub his eyes, but he didn't dare loosen his grip on the sword. All around him, he heard stones fall, plaster split, wood creak and snap, and he hunched his shoulders, expecting something to come crashing down on his head. "Scatty?" he called.

But there was no reply.

His voice rose. "Scatty!"

Squinting hard, blinking away the spots dancing before his eyes, he saw the monster dragging Scathach out of the house. Its tongue, now black and brown, was hanging loosely out of the side of its mouth. Holding the Warrior in a crushing grip, it turned on its own length and pushed through the devastated garden, its long tail slicing chunks out of the side of the house, smashing through the only unbroken window. Then the creature rose up on its two hind legs, like a collared lizard, and clattered down the alleyway, almost trampling underfoot the figure in white chain-mail armor standing guard. Without hesitation the figure disappeared after the creature.

Josh stumbled through the gaping hole in the side of the house and stopped. He glanced over his shoulder. The once-neat kitchen was a shredded ruin. Then he looked at the sword in his hand and smiled. He'd stopped the monster. His smile widened to a broad grin. He'd fought it off and saved his sister and everyone else in the house . . . except Scatty.

Taking a deep breath, Josh jumped down the steps and raced across the garden and out into the alley, following the monster. "I can't believe I'm doing this," he muttered. "I don't even like Scatty. Well . . . not that much," he amended.

CHAPTER THIRTY-TWO

*N*iccolò Machiavelli had always been a careful man.

He had survived and even thrived in the dangerous and deadly Medici court in Florence in the fifteenth century, a time when intrigue was a way of life and violent death and assassination was commonplace. His most famous book, *The Prince*, was one of the first to suggest that the use of subterfuge, lies and deceit was perfectly acceptable for a ruler.

Machiavelli was a survivor because he was subtle, cautious, clever and, above all else: cunning.

So what had possessed him to call upon the Disir? The Valkyries had no word for *subtle* in their language and didn't know the meaning of the word *caution*. Their idea of clever and cunning was to bring Nidhogg—an uncontrollable primeval monster—into the heart of a modern city.

And he had allowed them.

Now the street echoed with the sounds of breaking glass,

snapping wood and tumbling stone. Every car and house alarm in the district was blaring, and there were lights on in all the other houses lining the alleyway, though no one had ventured out yet.

"What is going on in there?" Machiavelli wondered aloud.

"Nidhogg is feasting off Scathach?" Dee suggested absently. His cell had started to buzz, distracting him.

"No, it's not!" Machiavelli suddenly shouted. He pushed open the car door, leapt out, grabbed Dee by the collar and dragged him out into the night. "Dagon! Out!"

Dee attempted to find his feet, but Machiavelli continued to drag him backward, away from the car. "Are you out of your mind?" the doctor shrieked.

There was a sudden explosion of glass as Dagon threw himself through the windshield. He slithered off the hood and landed alongside Machiavelli and Dee, but the Magician didn't even glance in his direction. He saw what had startled the Italian.

Nidhogg raced down the narrow alley toward them, standing tall on two powerful hind legs. A limp red-haired figure hung from its front claws.

"Back!" Machiavelli shouted, flinging himself to the ground, dragging Dee with him.

Nidhogg trampled over the long black German car. One hind paw landed directly in the center of the roof, crushing it to the pavement. Windows popped, spraying glass like shrapnel as the car buckled in the middle, the front and rear wheels lifting off the ground.

The creature disappeared into the night.

A heartbeat later, a white-clad Disir practically flew over the remains of the car, clearing it in a single leap, following the creature.

"Dagon?" Machiavelli whispered, rolling over. "Dagon, where are you?"

"I'm here." The driver came smoothly to his feet, brushing shards of sparkling glass from his black suit. He pulled off his cracked sunglasses and dropped them on the ground. Rainbow colors ran across round unblinking eyes. "It was holding Scathach," he said, loosening his black tie and popping open the top button of his white shirt.

"Is she dead?" Machiavelli asked.

"I'll not believe Scathach is dead until I see it for myself."

"Agreed. Over the years there have been too many reports of her death. And then she turns up! We need a body."

Dee climbed out of a mud-filled puddle; he suspected Machiavelli might have deliberately pushed him into it. He shook water from his shoe. "If Nidhogg has her, then the Shadow is dead. We've succeeded."

Dagon's fish eye swiveled down to look into the Magician's face. "You blinkered, arrogant fool! Something in the house frightened away Nidhogg—that's why it's running, and it can't be the Shadow because it's got her. And remember, this is a creature beyond fear. Three Disir went into that building—and only one came out! Something terrible happened in there."

"Dagon is right: this is a disaster. We need to completely rethink our strategy." Machiavelli turned to his driver. "I promised you that if the Disir failed, then Scathach was yours."

Dagon nodded. "And you have always kept your word."

"You have been with me now for close to four hundred years. You have always been loyal, and I owe you both my life and liberty. I free you from my service," Machiavelli said formally. "Find the Shadow's body . . . and if she is still alive, then do whatever you must do. Go now—and be safe, old friend."

Dagon turned away. Then he stopped suddenly and looked back at Machiavelli. "What did you call me?"

Machiavelli smiled. "Old friend. Be careful," he said gently. "The Shadow is beyond dangerous, and she's killed too many of my friends."

Dagon nodded. He pulled off his shoes and socks to reveal three-toed webbed feet. "Nidhogg will head for the comfort of the river." Abruptly, Dagon's tooth-filled mouth opened in what might have been a smile. "And the water is my home." Then he ran into the night, bare feet slapping the sidewalk.

Machiavelli glanced back toward the house. Dagon was right; something had terrified Nidhogg. What had happened in there? And where were the other two Disir?

Footsteps clattered on pavement and suddenly Josh Newman raced out of the alleyway, the stone sword in his hand streaming wisps of gold fire. Glancing neither left nor right, he ran around the destroyed car and followed the telltale trail of car alarms set off by the monster's passing.

Machiavelli looked at Dee. "I take it that was the American boy?"

Dee nodded.

"Did you see what he was holding? It looked like a sword," he said slowly. "A stone sword? Surely not Excalibur?"

"Not Excalibur," Dee said shortly.

"It was definitely a gray stone blade."

"It wasn't Excalibur."

"How do you know?" Machiavelli demanded.

Dee reached under his coat and pulled out a short stone sword, a match of the weapon Josh was carrying. The blade was trembling, vibrating almost imperceptibly. "Because I have Excalibur," Dee said. "The boy was holding its twin, Clarent. We always suspected Flamel had it."

Machiavelli closed his eyes and raised his face to the sky. "Clarent. No wonder Nidhogg fled from the house." He shook his head. Could this night get any worse?

Dee's cell buzzed again and both men jumped. The Magician almost snapped the phone in two opening it. "What?" he snarled. He listened for a moment, then closed the phone very gently, and when he spoke again, his voice was barely above a whisper. "Perenelle has escaped. She's free on Alcatraz."

Shaking his head, Machiavelli turned and walked down the alleyway, heading back toward the Champs-Elysées. His question was answered. The night had just gotten worse—much worse. Nicholas Flamel frightened Machiavelli, but Perenelle terrified him.

CHAPTER THIRTY-THREE

"*I*'m no little girl!" Sophie Newman was furious. "And I know more than just Fire magic. Disir." The name popped into her head, and suddenly Sophie knew everything the Witch of Endor knew about the creatures. The Witch despised them. "I know who you are," she snapped, her eyes glowing an ugly silver. "Valkyries."

Even amongst the Elders, the Disir were different. They had never lived on Danu Talis but had kept to the frozen northlands at the top of the world, at home in the bitter winds and sleeting ice.

In the terrible centuries after the Fall of Danu Talis, the world had shifted on its axis and the Great Cold had gripped most of the earth. From the north and south ice sheets flowed across the landscape, pushing humani into the thin unfrozen green belt that existed around the equator. Entire civilizations vanished, devastated by changing weather patterns, disease

284

and famine. Sea levels rose, flooding the coastal cities, altering the landscape, while inland the encroaching ice wiped away all traces of towns and villages.

The Disir soon discovered that their skills at surviving in the bitter northern climate gave them a special advantage over races and civilizations who could not cope with the deadly, never-ending winter. Gangs of savage female warriors quickly claimed most of the north, enslaving the cities that had escaped the ice. They ruthlessly destroyed anyone who stood against them, and soon the Disir had a second name: Valkyries, the Choosers of the Dead.

Very quickly the Valkyries controlled a frozen empire that encompassed most of the Northern Hemisphere. They forced their humani slaves to worship them as gods and even demanded sacrifices. Uprisings were brutally suppressed. As the Ice Age gripped harder, the Disir began to look farther south, setting their sights on the struggling remnants of civilization.

Images tumbling and dancing in her head, Sophie watched as the reign of the Disir was ended in a single night. She knew what had happened millennia past.

The Witch of Endor had worked with the repulsive Elder, Chronos, who could move through time itself. It had been necessary to sacrifice her eyes in order to see the twisting strands of time, but it was a sacrifice she had never regretted. Scouring ten thousand years of time, she had chosen a single warrior from each millennium, and then Chronos had dipped into each era to pull the warriors back to the age of the Great Cold.

Sophie knew that the Witch had especially requested that

her own granddaughter, Scathach, be brought back to fight the Disir.

It was the Shadow who had led the attack on the Disir stronghold, a city of solid ice close to the top of the world. She had slain the Valkyrie queen, Brynhildr, casting her into the heart of a flaming volcano.

By the time the sun had risen low over the horizon, the power of the Valkyries had been broken forever, their frozen city had lain in melted ruins, and less than a handful had survived. They fled into a terrifying icy Shadowrealm that even Scathach would not venture into. The surviving Disir called that night Ragnarök, the Doom of the Gods, and swore eternal vengeance on the Shadow.

Sophie brought her hands together and a miniature whirlwind appeared in her palms. Fire and ice had destroyed the Disir in the past. What would happen if she used a little Fire magic to heat up the wind? Even as the thought crossed Sophie's mind, the Disir leapt forward, her sword raised high over her head in a two-handed grip. "Dee wants you alive, but he didn't say unharmed . . . ," she snarled.

Sophie brought her hands to her mouth, pressed the thumb of her left had against the trigger on her wrist and blew hard. The whirlwind spiraled onto the floor and grew. It bounced once, twice . . . then hit the Disir.

Sophie had superheated the air until it was hotter than a furnace. The blistering whirlwind grabbed the Valkyrie, spun her around, rolled her over and tossed her high into the air. She crashed into the crystal chandelier, smashing all the bulbs save one. In the sudden gloom, the whirlwind dancing across the floor glowed with shimmering orange heat. The Valkyrie crashed to the ground but was immediately on her feet, even as shards of crystal crashed about her like glass rain. Her pale skin was bright red and looked badly sunburned, her blond eyebrows completely singed off. Without a word, she slashed out with her sword, the heavy blade cutting right through the banister rail at Sophie's hand.

"Scatty!"

Sophie heard her brother's voice calling from the kitchen. He was in trouble!

"Scatty!" she heard him call again.

The Valkyrie surged forward. Another superheated whirlwind caught her, ripping the sword from her hand and spinning her away, sending her tumbling into her sister, who had trapped Joan in a corner and battered her to her knees with a ferocious onslaught. The two Disir crashed to the floor in a clatter of weapons and armor.

"Joan—get back!" Sophie shouted.

Fog flowed from the girl's fingers and curled across the floor; thick ribbons and ropes of smoky air wrapped around the women, swathing them in chains of scalding hot air. It took an enormous effort of will, but Sophie managed to thicken the fog, spinning it faster and faster around the struggling Disir until they were shrouded in a thick mummylike cocoon, similar to the one the Witch had enfolded her in.

Sophie could feel herself weakening, leaden exhaustion making her eyes gritty and her shoulders heavy. Drawing upon the remnants of her power, she clapped her hands and lowered the temperature of the air in the foggy cocoon so quickly that it flash-froze into a crackling lump of solid ice.

"There. You should feel right at home," Sophie whispered hoarsely. She slumped, then forced herself to her feet and was about to dart into the kitchen when Joan stretched out her arm, stopping her. "Oh no you don't. Me first." The woman took a step toward the kitchen door, then glanced over her shoulder to the block of ice, with the two Disir partially visible within. "You saved my life," she said softly.

"You would have beaten her," Sophie said confidently.

"Maybe," Joan conceded, "and maybe not. I'm not as young as I once was. But you still saved my life," she repeated, "and that's a debt I'll never forget." Stretching out her left hand, she placed it flat against the kitchen door and applied a gentle pressure. The door clicked open.

And then fell off its hinges.

CHAPTER THIRTY-FOUR

*T*he Comte de Saint-Germain strolled downstairs from his studio, tiny noise-canceling earphones pushed into his ears, eyes fixed on the screen of the MP3 player in his hands. He was trying to create a new playlist: his top ten favorite sound tracks. *Gladiator,* naturally . . . *The Rock* . . . *Star Wars,* the first one only . . . *El Cid,* of course . . . *The Crow,* maybe . . .

He stopped at the bottom step and automatically straightened a picture that was hanging crooked on the wall. He took another step and realized that a framed gold disc was also slightly askew. Looking down the corridor, he suddenly noticed that all the pictures were at odd angles. Frowning, he pulled out his earphones . . .

And heard Josh call Scatty's name . . .

And heard the clatter of metal . . .

And realized that the air stank of vanilla and lavender . . .

Saint-Germain raced down the stairs to the next floor. He

found the Alchemyst slumped, exhausted, in the door to his room, and slowed, but Nicholas waved him on. "Quickly," he whispered. Saint-Germain darted past him and continued down the corridor and on to the stairs. . . .

The hallway was in ruins.

The remnants of the hall door hung off its hinges. All that remained of the antique crystal chandelier was a single buzzing lightbulb. Wallpaper hung in huge curling strips, revealing the cracked plaster beneath. Banisters were chopped through, tiles scored and chipped.

And there was a solid lump of ice sitting squarely in the center of the hall. Saint-Germain approached it cautiously and ran his fingers down the smooth surface. It was so cold his flesh stuck to it. He could make out two white-clad figures entwined within the block, faces frozen in ugly snarls; their startling blue eyes followed him.

Wood snapped in the kitchen and he turned and darted toward it, gloves of solid blue-white flame growing on his hands.

And if Saint-Germain thought that the damage to the hallway was bad, nothing prepared him for the devastation in the kitchen.

The entire side of the house was missing.

Sophie and Joan stood in the midst of the ruin. His wife was holding the shaking girl tightly, supporting her. Joan was wearing shiny blue-green satin pajamas and was still holding her sword in a metal gauntlet. She turned to look over her shoulder as her husband stepped into the room. "You missed the fun," she said in French.

"I heard nothing," he apologized, in the same language. "Tell me."

"It was all over in minutes. Sophie and I heard a disturbance at the back of the house. We ran downstairs just as two women smashed their way in through the hall door. They were Disir, they said they had come for Scathach. One attacked me, the other turned her attention to Sophie." Even though she was speaking an obscure variant of the French language, she dropped her voice to a whisper. "Francis . . . this girl. She is extraordinary. She combined the magics: she used Fire and Air to defeat the Disir. Then she wrapped them in fog and froze it to a lump of ice."

Saint-Germain shook his head. "It is physically impossible to use more than one magic at a time . . . ," he said, but his voice trailed away to a whisper. The evidence of Sophie's powers sat in the center of the hallway. There was a legend that the most powerful Elders were able to use all the elemental magics simultaneously. According to the most ancient myths, this was the reason—one of the reasons—that Danu Talis sank.

"Josh is gone." Sophie suddenly shook herself free of Joan's grip and spun around to face the count. Then she looked over his shoulder to where an ashen-faced Flamel stood leaning in the doorway. "Something's taken Josh," she said, desperately frightened now. "And Scatty's gone after him."

The Alchemyst shuffled into the center of the room, wrapped his hands around his body as if he was freezing and looked around. Then he bent to scoop up the Shadow's matching short swords from where they lay amongst the

291

rubble. When he turned to look back at the others, they were all startled to see that his eyes were bright with tears. "I am sorry," he said, "so terribly, terribly sorry. I have brought this terror and destruction to your home. It is unforgivable."

"We can rebuild," Saint-Germain said airily. "This will give us the excuse we needed to remodel."

"Nicholas," Joan said very seriously, "what happened here?"

The Alchemyst dragged up the only unbroken chair in the room and slumped into it. He hunched forward, elbows on his knees, looking at the Shadow's gleaming swords, turning them over and over in his hands. "Those are Disir in the block of ice. Valkyries. Scathach's sworn enemies, though she's never told me why. I know they have pursued her down through the centuries and have always allied themselves with her enemies."

"They did this?" Saint-Germain looked around the ruined kitchen.

"No. But they obviously brought something with them that did."

"What's happened to Josh?" Sophie demanded. She shouldn't have left him alone in the kitchen, she should have waited with him. She would have defeated whatever had attacked the back of the house.

Nicholas held up Scathach's weapon. "I think you should be asking what's happened to the Warrior. In the centuries I've known her, she's never let her swords out of her grasp. I fear she's been taken. . . ."

"Swords . . . swords . . ." Sophie pulled away from Joan and began desperately searching through the rubble. "When I went to bed, Josh had just come back from sword practice with Scatty and Joan. He had the stone sword you gave him." She summoned a wind to raise a chunk of heavy masonry and toss it aside, revealing the floor beneath. Where was the sword? She felt a flicker of hope. If he'd been captured, then surely the sword would be on the floor? She straightened and looked around the room. "Clarent isn't here."

Saint-Germain walked to the hole where the back door had been. The garden was a ruin. A chunk of stone had been ripped out of the fountain and the bowl cracked in half. It took him a moment to recognize the U-shaped hunk of metal that had been his back gate. Only then did it sink in that the entire back wall was missing. The nine-foot-tall wall was now little more than a stump. There were powdered and crushed bricks scattered all across the garden, almost as if the wall had been pushed down from outside.

"Something big—very big—has been in the garden," he said to no one in particular.

Flamel looked up. "Can you smell anything?" he asked.

Saint-Germain breathed deeply. "Snake," he said firmly. "But that's not Machiavelli's odor." He stepped out into the garden and drew in a deep lungful of cool air. "It's stronger out here." Then he coughed. "This stench is fouler, much fouler . . . ," he called. "This is the stink of something very, very old. . . ."

Drawn by the wailing car alarms, Saint-Germain crossed

the garden, clambered over the broken wall and looked up and down the alley. House and car alarms were ringing, mainly to his left, and there were lights on in the houses at that end of the street. In the mouth of the narrow alleyway, he could see the crushed remains of a black car.

"Whatever it was attacked this house," he said, darting back into the kitchen. "There's a two-hundred-thousand-euro car at the end of the street that's only fit for the scrap yard."

"Nidhogg," Flamel whispered in horror. He nodded; it made sense now. "The Disir brought Nidhogg," he said. Then he frowned. "But even Machiavelli wouldn't bring something like that into a major city. He's too cautious."

"Nidhogg?" Joan and Sophie asked simultaneously, looking at one another.

"Think of it as a cross between a dinosaur and a snake," Flamel explained. "But probably older than this planet. I think it's got Scathach and Josh went after it."

Sophie shook her head firmly. "He wouldn't do that—he couldn't—he's terrified of snakes."

"Then where is he?" Flamel asked. "Where is Clarent? It's the only explanation: he's taken the sword and gone in search of the Shadow."

"But I heard him calling to her for help. . . ."

"You heard him call her name. He might have been calling out to her."

Saint-Germain nodded. "It makes sense. The Disir only wanted Scathach. Nidhogg grabbed her and ran. Josh must have followed."

294

"Maybe it grabbed him and she followed," Sophie suggested. "That's the sort of thing she'd do."

"It had no interest in Josh. It would have just eaten him. No, he went of his own accord."

"That shows great courage," Joan said.

"But Josh isn't brave . . . ," Sophie began. Yet even as she was saying it, she knew it wasn't entirely true. He'd always stood up for her in school and protected her. But why would he go after Scatty? She knew he didn't even like her.

"People change," Joan said. "No one stays the same."

The noise was louder now, a mingled cacophony of police, ambulance and fire sirens drawing closer. "Nicholas, Sophie, you've got to go," Saint-Germain said urgently. "I think we're about to have police, lots and lots of police with far too many questions. And we have no answers. If they find you here—without papers or passports—I'm afraid they'll hold you for questioning." He tugged out a leather wallet attached to his belt on a long chain. "Here's some cash."

"I cannot . . . ," the Alchemyst began.

"Take it," Saint-Germain insisted. "Don't use your credit cards; Machiavelli can track your movements," he continued. "I don't know how long the police will be here. If I'm free, I'll meet you tonight at six at the glass pyramid outside the Louvre. If I'm not there at six, I'll try and get there at midnight, or failing that, at six tomorrow morning."

"Thank you, old friend." Nicholas turned to Sophie. "Grab your clothes, and Josh's too, and whatever else you need; we'll not be coming back here."

"I'll help you," Joan said, hurrying out of the room with Sophie.

The Alchemyst and his former apprentice stood in the ruins of the kitchen, listening to the two women run upstairs.

"What are you going to do with the block of ice in the hall?" Nicholas asked.

"We've got a big chest freezer in the cellar. I'll shove it in there until the police leave. What about the Disir, are they dead, do you think?"

"The Disir are practically impossible to kill. Just make sure that ice doesn't melt anytime soon."

"I'll drive it to the Seine one evening and drop it in the river. With luck it won't thaw till Rouen."

"What are you going to tell the police"—Nicholas waved a hand at the devastation—"about all this?"

"Gas explosion?" Saint-Germain suggested.

"Lame," Flamel said with a smile, remembering what the twins had said when he'd made the same suggestion.

"Lame?"

"Very lame."

"Then I think I just came home and found it like this," he said, "and it's close enough to the truth. I've no idea how it happened." He suddenly grinned mischievously. "I could sell the story and pictures to one of the tabloids. *Mysterious Forces Destroy Rock Star's House*."

"Everyone would think it was a publicity stunt."

"Yes, they would, wouldn't they? And you know what: I just happen to have a new album out. It'll be great advertising."

The kitchen door opened and Sophie and Joan walked

into the room. They had both changed into jeans and sweat-shirts and were wearing matching backpacks.

"I'm going with them," Joan said before Saint-Germain could ask the question that had started to form on his lips. "They'll need a guide and a bodyguard."

"Would it be worth my while arguing with you?" the count asked.

"No."

"Didn't think so." He hugged his wife. "Please be careful, be very careful. If Machiavelli or Dee is prepared to bring the Disir and Nidhogg into the city, then they are desperate. And desperate men do stupid things."

"Yes," Flamel said simply. "Yes, they do. And stupid men make mistakes."

CHAPTER THIRTY-FIVE

*J*osh kept looking over his shoulder, trying to orient himself. He was moving farther and farther away from Saint-Germain's house and was worried that he was going to get lost. But he couldn't turn back now; he couldn't leave Scatty to the creature. And so long as he could find the Arc de Triomphe at the end of the Champs-Elysées, he figured he'd be able to get back to the house. Alternatively, all he had to do was to follow the steady stream of police cars, fire trucks and ambulances that were racing down the main street, heading in the direction he was running from.

He tried not to think too much about what he was doing because if he thought about it—he was chasing a dinosaur-like monster through Paris—then he'd stop, and Scatty would . . . well, he wasn't sure what would happen to Scatty. Whatever it was, it wouldn't be good.

Following Nidhogg was simplicity itself. The creature ran

in a straight line, crashing through the countless small streets and alleyways that ran parallel to the Champs-Elysées. It left a trail of devastation in its wake, trampling through a side street filled with parked cars, running right over the top of them, leaving them crumpled, flattened wrecks. As it darted down a narrow alleyway, its wavering tail punched through the steel shutters on the fronts of shops on either side of the street, shattering the glass they protected. Burglar and car alarms added to the mayhem.

Suddenly, a flash of white ahead of him caught his attention.

Josh had briefly glimpsed the figure in white standing outside Saint-Germain's house. He guessed it was one of the monster's keepers. And now it looked as if they were also chasing the creature . . . which meant they had lost control. He glanced up, trying to gauge the time. Directly ahead of him, the sky was already paling toward the dawn, which meant that he was running east. What was going to happen when the city woke up to find a prehistoric monster rampaging through the streets? There'd be panic; no doubt the police and army would be brought in. Josh had hacked at it with his sword and that had done nothing—he had a horrible feeling that bullets would probably be just as useless.

The streets narrowed to little more than alleyways, and the creature was forced to slow down as he crashed off the walls. Josh discovered that he was catching up with the figure in white. He thought it was a man, but it was hard to be sure.

He was running easily now, not even breathing hard; he

299

guessed all the weeks and months of football practice were paying off. His sneakers made no sound on the streets and he assumed that the figure in white didn't even suspect they were being followed. After all, who would be crazy enough to run after a monster with nothing but a sword for protection? However, as he got closer, he could see that the figure was also carrying a sword in one hand and what looked like an oversized hammer in the other. He recognized the weapon from World of Warcraft: it was a war hammer, a ferocious and deadly variant of the mace. Drawing nearer still, he discovered that the person was wearing white chain-mail armor, metal boots and a rounded helmet with a veil of chain mail covering the neck. Somehow he wasn't even surprised.

Then, abruptly, the figure changed.

Right before his eyes, the figure transformed from an armored warrior into a blond-haired young woman, not much older than himself, in a leather jacket, jeans and boots. Only the sword and war hammer in her hands marked her as extraordinary. She disappeared around a corner.

Josh slowed: he didn't want to run into the woman with the sword and hammer. And, thinking about it, he guessed she probably wasn't a young woman at all.

There was an explosion of brick and glass ahead of him and Josh picked up his pace and darted around the corner, then stopped. The creature was stuck in an alley. Josh moved forward cautiously; it looked as if the monster had run down what looked like another arrow-straight street. But this particular street curved at the end and then narrowed, the upper stories of the two houses on either side projecting out over the sidewalk below. The monster had slammed into the opening, tearing a chunk out of both buildings. Attempting to push ahead, it had suddenly found itself wedged in. It thrashed from side to side, brick and glass raining down into the street below. There was a flash of movement in a nearby window, and Josh caught a glimpse of a man peering from one of the windows, eyes and mouth round with horror, frozen in place by the monster directly outside his window. A slab of concrete the size of a sofa fell on the creature's head, but it didn't even seem to notice.

Josh had no idea what to do. He needed to get to Scatty, but that meant getting around the creature, and there was simply no room. He watched as the blond woman raced down the alley. Without hesitation she leapt onto the monster's back and climbed nimbly toward its head, arms stretched out on either side, weapons poised.

She was going to kill it, Josh decided, relief washing over him. Maybe then he could get in and grab Scatty.

Sitting astride the creature's broad neck, the woman reached down and lashed out at Scathach's limp and unmoving body.

Josh's cry of horror was lost in the wail of sirens.

"Sir, we have a report of an . . . incident." The ashen-faced police officer handed the phone to Niccolò Machiavelli. "The RAID officer asked to speak to you personally."

Dee caught the man by the arm and spun him around.

"What is it?" he demanded in perfect French as Machiavelli listened intently to the call, one finger in his ear, trying to drown out the noise.

"I'm not sure, sir. A mistake, certainly." The police officer attempted a shaky laugh. "A few streets down, people are reporting that there is . . . a *monster* stuck in a house. Impossible, I know . . ." His voice trailed off as he turned to look toward what had once been a substantial three-story house that now had a gaping hole plowed through the side.

Machiavelli tossed the phone back to the police officer. "Get me a car."

"A car?"

"A car and a map," he snapped.

"Yes, sir. You can take mine." The police officer had been one of the first on the scene following dozens of calls from alarmed citizens. He'd spotted Machiavelli and Dee hurrying from the alley close to the source of the noise and had stopped them, convinced that they had something to do with what was being reported as an explosion. His bluster had turned to dismay when he'd discovered that the mud-spattered older man with white hair in the torn suit was actually the head of the DGSE.

The officer handed over his car key and a battered and torn Michelin map of Paris's city center. "I'm afraid this is all I have."

Machiavelli snatched it from his hand. "You're dismissed." He gestured toward the street. "Go and direct traffic; let no press or public near the house. Is that clear?"

"Yes, sir." The police officer raced away, thankful that he still had his job; no one wanted to upset one of the most powerful men in France.

Machiavelli spread the map across the hood of the car. "We're here," he explained to Dee. "Nidhogg is heading directly east, but at some stage, it's got to cross the Champs-Elysées and make for the river. If it continues on its present course, I've a reasonably good idea it will come out"—his finger stabbed the map—"close to here."

The two men climbed into the small car and Machiavelli looked around for a moment, trying to make sense of the controls. He couldn't remember the last time he'd driven a car; Dagon had always looked after that. Finally, with a grinding crunch of gears, he got the car moving and made an illegal turn that sent them fishtailing across the road, then roared down the Champs-Elysées, leaving rubber in their wake.

Dee sat silently in the passenger seat, one hand wrapped around the seat belt, the other braced against the dashboard. "Who taught you to drive?" he asked shakily as they bounced off the curb.

"Karl Benz," Machiavelli snapped. "A long time ago," he added.

"And how many wheels did that car have?"

"Three."

Dee squeezed his eyes shut as they roared across an intersection, barely missing a lumbering road-sweeper truck. "So what do we do when we get to Nidhogg?" he asked, focusing on the problem, trying to keep his mind off Machiavelli's terrible driving.

"That's your problem," Machiavelli retorted. "After all, you're the one who freed it."

"But you invited the Disir here. So it's partially your fault."

Machiavelli hit the brakes hard, sending the car into a long screeching slide. The engine cut out and the car jerked to a halt.

"Why have we stopped?" Dee demanded.

Machiavelli pointed out the window. "Listen."

"I can't hear anything over the noise of the sirens."

"Listen," Machiavelli insisted. "Something's coming." He pointed to the left. "Over there."

Dee rolled down his window. Over the police, ambulance and fire sirens, they could hear stones grinding, bricks falling and the sharp snap-crackle of breaking glass. . . .

Josh watched, powerless, as the woman sitting atop the monster lashed at Scatty with her sword.

At that moment the monster shrugged, still trying to free itself from the building that encased it, and the blade missed, whistling dangerously close to the unconscious Warrior's head. Edging higher on the monster's broad neck, the woman gripped a clump of thick skin, leaned sideways across a huge unblinking eye and jabbed the point of her sword at Scatty. Again the creature moved and the sword bit into its arm, close to the claw wrapped around the Warrior. The monster didn't react, but Josh saw how close the blade had come to

Scatty. The woman leaned down again, and this time, Josh knew, she'd hit the Warrior.

He had to do something! He was Scatty's only hope. He couldn't just stand here and watch someone he knew get killed. He started running. Back at the house, when he'd slashed at the creature, nothing had happened, but when he'd plunged the sword point first into its thick hide . . .

Holding Clarent in the two-handed grip Joan had taught him, Josh put on a final burst of speed and raced up to the creature. He could feel the sword humming in his hands just before he stabbed it into the monster's tail.

Instantly, heat flowed up through his arms and blossomed in his chest. The air filled with the tart smell of oranges in the heartbeat before his aura flared briefly golden and then faded to the same reddish-orange glow that was streaming off the sword protruding from the creature's thick knobbled skin.

Josh twisted Clarent and pulled it free. In the grayish brown hide, the wound burned bright red and immediately started to hardened into a black crust. It took a moment for the sensation to travel through the creature's primitive nervous system. Then the monster abruptly reared up on its hind legs, hissing and squealing in agony. It wrenched itself free of the house, the sudden rain of bricks, roof tiles and wooden beams sending Josh scrambling back, out of harm's way. He hit the ground, covering his head as debris crashed about him. He thought it would be just his luck to be killed by a roof tile. The unexpected movement almost dislodged the woman on the monster's back. Swaying, she dropped the war hammer and desperately grabbed at the creature's back to prevent herself from being thrown down directly in front of it. Lying on the ground, bricks raining around him, Josh watched as the thick black crust began to spread out from the wound and creep up the monster's tail. It reared again and then plowed right through the corner of the house and out across the Champs-Elysées. Josh was relieved to see that Scatty's limp form was still gripped in his front claws.

Taking a deep breath, Josh scrambled to his feet and snatched up the sword. Instantly, he felt power buzz through his body, heightening every sense. He stood swaying as raw power energized him; then he turned and raced after the monster. He felt amazing. Even though it was still not quite dawn, he could see clearly, though the colors were slightly off. He could smell the myriad scents of the city through the rancid serpent-stink of the creature. His hearing was so acute he could differentiate the sirens of the many different emergency services; he could even distinguish individual cars. He could actually feel the irregular indentations in the pavement beneath his feet through the rubber soles of his sneakers. He waved the sword in the air before him. It keened and hummed, and instantly, Josh imagined he could hear distant whispers and make out words he could almost understand. For the first time in his life, he felt truly alive: and he knew then that this was how Sophie had felt when she'd been Awakened. But whereas she'd been frightened, confused by the sensations . . . he felt exhilarated.

He wanted this. More than anything else in the world.

✧　✧　✧

Dagon padded into the alleyway, scooped up the Disir's fallen war hammer and raced after the boy.

Dagon had seen the flare of the boy's aura and knew that it was indeed powerful, though whether the boy and girl were the twins of legend was a different matter. Obviously, the Alchemyst, and Dee, too, seemed convinced that they were. But Dagon knew that even Machiavelli—one of the most brilliant humani he'd ever associated with—was unsure, and the brief glimpse he'd caught of the boy's aura wasn't enough to convince him either way. Gold and silver auras were rare—though not as rare as the black aura—and Dagon had encountered at least four sets of twins down through the ages with the sun and moon auras, as well as dozens of individuals.

But what neither Dee nor Machiavelli knew was that Dagon had seen the original twins.

He'd been on Danu Talis at the very end, for the Final Battle. He'd worn his father's armor on that auspicious day, when all knew that the fate of the island hung in the balance. Like everyone else, he'd cowered in terror as silver and gold lights blazed from the top of the Pyramid of the Sun in a display of primal power. The elemental magics had lain waste to the ancient landscape and sundered the island at the heart of the world.

Dagon rarely slept anymore; he didn't even possess a bed. Like a shark, he could sleep and continue to move about. He rarely dreamed, but when he did, the dreams were always the same: a vivid nightmare of those times when the skies had burned with gold and silver lights and the world had ended.

He'd spent many years in Machiavelli's service. He'd seen

both wonders and terrors during those centuries, and together, they'd been present for some of the most significant and interesting moments in the earth's recent history.

And Dagon was beginning to think that this night might be one of the most memorable.

"Now, that's something you don't see every day," Dee muttered.

The Magician and Machiavelli watched Nidhogg burst through a building on the left side of the Champs-Elysées, trample the trees that lined the street and career across the road. It still held red-haired Scatty in its claws, and the Disir was clinging to its back. The two immortals watched the huge swinging tail turn a set of traffic lights into a mangled ruin as the creature darted down another street.

"It's heading for the river," Machiavelli said.

"But what happened to the boy, I wonder?" Dee mused aloud.

"Maybe he got lost," Machiavelli began, "or was trampled by Nidhogg. Or maybe not," he added as Josh Newman stepped through the uprooted trees and out into the broad road. He looked left and right, but there was no traffic, and he didn't even glance at the police car badly parked against the curb. He darted across the wide avenue, the sword in his hand streaming smoky gold threads behind him.

"The boy's a survivor," Dee said admiringly. "Brave, too."

Seconds later, Dagon burst out of the side street, following Josh. He was carrying a war hammer. Spotting Dee and

Machiavelli in the car, he raised his other hand in what might have been a greeting, or a farewell.

"Now what?" Dee demanded.

Machiavelli turned the key in the ignition and wrenched the car into first gear. It jerked forward, bouncing a little; then the engine howled as he put his foot to the floor. "The Rue de Marignan comes out onto the Avenue Montaigne. I think I can get there before Nidhogg does." He hit the sirens.

Dee nodded. "Perhaps you might think about changing gear." His lips moved in a barely discernable smile. "You'll find the car will go faster that way."

CHAPTER THIRTY-SIX

"*Y*our garage isn't attached to your house?" Sophie asked, climbing into the back of a small red and black Citroën 2CV, taking up a position behind Nicholas, who was sitting up front with Joan.

"These are converted stables. In previous centuries, the stables were never too close to the house. I guess the rich didn't like living with the smell of horse manure. It's not so bad, though it can be a bit of an inconvenience on a rainy night, knowing you have to run three blocks home. If Francis and I go out for an evening, we usually take the Metro."

Joan eased the car out of the garage and turned right, moving away from the damaged house, which was quickly being surrounded by fire trucks, ambulances, police cars and press. When they'd left, Francis had been going upstairs to change; he reasoned that all the publicity would do wonders for the sale of his new album.

"We'll cut across the Champs-Elysées and then head down toward the river," Joan said, expertly maneuvering the Citroën through the narrow cobbled alleyway. "Are you sure that's where Nidhogg will go?"

Nicholas Flamel sighed. "I'm only guessing," he admitted. "I've never actually seen it—I don't know of anyone who has and lived—but I've come across creatures like it in my travels, and they are all related to the marine lizards, like the mosasaur. It's scared, maybe it's hurt. It'll head to the water, seeking cool, healing mud."

Sophie leaned forward between the front seats. She deliberately focused on Nidhogg, desperately sorting through the Witch's memories, looking for something that might help her. But even the Witch knew little about the primal creature except that it was locked in the roots of the World Tree, the tree that Dee had destroyed with . . .

"Excalibur," she whispered.

The Alchemyst swiveled in the seat to look at her. "What about it?"

Sophie frowned, trying to remember. "Josh told me earlier that Dee had destroyed Yggdrasill with Excalibur."

Flamel nodded.

"And you told me that Clarent is Excalibur's twin."

"It is."

"Does it share the same powers?" she asked.

Flamel's cool gray eyes flashed. "And you're wondering, if Excalibur could destroy something as ancient as the World Tree, could Clarent destroy Nidhogg?" He was nodding even as he was speaking. "The ancient weapons of power predate

311

the Elders. No one has any idea where they came from, though we do know that the Elders used some of them. The fact that the weapons are still around today proves just how indestructible they are." He nodded. "I'm sure Clarent could hurt and possibly even kill Nidhogg."

"And you believe Nidhogg is hurt now?" Joan spotted an opening in the light early-morning traffic and slotted neatly into it. Car horns blared behind her.

"Something drove it from the house."

"Then you know what you've just confirmed?" she said.

Flamel nodded. "We know Scatty would never touch Clarent. Therefore, Josh wounded the creature—enough to send it careering madly across Paris. And now he's chasing it."

"And Machiavelli and Dee?" Joan asked.

"Probably chasing him."

Joan cut across two lanes of traffic and roared down the Champs-Elysées. "Let's hope they don't catch up with him."

A sudden thought struck Sophie. "Dee met Josh. . . ." She stopped, realizing what she'd just said.

"In Ojai. I know," Flamel said, surprising her. "He told me."

Sophie sat back, surprised that her twin had told the Alchemyst. Color touched her cheeks. "I think Dee made an impression on him." She felt almost embarrassed saying this to the Alchemyst, as if she was betraying her brother, but she pressed on. This was no time for secrets. "Dee told him some things about you. I think . . . I think Josh sort of believed him," she finished in a rush.

"I know," Flamel said softly. "The English Magician can be very persuasive."

Joan slowed the car to a stop. "This isn't good," she muttered. "There should be virtually no one on the road at this hour."

They had driven right into a huge traffic jam. It stretched down the Champs-Elysées directly ahead of them. For the second day in a row, traffic on Paris's main thoroughfare had come to a complete halt. People were standing beside their cars looking at the gaping hole in the side of the building across the street. Police had just arrived and were quickly trying to take control, urging traffic to move on and allow the emergency services to get through to the building.

Joan of Arc leaned across the steering wheel, cool gray eyes assessing the situation. "It crossed the street and went this way," Joan said, signaling quickly and turning right, into the narrow Rue de Marignan, driving past a pair of mangled traffic lights. "I don't see them."

Nicholas rose in the seat, trying to see as far as possible down the long straight street. "Where does this come out?"

"On the Rue François, just before the Avenue Montaigne," Joan answered. "I've walked, cycled and driven through these streets for decades. I know them like the back of my hand." They drove past a dozen cars, each one bearing the marks of Nidhogg: metalwork crumpled like tinfoil, windows spider-webbed and smashed. A ball of metal that had once been a bicycle was now pressed deeply into the pavement, still attached to a railing by a length of chain.

"Joan," Nicholas said very softly, "I think you should hurry up."

"I don't like driving fast." She glanced sidelong at the Alchemyst, and whatever expression she saw on his face made her push her foot to the floor. The small engine howled and the car lurched forward. "What is it?" she demanded.

Nicholas chewed his bottom lip. "I've just thought of a potential problem," he admitted finally.

"What sort of problem?" Joan and Sophie asked simultaneously.

"A serious problem."

"Bigger than Nidhogg?" Joan jerked the stick shift and slammed the car into top gear. Sophie couldn't see that it made any difference; she still felt she could be walking faster. She pounded the back of the seat, frantic with worry. They needed to get to her brother.

"I gave Josh the two missing pages from the Codex," Flamel said. He twisted around in the seat to look at Sophie. "Do you think your brother has them with him?"

"Probably," she said immediately, and then nodded. "Yes, I'm sure he does. The last time we talked he was wearing the bag under his shirt."

"So how did Josh end up guarding the pages of the Codex?" Joan asked. "I thought you never let the book out of your sight."

"I gave them to him."

"You gave them?" she asked, surprised. "Why?"

Nicholas turned away and looked out at the street, now littered with the evidence of Nidhogg's passing. When he

314

looked back at Joan, his face was set in a grim mask. "I figured that since he was the only person amongst us who was neither immortal, Elder nor Awakened, he would not be involved in any of the conflicts we'd face, nor would he be a target: he's just a humani. I thought the pages would be safe with him."

Something about the statement bothered Sophie, but she couldn't put her finger on it. "Josh wouldn't give the pages to Dee," she announced confidently.

Nicholas twisted around to face the girl again, and the look in his pale eyes was terrifying. "Oh, believe me: Dee always gets what he wants," he said bitterly, "and what he cannot have—he destroys."

CHAPTER THIRTY-SEVEN

*M*achiavelli slid the car to a stop, half on, half off the curb. He pulled up the brake but left the car in gear, and it jerked forward and cut out. They were in a parking lot on the banks of the river Seine, close to where he'd anticipated Nidhogg would appear. For a moment, the only sound was the engine ticking softly, and then Dee let out his breath in a long sigh. "You are the worst driver I've ever come across."

"I got us here, didn't I? You do know that explaining all this is going to be very difficult," Machiavelli added, moving off the subject of his terrible driving. He had mastered the most arcane and difficult arts, had manipulated society and politics for half a millennium, was fluent in a dozen languages, could program in five different computer languages and was one of the world's experts on quantum physics. And he still couldn't drive a car. It was embarrassing. Rolling down the driver's window, he allowed cold air to wash into the vehicle. "I can impose a press blackout, of course, claiming it's a national security issue, but this is getting too public and way too messy." He sighed. "Video of Nidhogg is probably on the Internet right now."

"People will dismiss it as a prank," Dee said confidently. "I thought we were in trouble when Bigfoot was caught on camera. But that was quickly rejected as a hoax. If I've learned anything over the years, it is that the humani are masters at ignoring what is right in front of their noses. They've disregarded our existence for centuries, dismissing the Elders and their times as little more than myth and legend, despite all the evidence. Besides," he added smugly, absently stroking his short beard, "everything is coming together. We have most of the book; once we get the two missing pages, we will bring back the Dark Elders and return this world to its proper state." He waved a hand airily. "You'll not have to worry about minor issues like the press."

"You seem to be forgetting that we have some other problems, like the Alchemyst and Perenelle. They are not so minor."

Dee pulled his cell phone out of his pocket and waved it in the air. "Oh, I've taken care of that. I made a call."

Machiavelli glanced sidelong at the Magician but said nothing. In his experience, people often spoke merely to fill a silence in a conversation, and he knew that Dee was a man who liked to hear the sound of his own voice.

John Dee stared through the dirty windshield toward the Seine. A couple of miles downriver, just around the bend, the huge Gothic cathedral of Notre Dame de Paris would be slowly taking shape in the early dawn light. "I first met Nicholas and Perenelle in this city almost five hundred years ago. I was their student—you didn't know that, did you? That's not in your legendary files. Oh, don't look so surprised," he said, laughing at Machiavelli's stunned expression. "I've known about your files for decades. And my copies are even more up-to-date," he added. "But yes, I studied with the legendary Alchemyst, here in this very city. I knew within a very short time that Perenelle was more powerful—more dangerous—than her husband. Have you ever met her?" he asked suddenly.

"Yes," Machiavelli said shakily. He was astounded that the Elders—or was it just Dee?—knew about his secret files. "Yes. I met her just the once. We fought; she won," he said shortly. "She made quite an impression."

"She is an extraordinary woman; quite remarkable. Even in her own time, her reputation was formidable. What she would have achieved if only she'd chosen to side with us. I don't know what she sees in the Alchemyst."

"You never did understand the human capacity for love, did you?" Machiavelli asked softly.

"I understand that Nicholas survives and thrives because of the Sorceress. To destroy Nicholas, all we have to do is kill Perenelle. My master and I have always known that, but we thought that if we could capture both of them, their accumulated knowledge was worth the risk of leaving them alive."

"And now?"

"It is no longer worth the risk. Tonight," he added, very

softly, "I finally did something that I should have done a long time ago." He sounded almost regretful.

"John," Machiavelli barked urgently, swiveling in the seat to look at the English Magician. "What have you done?"

"I've sent the Morrigan to Alcatraz. Perenelle will not see another dawn."

CHAPTER THIRTY-EIGHT

*J*osh finally caught up with the monster on the banks of the Seine.

He didn't know how far he'd run, miles probably—but he knew that he shouldn't have been able to do it. He'd sprinted the entire length of the last street—he'd thought the street sign said Rue de Marignan—without any effort, and now, swinging left onto the Avenue Montaigne, he wasn't even breathless.

It was the sword.

He'd felt it buzz and hum in his hands as he'd run, heard it whisper and sigh what sounded like vague promises. When he held it directly in front of him, toward the monster, the whispers grew louder and it visibly trembled in his hand. When he moved it away, they faded.

The sword was drawing him toward the creature.

Following the monster's trail of destruction down the

narrow street, racing past confused, shocked and horrified Parisians, Josh found strange and disturbing thoughts flickering at the very edges of his consciousness:

. . . he was in a world without land, swimming in an ocean vast enough to swallow whole planets, filled with creatures that made the monster he was chasing look tiny. . . .

. . . he was dangling high in the air, wrapped in thick roots that bit into his flesh, looking down over a blasted, fiery wasteland. . . .

. . . he was lost and confused, in a place filled with small buildings and even tinier creatures, and he was in pain, an incredible fire searing the base of his spine. . . .

. . . he was . . .

Nidhogg.

The name snapped into his consciousness, and the shock that he was somehow experiencing the monster's thoughts almost stopped him in his tracks. He knew the phenomenon had to be connected to the sword. Earlier, when the creature's tongue had touched the blade, he'd glimpsed a snapshot of an alien world, shocking images of a bizarre landscape, and now, having stabbed the creature again, he caught hints of a life completely beyond his experience.

It dawned on him that he was seeing what the creature—Nidhogg—had seen at some time in the past. He was experiencing what it was feeling now.

It had to be connected to the sword.

And if this was Excalibur's twin, Josh suddenly wondered, then did *that* ancient weapon also transfer feelings, emotions, and impressions when it was used? What had Dee felt when he had plunged Excalibur into the ancient Yggdrasill? What sights had he seen, what had he experienced and learned? Josh found himself wondering if that was the real reason Dee had destroyed the Yggdrasill: had he killed it to experience the incredible knowledge it contained?

Josh glanced quickly at the stone sword and a shudder ran through him. A weapon like this gave the wielder unimaginable powers—and what a frightening temptation it was. Surely the urge to use it again and again to gain more and more knowledge would become uncontrollable? It was a terrifying thought.

But why had the Alchemyst given it to him?

The answer came immediately: because Flamel didn't know! The sword was a dead lump of stone until it stabbed or cut something—only then did it come alive. Josh nodded to himself; now he knew why Saint-Germain, Joan and Scatty would not touch the weapon.

As he raced down the street toward the river, he wondered what would happen if he managed to kill Nidhogg with Clarent. What would he feel, what would he experience?

What would he know?

Nidhogg burst through a stand of trees and darted across the road and down onto the Port des Champs-Elysées. It stopped in the parking lot on the quayside almost directly in front of Dee and Machiavelli and dropped onto all fours, huge head swaying from side to side, tongue lolling out of its mouth. It was so close they could see Scatty's limp body caught in its claws and the Disir astride its neck. Nidhogg's tail lashed, buffeting parked cars and smashing into a long tour bus, staving in the engine. A tire popped with a deep boom.

"I think we should get out of the car . . . ," Dee began, reaching for the door, eyes fixed on the swinging tail as it flipped a heavy BMW onto its roof.

Machiavelli's arm shot out, fingers closing on the Magician's arm in a painful viselike grip. "Do not even think about moving. Do nothing that will attract its attention."

"But the tail . . ."

"It's in pain, that's why the tail is thrashing about. But it seems to be slowing down."

Dee turned his head slightly. Machiavelli was correct: there was something wrong with Nidhogg's tail. About one-third of its total length had turned black—it looked almost stonelike. Even as Dee watched, tendrils and veins of bubbling black liquid crept over the creature's hard flesh, slowly encasing it in a solid crust. Dr. John Dee immediately knew what had happened.

"The boy stabbed it with Clarent," he said, not even turning his head to look at Machiavelli. "That's what caused the reaction."

"I thought you said Clarent was the Sword of Fire, not the Sword of Stone."

"There are many different forms of fire," Dee said. "Who knows how the blade's energy reacted with something like Nidhogg?" He stared at the tail, watching as more of the thick black crust grew on the skin. As it hardened, he caught a brief glimpse of red fire. "Lava crust," he said, voice hushed in wonder. "It's lava crust. The fire is burning *within* the creature's skin."

"No wonder it's in pain," Machiavelli muttered.

"You sound almost sorry for it," Dee snapped.

"I never traded my humanity for my long life, Doctor. I've always remembered my roots." His voice hardened, turned contemptuous. "You worked so hard to be like your Elder master that you've forgotten what it is like to feel human—to be human. And we *humans*"—he stressed the last word—"have the capacity to feel another creature's pain. It is what lifted humani above the Elders, it is what made them great."

"And it's the weakness that will ultimately destroy them," Dee said simply. "Let me remind you that this creature is not human. It could crush you underfoot and not even notice. However, let us not argue now; not when we're about to be victorious. The boy might have solved our problem for us," Dee said. "Nidhogg is slowly turning to stone." He laughed delightedly. "If it jumps into the river now, the weight of its tail will drag it to the bottom—and take Scathach with it." He looked slyly at Machiavelli. "I take it your humanity does not extend to feeling sorry for the Shadow."

Machiavelli grimaced. "Knowing Scathach is lying at the bottom of the Seine wrapped in the creature's claws would make me very happy indeed."

The two immortals sat unmoving in the car, watching as the creature lurched forward, moving more slowly now, the weight of its tail dragging behind it. All that stood between it and the water was one of the glass-enclosed boats—the bateaux-mouches—that took tourists up and down the river.

Dee nodded toward the boat. "Once it climbs onto that, the boat will sink, and Nidhogg and Scathach will disappear into the Seine forever."

"And what about the Disir?"

"I'm sure she can swim."

Machiavelli allowed himself a wry smile. "So all we're waiting for now . . ."

". . . is for it to reach the boat," Dee finished, just as Josh appeared through the gaping hole in the tree-lined quayside and darted across the parking lot.

As Josh raced up to the creature, the sword in his right hand began to burn, long streamers of orange fire curling off the blade. His aura started to crackle a matching golden color, suffusing the air with the smell of oranges.

Abruptly, the Disir slid off the monster's back, flickering back into her white chain mail in the instant before her feet touched the ground. She rounded on Josh, her features locked into an ugly, savage mask. "You are becoming a nuisance, boy," she snarled in barely comprehensible English. Lifting her great broadsword in both hands, she threw herself toward Josh. "This will just take a moment."

CHAPTER THIRTY-NINE

*H*uge sweeping banks of fog rolled across San Francisco Bay.

Perenelle Flamel folded her arms across her chest and watched the night sky fill with birds. A great wheeling flock rose over the city, gathered in a thick moving cloud, and then, like tendrils of spilled ink, three separate streams of birds set out across the bay, heading directly for the island. And she knew that somewhere in the heart of the great flock was the Crow Goddess. The Morrigan was coming to Alcatraz.

Perenelle was standing in the burned-out ruins of the warden's house, where she'd finally managed to escape the masses of spiders. Although it had burned more than three decades ago, she could smell the ghost-odors of charred wood, cracked plaster and melted piping lingering in the air.

The Sorceress knew that if she lowered her defenses and concentrated, she would be able to hear the voices of the wardens
and their families who had occupied the building through the
years.

Shading her bright green eyes and squinting hard, Perenelle
concentrated on the approaching birds, trying to distinguish
them from the night and work out just how much time she
had before they arrived. The flock was huge, and the thickening fog made it impossible to guess either size or distance.
But she guessed she had perhaps ten or fifteen minutes before
they reached the island. She brought her little finger and
thumb close together. A single white spark cracked between
them. Perenelle nodded. Her powers were returning, just not
fast enough. They would continue to strengthen now that
she was away from the sphinx, but her aura would recharge
more slowly at night. She also knew that she was still nowhere
near strong enough to defeat the Morrigan and her pets.

But that didn't mean she was defenseless; a lifetime of
study had taught her many useful things.

The Sorceress felt a chill breeze ruffle her long hair in the
instant before the ghost of Juan Manuel de Ayala flickered
into existence beside her. The ghost hung in the air, taking
substance and definition from a host of dust particles and
water droplets in the gathering fog. Like many of the ghosts
she'd encountered, he was wearing the clothes he had felt
most comfortable in while he was alive: a loose white linen
shirt tucked into knee-length trousers. His legs tapered away
below his knees, and, like a lot of spirits, he had no feet. While

they were alive, people rarely looked down at their feet. *"This was once the most beautiful spot on this earth, was it not?"* he asked, flat moist eyes fixed on the city of San Francisco.

"It still is," she said, turning to look across the bay to where the city sparkled and glittered with countless tiny lights. "Nicholas and I have called it home for many years."

"Oh, not the city!" de Ayala said dismissively.

Perenelle glanced sidelong at the ghost. "What are you talking about?" she asked. "It looks beautiful."

"I once stood here, close to this very spot, and watched perhaps a thousand fires burning on the shores. Each fire represented a family. In time I came to know all of them." The Spaniard's long face grimaced in what might have been pain. *"They taught me about the land, and about this place, spoke to me of their gods and spirits. I think it was those people who bound me to this land. All I see now are lights; I cannot see the stars, I cannot see the tribes or individuals huddling around their fires. Where is the place I loved?"*

Perenelle nodded toward the distant lights. "It's still there. Just grown."

"It's changed out of all recognition," de Ayala said, *"and not for the better."*

"I've watched the world change too, Juan." Perenelle spoke very softly. "But I like to believe that it *has* changed for the better. I am older than you. I was born into an age when a toothache could kill you, when life was short and brutal and death was often painful. Around the same time you were discovering this island, the average life expectancy of a healthy adult was no more than thirty-five years. Now it is double

328

that. Toothaches no longer kill—well, not usually," she added with a laugh. Getting Nicholas to go to the dentist was practically impossible. "Humans have made astonishing strides in the last few hundred years; they have created wonders."

De Ayala floated around to hover directly in front of her. *"And in their rush to create wonders, they have ignored the wonders all around them, ignored the mysteries, the beauty. Myths and legends walk unseen amongst them, ignored, unrecognized. It was not always so."*

"No, it wasn't," Perenelle agreed sadly. She looked across the bay. The city was fast disappearing into the mist, the lights taking on a magical, ethereal quality. It was easy now to see what it must have looked like in the past . . . and what it might look like again if the Dark Elders reclaimed the earth. In past ages, mankind had recognized that there really were creatures and other races—the Vampire, the Were, the Giants—living in the shadows. Sometimes beings as powerful as gods lived in the heart of the mountains or deep in the impenetrable forests. There were ghouls in the earth, wolves really did roam the forest, and there were creatures much worse than trolls under bridges. When travelers had returned from distant lands, bringing with them stories of the monsters and creatures they had met, the wonders they had seen, no one doubted them. Nowadays, even with photographs, videos or eyewitness accounts of something extraordinary or otherworldly, people still doubted—dismissing everything as a hoax.

"And now one of those terrible wonders is coming to my island," Juan said sadly. *"I can feel it approach. Who is it?"*

"The Morrigan, the Crow Goddess."

Juan turned to Perenelle. *"I've heard of her; some of the Irish and Scottish sailors in my crews feared her. She's coming for you, isn't she?"*

"Yes." The Sorceress smiled grimly.

"What will she do?"

Perenelle tilted her head to one side, considering. "Well, they've tried imprisoning me. That's failed. I imagine Dee's masters have finally sanctioned a more permanent solution." She laughed shakily. "I've been in trickier situations. . . ." Her voice cracked and she swallowed hard and tried again. "But I've always had Nicholas by my side. Together we were undefeatable. I wish he were here with me now." She took a deep breath, steadying her breathing and raising both hands in front of her face. Smoking wisps of her ice white aura curled off her fingertips. "But I am the immortal Perenelle Flamel, and I will not go down without a fight."

"Tell me how I can help you," de Ayala said formally.

"You have done enough for me already. Because of you I escaped the Sphinx."

"This is my island. And you are under my protection now." He smiled ruefully. *"However, I'm not sure the birds will be frightened by a few banging doors. And there's not a lot else I can do."*

Perenelle carefully picked her way from one side of the ruined house to the other. Standing in one of the tall rectangular windows, she stared back at the prison. Now that night had fallen, it was little more than a vague and ominous outline against the purple sky. She took stock of her situation: she was trapped on an island crawling with spiders, there was a sphinx wandering loose in the corridors below, and the cells were filled with creatures from some of the darkest myths she had ever encountered. Plus, her powers were incredibly diminished and the Morrigan was coming. She'd told de Ayala that she'd been in trickier situations, but right now she couldn't remember one.

The ghost appeared alongside Perenelle, its outline distorting the shape of the building beyond. *"What can I do to help?"*

"How well do you know this island?" she asked.

"Ha! I know every inch. I know the secret places, the half-completed tunnels dug by the prisoners, hidden corridors, walled-up rooms, the old Indian caves cut deep into the rock below. I could hide you and no one would ever find you."

"The Morrigan is resourceful . . . and then there are the spiders. They'd find me."

The ghost floated around to place himself directly in front of her again. Only his eyes—a deep rich brown—were visible in the night. *"Oh, the spiders are not under Dee's control."*

Perenelle took a step back in surprise. "They're not?"

"They only began to appear a couple of weeks ago. I started to notice the webs over the doors, coating the stairs. Every morning, there were more and more spiders. They'd float in on the wind, carried by strands of thread. There were humanlike guards on the island then . . . though they were not human," he added quickly. *"Terrible blank-faced creatures."*

"Homunculi," Perenelle said with a shudder. "Creatures Dee grows in bubbling vats of fat. What happened to them?"

"*They were given the task of sweeping clean the spiders' webs, keeping the doors clear. One stumbled and fell into a web,*" de Ayala said, his teeth appearing out of the gloom in a quick smile. "*All that was left of it were scraps of cloth. Not even bones,*" he told her in a horrified whisper.

"That's because homunculi have no bones," she said absently. "So what is calling the spiders here?"

De Ayala turned to look at the prison. "*I'm not sure. . . .*"

"I thought you knew all there was to know about this island?" Perenelle said with a smile.

"*Far below the prison, cut deep into the bedrock by the waves, is a series of subterranean caves. I believe the first native inhabitants of the island used them for storage. About a month ago, the small Englishman—*"

"Dee?"

"*Yes, Dee, brought something to the island in the dead of night. It was sealed away in those caves, and then he blanketed the entire area with magical sigils and Wards. Even I cannot penetrate the layers of protection. But I am convinced that whatever is drawing the spiders to the island is locked in those caves.*"

"Can you get me to the caves?" Perenelle asked urgently. She could hear the rasp and clatter of thousands of birds' wings, drawing ever closer.

"*No,*" de Ayala snapped. "*The corridor is thick with spiders, and who knows what other traps Dee has put into place.*"

Perenelle automatically reached for the sailor's arm, but her hand passed right through him, leaving a swirl of water droplets in her wake. "If Dee has buried something in Alcatraz's hidden dungeons, and then protected it with magic so potent that even an insubstantial spirit cannot get through it, then we need to know what it is." She smiled. "Have you never heard the saying 'the enemy of my enemy is my friend'?"

"No, but I have heard 'fools rush in where angels fear to tread.' "

"Come, then—quickly, before the Morrigan arrives. Take me back into Alcatraz."

CHAPTER FORTY

*T*he Disir's sword flashed toward Josh's head.

Everything was happening so fast, he didn't have time to be afraid. Josh saw the flicker of movement and reacted instinctively, bringing Clarent up and around, holding it horizontally over his head. The Disir's broadsword struck the short stone blade and screamed along it in an explosion of sparks. They rained down over Josh's hair, stinging where they touched his face. The pain made him angry, but the force of the blow drove him to his knees, and then the Disir stepped back and brought her weapon around in a wide sweeping cut. It whined as it sliced through the air toward him . . . and Josh knew with a sickening feeling in the pit of his stomach that he would not be able to avoid it.

Clarent trembled in Josh's palm.

Twitched.

And moved.

A surge of tingling heat shot into his hand, shocking him, the spasm tightening his fingers around the hilt. Then the sword jerked, shooting out to meet the Disir's metal blade, turning it aside at the last moment in another explosion of sparks.

Blue eyes wide with shock, the Disir danced away. "No humani possesses such skill," she wondered aloud, her voice barely above a whisper. "Who are you?"

Josh got shakily to his feet, not entirely sure what had just happened, knowing only that it was something to do with the sword. It had taken control; it had saved him. His eyes went to the terrifying warrior maid, flickering between her masked face and her gleaming silver sword. He held Clarent before him in both hands, trying to mimic the stance he'd seen Joan and Scatty use, but the sword kept shifting in his grip, moving and shivering of its own accord. "I am Josh Newman," he said simply.

"Never heard of you," the woman said dismissively. She snapped a quick look over her shoulder to where Nidhogg was crawling toward the water. Its tail was now so heavily encrusted with black stone that it could barely move.

"Maybe you've never heard of me," Josh said, "but this"—he tilted the sword blade upward—"is Clarent." He watched the woman's bright blue eyes widen slightly. "And I see you *have* heard of it!"

Spinning her sword loosely in one hand, the Disir began to edge around Josh. He kept turning to face her. He knew what she was doing—moving him so that his back would be to the monster—but he didn't know how to prevent it from happening. When his back was almost touching Nidhogg's stone skin, the Disir stopped.

"In the hands of a master, the sword might be dangerous," the Disir said.

"I'm no master," Josh said loudly, delighted that his voice didn't tremble. "But I don't need to be. Scathach told me that this weapon really could kill her. I didn't understand what she meant, but now I do. And if it could kill her, then I'm guessing it could do the same to you." He jerked his thumb over his shoulder. "Look what I did to this monster with just a single cut. All I have to do is to scratch you with it." The blade actually shivered in his hands, humming in what almost sounded like agreement.

"You could not even get close to me," the Disir mocked, swooping in, the broadsword weaving before her in a mesmerizing pattern. She suddenly attacked with a quick flurry of blows.

Josh didn't even have time to catch his breath. He managed to stop three of them, Clarent moving to intercept each strike, the Disir's metal blade slamming off his stone sword in a shower of sparks, each blow driving him back, the force vibrating through his entire body. The Disir was just too fast. The next swipe struck his bare arm between the shoulder and elbow. Clarent managed to nudge the sword at the last instant, so it was only the flat of the blade, rather than the razor-sharp edge, that hit him. Instantly, his entire arm went numb from shoulder to fingertips and he felt a sudden wash of nausea from the pain, the fear and the sudden realization that he was going to die. Clarent fell from his grasp and clattered to the ground.

When the woman smiled, Josh saw that her teeth were thin needle points. "Easy. Too easy. A legendary sword does not make you a swordsman." Hefting the broadsword, she advanced on the boy, driving him right up against Nidhogg's stone-flesh. Josh squeezed his eyes shut as she raised her arms high and screamed a hideous war cry. *"Odin!"*

"Sophie," he whispered.

"Josh!"

Two blocks away, stuck in unmoving traffic, Sophie Newman sat bolt upright in the backseat of the car, a sudden stomach-churning feeling of terror catching her in her chest, setting her heart pounding madly.

Nicholas spun around and caught the girl's hand. "Tell me!"

Tears filled her eyes. "Josh," she gasped, almost unable to speak with the lump in her throat. "Josh is in danger, terrible danger." The car filled with the overpowering smell of rich vanilla as her aura blossomed. Tiny sparks danced on the end of her blond hair, crackling like cellophane. "We've got to get to him!"

"We're going nowhere," Joan said grimly. Traffic on the narrow street was at a complete standstill.

A chill settled in Sophie's stomach: it was the appalling fear that her brother was going to die.

"Sidewalk," Nicholas said decisively. "Take it."

"But the pedestrians—"

"Can get out of the way. Use your horn." He swiveled back around to Sophie. "We're minutes away," he said as Joan bumped the small car up off the pavement and roared down the sidewalk, horn squeaking plaintively.

"That's going to be too late. There must be something you can do?" Sophie pleaded desperately. "Anything?"

Looking old and tired, lines etched into his forehead and around his eyes, Nicholas Flamel shook his head miserably. "There is nothing I can do," he admitted.

Sparking, crackling, snapping, a sheet of stinking yellow-white flame winked into existence between Josh and the Disir. The heat was so intense it drove him back onto Nidhogg's clawed feet and crisped his hair, scorching his eyebrows and eyelashes. The Disir too staggered back, blinded by the foul flames.

"Josh!"

Someone called his name, but the terrifying flames were roaring right in front of his face.

The proximity of the fire roused the monster. It took a shuddering step, the movement of its leg thrusting Josh forward onto his hands and knees, pitching him dangerously close to the flames . . . which died as abruptly as they had risen. He hit the ground hard, hands and knees stinging with the contact. The smell of rotten eggs was appalling and his eyes and nose were streaming, but through his tears, he saw Clarent and attempted to reach for it just as someone shouted at him again.

"Josh!"

The Disir threw herself at Josh once more, sword thrusting at him. A solid spear of yellow flame struck the woman, exploding over her chain mail, which immediately started to rust and fall away. And then another wall of flame roared into existence between the boy and the warrior.

"Josh." A hand fell on Josh's shoulder and he jumped, shouting aloud with fright and the pain in his bruised shoulder. He looked up to find Dr. John Dee leaning over him.

Dirty yellow smoke dribbled from the Magician's hands, which were barely covered in torn gray gloves, and his once-elegant suit was now a ruined mess. Dee smiled kindly. "It would be best if we left right now." He gestured toward the flames. "I can't keep this up forever." Even as he was speaking, the Disir's blade cut blindly through the fire, flames curling around the metal as it sought a target. Dee hauled Josh to his feet and dragged him backward.

"Wait," Josh said hoarsely, voice raw with a combination of fear and the smoke. "Scatty . . ." He coughed and tried again. "Scatty is trapped. . . ."

"Escaped," Dee said quickly, putting an arm around the boy's shoulder, supporting him, leading him toward a police car.

"Escaped?" Josh mumbled, confused.

"Nidhogg lost its grip on her when I created the curtain of fire between you and the Disir. I saw her roll away from its claws, jump to her feet and race down the quay."

"She ran . . . she ran away?" That didn't sound right. She'd been limp and unconscious the last time he'd seen her.

He tried to concentrate, but his head was throbbing, and the flesh on his face felt tight from the flames.

"Even the legendary Warrior could not stand against Nidhogg. Heroes survive to fight again because they know when to run."

"She left me?"

"I doubt she even knew you were there," Dee said quickly, bundling Josh into the back of a badly parked police car and sliding in beside him. He tapped the white-haired driver on the shoulder. "Let's go."

Josh sat up straight. "Wait . . . I dropped Clarent," he said.

"Trust me," Dee said, "you don't want to return for it." He leaned back so that Josh could look out the window. The Disir, her once-pristine white chain mail now hanging in tattered and rotting shreds about her, strode through the dying yellow flames. She spotted the boy in the back of the car and raced toward it, shouting unintelligibly in a language that sounded like wolves howling.

"Niccolò," Dee said quickly. "She's rather upset. We really should be going now, right now."

Josh looked away from the approaching Disir at the driver and was horrified to discover that it was the same man he'd seen on Sacré-Coeur's steps.

Machiavelli turned the key in the ignition so savagely that the starter screeched. The car lurched, jerked forward, then died.

"Oh great," Dee muttered. "That's just great." Josh watched as the Magician leaned out the window, brought his

340

hand to his mouth and blew sharply into it. A yellow sphere of smoke rolled from his palm and dropped onto the ground. It bounced twice like a rubber ball, then exploded at head height just as it reached the Disir. Thick, sticky strands the color and consistency of dirty honey splashed over the Disir, then dripped down in long streamers, gluing her to the ground. "That should hold her . . . ," Dee began. The Disir's broadsword sliced easily through the strands. "Or maybe not."

Through his pain, Josh realized that Machiavelli had tried—and failed—to get the car started again. "Let me," he muttered, scrambling over the back of the seat as Machiavelli slid over to the passenger side. His right shoulder was still aching, but at least feeling had returned to his fingers, and he didn't think anything was broken. He was going to have a massive bruise to add to his growing collection. Turning the key in the ignition, he floored the accelerator and simultaneously slammed the car into reverse just as the Disir reached it. He was suddenly thankful that he'd learned to drive a stick shift on his father's old battered Volvo. The warrior's flailing sword struck the door, puncturing the metal, the tip of the blade inches from Josh's leg. As the car screeched backward, the Disir set her feet firmly and held on to her sword with both hands. The blade tore a horizontal rip right across the door and into the wing over the engine, peeling back the metal as if it were paper. It also tore apart the front driver's-side tire, which exploded with a dull bang.

"Keep going!" Dee shouted.

"I'm not stopping," Josh promised.

With the engine whining in protest and the front tire flapping and banging off the ground, Josh tore away from the quayside . . .

. . . just as Joan wheeled the slightly scratched Citroën in at the other end.

Joan hit the brakes and the car screeched to a halt on the morning-wet stones. Sophie, Nicholas and Joan watched in confusion as Josh reversed a battered police car at high speed away from Nidhogg and the Disir. They could clearly see Dee and Machiavelli in the car as he executed a clumsy handbrake turn and sped from the parking lot.

For a single heartbeat, the Disir stood on the quayside, looking lost and bewildered. Then she spotted the newcomers. Turning, she raced toward them, sword held high over her head, screeching a barbaric war cry.

CHAPTER FORTY-ONE

"*I*'ll take care of this," Joan said, sounding almost pleased at the prospect. She touched Flamel's sleeve and nodded to where the Warrior was still wrapped in Nidhogg's claws. "Get Scathach." The monster was now less than six feet from the edge of the quay and edging ever closer to the safety of the water.

The tiny Frenchwoman grabbed her sword and leapt out of the car.

"More humani with swords," the Disir spat, blade falling toward the woman.

"Not just any humani," Joan said, easily turning the weapon aside, her own sword then flicking out to clink against the remains of the rusted mail on the Disir's shoulders. "I am Joan of Arc!" The longsword in her hands twirled and twisted, creating a spinning wheel of steel that drove the Disir back with the ferocity of its attack. "I am the Maid of Orléans."

✦ ✦ ✦

Sophie and Nicholas moved cautiously toward Nidhogg. Sophie noted that its entire tail was coated with heavy black stone, which had now started to creep up its back and down its hind legs. The weight of the stone tail anchored the creature to the ground, and Sophie saw its huge muscles bunching and rippling as it tugged itself toward the water. She could see where its claws and dragging tail left deep indentations in the pavement.

"Sophie," Flamel shouted, "I need some help!"

"But Josh . . . ," she began, distracted.

"Josh is gone," he snapped. He swooped in to snatch Clarent off the ground, hissing in surprise at the heat of the weapon. Darting forward, he slapped at Nidhogg with the sword. The blade bounced harmlessly off the stone-sheathed skin. "Sophie, help me free Scatty and then we'll go after Josh. Use your powers."

The Alchemyst hacked at Nidhogg again but without any effect. His worst fears had been realized: Dee had gotten his hands on Josh . . . and Josh had the last two pages from the Codex. Nicholas looked over his shoulder. Sophie was standing still, looking frightened and completely bemused.

"Sophie! Help me."

Sophie obediently raised her hands, pressed her thumb against her tattoo and tried to call on her Fire magic. Nothing happened. She couldn't concentrate; she was too worried about her brother. What was he doing? Why had he gone with Dee and Machiavelli? It didn't look as though they had forced him to—he'd been driving them!

"Sophie!" Nicholas called.

But she knew he'd been in danger—real and terrible danger. She'd felt the emotion deep within her, recognized it for what it was. Whenever Josh was in trouble, she knew. When he'd nearly drowned off Pakala Beach on Kauai, she'd woken up breathless and gasping; when he'd broken his ribs on the football field in Pittsburgh, she'd distinctly felt the sharp pain in her left side, felt the sting with every breath she took.

"Sophie!"

What had happened? One moment he was in mortal danger . . . and the next . . . ?

"Sophie!" Flamel snarled.

"What?" she snapped, turning on the Alchemyst. She felt a quick surge of anger; Josh was right—he'd been right all along. This was the Alchemyst's fault.

"Sophie," he said more gently. "I need you to help me. I can't do this on my own."

Sophie turned to look at the Alchemyst. He was crouched on the ground, cool green vapor puddling around him. A thick emerald cord of smoke wrapped around one of Nidhogg's huge legs and disappeared deep into the earth, where it looked as if Flamel had attempted to trap it. Another rope of smoke, thinner, less substantial than the first, was loosely wrapped around one of the creature's hind legs. Nidhogg inched forward and the green cord snapped and dissolved into the air. Another few steps and it would carry Scathach—her friend—into the river. Sophie wasn't going to let that happen.

Her fear and anger lent her focus. When she pressed her

tattoo, flames popped alight on each finger. She splashed silver fire across Nidhogg's back, but it had no effect. Then she peppered the monster with tiny fiery hailstones, but it didn't even seem to notice. It continued to edge nearer to the water.

Fire didn't work, so she tried wind. But the miniature tornados she threw bounced harmlessly off the creature. Scouring the Witch's memories, she tried a trick Hekate had used against the Mongol Horde. She whipped up a sharp wind that drove stinging grit and dirt into Nidhogg's eyes. The creature merely blinked and a second, protective eyelid slid down over its huge eye.

"Nothing's working!" she screamed as the monster dragged Scatty ever closer to the edge. "Nothing's working!"

The Disir's sword slashed out. Joan ducked, and the heavy blade whistled over her head and sliced into the Citroën, turning the windshield into white powder, popping off the tiny windshield wipers.

Joan was furious; she loved her 2CV Charleston. Francis had wanted to buy her a new car for her birthday, in January. He'd given her a pile of glossy car catalogs and told her to pick one. She'd pushed the catalogs aside and told him she'd always wanted the little classic French car. He'd searched all over Europe for the perfect model and then spent a small fortune having it restored to its original pristine condition. When he'd presented it to her, it had been wrapped in three thick ribbons of blue, white and red.

Another wide slash from the Disir scored a rent on the

hood of the car, and then another cut off the small round headlight that perched over the right front wheel arch like an eye. The light bounced away and shattered.

"Do you know," Joan asked, her huge eyes dark with fury, renewing her attack on the Disir, every word matched by a hammer blow from her sword, "how difficult it is to find original parts for this car?"

The Disir fell back, desperately trying to defend herself from Joan's whirling blade, pieces of her rotting chain mail flying away as the small Frenchwoman's sword struck closer and closer. She kept trying different fighting styles to defend herself, but nothing was effective against the ferocious onslaught.

"You will notice," Joan continued, pushing the warrior back toward the river, "that I have no fighting style. That is because I was trained by the greatest warrior of all. I was trained by Scathach the Shadow."

"You may defeat me," the Disir said grimly, "but my sisters will avenge my death."

"Your sisters," Joan said, with a final savage cut that snapped the Disir's blade in two. "Would they be the two Valkyries currently frozen into their own personal iceberg?"

The Disir faltered, swaying on the edge of the wall along the river. "Impossible. We are undefeatable."

"Everyone can be defeated." The flat of Joan's blade clanged against the Disir's helmet, stunning her. Then Joan darted forward, her shoulder catching the swaying Disir in the chest, knocking her backward into the Seine. "Only ideas are immortal," she whispered.

Still clutching the broken remains of her sword, the Valkyrie disappeared into the murky river in a huge splash that drenched Joan from head to toe.

Sophie was puzzled. Her magic had failed against Nidhogg . . . but how had Josh . . . ? He had no powers.

The sword: he had the sword.

Sophie snatched Clarent from Flamel's hand. And instantly her aura snapped to life, sparking, crackling, long streamers of icy light spinning around her body. She felt a rush of emotions, a swirling mess of thoughts, ugly thoughts, dark thoughts, the memories and emotions of those men and women who had carried the sword in ages past. She was about to fling the weapon away in disgust, but she knew it was probably Scatty's only chance. Nidhogg's tail was wounded, so Josh must have cut it there. But she'd seen the Alchemyst hack at the tough hide with no result.

Unless . . .

Racing up to the monster, she plunged the weapon point first into its shoulder.

The effect was immediate. Red-black fire burned along the length of the blade, and the monster's skin immediately started to harden. Sophie's aura blazed brighter than it had ever been before, and instantly her brain was filled with impossible visions and incredible memories. Then her aura overloaded and winked out in an explosion that picked her up and sent her sailing through the air. She managed to scream once before she came crashing down onto the canvas roof of Joan's

Citroën, which slowly and gently ripped along its seams and deposited her neatly in the front passenger seat.

Nidhogg spasmed, great claws opening as its flesh hardened.

Joan of Arc darted through the monster's legs, grabbed Scatty around the waist and jerked her free, oblivious to the creature's huge feet stamping inches from her head.

Nidhogg bellowed, a sound that set house alarms clanging across the city. Every car alarm in the parking lot burst to life. The beast attempted to turn its head, to follow Joan as she dragged Scatty away, but its ancient flesh was solidifying into thick black stone. Its mouth opened, revealing its daggerlike teeth.

Abruptly, a huge section of the quayside cracked; rock pulverized to dust, crumpling to powder beneath the creature's weight. Nidhogg tilted forward and crashed down through the moored tourist boat, snapping it in two, disappearing into the Seine in an enormous explosion of water that sent a huge wave racing down the river.

Lying on the quayside, close to the water's edge, soaked through, Scathach came slowly, groggily awake. "I haven't felt this bad in centuries," she mumbled, attempting but failing to sit up. Joan eased her into a sitting position and held her tightly. "The last thing I remember . . ." Scatty's green eyes snapped open. "Nidhogg . . . Josh."

"He tried to save you," Flamel said, limping up to Scatty and Joan. He snatched Clarent from the quayside. "He stabbed Nidhogg, slowed it down long enough for us to get here. Then Joan fought the Disir for you."

"We all fought for you," Joan said. She put her arm around Sophie, who had staggered from the wrecked car, bruised and battered, with a long scrape along her forearm but otherwise unharmed. "Sophie finally defeated Nidhogg."

The Warrior slowly got to her feet, turning her head from side to side, working her stiff neck muscles. "And Josh?" she asked, looking around. Her eyes went wide with alarm. "Where's Josh?"

"Dee and Machiavelli have him," Flamel said, his face gray with exhaustion. "We're not sure how."

"We have to go after them now," Sophie said urgently.

"Their car's not in good shape, they cannot have gotten far," Flamel said. He turned to look at the Citroën. "I'm afraid yours has taken a battering as well."

"And I did so love that car . . . ," Joan murmured.

"Let's get out of here," Scatty said decisively. "We're about to be inundated with police."

And then, like a shark erupting from the waves, Dagon exploded out of the Seine. Rearing up, more fish now than man, gills open on his long neck, round eyes bulging, he wrapped webbed claws around Scathach and dragged her backward into the river. "Finally, Shadow. Finally."

They disappeared into the water with barely a splash and didn't reappear.

CHAPTER FORTY-TWO

$\mathcal{P}$erenelle followed de Ayala's ghost as he led her through the maze of Alcatraz's ruined buildings. She tried to keep to the shadows, ducking under shattered walls and empty doorways, constantly alert for creatures moving in the night. She didn't think the sphinx would dare venture out of the prison—despite their terrifying appearance, sphinxes were cowardly creatures, fearful of the dark. However, many of the beings she'd seen in the spiderwebbed cells below were creatures of the night.

The entrance to the tunnel was almost directly under the tower that had once held the island's only fresh water supply. Its metal framework was rusted, eaten away by the salt sea, acid bird droppings and countless tiny leaks from the huge water tank. However, the ground directly beneath the tower was lush with growth, fed by the same dripping water.

De Ayala pointed out an irregular patch of earth close to

351

one of the metal legs. *"You will find a shaft leading down to the tunnel under here. There is another entrance to the tunnel cut into the cliff face,"* he said, *"but it is only accessible by boat at low tide. That is how Dee brought his prisoner to the island. He doesn't know about this entrance."*

Perenelle found a rusted length of metal and used it to scrape away the dirt, revealing broken and cracked concrete beneath the soil. Using the edge of the metal bar, she began to dig away at the dirt. She kept glancing up, trying to gauge how close the birds had come to the island, but with the wind whipping in over the ruined buildings and keening through the rusted metal struts of the water tower, it was impossible to make out any other noises. Tendrils of the thick fog that had claimed San Francisco and the Golden Gate Bridge had now reached the island, coating everything in a dripping, salt-smelling cloud.

When she had scraped back the earth, de Ayala drifted over one particular spot. *"Just here,"* he said, his voice a breath in her ear. *"The prisoners discovered the existence of the tunnel and managed to dig a shaft down to it. They understood that decades of water dripping from the tower had softened the soil and even eaten away at the stones beneath. But when they eventually broke through to the tunnel below, it was at high tide, and they found that it was flooded. They abandoned their efforts."* He showed his teeth in a perfect smile he had not possessed in life. *"If only they had waited until the tide turned."*

Perenelle scraped away more soil, revealing more broken stone. Jamming the metal bar under the edge of a block, she leaned hard on it. The stone didn't budge. She pressed again with both hands, and then, when that didn't work, lifted a boulder and hammered once on the metal bar: the clink rang out across the island, tolling like a bell.

"Oh, this is impossible," she muttered. She was reluctant to use her powers, since it would reveal her location to the sphinx, but she had no other choice. Cupping her right hand, she allowed her aura to gather in her palm, where it puddled like mercury. She rested her hand lightly, almost gently, on the stone, then turned her hand over and allowed the raw power to pour from her palm and seep into the granite. The stone turned soft and soapy and then melted like candle wax. Thick globs of liquid rock fell away and disappeared into the darkness below.

"I've been dead a long time; I thought I'd seen wonders, but I've never seen anything like that," de Ayala said in awe.

"A Scythian mage taught me the spell in return for saving his life. It's quite simple, really," she said. She leaned over the hole and then jerked back, eyes watering. "Oh my: it stinks!"

The ghost of Juan Manuel de Ayala hovered directly over the hole. He turned and smiled, showing his perfect teeth again. *"I can't smell anything."*

"Trust me, be glad you cannot," Perenelle muttered, shaking her head; ghosts often had a peculiar sense of humor. The tunnel reeked of rotting fish and ancient seaweed, of rancid bird and bat droppings, of pulped wood and rusting metal. There was another scent also, bitter and acrid, almost like vinegar. Bending down, she tore a strip off the bottom of her dress and wrapped it around her nose and mouth as a crude mask.

"There is a ladder of sorts," de Ayala said, *"but be careful, I'm sure it's rusted through."* He suddenly glanced up. *"The birds have reached the southern end of the island. And something else. Something evil. I can feel it."*

"The Morrigan." Perenelle leaned over the hole and snapped her fingers. A slender feather of soft white light peeled off her fingertips and drifted down the hole, disappearing into the gloom below, shedding a flickering milky light on the streaked and dripping walls. The light had also revealed the narrow ladder, which turned out to be little more than spikes driven at irregular angles into the wall. The spikes, each no longer than four inches, were thick with rust and dripping moisture. Leaning over, she caught the first spike and tugged hard. It seemed solid enough.

Perenelle twisted around and slid one leg into the opening. Her foot found one of the spikes and immediately slipped off. Drawing her leg back out of the hole, she tugged off her sandals and tucked them into her belt. She could hear the flapping of birds—thousands, perhaps tens of thousands of them—drawing closer. She knew her tiny expenditure of power to melt the stone and light up the interior of the tunnel would have alerted the Morrigan to her position. She had only moments before the birds arrived. . . .

Perenelle put her leg into the shaft again, her bare foot touching the spike. It was cold and slimy beneath her skin, but at least she was able to get a better grip. Grasping handfuls of tough grass, she lowered herself, her foot finding another spike, and then she reached down and caught a spike in her left hand. She winced. It felt disgusting, squelching beneath her fingers. And then she smiled; how she'd changed. When she was a girl, growing up in Quimper in France all those years ago, she'd gone paddling in rock pools, picking and eating raw shellfish. She'd wandered barefoot through streets that were ankle deep in mud and filth.

Testing each step, Perenelle climbed down the length of the shaft. At one point a spike broke away beneath her foot and went clanging into the darkness. It seemed to fall for a long time. She lay back against the foul wall, feeling the damp soak through her thin summer dress. Holding on desperately, she sought another spike. She felt the metal nail in her hand shift, and for a heart-stopping moment, she thought it was going to pull free of the wall. But it held.

"A close call. I thought you were going to be joining me," the ghost of de Ayala said, materializing out of the gloom directly before her face.

"I'm not that easy to kill," Perenelle said grimly, continuing to climb down. "Though it would be funny if, having survived decades of concentrated attacks from Dee and his Dark Elders, I was to die in a fall." She looked at the vague shape of the face before her. "What's happening up there?" She jerked her head in the direction of the opening of the shaft, visible only because of the wisps of gray fog that curled and dribbled into it.

"The island is covered with birds," de Ayala said. *"Perhaps a hundred thousand of them; they are perched on every available surface. The Crow Goddess has gone into the heart of the prison, no doubt in search of the sphinx."*

"We don't have much time," Perenelle warned. She took

another step and her foot sank up to the ankle in thick gooey mud. She had reached the bottom of the shaft. The mud was icy cold, and she could feel the chill seeping into her bones. Something crawled over her toes. "Which way?"

De Ayala's arm appeared, ghostly white, directly in front of her, pointing to the left. She realized that she was standing at the mouth of a tall, roughly hewn tunnel that sloped gently downward. De Ayala's ghostly luminescence lit up the coating of spiders' webs that sheathed the walls. They were so thick that it looked as if the walls were painted silver.

"I cannot go any farther," the ghost said, his voice rasping around the walls. *"Dee has placed incredibly powerful warding spells and sigils in the tunnel; I cannot get past. The cell you are looking for is about ten paces ahead and on your left-hand side."*

Although Perenelle was reluctant to use her magic, she knew she had no choice. She was certainly not going to wander into a tunnel in pitch-darkness. She snapped her fingers and a globe of white fire winked to life over her right shoulder. It shed a soft opalescent glow over the tunnel, picking out each spider's web in intricate detail. The webs stretched in a thick curtain right across the opening. She could see webs woven on top of webs and wondered how many spiders were down here.

Perenelle stepped forward, the light moving with her, and she suddenly saw the first of the Wards and protections Dee had placed along the tunnel. A series of tall metal-tipped wooden spears had been implanted deep in the muddy floor. The flat metal head of each spear was painted with an ancient symbol of power, a square hieroglyph that would have been familiar to the ancient Maya peoples of Central America. She could see at least a dozen spears, each painted with a different symbol. She knew that individually the symbols were meaningless, but together they set up an incredibly powerful zigzagging network of raw power that crisscrossed the corridor with invisible beams of black light. It reminded her of the complicated laser alarms banks used. The power had no effect on humans—all she could feel was a dull buzzing and a tension at the back of her neck—but it was an impenetrable barrier to any of the Elder Race, the Next Generation and the Creatures of the Were. Even de Ayala, a ghost, was affected by the barrier.

Perenelle recognized some of the symbols on the spearheads; she had seen them in the Codex and etched onto the walls of the ruins at Palenque in Mexico. Most of them predated mankind; many of them were even older than the Elders and belonged to the race that had inhabited the earth in the far-distant past. They were the Words of Power, the ancient Symbols of Binding, designed to protect—or trap—something either incredibly valuable or extraordinarily dangerous.

She had a feeling this was going to be the latter.

And she also wondered where Dee had discovered the ancient words.

Sloshing through the thick mud, Perenelle took her first step into the tunnel. All the spiderwebs rustled and trembled, a sound like the whispering rustle of leaves. There must be millions of spiders in here, she thought. They didn't frighten her; she'd come up against creatures much more frightening than spiders, but she was aware that there were probably poisonous brown recluses, black widows or even South American hunting spiders amongst the mass of arachnids. A bite from one of them would certainly incapacitate her, possibly even kill her.

Perenelle jerked one of the spears out of the mud and used it to swipe away the web. The square symbol on the spearhead glowed red and the gossamer webs hissed and sizzled where the spear touched them. A thick shadow that she knew was a mass of spiders flowed backward into the gloom. Advancing slowly down the narrow tunnel, she knocked over each spear she came to, allowing the filthy mud to wash away the Words of Power, gradually dismantling the intricate pattern of magic. If Dee had gone to all this trouble to trap something in the cell, it meant that he couldn't control it. Perenelle wanted to find out what it was and free it. But as she drew nearer, the globe over her shoulder throwing a flickering light across the corridor, another thought crossed her mind: had Dee imprisoned something that even she should be afraid of, something ancient, something horrible? Suddenly, she didn't know if she was making a terrible mistake.

The doorposts and the entrance to the cell had been painted with symbols that hurt her eyes to look at. Harsh and angular, they seemed to shift and twist on the rock, not unlike the writing in the Book of Abraham. But whereas the letters in the ancient book formed words in languages she mostly understood, or at least recognized, these symbols twisted into unimaginable shapes.

She bent down, scooped up some of the mud and

splashed it over the letters, erasing them. Only when she had completely cleaned away the primeval Words of Power did she step forward and send the globe of light twisting and bobbing into the cell.

It took Perenelle a single heartbeat to make sense out of what she was seeing. And in that moment, she realized that dismantling the protective pattern of power might indeed have been a terrible mistake.

The entire cell was a thick cocoon of spiders' webs. In the center of the cell, dangling from a single strand of silk no thicker than her index finger, was a spider. The creature was enormous, easily the same size as the huge water tower that dominated the island above her head. It vaguely resembled a tarantula but bristling purple hair tipped with gray covered its entire body. Each of its eight legs was thicker than Perenelle. Set in the center of its body was a huge, almost human head. It was smooth and round, with no ears, no nose and only a horizontal slash for a mouth. Like a tarantula, it had eight tiny eyes set close to the top of the skull.

And one by one, the eyes slowly opened, each the color of an old bruise. They fixed on the woman's face. Then the mouth widened, and two long spearlike fangs appeared. "Madame Perenelle. Sorceress," it lisped.

"Areop-Enap," she said in wonder, acknowledging the ancient spider Elder. "I thought you were dead."

"You mean you thought you'd killed me!"

The web twitched and suddenly the hideous creature launched itself at Perenelle.

CHAPTER FORTY-THREE

Dr. John Dee leaned across the backseat of the police car. "Turn here," he said to Josh. He saw the expression on the young man's face and added, "Please."

Josh hit the brakes and the car slid and screeched, the front tire now completely torn away and the wheel running on the metal rim, kicking up sparks.

"Now here." Dee pointed to a narrow alleyway lined on both sides with rows of plastic trash cans. Watching him in the rearview mirror, Josh could see that he kept twisting in the seat to look behind him.

"Is she following?" Machiavelli asked.

"I can't see her," Dee said crisply, "but I think we need to get off the streets."

Josh struggled to control the car. "We won't get much farther in this," he began, and then hit the first trash can, which toppled into a second and then a third, scattering rubbish across the alley. He turned the steering wheel sharply to avoid running over one of the fallen bins and the engine began to bang alarmingly. The car wobbled and then suddenly stopped, smoke billowing from the hood. "Out," Josh said quickly. "I think we're on fire." He scrambled out of the car, Machiavelli and Dee exiting on the other side. Then they turned and ran down the alley, away from the car. They had taken perhaps half a dozen steps when there was a dull thump and the car burst into flames. Thick black smoke began spiraling upward into the sky.

"Wonderful," Dee said bitterly. "So now the Disir definitely knows where we are. And she's not going to be happy."

"Well, not with you, that's for sure," Machiavelli said with a wry smile.

"Me?" Dee looked surprised.

"I'm not the one who set fire to her," Machiavelli reminded him.

It was like listening to children. "Enough, already!" Josh rounded on the two men. "Who was that . . . that woman?"

"That," Machiavelli said with a grim smile, "was a Valkyrie."

"A Valkyrie?"

"Sometimes called a Disir."

"A Disir?" Josh found that he wasn't even surprised by the response. He didn't care what the woman was called; all he cared about was that she'd tried to slice him in two with a sword. Maybe this was a dream, he thought suddenly, and everything that had happened from the moment Dee and the Golems had stepped into the bookshop was nothing more than a nightmare. And then he moved his right arm and his bruised shoulder protested. He winced in pain. The skin on his burned face felt tight and stiff, and when he licked his dry, cracked lips, he realized that this was no dream. He was wide awake—this was a living nightmare.

Josh stepped back from the two men. He looked up and down the narrow alley. There were tall houses on one side, and what looked like a hotel was on the other. The walls were daubed with layers of cursive and ornate graffiti, some of which had even been sprayed onto the trash cans. Standing on his toes, he tried to see the skyline, looking for the Eiffel Tower or Sacré-Coeur, something to give him an idea where he was. "I've got to get back," he said, edging farther from the two disheveled men. According to Flamel, they were the enemy—especially Dee. And yet Dee had just saved him from the Disir.

Dee turned to look at him, gray eyes twinkling kindly. "Why, Josh, where are you going?"

"Back to my sister."

"And Flamel and Saint-Germain too? Tell me; what are they going to do for you?"

Josh took another step backward. He had seen Dee throw spears of fire on two occasions—in the bookshop and at the Disir—and he was unsure how far the Magician could actually toss them. Not far, he figured. Another step or two and he would turn and run down the alleyway. He could stop the first person he met and ask directions to the Eiffel Tower. He thought the French for "where is?" was *"où est?"* or maybe it was *"qui est?"* Or did that mean "who is?" He shook his head slightly, regretting not having paid attention in French class. "Don't try and stop me," he began, turning away.

"What did it feel like?" Dee asked suddenly.

Josh slowly turned to look at the Magician. He knew instantly what he was talking about. He found that his fingers had automatically curled, as if he were holding the hilt of a sword.

"What was it like holding Clarent, feeling that raw power running through you? What was it like knowing the thoughts and emotions of the creature you'd just stabbed?" Dee reached under his tattered suit coat and pulled out Clarent's twin: Excalibur. "It is an awe-inspiring feeling, is it not?" He turned the blade in his hand, a blue-black trickle of energy shivering across the stone sword. "I know you must have experienced Nidhogg's thoughts . . . emotions . . . memories?"

Josh nodded. They were still fresh—startlingly vivid—in his head. The thoughts, the sights, were so alien, so bizarre, that he knew he'd never have been able to imagine them himself.

"For an instant you knew what it was to be godlike: to see worlds beyond imagination, to experience alien emotions. You saw the past, the very distant past . . . you might even have seen Nidhogg's Shadowrealm."

Josh nodded slowly, wondering how Dee knew.

The Magician took a step closer to the boy. "For an instant, Josh, the merest instant, it was like being Awakened—

363

though nowhere near as intense," he added quickly. "And you *do* want to have your powers Awakened?"

Josh nodded. He felt breathless, his heart hammering in his chest. Dee was right; in those moments he'd held Clarent, he'd felt alive, truly alive. "But it can't be done," he said quickly.

Dee laughed. "Oh yes, it can. It can be done here, today," he finished triumphantly.

"But Flamel said . . . ," Josh began, and then stopped, realizing what he'd just said. If he could be Awakened . . .

"Flamel says many things. I doubt even he knows what is the truth anymore."

"Do you?" Josh snapped.

"Always." Dee jerked his thumb over his shoulder at Machiavelli. "The Italian is no friend of mine," he said quietly, staring directly into Josh's troubled eyes. "So ask him the question: ask him if your powers could be Awakened this very morning."

Josh turned to regard Niccolò Machiavelli. The tall white-haired man looked vaguely troubled, but he nodded in agreement. "The English Magician is correct: your powers could be Awakened today. I imagine we could probably find someone to do it within the hour."

Smiling triumphantly, Dee turned back to Josh. "It's your choice. So, give me your answer—do you want to go back to Flamel and his vague promises, or do you want to have your powers Awakened?"

Even as he was turning to follow the black threads of dark energy that drifted off Excalibur's stone blade, Josh knew the answer. He remembered the feelings, the emotions, the power, that had coursed through his body when he'd held Clarent. And Dee had said those feelings were nowhere near as intense as being Awakened.

"I need an answer," Dee said.

Josh Newman took a deep breath. "What do I have to do?"

CHAPTER FORTY-FOUR

Joan swung the battered Citroën into the mouth of the alleyway and eased the car to a halt, blocking the entrance. Leaning over the steering wheel, she scoured the alley, looking for movement, wondering if this was a trap.

Following Josh had been remarkably easy; all she'd had to do was to follow the gouge cut into the street by the metal rim of his car's front wheel. She'd had a brief moment of panic when she'd lost him in a maze of back streets, but then a thick plume of black smoke rose over the rooftops and she'd followed that: it had led her to the alley and the burning police car.

"Stay here," she commanded the exhausted Flamel and the ashen-faced Sophie as she climbed out of the car. She carried her sword loosely in her right hand as she walked down the alley, tapping the blade gently against the palm of her left hand. She was fairly sure that they were too late and that Dee,

Machiavelli and Josh were gone, but she wasn't prepared to take any risks.

Padding silently down the center of the alley, wary of the piles of trash cans that could be hiding an assailant, Joan realized she was still in a state of shock following Scatty's disappearance. One moment Joan had been standing in front of her old friend, and the next, the creature that was more fish than man had reared up out of the water and dragged Scatty down with him.

Joan blinked away tears. She had known Scathach for more than five hundred years. In those early centuries they'd been inseparable, adventuring together across the world into countries yet to be explored by the West, encountering tribes that still lived as their ancestors had thousands of years in the past. They'd discovered lost islands, hidden cities and forgotten countries, and Scatty had even taken her into some of the Shadowrealms, where they had fought creatures that had long been extinct on the earth. In the Shadowrealms, Joan had seen her friend fight and defeat creatures that existed only in the darkest human myths. Joan knew that nothing could stand against the Shadow . . . and yet Scatty herself had always said that she could be defeated, that she was immortal but not invulnerable. Joan had always imagined that when Scatty finally laid down her life it would be in one final dramatic and extraordinary event . . . not by being dragged into a dirty river by an overgrown fish-man.

Joan grieved for her friend, and she would weep for her, but not now. Not yet.

Joan of Arc had been a warrior from the time she was barely a teenager, riding into battle at the head of a massive French army. She had seen too many friends fall in battle and had learned that if she concentrated on their deaths she would be incapable of fighting. Right now she knew she needed to protect Nicholas and the girl. Later, there would be time to grieve for Scathach the Shadow, and there would also be time to go in search of the creature Flamel had called Dagon. Joan hefted the sword in her hand. She would avenge her friend.

The petite Frenchwoman walked past the blazing remains of the police car and crouched on the ground, expertly reading the traces and signs on the damp stones. She heard Nicholas and Sophie climb out of the battered Citroën and walk down the alley, stepping around puddles of oil and dirty water. Nicholas was carrying Clarent. Joan distinctly heard it buzz as he approached the burning car, and she wondered if it was still connected to the boy.

"They ran from the car and stopped here," she said, without looking up, as they stopped beside her. "Dee and Machiavelli were facing Josh. He stood over there." She pointed. "They ran through the water back there; you can clearly see the outlines of their shoes on the ground."

Sophie and Flamel leaned over and looked at the ground. They nodded, though she knew they could see nothing.

"Now, this is interesting," she continued. "At one stage Josh's footsteps are pointing down the alley, and he's on the balls of his feet, almost as if he was thinking about running. But look here." She pointed to traces of heel prints on the ground that only she could see. "The three of them walked off together, Dee and Josh first, Machiavelli following behind."

"Can you track them?" Flamel demanded.

Joan shrugged. "To the end of the alley, maybe, but beyond that . . ." She shrugged again and straightened up, dusting off her hands. "Impossible; there will be too many other prints."

"What are we going to do?" Nicholas whispered. "How are we going to find the boy?"

Joan's eyes drifted from Flamel's face to Sophie. "We can't . . . but Sophie can."

"How?" he asked.

Joan moved her hand in a horizontal line in front of her. It left the faintest tracery of light in the air, and the foul alley briefly smelled of lavender. "She's his twin: she'll be able to follow his aura."

Nicholas Flamel caught both of Sophie's shoulders, forcing the girl to look into his eyes. "Sophie!" he snapped. "Sophie, look at me."

Sophie raised red-rimmed eyes to look at the Alchemyst. She was completely numb. Scatty was gone, and now Josh had vanished, kidnapped by Dee and Machiavelli. Everything was falling apart.

"Sophie," Nicholas said very quietly, his pale eyes catching and holding hers. "I need you to be strong now."

"What's the point?" she asked. "They're gone."

"They're not gone," he said confidently.

"But Scatty . . ." The girl hiccupped.

". . . is one of the most dangerous women in the world,"

he finished. "She's survived for over two thousand years and fought creatures infinitely more dangerous than Dagon."

Sophie wasn't sure if he was trying to convince himself or her. "I saw that thing drag her into the river, and we waited for at least ten minutes. She didn't come back up. She *must* have drowned." Her voice caught and she could feel the tears pricking at the back of her eyes again. Her throat felt as if it were on fire.

"I've seen her survive worse, much worse." Nicholas attempted a wan smile. "I think Dagon is in for a surprise! Scatty's like a cat: she hates getting wet. The Seine runs very fast; they were probably swept downriver. She'll contact us."

"But how? She'll have no idea where we are." Sophie really hated the way adults lied. They were just so transparent.

"Sophie," Nicholas said seriously. "If Scathach is alive, she will find us. Trust me."

And in that moment, Sophie realized that she did not trust the Alchemyst.

Joan put her arm on Sophie's shoulder and squeezed gently. "Nicholas is right. Scatty is . . ." She smiled, and her entire face lit up. "She is extraordinary. Her aunt once abandoned her in one of the Underworld Shadowrealms: it took her centuries to find her way out. But she did it."

Sophie nodded slowly. She knew that what they were saying was true—the Witch of Endor knew more about Scathach than either the Alchemyst or Joan—but she could also tell that they were very worried.

"Now, Sophie," Nicholas resumed. "I need you to find your brother."

"How?"

"I'm hearing sirens," Joan said urgently, looking back down the alley. "Lots of sirens."

Flamel ignored her. He stared deep into Sophie's bright blue eyes. "You can find him," he insisted. "You are his twin; it is a connection that goes even deeper than blood. You've always known when he was in trouble, haven't you?"

Sophie nodded.

"Nicholas . . . ," Joan prodded, "we are running out of time."

"You've always felt his pain, known when he was unhappy or upset?"

Sophie nodded again.

"You are connected to him, you can find him." The Alchemyst turned the girl around so that she was facing down the alleyway. "Josh was standing here," he said, pointing. "Dee and Machiavelli were standing about here."

Sophie was confused and getting irritated. "But they're gone now. They took him away."

"I don't think they forced him to go anywhere, I think he went with them of his own free will," Nicholas said very softly.

The words hit Sophie like a blow. Josh wouldn't leave her, would he? "But why?"

Flamel shrugged slightly. "Who knows? Dee has always been very persuasive, and Machiavelli is a master manipulator. But we can find them, I'm sure of it. Your senses have been Awakened, Sophie. Look again; imagine Josh standing in front of you, *see* him. . . ."

Sophie took a deep breath and closed her eyes, then opened them again. She could see nothing out of the ordinary; she was standing in a dirty trash-strewn alley, the walls covered with curling ornate graffiti, with the smoke of the burning car whirling around her.

"His aura is gold," Flamel continued. "Dee's is yellow . . . Machiavelli's gray or dirty white. . . ."

Sophie started to shake her head. "I can't see anything," she began.

"Then let me help you." Nicholas put his hand on her shoulder and suddenly the stink of the burning car was replaced with the fresh sharp smell of mint. Instantly, her aura flared around her body, crackling and spitting like a firework, the pure silver now tinged with the emerald green of Flamel's aura.

And then she *saw* . . . something.

Directly in front of her she could make out the merest hint of Josh's outline. It was ghostly and insubstantial, composed of little more than threads and sparkling dust motes of gold, and when he moved he trailed streaked lines of gossamer color in the air behind him. Now that she knew what she was looking for, she could also make out the traces of Dee's and Machiavelli's outlines in the air.

She blinked slowly, afraid that the images would vanish, but they remained hanging in the air before her, and if anything, the colors grew even more intense. Josh's aura was the brightest of all. She reached out blindly, her fingers touching the golden edge of her brother's arm. The smoky outline twisted away as if blown by a breeze.

"I see them," she said in awe, her voice barely above a whisper. She'd never imagined she'd be able to do anything like this. "I can see their outlines."

"Where did they go?" Nicholas asked.

Sophie followed the colored streaks in the air; they led to the end of the alley. "This way," she said, and set off down the alleyway toward the street, with Nicholas close on her heels.

Joan of Arc took one last lingering look at her battered car and then followed.

"What are you thinking?" Flamel asked.

"I'm thinking that when this is all over, I'm going to return the car to its former pristine condition. And then never take it out of the garage again."

"Something's wrong," Flamel said as they wove their way through the streets.

Sophie was concentrating fiercely on following her twin and ignored him.

"I've just been thinking the same thing," Joan said. "The city is too quiet."

"Exactly." Flamel looked around. Where were the Parisians on their way to work and the tourists determined to get to see the sights before the city grew stifling hot and crowded? The few people on the street hurried past, talking excitedly together. The air was filled with sirens, and there were police everywhere. And then Nicholas realized that Nidhogg's rampage through the city had probably hit the news and people were being warned to stay off the streets. He wondered what excuse the authorities would make to explain the chaos.

Sophie pushed her way blindly down the street, following the gossamer threads that Josh's, Dee's and Machiavelli's auras had left in the air behind them. She kept bumping into people and apologizing, but she never took her eyes off the sparkles of light. And then she noticed that as the sun rose higher in the heavens, it was becoming harder and harder to make out the pinpoints of colored light. She realized she was running out of time.

Joan of Arc caught up with the Alchemyst. "Can she really see the afterimages left by their auras?" she asked in archaic French.

"She can," Nicholas replied in the same language. "The girl is extraordinarily powerful: she has no idea of the extent of her powers."

"Have you any clue where we're going?" Joan asked, looking around. She thought they were somewhere in the vicinity of the Palais de Tokyo, but she'd been concentrating on the marks on the road left by the police car and hadn't been paying too much attention to their whereabouts.

"None," Nicholas said, frowning. "I'm just wondering why we seem to be heading into the back streets. I would have thought that Machiavelli would want to take the boy into custody."

"Nicholas, they want the boy for themselves, or rather, the Elders do. What does the prophecy say? 'The two that are one, the one that is all.' One to save the world, one to destroy it. The boy is a prize." Without moving her head, her eyes flickered toward Sophie. "And the girl, too."

"I know that."

Joan rested her hand lightly on the Alchemyst's arm. "You know that we must never allow both of them to fall into Dee's hands."

Flamel's face hardened into a mask. "I know that, too."

"What will you do?"

"Whatever is necessary," he said grimly.

Joan pulled out a black cell phone. "I'm calling Francis; I'll let him know we're OK." She looked around for a landmark. "Maybe he'll know where we are."

Sophie turned into a narrow alleyway, barely wide enough for two people to pass side by side. In the gloom, she could see the threads and speckled light more clearly now. She even caught ghostly flashes of her brother's outline. She felt her spirits lift; maybe they were going to catch up with him.

Then, abruptly, the auras vanished.

She stopped, confused and frightened. What had happened? Looking back down the alley, she could see the traces of their auras in the air, gold and yellow—Josh and Dee, side by side—Machiavelli's gray following along behind. They reached the center of the alleyway and stopped, and she could distinctly see the outline of her brother's body picked out in gold standing almost directly in front of her. Squinting, concentrating hard, she attempted to bring his aura into focus. . . .

He was looking down, mouth open.

Sophie stepped back. Directly under her feet was a large manhole cover, with the letters *IDC* pressed into the metal. Tiny speckles of the three auras were streaked across the cover, outlining each letter in a different color.

"Sophie?" Nicholas began.

She felt a rush of excitement: relief that she hadn't lost him. "They've gone down," she said.

"Down?" he asked, turning a sickly pale color. His voice dropped to little more than a whisper. "Are you sure?"

"Positive," she said, alarmed at the expression on his face. "Why, what's wrong? What's down there? Sewers?"

"Sewers . . . and worse." The Alchemyst suddenly looked very old and tired. "Below us are the legendary Catacombs of Paris," he whispered.

Joan crouched down and pointed to where the mud around the edge of the manhole cover was disturbed. "This was opened very recently." She looked up, her expression grim. "You're right; they've taken him down into the Empire of the Dead."

CHAPTER FORTY-FIVE

"*O*h, stop that!" Perenelle bashed the spider Elder on the top of the head with the flat side of the spear in her hand. The ancient symbol of power blazed white-hot and the spider darted back into the cell, the top of its skull sizzling, gray smoke curling upward.

"That hurt!" Areop-Enap snapped, more irritated than wounded. "You're always hurting me. You nearly killed me the last time I saw you."

"And let me remind you that the last time we met, your followers attempted to sacrifice me to activate an extinct volcano. Naturally, I was a little upset."

"You brought down an entire mountain on top of me," Areop-Enap said in a peculiar lisp caused by its overlong fangs. "You could have killed me."

"It was only a small mountain," Perenelle reminded the

creature. She thought Areop-Enap was female but couldn't be entirely sure. "You've survived worse."

All of Areop-Enap's eyes were on the spear in Perenelle's hand. "Can you at least tell me where I am?"

"On Alcatraz. Or rather, below Alcatraz, an island in the San Francisco Bay on the West Coast of the Americas."

"The New World?" Areop-Enap asked.

"Yes, the New World," Perenelle said, smiling. The reclusive spider Elder often hibernated for centuries and missed huge chunks of human history.

"What are you doing here?" Areop-Enap asked.

"I am a prisoner—like you." She stepped back. "If I lower the spear, are you going to do something stupid?"

"Like what?"

"Like jump at me."

All the hairs on Areop-Enap's legs rose and fell in unison. "Truce?" the spider Elder suggested.

Perenelle nodded. "Truce," she agreed. "It seems we have a common enemy."

Areop-Enap moved to the door of the cell. "Do you know how I got here?"

"I was rather hoping you would be able to tell me that," Perenelle said.

Keeping several wary eyes on the glowing spear, the spider took a tentative step out into the corridor. "The last place I remember was Igup Island. It's part of Polynesia," it added.

"Micronesia," Perenelle said. "The name changed more than one hundred and fifty years ago. Just how long have you been asleep, Old Spider?" she asked, calling the creature by its common name.

"I'm not sure . . . when did we last meet and have our little misunderstanding? In humani years, Sorceress," it added.

"When Nicholas and I were on Pohnpei investigating the ruins of Nan Madol," Perenelle said immediately. She had an almost perfect memory. "That was about two hundred years ago," she added.

"I probably took a nap sometime about then," Areop-Enap said, stepping out into the corridor. Behind it, the cell came alive with millions of spiders. "I remember waking from a very nice nap," it said slowly. "I saw the Magician Dee . . . but he was not alone. There was someone else—*something* else—with him. Instructing him."

"Who?" Perenelle asked urgently. "Try and remember, Old Spider, this is important."

Areop-Enap closed each of its eyes as it tried to recall what had happened. "Something is preventing me," it said, all its eyes opening simultaneously. "Something powerful. Whoever was with him was protected by an extraordinarily powerful magical shield." Areop-Enap looked up and down the corridor. "That way?" it asked.

"This way." Perenelle pointed with the spear. Even though Areop-Enap had called a truce, Perenelle was not prepared to stand unarmed before one of the most powerful of the Elders. "I wonder why he wanted you prisoner." A sudden thought struck her and she stopped so quickly that Areop-Enap brushed against her, almost sending her face-first onto the muddy floor. "If you had to make a choice, Old Spider, if you had to choose between returning the Elders to this world or leaving it in the hands of the humani, who would you choose?"

"Sorceress," Areop-Enap said, mouth gaping to reveal its terrifying teeth in what might have been a smile, "I was one of the Elders who voted that we should leave the earth to the ape-kin. I recognized that our time on this planet was over; and in our arrogance we had almost destroyed it. It was time to step back and leave it to the humani."

"So you would not be in favor of the return of the Elders?"

"No."

"And if there was a fight, who would you stand with—the Elders or the humani?"

"Sorceress," Areop-Enap said very seriously, "I've stood with the humani before. Along with my kin, Hekate and the Witch of Endor, I helped bring civilization to this planet. Despite my appearance, my loyalties are with the humani."

"And that's why Dee had to capture you now. He couldn't afford to have someone as powerful as you fight alongside humankind."

"Then the confrontation must be very close indeed," Areop-Enap said. "But there's nothing Dee and the Dark Elders can do until they secure the Book of . . ." Areop-Enap's voice trailed away. "They've got the Book?"

"Most of it," Perenelle confirmed miserably. "And you should know the rest of it. You are familiar with the prophecy of the twins?"

"Of course. That old fool, Abraham, was always twittering on about the twins and scribbling down his indecipherable prophecies in the Codex. I never believed a word of them myself. And in all the years I knew him, he never got a single thing right."

"Nicholas found the twins."

"Ah." Areop-Enap was silent for a moment, then shrugged what shoulders it had, eyes blinking in unison. "So Abraham was right about something; well, that's a first."

While Perenelle slogged through ankle-deep mud, recounting what she had discovered in the cells above, she noticed that despite its enormous size, the spider Elder glided over the top of the muck. Behind them, the walls and ceilings pulsed with millions of spiders as they followed the Elder. "I wonder why Dee didn't kill you."

"He couldn't," Areop-Enap said matter-of-factly. "My death would send ripples through myriad Shadowrealms. Unlike Hekate, I have friends, and too many of them would come to investigate. Dee would not want that." Areop-Enap stopped when it came to the first of the spears Perenelle had pushed down. A huge leg turned it over, and the spider examined the faint traces of the hieroglyph painted on the spearhead. "I'm curious," it lisped. "These Words of Power. They were ancient when the Elders ruled the earth. And I thought we had destroyed both them and all record of them. How did the English Magician rediscover them?"

"I was wondering the same thing," Perenelle said. She turned the spear in her hand to look at the single square hieroglyph. "Maybe he copied the spell from somewhere."

"No," Areop-Enap said. "The individual words are powerful, it is true, but Dee set them up in the particular pattern that kept me trapped in the cell. Every time I tried to escape, it was as if I ran into a solid wall. I've seen that pattern before, but it was in the days before the Fall of Danu Talis. In fact, now that I think of it, the last time I saw that pattern was before we had even created the island continent and dragged it up from the ocean floor. Someone instructed Dee; someone knew how to create these magical Wards, someone who'd seen them."

"No one knows who Dee's Elder is, whom he serves," Perenelle said thoughtfully. "Nicholas spent decades vainly trying to discover who, ultimately, controls the Magician."

"Someone old," Areop-Enap said. "As old as me, or even older. One of the Great Elders, perhaps." All of the spider Elder's eyes blinked. "But it cannot be; none of them survived the Fall of Danu Talis."

"You did."

"I'm not one of the Great Elders," Areop-Enap said simply.

They reached the end of the tunnel and de Ayala winked into existence directly before them. He had been a ghost for centuries and had seen wonders and monsters, but he had never seen anything like Areop-Enap, and the sight of the enormous creature shocked him speechless.

"Juan," Perenelle said gently. "Talk to me."

"The Crow Goddess is here," he said finally. *"She is almost directly above us, perched on top of the water tower like a huge vulture. She's waiting for you to climb out. She had an argument*

with the sphinx," the ghost added. *"The sphinx said that the Elders had given you to her; the Morrigan claimed that Dee said you were hers."*

"So nice to be in demand," Perenelle said, looking up the length of the shaft into the darkness. She glanced sidelong at Areop-Enap. "I wonder if she knows you're here."

"Unlikely," Old Spider said. "Dee would have no reason for telling her, and with so many magical and mythical creatures on the island, she'll not be able to pick out my aura."

Perenelle's lips twisted in a quick smile that lit up her face. "Shall we surprise her?"

CHAPTER FORTY-SIX

*J*osh Newman stopped and swallowed hard. Any moment now, he was going to throw up. Although it was cool and damp underground, he was sweating, his hair plastered to his skull, his shirt lying icy and clinging along the length of his spine. He had gone beyond frightened, past terrified and straight to petrified.

Descending into the sewers had been bad enough. Dee had wrenched the manhole cover out of the ground without any effort, and they'd jerked back as a plume of filthy, foul-smelling gas vented into the street. When it had drifted away, Dee had slipped into the opening, followed a moment later by Josh and finally Machiavelli. They'd climbed down a short metal ladder and ended up standing in a tunnel that was so narrow they had to march single file and so low that only Dee could walk upright. The tunnel dipped, and Josh gasped as ice-cold water suddenly flooded his sneakers. The smell was appalling, and he desperately tried not to think about what he might be wading through.

The rotten-egg stink of sulfur briefly masked the smells in the sewer as Dee created a globe of cold blue-white light. It hovered and danced in the air about twelve inches in front of the Magician, painting the interior of the narrow arched tunnel in stark ashen light and deep impenetrable shadows. As they sloshed forward, Josh could hear things moving and glimpsed sparkling points of red light shifting in the blackness. He hoped they were only rats.

"I don't . . . ," Josh began, his voice echoing distortedly in the narrow tunnel. "I really don't like small spaces."

"Neither do I," Machiavelli added tightly. "I spent a little time in prison, a long time ago. I've never forgotten it."

"Was it as bad as this?" Josh asked shakily.

"Worse." Machiavelli was walking behind Josh and he leaned forward to add, "Try and stay calm. This is just a maintenance tunnel; we'll get into the proper sewers in a few moments."

Josh took a deep breath and gagged on the smell. He had to remember to breathe only through his mouth. "And how is that going to help?" he muttered through clenched teeth.

"The sewers of Paris are mirrors of the streets above," Machiavelli explained, his breath warm against Josh's ear. "The bigger sewers are fifteen feet high."

Machiavelli was correct; moments later they came out of

the cramped and claustrophobic service tunnel into a tall arched sewer wide enough to drive a car through. The high brick walls were brightly lit and lined with black pipes of various thicknesses. Somewhere in the distance, water splashed and gurgled.

Josh felt the claustrophobia ease a little. Sophie sometimes got scared in wide-open spaces; he was afraid of tightly enclosed spots. Agoraphobia and claustrophobia. He took a deep breath; the air was still tainted with effluent, but at least it was breathable. He lifted the front of his black T-shirt to cover his face and breathed in: it stank. When he got out of here—*if* he got out of here—he'd have to burn everything, including the fancy designer jeans Saint-Germain had given him. He quickly dropped the shirt, realizing that he'd nearly exposed the bag he wore on the cord around his neck containing the pages from the Codex. No matter what happened now, he was determined that he wasn't going to give up the pages to Dee, not until he was sure—very, very, very sure— that the Magician's motives were honest.

"Where are we?" he wondered aloud, looking back at Machiavelli. Dee had walked out into the center of the sewer, the solid white ball now spinning just above the palm of his outstretched hand.

The tall Italian glanced around. "I've no idea," he admitted. "There are about twenty-one hundred kilometers of sewers—around thirteen hundred miles," he amended, seeing the blank look on Josh's face. "But don't worry, we'll not get lost. Most have their own street signs."

"Street signs in the sewers?"

"The sewers of Paris are one of the great wonders of this city." Machiavelli smiled.

"Come!" Dee's voice cracked out, echoing in the chamber.

"Do you know where we're going?" Josh asked quietly. He knew from experience that he needed to keep distracted; once he started thinking about the narrowness of the tunnels and the weight of the earth above him, his claustrophobia would reduce him to a wreck.

"We're going down, into the deepest, oldest part of the catacombs. You're going to be Awakened."

"Do you know who we're going to see?"

Machiavelli's usually impassive face twitched in a grimace. "Yes. By reputation only. I've never seen it." He lowered his voice to little more than a whisper and caught Josh's sleeve, pulling him back. "It's not too late to turn back," he said.

Josh blinked in surprise. "Dee wouldn't like that."

"Probably not," Machiavelli agreed with a wry smile.

Josh was puzzled. Dee had said Machiavelli wasn't his friend, and it had been obvious that the two men didn't agree. "But I thought you and Dee were on the same side."

"We are both in the service of the Elders, it is true . . . but I have never approved of the English Magician and his methods."

Ahead of them, Dee turned into a smaller tunnel and stopped before a narrow metal door that was secured by a thick padlock. He pinched through the hasp of the metal lock with fingernails that stank of foul yellow power and pulled open the door. "Hurry," he called back impatiently.

"This . . . this person we're going to see," Josh said slowly, "can they really Awaken my powers?"

"I have no doubt about it," Machiavelli said softly. "Is the Awakening so important to you?" he asked, and Josh was aware that Machiavelli was watching him closely.

"My sister was Awakened—my twin sister," he explained slowly. "I want . . . I *need* to have my powers Awakened so we're alike again." He looked at the tall white-haired man. "Does that make sense?"

Machiavelli nodded, his face an unreadable mask. "But is that the only reason, Josh?"

The boy looked at him for a long moment before he turned away. Machiavelli was right; it wasn't the only reason. When he'd held Clarent, he'd briefly experienced a hint of what it must be like to have Awakened senses. For a few moments, he'd felt truly alive, he'd felt complete . . . and more than anything else, he wanted to experience that feeling again.

Dee led them into another tunnel, which was, if anything, even narrower than the first. Josh felt his stomach clench and his heart start to thump. The tunnel turned and twisted downward in a series of slender stairs. The stones here were older, the steps irregularly shaped, the walls soft and crumbling as they brushed past. In some places it was so narrow that Josh had to turn sideways to slip through. He got stuck in a particularly confined corner and immediately started to feel breathless panic bubbling in his chest. Then Dee caught one arm and unceremoniously yanked him through, tearing a long strip off the back of his T-shirt. "Nearly there," the Magician muttered. He raised his arm slightly and the bobbing ball of silver light rose higher into the air, revealing the tunnel's pitted brickwork.

"Hang on a second; let me catch my breath." Josh bent over, hands on his knees, breathing deeply. He realized that as long as he concentrated on the ball of light and didn't think about the walls and ceiling closing in on him, he was OK. "How do you know where we're going?" he panted. "Have you been here before?"

"I was here once before . . . a long time ago," Dee said with a grin. "Right now, I'm just following the light." The harsh white light turned the Magician's smile into something terrifying.

Josh remembered a trick his football coach had taught him. He wrapped his hands around his stomach and squeezed hard as he breathed in and straightened up. The feeling of queasiness immediately eased. "Who are we going to see?" he asked.

"Patience, humani, patience." Dee looked past Josh to where Machiavelli was standing. "I'm sure our Italian friend will agree. One of the great advantages of immortality is that one learns patience. There is a saying: 'good things come to those who wait.' "

"Not always good things," Machiavelli muttered as Dee turned away.

At the end of the narrow tunnel was a low metal door. It

looked as if it hadn't been opened in decades and had rusted solid into the weeping limestone wall. In the white light, Josh saw that the rust had stained the off-white stone the color of dried blood.

The ball of light bobbed in the air while Dee ran his glowing yellow fingernail around the edge of the door, cutting it out of the frame, the stink of rotten eggs blanketing the odor of sewage.

"What's through here?" Josh asked. Now that he'd started to get his fear under control, he was beginning to feel a little excitement. Once he was Awakened, he'd slip away and get back to Sophie. He turned to look at Machiavelli, but the Italian shook his head and pointed to Dee. "Dr. Dee?" Josh asked.

Dee broke open the low door and jerked it out of its frame. Soft stone crumbled and flaked away around it. "If I am correct—and I almost always am," the Magician added, "then this will lead us into the Catacombs of Paris." Dee leaned the door against the wall and then stepped through the opening.

Josh ducked to follow him. "I've never heard of them."

"Few people outside Paris have," Machiavelli said, "and yet, along with the sewers, they are one of the marvels of this city. Over a hundred seventy miles of mysterious and labyrinthine tunnels. The catacombs were once limestone quarries. And now they are filled . . ."

Josh stepped through the opening, straightened up and looked around.

". . . with bones."

The boy felt something twist in the pit of his stomach and he swallowed hard, a sour and bitter taste at the back of his throat. Directly ahead, as far as he could see in the gloomy tunnel, the walls, the curved ceiling and even the floor were composed of polished human bones.

CHAPTER FORTY-SEVEN

*N*icholas had just levered up the manhole cover when Joan's phone rang, the high-pitched warbling scale making them all jump with fright. The Alchemyst dropped the cover back into place with a clang, dancing back before it fell on his toes.

"It's Francis," Joan told them, flipping open the phone. She spoke to Saint-Germain in rapid-fire French and then snapped the cell closed. "He's on his way," she said. "He said that on no account are we to go down into the catacombs without him."

"But we can't wait," Sophie protested.

"Sophie's right. We should—" Nicholas started to say.

"We wait," Joan said firmly in the voice that had once commanded armies. She placed her tiny foot on the manhole cover.

"They'll get away," Sophie said desperately.

"Francis said he knows where they're going," Joan said very softly. She turned to look at the Alchemyst. "He said you do too. Do you?" she demanded.

Nicholas took a deep breath and then nodded grimly. The early-morning light washed all the life from his face, leaving it the color of faded parchment. The circles beneath his eyes were bruise dark and baggy. "I believe so."

"Where?" Sophie asked. She tried to stay calm. She'd always been better at controlling her temper than her brother was, but right now she was close to throwing back her head and screaming in frustration. If the Alchemyst knew where Josh was going, why weren't they heading there now?

"Dee is taking Josh to have his powers Awakened," Flamel said slowly, obviously choosing his words with care.

Sophie frowned, confused. "Is that so bad? Isn't that what we wanted?"

"Yes, it's what we wanted, but not *how* we wanted it." Although his face was expressionless, there was pain in his eyes. "Much depends on who—or what—Awakens a person's powers. It is a dangerous process. It can even be deadly."

Sophie slowly turned to look at him. "And yet you were willing to allow Hekate to Awaken both Josh and me." Her brother had been right all along: Flamel had put them both in danger. She could see that now.

"It was necessary for your own protection. There were dangers, yes, but neither of you was in any danger from the Goddess herself."

"What sort of dangers?"

"Most of the Elders were never generous toward what

they called humani. Very few of them were prepared to give without attaching some sort of conditions," Flamel explained. "The greatest gift the Elders can bestow is that of immortality. Humans want to live forever. Both Dee and Machiavelli are in service to their Dark Elders who gifted them with immortality."

"In service?" Sophie asked, looking from the Alchemyst to Joan.

"They are servants," Joan said gently, "some would say slaves. It is the price of their immortality and powers."

Joan's phone rang again with the same ring tone and she flipped it open. *"François?"*

"Sophie," Flamel continued quietly, "the gift of immortality can be withdrawn from a person at any time, and if that happens then all of their unnatural years will catch up with them in a matter of moments. Some Elders enslave the humani they Awaken, turn them into little better than zombies."

"But Hekate didn't make me immortal when she Awakened me," Sophie argued.

"Unlike the Witch of Endor, Hekate had no interest in humani for countless generations. She always remained neutral in the wars between those of us who defend humanity and the Dark Elders." A bitter smile twisted his thin lips. "Perhaps if she had chosen a side, she would still be alive today."

Sophie looked into the Alchemyst's pale eyes. She was thinking that if Flamel had not gone into Hekate's Shadowrealm, the Elder would still be alive. "You're saying Josh is in danger," she said finally.

"Terrible danger."

Sophie's gaze never left Flamel's face. Josh was in danger not because of Dee or Machiavelli, but because Nicholas Flamel has placed the two of them in this terrible situation. He was protecting them, he said, and once she had believed that without question. But now . . . now she didn't know what to think.

"Come." Joan snapped her phone shut, caught Sophie's hand and dragged her down the alleyway toward the street. "Francis is on the way."

Flamel took one final look at the manhole cover, then tucked Clarent under his coat and hurried after them.

Joan led them out of the narrow side street onto the Avenue du President Wilson, then quickly turned left onto Rue Debrousse and headed back toward the river. The air was filled with the sounds of countless police and ambulance sirens, and in the skies overhead police helicopters buzzed low over the city. The streets were almost completely empty, and no one paid any attention to three people running for shelter.

Sophie shivered; the whole scene was so surreal. It was like something she'd see in a war documentary on the Discovery Channel.

At the bottom of the Rue Debrousse, they found Saint-Germain waiting in a nondescript black BMW badly in need of washing. The front and rear passenger doors were open slightly, and the tinted driver's window hummed down as they approached. Saint-Germain was grinning delightedly. "Nicholas, you should come home more often; the city is in chaos. It's all terribly exciting. I've not had so much fun in centuries."

Joan slid in beside her husband, while Nicholas and Sophie climbed into the back. Saint-Germain gunned the engine, but Nicholas leaned forward and squeezed his shoulder.

"Not so fast. We don't need to draw any attention to ourselves," he warned.

"But with the panic on the streets, we shouldn't be driving slowly, either," Saint-Germain pointed out. He eased the car away from the curb and set off down the Avenue de New York. He drove with one hand on the steering wheel, the other draped over the seat as he kept twisting around to talk to the Alchemyst.

Completely numb, Sophie slumped against the window, staring out at the river flashing by on her left. In the distance, on the opposite side of the Seine, she could make out the now familiar shape of the Eiffel Tower rising over the rooftops. She was exhausted and her head was spinning. She was confused about the Alchemyst. Nicholas couldn't be bad, could he? Saint-Germain and Joan—Scatty, too—obviously respected him. Even Hekate and the Witch liked him. Flickering thoughts that she knew were not hers hovered at the very edge of her consciousness, but when she tried to focus, they drifted away. They were the Witch of Endor's memories, and she knew instinctively that they were important. They were something to do with the catacombs, and the creature who lived in the depths. . . .

"Officially, the police are reporting that a portion of the catacombs has caved in and brought down some houses with it," Saint-Germain was saying. "They're claiming that the sewers have ruptured and that methane, carbon dioxide and carbon monoxide gas have escaped into the city. The center of Paris is being sealed off and evacuated. People are being advised to remain indoors."

Nicholas leaned back against the leather seats and closed his eyes. "Has anyone been injured?" he asked.

"A few cuts and bruises, but nothing more serious has been reported."

Joan shook her head in amazement. "Considering what's just tromped through the city, that's a minor miracle."

"Any sightings of Nidhogg?" Nicholas asked.

"Not on any of the main news channels yet, but some grainy cell phone images have turned up on blogs, and *Le Monde* and *Le Figaro* are both claiming to have exclusive images of what they are calling 'The Creature from the Catacombs' and 'The Beast from the Pit.' "

Sophie leaned forward, following the conversation. She looked from Nicholas to Saint-Germain and then back at the Alchemyst. "Soon the whole world will know the truth. What happens then?"

"Nothing," the two men said simultaneously.

"Nothing? But that's not possible."

Joan swiveled around in the passenger seat. "But that is what is going to happen. This will be covered up."

Sophie looked at Flamel. He nodded in agreement. "Most people simply won't believe it anyway, Sophie. It will be dismissed as a hoax or a prank. Those who do think it true will be called conspiracy theorists. And you can be sure that

Machiavelli's people are already working to confiscate and destroy every image."

"Within a couple of hours," Saint-Germain added, "the events of this morning will simply be reported as an unfortunate accident. Sightings of a monster will be laughed at and dismissed as hysteria."

Sophie shook her head in disbelief. "You can't hide something like that forever."

"The Elders have been doing it for millennia," Saint-Germain said, tilting the rearview mirror so that he could look at Sophie. In the dark interior of the car, she thought his bright blue eyes were glowing slightly. "And you have to remember that humankind really does not want to believe in magic. They don't want to know that myths and legends were almost always based on the truth."

Joan reached over and laid her hand gently on her husband's arm. "But I do not agree; humans have always believed in magic. It is only in these last few centuries that the belief has fallen away. I think that they really want to believe, because in their hearts they know it to be true. They know that magic really exists."

"I used to believe in magic," Sophie said very quietly. She had turned to look out at the city again, but reflected in the glass, she saw a brightly painted child's bedroom: her bedroom, five, perhaps six years ago. She had no idea where it was—the house in Scottsdale, maybe, or it might have been Raleigh; they'd moved around so much then. She was sitting in the middle of her bed, surrounded by her favorite books. "When I was younger, I read about princesses and wizards and knights and magicians. Even though I knew they were just stories, I wanted the magic to be real. Until now," she added bitterly. She moved her head to glance at the Alchemyst. "Are all the fairy tales true?"

Flamel nodded. "Not every fairy tale, but just about every legend is based on a truth; every myth has a basis in reality."

"Even the scary ones?" she whispered.

"Especially the scary ones."

A trio of news helicopters buzzed low overhead, the noise of their rotors vibrating the interior of the car. Flamel waited until they had passed and then leaned forward. "Where are we going?"

Saint-Germain pointed straight ahead and to the right. "There's a secret entrance to the catacombs in the Trocadéro Gardens. It leads straight down into the forbidden tunnels. I've checked the old maps; I think Dee's route will take them through the sewers first and then down into the lower tunnels. We'll make up some time this way."

Nicholas Flamel sat back in the seat and then reached over and squeezed Sophie's hand. "It's going to be all right," he said.

But Sophie didn't believe him.

The entrance to the catacombs was through a rather ordinary-looking metal grate set into the ground. Partially covered in moss and grass, it was hidden in a stand of trees behind a richly carved and beautifully painted carousel at one end of the Trocadéro Gardens. Usually, the stunning gardens would have been overrun with tourists, but this morning they were deserted, and the carousel's empty wooden horses bobbed up and down below their blue and white striped awning.

Saint-Germain cut across a narrow path and led them into a patch of grass burned brown by the summer sun. He stopped over an unmarked rectangular metal grate. "I haven't used this since 1941." He knelt down, grabbed the bars and tugged. It didn't move.

Joan glanced sidelong at Sophie. "When Francis and I fought with the French Resistance against the Germans, we used the catacombs as a base. We could pop up anywhere in the city." She tapped the metal grate with the toe of her shoe. "This was one of our favorite spots. Even during the war the gardens were always full of people, and we could mingle easily with the crowds."

The air was suddenly touched with the rich autumnal scent of burnt leaves, and then the metal bars in Francis's hands began to glow with a rich red-hot, then white-hot, heat. The metal turned to liquid and melted away, thick blobs disappearing down into the shaft. Saint-Germain wrenched the remainder of the grating out of the hole and tossed it to one side, then swung himself into the opening. "There's a ladder here."

"Sophie, you go next," Nicholas said. "I'll come after you. Joan, will you take up the rear?"

Joan nodded. She caught the edge of a nearby wooden park bench and dragged it across the grass. "I'll pull it over the opening before I climb down. We don't want any unexpected visitors dropping in, do we?" She smiled.

Sophie gingerly climbed into the opening, her feet finding the rungs of the ladder. She carefully lowered herself. She'd been expecting it to be foul and horrible, but it just smelled dry and musty. She started counting the steps but lost count somewhere around seventy-two, though she could tell by the rapidly diminishing square of sky above their heads that they were climbing deep underground. She wasn't scared—not for herself. Tunnels and narrow spaces held no fears for her, but her brother was terrified of small spaces: how was he feeling now? Butterflies shifted in her stomach; she felt queasy. Her mouth went dry and she knew—instinctively, unquestioningly—that this was how her brother was feeling right at that moment. She knew that Josh was terrified.

CHAPTER FORTY-EIGHT

"Bones," Josh said numbly, looking up and down the tunnel.

The wall directly before him was created from hundreds of stained-yellow and bleached-white skulls. Dee strode down the corridor and his sphere of light sent shadows dancing and twitching, making it appear as if the empty eye sockets were moving, following him.

Josh had grown up with bones; he knew they were nothing to be frightened of. His father's study was full of skeletons. As children, both he and Sophie had played in museum storerooms full of skeletal remains, but they had all been animal and dinosaur bones. Josh had even helped piece together the tailbone of a raptor that had gone on display in the American Museum of Natural History. But these bones . . . these were . . . these were . . .

"Are these all human bones?" he whispered.

"Yes," Machiavelli said softly, his voice now touched with a trace of his Italian accent. "There are the remains of at least six million bodies down here. Maybe more. The catacombs were originally huge limestone quarries." He jerked his thumb upward. "The same limestone used to build the city. Paris is built over a warren of tunnels."

"How did they get down here?" Josh's voice trembled. He coughed, wrapped his arms tightly around his body and tried to look nonchalant, as if he weren't completely terrified. "They look ancient; how long have they been here?"

"A couple of hundred years only," Machiavelli said, surprising him. "By the end of the eighteenth century, the graveyards of Paris were overflowing. I was in the city then," he added, mouth twisting in disgust. "I'd never seen anything like it. There were so many dead in the city that the graveyards were often just huge mounds of piled earth with bones visible in them. Paris might have been one of the most beautiful cities in the world, but it was also the foulest. Worse than London—and that's saying something!" He laughed, and the sound echoed and reechoed off the bone walls and was distorted into something hideous. "The stink was indescribable, and there truly were rats as big as dogs. Disease was rife and outbreaks of plague were common. Finally, it was recognized that the overflowing graveyards must have something to do with the contagion. So it was decided to empty the graveyards and move the remains down into the empty quarries."

Trying not to think about the fact that he was surrounded by the bones of people who had most likely died from some terrible disease, Josh focused on the walls. "Who made the patterns?" he asked, pointing to a particularly ornate sunburst design that had been created using human bones of various length to represent the sunbeams.

Machiavelli shrugged. "Who knows? Someone who wished to honor the dead, perhaps; someone trying to make sense out of what must have been incredible chaos. Humans are always looking to make order out of chaos," he added softly.

Josh looked at him. "You call them . . . *us,* 'humans.' " He turned to look for Dee, but the Magician had almost reached the end of the corridor and was out of earshot. "Dee calls us humani."

"Don't confuse me with Dee," Machiavelli said with an icy smile.

Josh was confused. Who was the more powerful here— Dee or Machiavelli? He'd thought it was the Magician, but he was beginning to suspect that the Italian was much more in control. "Scathach told us you were more dangerous and more cunning than Dee," he said, thinking aloud.

Machiavelli's smile turned to a delighted grin. "That's the nicest thing she's ever said about me."

"Is it true? Are you more dangerous than Dee?"

Machiavelli took a moment to consider. Then he smiled and the faintest hint of serpent filled the tunnel. "Absolutely."

"Hurry; this way," Dr. Dee called back, voice flattened by the narrow walls and low ceiling. He turned and headed off down the bone-lined tunnel, taking the light with him. Josh was tempted to run after him, unwilling to be alone in the utter darkness, but then Machiavelli snapped his fingers and an elegant candle-thin flame of gray-white light appeared in the palm of his hand.

"Not all the tunnels are like this," Machiavelli continued, indicating the neatly set bones in the walls, the regular shapes and patterns. "Some of the small tunnels are simply piled high with assorted bits and pieces."

They rounded a curve in the tunnel and found Dee waiting for them, tapping his foot impatiently. He turned and marched away without saying a word.

Josh concentrated on Dee's back and the globe of light bobbing over his shoulder as they wound deeper and deeper into the catacombs; doing that helped him to ignore the walls that seemed to be closing in with every step. He noticed as he walked along that some of the bones lining the tunnel had dates scratched on them, centuries-old graffiti, and he was conscious too that the only footsteps in the thick layer of dust on the floor were the imprints of Dee's small feet. These tunnels had not been used in a very long time.

"Do people ever come down here?" he asked Machiavelli, making conversation just for the sake of hearing a sound in the oppressive silence.

"Yes. Portions of the catacombs are open to the public," Machiavelli said, holding his hand high, the thin flame picking out the ornate patterns of bones set in the walls, dancing shadows bringing them to flickering life. "But there are many kilometers of catacombs beneath the city, and vast tracts of it have not been mapped. Exploring those tunnels is dangerous and illegal, of course, but people still do it. Those people are called cataphiles. There's even a special police unit, the cataflics, that patrols these tunnels." Machiavelli waved an arm at the surrounding walls, the flame dancing wildly but not extinguishing. "But we'll run into neither group down here. This area is completely unknown. We are deep below the city now, in one of the very first quarries excavated many centuries ago."

"Deep below the city," Josh repeated slowly. He hunched his shoulders, imagining he could actually feel the weight of Paris over his head, the many tons of earth, concrete and steel pressing down on him. Claustrophobia threatened to overwhelm him, and he felt as if the walls were throbbing, pulsing. His throat was dry, his lips cracked, and his tongue felt too big in his mouth. "I think," he whispered to Machiavelli, "I think I'd like to head back up to the surface now, if that's OK."

The Italian blinked in genuine surprise. "No, Josh, no, it's not OK." Machiavelli reached out and squeezed Josh's shoulder and the boy felt a rush of warmth flow through his body. His aura crackled, and the close air in the tunnel was touched with the scent of orange and the rank odor of snake. "It's too late for that," Machiavelli said gently. He lowered his voice to a whisper. "We've gone too deep . . . there's no turning back. You will leave these catacombs Awakened or . . ."

"Or what?" Josh asked, when he realized, with a growing sense of horror, how the Italian was going to finish the sentence.

"Or you will not leave them at all," Machiavelli said simply.

They rounded a curve and started down a long arrow-straight tunnel. The walls here were even more ornately decorated in bone but with strange square patterns that Josh almost recognized. They were similar to drawings he'd seen in his father's study and looked like Maya or Aztec glyphs; but what were Meso-American hieroglyphs doing in the Catacombs of Paris?

Dee was waiting for them at the end of the tunnel. His gray eyes sparkled in the reflected light, which also lent his skin an unhealthy glow. When he spoke, his English accent had thickened, and the words tumbled so quickly it was difficult to comprehend what he was saying. Josh couldn't tell if the Magician was excited or nervous, and that made him even more afraid.

"This is now a momentous day for you, boy, a momentous day. For not only will your powers be Awakened, but you will also meet one of the few Elders who is still remembered by humanity. It is a great honor." He clapped his hands together. Ducking his head, he raised his hand, bringing up the globe of light, and revealed two tall arched columns of bones that had been shaped to form a doorframe. Beyond the opening, there was utter blackness. Stepping back, he directed, "You first."

Josh hesitated and Machiavelli caught his arm and squeezed tightly. When he spoke, his voice was low and urgent. "Whatever happens, you must not show fear, and do not panic. Your life, your very sanity, depends on it. Do you understand?"

"No fear, no panic," Josh repeated. He was starting to hyperventilate. "No fear, no panic."

"Go now." Machiavelli released the boy's arm and pushed

him forward toward Dee and the bone doorway. "Have your powers Awakened," he said, "and I hope it will be worth it."

Something in Machiavelli's voice made Josh look back. There was a look almost of pity on the Italian's face, and Josh stopped. Dee looked at him, gray eyes glittering, lips twisted in an ugly smile. He raised his eyebrows. "Don't you want to be Awakened?"

And Josh really had only one answer to that.

Glancing back at Machiavelli again, he half raised a hand in farewell, took a deep breath and stepped through the arched doorway into the pitch-black. Light blossomed as Dee followed him, and the boy discovered that he was standing in a vast circular chamber that seemed to be carved entirely out of one enormous bone—the smoothly curved walls, the polished yellow ceiling, even the parchment-colored floor were the same shade and texture as the bone-filled walls outside.

Dee put his hand on the small of Josh's back and urged him forward. Josh took two steps and stopped. The past few days had taught him to expect surprises—wonders, creatures and monsters: but this, this was . . . disappointing.

The chamber was empty except for a long rectangular raised stone plinth in the center of the room. Dee's globe of light bobbed over the platform, harshly illuminating every carved detail. Lying flat on the top of a pitted slab of limestone was a huge statue of a man in ancient-looking metal and leather armor, gauntleted hands wrapped around the thick hilt of a broadsword that was at least six feet long. Rising up on his toes, Josh could see that the statue's head was covered in a helmet that completely concealed the face.

Josh looked around. Dee was standing to the right of the doorway and Machiavelli had stepped into the room and taken up a position on the left. They were both watching him intently. "What . . . what happens now?" he asked, his voice flat and muffled in the chamber.

Neither man responded. Machiavelli folded his arms and tilted his head slightly to one side, eyes narrowing.

"Who's this?" Josh asked, jerking a thumb at the statue. He didn't expect to get an answer from Dee, but when he turned to the Italian he realized that Machiavelli wasn't looking at him, he was looking *beyond* him. Josh spun around . . . just as two nightmarish creatures materialized out of the shadows.

Everything about them was white, from their almost transparent skin to the long fine hair that flowed down their backs and brushed the floor behind them. It was impossible to say whether they were male or female. They were the size of small children, unnaturally thin, with bulbous heads, broad foreheads and pointed chins. Overlarge ears and tiny nubs of horn grew out of the top of their skulls. Huge circular eyes without any pupils fixed on him, and when the creatures stepped forward, he realized that there was something wrong with their legs. Their thighs curved backward, and then the legs jutted forward at the knee and ended in goatlike hooves.

They separated as they came around the slab, and Josh's instinct was to back away from them, but then he remembered Machiavelli's advice and stood his ground. Taking a deep breath, he looked closely at the nearer creature and discovered that it was not quite as terrifying as it looked at first: it was so small it appeared almost fragile. He thought he knew what they were; he'd seen images of them on fragments of Greek and Roman pottery on the bookshelves in his mom's study. They were fauns, or maybe satyrs; he wasn't sure what the difference was.

The creatures slowly circled Josh, reaching for him with icy long-fingered hands tipped with filthy black nails, stroking his torn T-shirt, pinching the fabric of his jeans. They spoke together, chattering in high-pitched, almost inaudible voices that set his teeth on edge. One bone-chilling finger touched the flesh of his stomach and his aura spat and crackled gold sparks. "Hey!" he shouted. The creatures jumped back, but that single touch had set Josh's heart racing. He was abruptly gripped by every nameless fear he'd ever imagined, and all the nightmares that most terrified him flooded to the surface, leaving him gasping and shaking, bathed in a bitter icy sweat. The second faun darted forward and laid a cold hand on Josh's face. Suddenly, his heart was tripping madly, his stomach churning with mindless panic.

The two creatures held each other and jumped up and down, shaking with what could only be laughter.

"Josh." Machiavelli's commanding voice broke through the boy's rising panic and silenced the creatures. "Josh. Listen to me. Hear my voice, concentrate on it. The satyrs are simple creatures and feed off the most basic of human emotions: one gorges itself on fear, the other delights in panic. They are Phobos and Deimos."

At the mention of their names, the two satyrs started

back, fading into the shadows, until only their huge liquid eyes were visible, black and shining in the light of the hovering globe.

"They are the Guardians of the Sleeping God."

And then, with a grinding of ancient stone, the statue sat up and swiveled its head to look at Josh. Within the helmet, two eyes blazed bloodred.

CHAPTER FORTY-NINE

"*I*s this a Shadowrealm?" Sophie asked in a horrified whisper, her breath catching in her throat.

She was standing at the entrance to a long straight tunnel whose walls were decorated and lined with what looked like human bones. A single low-wattage bulb lit the space with a dull yellow light.

Joan squeezed her arm and laughed gently. "No. We're still in our world. Welcome to the Catacombs of Paris."

Sophie's eyes flickered silver as the Witch's knowledge flowed through her. The Witch of Endor knew these catacombs well. Sophie rocked back on her heels as a sudden array of images engulfed her: men and women wearing little more than rags quarrying stone from huge pits in the ground, watched over by guards wearing the uniforms of Roman centurions. "These were quarries," she whispered.

"A long time ago," Nicholas said. "And now it is a tomb for millions of Parisians and one other. . . ."

"The Sleeping God," Sophie said, her voice cracking. This was an Elder the Witch both loathed and pitied.

Saint-Germain and Joan were shocked by the girl's knowledge. Even Flamel looked startled.

Sophie started shivering. She wrapped her arms around her body, trying to stand upright as dark thoughts crashed through her brain. The Sleeping God had once been an Elder. . . .

. . . On a burning battlefield, she saw a lone warrior in metal and leather armor, wielding a sword almost as tall as he, fighting off creatures straight out of the Jurassic Age.

. . . At the gates of an ancient city, the warrior in metal and leather stood alone against a vast horde of apelike beast-men while a column of refugees escaped through another gate.

. . . On the steps of an impossibly high pyramid, the warrior defended a lone woman and child from creatures that were a cross between serpents and birds.

"Sophie . . ."

She shivered, ice-cold now, teeth chattering. The images changed; the warrior's polished leather and metal armor had turned filthy, encrusted with mud, streaked and stained. The warrior, too, was changed.

. . . The warrior raced through a primitive ice-locked village, howling like a beast, while fur-wrapped humans fled from him or cowered in fear.

. . . The warrior rode at the head of a vast army that was a mongrel mix of beasts and men bearing down on a sparkling city in the heart of an empty desert.

. . . The warrior stood in the middle of an enormous library filled with charts, scrolls and books of metal, cloth and bark. The library was burning so intensely that the metal books flowed liquid. Slashing his sword through a series of shelves, he swept more books onto the flames.

"Sophie!"

The girl's aura flickered and crackled as the Alchemyst gripped her shoulders and squeezed hard.

"Sophie!"

Flamel's voice snapped her out of her trance. "I saw . . . I saw . . . ," she began hoarsely. Her throat felt raw, and she'd bitten down so hard on the inside of her cheek that there was the disgusting metallic taste of blood in her mouth.

"I cannot even imagine what you saw," he said gently. "But I think I know *who* you saw. . . ."

"Who was it?" she panted, breathless now. "Who was the warrior in the metal and leather armor?" She knew if she thought hard about him, the Witch's memories would supply his name, but that would also draw her back into the warrior's violent world, and she didn't want that.

"The Elder, Mars Ultor."

"The God of War," Joan of Arc added bitterly.

Without looking or turning her head, Sophie raised her left hand and pointed down a narrow corridor. "He's down there," she said quietly.

"How do you know?" Saint-Germain asked.

"I can feel him," the girl said with a shudder. She rubbed her arms furiously. "It's like something cold and sticky is running down my skin. It's coming from there."

"This tunnel leads us into the secret heart of the catacombs," Saint-Germain said, "into the lost Roman city of Lutetia." He brushed his hands briskly together, showering sparks onto the ground, and then set off down the tunnel, followed by Joan. Sophie was about to follow them when she stopped and looked at the Alchemyst. "What happened to Mars? When I saw him first, I thought he was the defender of humanity. What changed him?"

Nicholas shook his head. "No one knows. Perhaps the answer lies in the Witch's memories?" he suggested. "They must have known one another."

Sophie started to shake her head. "Don't make me think about him . . . ," she began, but it was too late. Even as the Alchemyst was asking the question, a series of terrible images flashed through Sophie's mind. She saw a tall, handsome man standing alone on the top of a dizzyingly high stepped pyramid, arms raised to the heavens. Across his shoulders he wore a spectacular cloak of multicolored feathers. Spread out below the pyramid was a huge stone city, surrounded by a thick jungle. The city was celebrating, the broad streets thronged with people wearing brightly colored clothes, ornate jewelry and extravagant feathered cloaks and headdresses. The only absence of color was in the line of white-clad men and women stretching down the center of the wide main street. Looking more closely, she realized that they were chained together with ropes of leather and vine around their necks. Guards wielding whips and spears were driving them toward the pyramid.

Sophie drew in a deep shuddering breath and blinked away the images. "She knew him," she said coldly. She didn't tell the Alchemyst that the Witch of Endor had once loved Mars . . . but that had been a long time ago, before he had changed, before he had become known as Mars Ultor. The Avenger.

CHAPTER FIFTY

"Hail, Mars, the Lord of War," Dee said loudly.

Completely numb with fright, Josh watched as the huge helmeted head slowly turned to look at Dee. The Magician's aura immediately snapped alight, sizzling yellow and vaporous around him. Within the god's helmet, red light glowed. The head turned again with the sound of grinding stone, and blazing crimson eyes looked at the boy. The two ghost-white satyrs, Phobos and Deimos, crept out of the shadows and crouched behind the stone pedestal, watching Josh intently. Even glancing at them sent waves of panic and fear coursing through his entire body, and he was sure he saw one of them lick thin lips with a tongue the color of an old bruise. Deliberately looking away, he concentrated on the ancient Elder.

"You must show no fear," Machiavelli had said, "and do not panic." But that was easier said than done. Directly in front of him, close enough to touch, was the Elder the

Romans had worshipped as the God of War. Josh had never heard of Hekate or the Witch of Endor, and because he knew nothing about them, they hadn't had the same effect on him. This Elder was different. Now he knew what Dee had meant when he said that this was the Elder remembered by humankind. This was Mars himself, the Elder with a month and a planet named after him.

Josh tried to draw in a deep breath and settle his thumping heart, but he was shaking so hard he could barely breathe. His legs were like jelly, and he felt that at any moment, he could crumple to the ground. Squeezing his mouth shut, he forced himself to draw in air through his nose, trying to remember some of the breathing exercises he'd learned in martial arts class. He closed his eyes tight and wrapped his arms around his body, hugging himself hard. He should be able to do this: he'd seen Elders before; he'd faced the undead and even fought a primeval monster. How hard could this be?

Josh straightened, opened his eyes and looked at the statue of Mars . . . except that it wasn't a statue. This was a living being. There was a thick hard gray crust over his skin and clothing. The only touch of color about the god was in his eyes, which glowed red behind a full-face visor that completely concealed his face.

"Great Mars, it is almost time," Dee said quickly, "time for the Elders to return to the world of the humani." He took a breath and announced dramatically, "We have the Codex."

Josh felt the crackle of parchment under his T-shirt. What would happen to him if they knew he had the two missing pages? Would they still Awaken him?

At the mention of the Codex, the Elder's head snapped toward Dee, eyes blazing, wisps of red smoke drifting from the slit in the helm.

"The prophecy is almost fulfilled," Dee continued quickly. "Soon we will make the Final Summoning. Soon we will free the Lost Elders and return them to their rightful place as rulers of the world. Soon we will return the world to the paradise it once was."

With the sound of grinding stone, Mars swung his legs off the plinth and turned so that he was sitting facing the boy. Josh noticed that every movement sent tiny flakes of what looked like stone skin onto the ground.

Dee's voice rose almost to a shout. "And the first prophecy of the Codex has come to pass. We have found the two that are one. We have found the twins of legend." He waved a hand toward Josh. "This humani possesses an aura of pure gold; his twin sister's aura is unblemished silver."

Mars tilted his head to look at Josh again and then stretched out a gloved hand. It was still a foot and a half away from the boy's shoulder when his aura bloomed silently around him, the bright glow lighting up the interior of the chamber, turning the polished bone walls golden, sending Phobos and Deimos scuttling for shelter in the deepest shadows behind the plinth. The dry air was suddenly rich with the scent of orange.

Squinting against the glow given off by his own skin, feeling the hair on his head standing up, crackling with static, Josh watched in awe as the hardened crust began to fall away from Mars's fingertips to reveal deeply tanned, muscled flesh beneath. The god's own aura flared, outlining the statue in a thick purple-red mist and his healthy skin started to glow an angry red as tiny sparks curled off the aura and stuck to his flesh, quickly cooling and coating it in a gray-white stonelike scab. Josh frowned; it looked as if the god's aura was hardening into a thick shell around him, slowly turning him to stone again.

"The girl's powers have been Awakened," Dee continued, his voice echoing in the chamber. "The boy's have not. If we are to succeed, if we are to bring back the Elders, this boy's powers must be Awakened. Mars Ultor, will you Awaken the boy?"

The god planted his tall broadsword on the ground, the point sinking easily into the bone floor, wrapped both hands around the hilt and leaned forward to look at Josh.

Show no fear and don't panic. Josh straightened and stood tall, then stared directly into the narrow rectangular opening in the stone helm. For the space of a single heartbeat, he thought he caught a flash of brilliantly bright blue eyes in the shadows, before they turned red and glowing again. Josh's aura faded to a dull glow and the two satyrs immediately crept forward, climbing onto the plinth to peer around the god at the boy. The hunger in their eyes was unmistakable now.

"Twins."

It took Josh a moment to realize that Mars had spoken. The god's voice was surprisingly soft and sounded incredibly weary. "Twins?" The question in his voice was unmistakable.

"Y-yes," Josh stammered. "I have a twin sister, Sophie."

"I had twin boys once . . . a long time ago," Mars said, his voice lost and distant. The red glow inside his helm faded and blue eyes blinked again. "Good boys, fine boys," he added, and Josh was unsure whom he was speaking to. "Who is the elder?" he asked. "You or your sister?"

"Sophie," Josh said, lips curling in a sudden smile at the thought of his sister. "But only by twenty-eight seconds."

"And do you love your sister?" Mars asked.

Taken by surprise, Josh said, "Yes . . . well, I mean, yes, of course I do. She's my twin."

Mars nodded. "Romulus, my younger boy, said that too. He swore to me that he loved his brother, Remus. And then he killed him."

The bone chamber fell deathly silent.

Looking into the helmet, Josh saw Mars Ultor's eyes turn blue and wet, and he felt his own eyes fill with tears in sympathy. Then the god's tears hissed to steam as his eyes blazed red again. "I had Awakened my sons' auras, gave them access to powers and abilities beyond those of the humani. All their senses and emotions were heightened . . . including the emotions of hate, fear and love." He paused, and then added, "They had been close—so close—until I Awakened their senses. That destroyed them." There was another, longer pause. "Perhaps it would be better if I did not Awaken you. For your own sake and the sake of your sister."

Josh blinked in surprise and looked over his shoulder at Dee and Machiavelli. The Italian's face was impassive, but Dee looked as stunned as Josh felt. Was Mars refusing to Awaken him?

"Lord Mars," the Magician began, "the boy must be Awakened. . . ."

"It will be his choice," Mars said mildly.

"I demand—"

The glow within the god's helm turned incandescent. "*You* demand!"

"In my master's name, of course," Dee said quickly. "My master demands—"

"Your master can make no demands of me, Magician," Mars whispered. "And if you speak again," he added, "I will loose my companions on you." Phobos and Deimos clambered over the god's shoulders to peer at Dee. They were both drooling. "It is a terrible death." He looked back at Josh. "This is your choice and yours alone. I can Awaken your powers. I can make you powerful. Dangerously powerful." Red eyes blazed brightly, the centers burning yellow hot. "Is this what you want?"

"Yes," Josh said without hesitation.

"There is a price, for everything has a price."

"I'll pay it," Josh said immediately, though he had no idea what that payment might be.

Mars nodded his great head, stone cracking and grinding. "A good response, the correct response. Asking me about the price would have been a mistake."

Phobos and Deimos cackled in what Josh assumed was a laugh, and he immediately knew that others had paid the price for trying to negotiate with the Sleeping God.

"There will come a time when I will remind you that you

are in debt to me." The god looked over Josh's head. "Who will mentor the boy?"

"I will," Dee and Machiavelli said simultaneously.

Josh turned to look at the two immortals, surprised by their response. Of the two, he thought he would prefer to be mentored by Machiavelli.

"Magician, he is yours," Mars said after a moment's consideration. "I can read your intent and your motives clearly. You intend to use the boy to bring back the Elders; I have no doubt of that. But you . . . ," he added, his head swiveling to look at Machiavelli. "I cannot read your aura; I do not know what you want. Perhaps because you have not yet decided."

Rocks snapped and creaked as the god stood. He was at least seven feet tall, his helmeted head almost brushing the ceiling. "Kneel," he said to Josh, who folded to his knees. Mars tugged his huge sword free from the floor and spun it until it was directly in front of the boy's face. Josh went crosseyed looking at the blade. It was so close that he could see where the edge was chipped and pitted and was able to make out the faintest trace of a spiraling pattern down the center of the sword.

"What are your clan name and your parents' names?"

Josh's mouth was so dry he could barely speak. "The clan name? Oh, the family name is Newman. My father is Richard and my mother is Sara." He had a sudden memory of Hekate asking Sophie the same questions. It had been only a couple of days ago, and yet it felt like a lifetime.

The timbre of the god's voice changed, becoming stronger,

loud enough for Josh to feel the vibrations in his bones. "Josh, son of Richard and Sara of the Clan Newman, of the race humani, I will grant you an Awakening. You have acknowledged that this is no gift and there will be a price to pay. If you do not pay it, I will destroy you and everything you hold dear."

"I'll pay," Josh said thickly, blood thundering in his head, adrenaline coursing through his body.

"I know you will." The huge sword moved, first touching Josh's right shoulder, then his left before moving back to his right. The faintest outline of his aura winked into existence around his body. Wisps of gold smoke started to curl off his blond hair, and the scent of citrus grew stronger. "Henceforth you will see with acuity. . . ."

Josh's bright blue eyes turned into solid gold discs. Immediately, tears gathered and ran down his face. They were the color and texture of liquid gold.

"You will hear with clarity. . . ."

Smoke coiled from the boy's ears.

"You will taste with purity. . . ."

Josh opened his mouth and coughed. A puff of saffron-colored mist appeared, and tiny amber sparks danced between his tongue and teeth.

"You will touch with sensitivity. . . ."

The boy brought his hands up to his face. They were glowing so brightly that they were almost transparent. Sparks leapt and curled between each finger, and his badly chewed fingernails were polished mirrors.

"You will smell with intensity. . . ."

424

Josh's head was almost completely enveloped in golden smoke now. It trickled from his nostrils, making it look as if he were breathing fire. His aura had thickened, solidified around his shoulders and across his chest, becoming shiny and reflective.

The god's sword moved again, tapping lightly against the boy's shoulders. "Truly, yours is one of the most powerful auras I have ever encountered," Mars said quietly. "There is something else I can give you—a gift—and this I give freely. You may find it of use in the days to come." Stretching out his left hand, he rested it on top of the boy's head. Instantly, Josh's aura burst into incandescent light. Streamers and globes of yellow fire curled from his body and bounced around the room. Phobos and Deimos were caught by the blast of light and heat, and it sent them squealing and scrambling behind the stone plinth, but not before their pale skin had reddened and the tips of their snow white hair had darkened and crisped. The searing light drove Dee to his knees, gloved hands pressed against his eyes. He rolled over, burying his face in his hands as spheres of fire bounced off the floor and ceiling, spattering against the walls, leaving scorch marks on the polished bone.

Only Machiavelli had escaped the full force of the explosion of light. He'd turned away and ducked out of the room in the last instant before Mars had touched the boy. Curling up in a ball, he hid in the deep shadows outside the door while streamers of yellow light ricocheted off the walls and hissing balls of solid energy blazed out into the corridor. He blinked hard, trying to clear the streaked afterimages seared onto his retinas. Machiavelli had seen Awakenings before, but never anything this dramatic. What was Mars doing to the boy, what gift was he giving him?

Then, through his blurring vision, he saw a vague silvery shape materialize at the other end of the corridor.

And the scent of vanilla filled the catacombs.

CHAPTER FIFTY-ONE

Perched on top of the water tower on Alcatraz, surrounded by huge Dire-Crows, the Morrigan sang softly to herself. It was a song first heard by the most primitive of ancient men, now imprinted deep into humankind's DNA. It was slow and gentle, lost and plaintive, beautiful . . . and utterly terrifying. It was the Song of the Morrigan: a cry designed to inspire fear and terror. And on battlefields across the world and down through time, it was often the last sound a human heard in this life.

The Morrigan drew her black feathered cloak about her and gazed out across the fog-locked bay toward the city. She could feel the heat of the mass of humani, could see the seething glow of almost a million auras within San Fancisco itself. And every aura was wrapped around a humani, each one rich with fears and worries, filled with succulent, tasty emotions. She pressed her hands together and brought the tips of her fingers to her thin black lips. Her ancestors had fed off humankind, had drunk their memories, savored their emotions like fine wines. Soon . . . oh, so very soon, she would be free to do it again.

But before that she had a banquet to enjoy.

Earlier, she'd received a call from Dee. Finally, he and his Elders had been forced to agree that it was now too dangerous to allow both Nicholas and Perenelle to survive; he had given her permission to slay the Sorceress.

The Morrigan had an eyrie high in the San Bernardino Mountains. She would carry Perenelle there and over the next few days drain every last one of the woman's memories and emotions. The Sorceress had lived for almost seven hundred years; she had traveled across the globe and into Shadowrealms, had seen wonders and experienced terrors. And the woman had an extraordinary memory; she would have remembered everything, every emotion, every thought and fear. And the Morrigan would relish them all. When she was finished, the legendary Perenelle Flamel would be little more than a mindless babe. The Crow Goddess threw back her head and opened her mouth wide, her long incisors white and stark against her dark lips, her tongue tiny and black. Soon.

The Morrigan knew that the Sorceress was in the tunnels beneath the water tower. The only other entrance was through a tunnel that was accessible only at low tide. And although the tide would not turn for hours, the rocks and cliff face around the cave mouth were covered with razor-billed crows.

Then the Morrigan's nostrils flared.

Over the salt and iodine smell of the sea, the metallic stink of rusted metal and rotting stone and the musty scent of countless birds, she suddenly smelled something else . . . something that didn't belong, not in this place, not in this age. Something ancient and bitter.

The wind shifted, and the fog curled with it. Beads of salty moisture suddenly glistened on a thread of silver hanging in the air before her. The Morrigan blinked her jet-black eyes. Another thread wavered in the air, and then another and another, crisscrossed in a series of circles. They looked like webs.

They *were* webs.

She was coming to her feet when a monstrous spider erupted from the shaft below her and landed squarely on the side of the water tower, its huge barbed feet biting into the metal. It scuttled toward the Crow Goddess.

The mass of birds ringing the water tower spiraled skyward, screaming raucously . . . and were instantly trapped in the enormous web floating overhead. They fell back on top of their dark mistress, entangling her in a writhing mass of feathers and sticky web. The Morrigan slashed her way free with razor-tipped nails, gathered her cloak about her and was about to take to the air when the spider climbed over the top of the water tower and drove her back, pinning her down with a huge barbed foot.

Perenelle Flamel, astride the spider's back, a blazing spear in her hand, leaned forward and smiled at the Morrigan. "You were looking for me, I believe."

CHAPTER FIFTY-TWO

Sophie ran.

She was no longer afraid; she didn't feel sick or weak anymore. She just had to get to her brother. Josh was directly ahead of her, in a room at the end of the tunnel. She could see the golden glow of his aura lighting up the darkness, smell the mouthwatering scent of oranges.

Pushing past Nicholas, Joan and Saint-Germain, ignoring their cries to stop, Sophie raced for the glowing arched doorway. She had always been a good runner and held track records for the hundred-meter in most of the schools she'd attended, but now she practically flew down the corridor. And with every step, her aura—fueled by anger and determination—grew around her, sparking, crackling and metallic. Her enhanced senses flared, her pupils shrinking to dots and then expanding to silver discs, and instantly the shadows vanished and she could see the gloomy catacomb in all its shocking detail. Her nostrils were assaulted with a variety of smells—snake and sulfur, rot and mold—but stronger than all the others was the orange scent of her brother's aura.

And she knew she was too late: he had been Awakened.

Ignoring the man crouching on the ground outside the chamber, Sophie raced through the doorway . . . and her aura instantly hardened to a metallic shell as blazing arcs of gold fire bounced off the walls to spatter against her. She staggered, battered by the energy. Gripping the edge of the door, she held on to prevent herself from being pushed back out into the corridor.

"Josh," she said, awed by the sight before her.

Josh was kneeling on the ground before what could only be Mars. The huge Elder was holding a broadsword aloft in his left hand, the point touching the ceiling, while his right was clamped onto her brother's head. Josh's aura was blazing like wildfire, cocooning him in golden light. Yellow fire spun around him, throwing off spheres and whips of energy. They splashed against the walls and ceilings, cutting away chunks of time-yellowed bone to reveal the white beneath.

"Josh!" Sophie screamed.

The god slowly turned his head and fixed her with glowing red eyes. "Leave," Mars commanded.

Sophie shook her head. "Not without my twin," she said through gritted teeth. She wasn't going to abandon her brother; she'd never do that.

"He is no longer your twin," Mars said mildly. "You are different now."

"He will always be my twin," she said simply.

Pushing into the room, she sent a wave of ice-cold silver fog rolling out from her body to wash over her brother and the Elder. It hissed and sizzled where it touched Josh's aura, dirty white smoke curling up to gather at the ceiling. It frosted over Mars's hard skin, and ice crystals sparkled in the amber light.

The god slowly lowered his sword. "Have you any idea who I am?" he asked, his voice soft, almost gentle. "If you did, you would fear me."

"You are Mars Ultor," Sophie said slowly, the Witch of Endor's knowledge informing her. "And before the Romans worshipped you, the Greeks knew you as Ares, and before that the Babylonians called you Nergal."

"Who are you?" The Elder's hand dropped away from Josh's head, and instantly, the boy's aura winked out and the fires died.

Josh swayed and Sophie swooped in to catch him before he hit the ground. The moment she touched him, her own aura disappeared, leaving her defenseless. But she'd gone beyond fear now; she felt nothing, only relief that she'd been reunited with her twin. Crouching on the ground, cradling her brother in her arms, Sophie looked up at the towering war god. "And before you were Nergal, you were the champion of the humankind: you were Huitzilopochtli. You led the human slaves to safety when Danu Talis sank beneath the waves."

The god staggered away. The backs of his knees hit the plinth and he sat down suddenly, the massive stone cracking beneath his great weight. "How do you know this?" he asked, and what sounded like fear rattled in his voice.

"Because you walked with the Witch of Endor." She straightened, hauling her brother to his feet. His eyes were open but had rolled back in his head, leaving only the whites showing. "The Witch of Endor gave me all her memories," Sophie said. "I know what you did . . . and why she cursed you." Stretching out her hand, she touched the god's stone-hard skin with her fingertip. A spark snapped. "I know why she did this to your aura."

Draping her brother's arm over her shoulder, she turned her back on the war god. Flamel, Saint-Germain and Joan had arrived and had gathered in the doorway. Joan's sword was loosely pointed at Dee, who was lying unmoving on the floor. No one spoke.

"If you have the Witch's knowledge within you," Mars said urgently, almost pleadingly, "then you know her incantations and cantrips. You know how to lift this curse."

Nicholas hurried forward to lift Josh from Sophie's arms, but she refused to let her brother go. Glancing over her shoulder at the god, she said very softly, "Yes, I know how to lift it."

"Then do it," Mars commanded. "Do it and I will give you everything you want. I can give you anything!"

Sophie thought for a moment. "Can you take away my Awakened senses? Can you make me and my brother normal again?"

There was a long moment of silence before the god spoke again. "No. I cannot do that."

"Then there is nothing you can do for us." Sophie turned away and, with Saint-Germain's assistance, helped Josh out into the corridor. Joan ducked out, leaving only Flamel standing in the doorway.

"Wait!" The god's voice rose and the entire chamber trembled with the sound. Phobos and Deimos slunk out from behind the cracked plinth, chattering noisily. "You will reverse this curse, or . . . ," the god began.

Nicholas stepped forward. "Or what?"

"None of you will leave these catacombs alive," Mars barked. "I will not permit it. And I am Mars Ultor!" The god's hidden eyes blazed bloodred and he took a step forward, swinging the huge sword before him. "Who are you to deny me?"

"I am Nicholas Flamel. And you," he added, "are an Elder who made the mistake of believing that you were a god." He snapped his fingers and dust motes of glittering emerald drifted to the bone floor. They raced across the smoothly polished surface, leaving tiny threads of green in the aged yellow. "I am the Alchemyst . . . and let me introduce you to the greatest secret of alchemy: transmutation." And then he turned back to the corridor and disappeared into the shadows.

"No!" Mars took a step forward and instantly sank up to his ankle in the floor, which had suddenly turned soft and gelatinous. The god took another shuddering step and then lost his footing as the ground melted beneath his weight. He crashed forward, hitting the floor hard enough to send splashes of jellylike bone onto the walls. His sword bit a huge chunk out of the wall where, a moment earlier, Flamel had been standing. Mars struggled to regain his footing, but the floor was a shifting quagmire of sticky semiliquid bone. Rising to his hands and knees, Mars thrust his head forward to glare at Dee, who was slowly crawling out of the liquid toward the door. "This is your doing, Magician!" he howled savagely, the entire chamber vibrating with his rage. Bone dust and chips of ancient stone rained down. "I hold you responsible."

Dee staggered to his feet and leaned against the door-frame, shaking glutinous jelly off his hands, brushing it off his ruined trousers.

"Bring me the girl and the boy," Mars snarled, "and I may forgive you. Bring me the twins. Or else."

"Or else—what?" Dee asked mildly.

"I will destroy you: not even your Elder master will be able to protect you from my wrath."

"Don't you dare threaten me!" Dee said, his voice an ugly snarl. "And I don't need my Elder to protect me."

"Fear me, Magician, for you have made an enemy of me."

"Do you know what I do to those who frighten me?" Dee demanded, his accent thickening. "I destroy them!" The room suddenly filled with the stench of sulfur, and then the bone walls began to run and melt like soft ice cream. "Flamel is not the only alchemist who knows the secret of trans-mutation," he said as the ceiling turned soft and liquid, long strands dripping down to the floor, covering Mars in sticky fluid. Then it began to rain bone in huge yellow drops.

"Destroy him!" Mars howled. Phobos and Deimos leapt from the plinth onto the Elder's back, teeth and claws extended, huge eyes fixed on Dee.

The Magician spoke a single word of power and snapped his fingers: the liquid bone instantly hardened.

Niccolò Machiavelli appeared in the doorway. He folded his arms and looked into the chamber. In the center of the room, caught as he tried to rise from the floor, the two satyrs on his back, was Mars Ultor, frozen in bone.

"So the catacombs of Paris have yet another mysterious bone statue," the Italian said mildly. Dee turned away. "First you kill Hekate and now Mars," Machiavelli continued. "And I thought you were supposed to be on our side. You do realize," he called after Dee, "that we are both dead men. We've failed to capture Flamel and the twins. Our masters will not forgive us."

"We've not failed yet," Dee called back. He was almost at the end of the corridor. "I know where this tunnel comes out. I know how we can capture them." He stopped and looked back, and when he spoke, the words came slowly, almost reluctantly. "But . . . Niccolò . . . we will need to work together. We will need to combine our powers."

"What do you intend to do?" Machiavelli asked.

"Together, we can loose the Guardians of the City."

CHAPTER FIFTY-THREE

$\mathcal{T}$he Morrigan managed to struggle to her feet, but a spiderweb as thick as her arm wrapped around her waist and twisted between her legs, entangling them, and she fell. She started to slide over the side of the water tower when a second and then a third web caught her, curling around her body, wrapping it from neck to toes in a thick mummylike shell. Perenelle leapt off Areop-Enap's back and crouched beside the Crow Goddess. The head of her spear vibrated with energy, and red and white smoke coiled into the damp night air. "You probably feel like screaming right now," Perenelle said with a wry smile. "Go ahead."

The Morrigan obliged. Her jaws unhinged, black lips parted to reveal her savage teeth and she howled.

The nerve-shattering cry echoed across the island. Every unbroken pane of glass on Alcatraz shattered into powder, and the entire water tower swayed. Across the bay, the city came awake as business, house and car alarms along the waterfront burst into cacophonous life. Every dog within a hundred-mile radius of the island started yowling piteously.

But the scream also brought the rest of the huge flock of gathered birds surging into the night sky in a thunderous explosion of flapping wings and raucous cries. Most were immediately entangled and brought down by a thick cloud of spiderwebs hanging in the air between the desolate buildings, draped across every open window, spun from pole to pole. The moment the ensnared birds hit the ground, spiders of every shape and size swarmed over them, cocooning them in thick silver webs. Within moments, the island fell silent again.

A handful of Dire-Crows escaped. Six of the huge birds swooped low over the island, avoiding the festoons and nets of sticky web. The birds curled out over San Francisco Bay toward the bridge, soared high and then swung back to attack. Now they were above the entangling spiderwebs. They circled over the water tower. Twelve pitch-black eyes fixed on Perenelle, and razor beaks and dagger-tipped claws opened as they dropped silently toward the woman.

Crouched over the Morrigan, Perenelle caught the flickering hint of movement reflected in her adversary's black eyes. The Sorceress brought the spearhead to blazing life with a single word and spun it in her hand, leaving a red triangle burning in the foggy air. The savage birds flew through the red fire . . . and *changed*.

Six perfect eggs dropped out of the sky and were plucked out of midair by strands of gossamer-thin spiderweb.

"Breakfast," Areop-Enap said delightedly, clambering down the side of the tower.

Perenelle sat down beside the struggling Crow Goddess. Resting the spear on her knees, she looked out across the bay in the direction of the city she called home.

"What will you do now, Sorceress?" the Morrigan demanded.

"I have no idea," Perenelle said truthfully. "It seems Alcatraz is mine." She sounded almost bemused by the idea. "Well, mine and Areop-Enap's."

"Unless you've managed to master the art of flight, you are trapped here," the Morrigan snarled. "This is Dee's property. No tourists come here now; there are no sightseers, no fishing boats. You are still as much a prisoner as when you were in your cell. And the sphinx patrols the corridors below. She'll be coming for you."

The Sorceress smiled. "She can try." She twirled the spear. It hummed in the air. "I wonder what this would turn her into: baby girl, lion cub or bird egg."

"You know that Dee will return—and in force. He'll want his army of monsters."

"I'll be waiting for him, too," the Sorceress promised.

"You cannot win," the Morrigan spat.

"People have been telling Nicholas and me that for centuries. And yet, we're still here."

"What will you do with me?" the Crow Goddess asked eventually. "Unless you kill me, you know I'll never rest until you are dead."

Perenelle smiled. She brought the spearhead close to her

lips and blew gently on it until it glowed white-hot. "I wonder what this would turn *you* into?" she asked absently. "Bird or egg?"

"I was born, not hatched," the Morrigan said simply. "You cannot threaten me with death. It holds no fear for me."

Perenelle got to her feet and planted the butt of the spear on the ground. "I'm not going to kill you. I've got a much more suitable punishment in store for you." She looked toward the skies, and the wind took her long hair, blowing it straight out behind her. "I've often wondered what it would be like to be able to fly, to soar silently through the heavens."

"There is no greater feeling," the Morrigan said honestly.

Perenelle's smile was icy. "That's what I thought. So I'm going to take away that which you hold most precious: your freedom and your ability to fly. I have the most wonderful cell just for you."

"No prison can hold me," the Morrigan said contemptuously.

"It was designed to hold Areop-Enap," Perenelle said. "Deep underground, you will never see the sunlight or fly in the air again."

The Morrigan howled again and thrashed from side to side. The water tower shifted and trembled, but the Old Spider's web was unbreakable. Then the Crow Goddess abruptly fell silent. The wind picked up, and fog swirled around the two women. They could hear the clanging of distant alarms from San Francisco.

The Morrigan began to heave a series of hacking coughs,

and it took Perenelle a moment before she realized that the Crow Goddess was laughing. Although she had an idea she was not going to like the answer, Perenelle asked, "And do you want to tell me what you find so amusing?"

"You may have defeated me," the Morrigan heaved, "but you are already dying. I can see the age on your face and hands."

Perenelle raised her hand to her face and moved the spearhead so that it shed light on her flesh. She was shocked to discover a speckling of brown spots on the back of her hand. She touched her face and neck, fingers tracing the lines of new wrinkles.

"How long before the alchemical formula wears off, Sorceress? How long before you wither into shriveled old age? Is it measured in days or weeks?"

"A lot can happen in a few days."

"Sorceress, listen to me now. Listen to the truth. The Magician is in Paris. He has captured the boy and loosed Nidhogg on your husband and the others." She coughed another laugh. "I was sent here to kill you because you and your husband are worthless. The twins are the key to the future."

Perenelle leaned close to the Morrigan. The spearhead shed a crimson glow over both their faces, making them look like hideous masks. "You're right. The twins are the key to the future—but whose: the Dark Elders' or humankind's?"

CHAPTER FIFTY-FOUR

*N*iccolò Machiavelli took a tentative step forward and looked down over the city of Paris. He was standing on the roof of the great Gothic cathedral of Notre Dame; below was the river Seine and the Pont au Double, and directly spread out before him was the broad *parvis*, the square. Holding tightly to the ornate brickwork, he drew in a deep shuddering breath and willed his thumping heart to slow. He had just climbed one thousand and one steps up out of the catacombs onto the roof of the cathedral, following a secret route Dee claimed he'd used before. His legs were trembling with the effort and his knees ached. Machiavelli liked to think that he kept himself in good condition—he was a strict vegetarian and exercised every day—but the climb had exhausted him. He was also vaguely irritated that the strenuous climb hadn't affected Dee in the slightest. "When did you say you were last up here?" he asked.

"I didn't say," the Magician snapped. He was standing to Machiavelli's left, in the shadow of the south tower. "But if you must know, it was in 1575." He pointed off to one side. "I met the Morrigan right there. It was on this roof that I first learned of the true nature of Nicholas Flamel and the existence of the Book of Abraham. So perhaps it is fitting that it ends here too."

Machiavelli leaned out and looked down. He was standing almost directly above the west rose window. The square below him should have been thronged with tourists, but it was eerily deserted. "And how do you know Flamel and the others will come out here?" he asked.

Dee's small teeth flashed in an ugly grin. "We know the boy is claustrophobic. His senses have just been Awakened. When he comes out of whatever trance Mars left him in, he's going to be terrified, and his heightened senses will only add to that terror. For the sake of his sanity, Flamel will have to get him above ground as quickly as possible. I know that there is a secret passage leading from the buried Roman city into the cathedral." He suddenly pointed down as five figures stumbled out of the central door directly below them. "You see?" he said triumphantly. "I'm never wrong." He looked at Machiavelli. "You know what we have to do?"

The Italian nodded. "I know."

"You don't look too happy about it."

"Defacing a beautiful building is a crime."

"But killing people is not?" Dee asked.

"Well, people can always be replaced."

❖　❖　❖

"Let me just sit," Josh gasped. Without waiting for a response, he crumpled out of his sister's and Saint-Germain's hands and sat down on a smooth circular stone set into the cobbled square. Bringing his knees up to his chest, he rested his chin on his kneecaps and wrapped his arms around his shins. He was shaking so hard that his heels were tapping off the stone.

"We really need to keep moving," Flamel said urgently, looking around.

"Give us a minute," Sophie snapped. Kneeling beside her brother, she reached out to touch him, but a spark cracked between her fingertips and his arm and they both jumped. "I know what you're feeling," she said gently. "Everything is so . . . so bright, so loud, so sharp. Your clothes feel so heavy and rough against your skin, your shoes are too tight. But you do get used to it. The feelings do go away." He was undergoing what she'd experienced only a couple of days ago.

"My head is throbbing," Josh mumbled. "It feels like it's about to explode, like it's crammed with too much information. I keep thinking these strange thoughts. . . ."

The girl frowned. That didn't sound right. When she'd been Awakened, her senses had been overwhelmed, but it was only when the Witch of Endor had poured knowledge into her that she'd felt as if her brain were about to burst. A sudden thought struck her, and she remembered that when she'd raced into the chamber, she'd seen the Elder's huge hand pressing on her brother's head. "Josh," she said quietly. "When Mars Awakened you, what did he say?"

Her brother shook his head miserably. "I don't know."

444

"Think," she said sharply, and saw him wince at the sound of her voice. "Please, Josh," she said quietly. "This is important."

"You're not the boss of me," he muttered with a trace of a smile.

"I know." She grinned. "But I'm still your big sister— now tell me!"

Josh frowned, but the effort hurt his forehead. "He said . . . he said that the Awakening wasn't a gift, that it was something I would have to pay for later."

"What else?"

"He said . . . he said that mine was one of the most powerful auras he'd ever encountered." Josh had been looking at the god as he'd spoken the words, seeing him for the first time with Awakened eyes, noticing the intricate detail on his helm and the ornate design on his leather breastplate and hearing clearly the pain in his voice. "He said he was going to give me a gift, something I might find useful in the days to come."

"And?"

"I have no idea what that was. When he put his hand on my head, I felt as if he was trying to push me through the floor. The pressure was incredible."

"He's passed something to you," Sophie said, worried. "Nicholas," she called.

But there was no response, and when she turned to look for the Alchemyst she found him, Saint-Germain and Joan staring back at the great cathedral.

"Sophie," Nicholas said calmly, without turning around,

"help your brother to his feet. We need to get out of here right now. Before it's too late."

His calm, reasoned tone frightened her more than if he had shouted. Catching her brother under both arms, ignoring the rattling snap of their auras, she hauled him upright and turned around. Facing them were three squat mismatched monsters.

"I think it's already too late," she said.

Over the centuries, Dr. John Dee had learned how to animate Golems and had also managed to create and control simulacra and homunculi. One of the earliest skills Machiavelli had mastered was the ability to control a tulpa. The process was surprisingly similar; all that really differed were the materials.

They could both bring the inanimate to life.

Now the Magician and the Italian stood side by side on the roof of Notre Dame and focused their wills.

And one by one, the gargoyles and grotesques of Notre Dame came to creaking life.

The gargoyles—the water spouts—moved first.

Singly and in pairs, then in dozens and suddenly in hundreds, they broke free of the cathedral walls. Crawling out from the hidden places—the unseen eaves, the forgotten gutters—stone dragons and serpents, goats and monkeys, cats, dogs and monsters slithered down the front of the building.

Then the grotesques—the hideous carved statues—came to lumbering life. Lions, tigers, apes and bears tore themselves free from the medieval stonework and clambered down the building.

"This is really very, very bad," Saint-Germain muttered.

A crudely carved lion dropped to the ground directly in front of the cathedral door and padded forward, stone claws clicking and sliding on the smooth cobbles.

Saint-Germain threw out his hand and the lion was engulfed in a ball of fire . . . which had no effect on it, other than to burn off centuries of dirt and bird droppings. The lion kept coming. Saint-Germain tried different types of fire—darts and sheets of flame, fire balls and whips—but to no avail.

More and more of the gargoyles dropped to the ground. A few shattered on impact, but most survived. They spread out, filling the square, and then they started to close in, tightening the noose. Some of the creatures were intricately and beautifully carved; others had been weathered to little more than anonymous lumps. The bigger gargoyles lumbered slowly while the smaller grotesques darted about. But they all moved in absolute silence, save for the grinding scrape of stone on stone.

A creature that was half man, half goat shuffled out of the approaching crowd, dropped to all fours and trotted forward, wickedly curved stone horns slashing at Saint-Germain. Joan jumped forward and chopped at the creature, her sword striking sparks off its neck. The blow didn't even slow it down. Saint-Germain managed to throw himself to one side at the last minute, then made the mistake of slapping the beast on the rump as it went past. His hand stung. The goat-man tried to stop on the cobbles and slipped, crashing to the ground and cracking off one of his horns.

Nicholas drew Clarent and spun around, holding the sword in both hands, wondering which creature would attack first. A bear with the head of a woman lumbered forward, claws extended. Nicholas jabbed with Clarent, but the sword screamed harmlessly off the creature's stone hide. He quickly cut at the beast with the edge of the sword, but the vibration numbed his entire arm, almost knocking the sword from his grip. The bear swiped a massive paw that whispered over the Alchemyst's head. It teetered off balance, and Nicholas rushed forward to throw his weight against it. The bear crashed to the ground. Its claws beat against the cobblestones, shattering them to dust as it attempted to regain its feet.

Standing before her brother, desperately trying to shield him, Sophie loosed a series of small whirlwinds. They bounced harmlessly off most of the stones and did nothing more than send a newspaper spiraling high into the sky.

"Nicholas," Saint-Germain said desperately as the circle of stone creatures drew even closer. "A little magic, some alchemy, would be good now."

Nicholas held out his right hand. A tiny sphere of green glass formed in it. Then it cracked and the liquid contents flowed back into his skin. "I'm not strong enough," the Alchemyst answered sadly. "The transmutation spell in the catacombs exhausted me."

The gargoyles shuffled closer, stone grinding, cracking with every step. Small grotesques were pulverized to dust if they were caught under the bigger creatures' feet.

"They'll just roll right over us," Saint-Germain muttered.

"Dee must be controlling them," Josh mumbled. He slumped against his sister, hands pressed against his ears. Every grinding footstep, every crack of stone, was agony to his Awakened hearing.

"There's too many here for just one man," Joan said. "It has to be Dee *and* Machiavelli."

"But they must be close by," Nicholas said.

"Very close," Joan agreed.

"A commander always takes the high ground," Josh said suddenly, surprising himself with the knowledge.

"Which means they're on the roof of the cathedral," Flamel concluded.

Then Joan pointed. "I see them. There, between the towers, directly above the center of the West Rose Window." She tossed her sword to her husband, and then her aura flowed silver around her body and the air filled with the scent of lavender. Her aura hardened, taking on shape and substance, and suddenly a longbow grew out of her left hand while a shining arrow appeared in her right. Drawing back her right arm, she sighted and loosed the arrow, sending it arcing high into the air.

"They've spotted us," Machiavelli said. Huge beads of sweat rolled down his face, and his lips were blue with the effort of controlling the stone creatures.

"It is no matter," Dee said, peering over the edge. "They are powerless." In the square below, the five humans were standing in a circle as the crushing stone statues closed in.

449

"Then let us finish it," Machiavelli said through gritted teeth. "But remember, we need the children alive." He broke off as something slender and silver arced through the air before his face. "It's an arrow," he began in wonder, and then stopped and grunted as the arrow plunged deep into his thigh. His entire leg from hip to toe went dead. He staggered back and fell onto the cathedral roof, hands pressed against his leg. Surprisingly, there was no blood, but the pain was excruciating.

On the ground far below, at least half the creatures suddenly froze or toppled over. They crashed to the ground, and those behind tumbled over them. Rock shattered, weathered stone exploding to dust. But still the rest of the creatures pressed on, closing in.

Another dozen silver arrows arced up from below. They pinged and shattered harmlessly against the brickwork.

"Machiavelli!" Dee howled.

"I can't . . ." The pain in his leg was indescribable, and tears rolled down his cheeks. "I can't concentrate. . . ."

"Then I'll finish it myself."

"The boy and girl," Machiavelli said weakly. "We need them alive. . . ."

"Not necessarily. I am a necromancer. I can reanimate their corpses."

"No!" Machiavelli screamed.

Dee ignored him. Focusing his extraordinary will, the Magician issued the gargoyles a single command. "Kill them. Kill them all."

The creatures surged forward.

⬧ ⬧ ✧

"Again, Joan!" Flamel shouted. "Fire again!"

"I cannot." The tiny Frenchwoman was gray with exhaustion. "The arrows are shaped from my aura. I have nothing left."

The gargoyles pressed in, closer and closer, stone grinding and scraping as they shuffled on. Their range of movement was limited; some had claws and teeth, others horns or barbed tails, but they would simply crush the humans.

Josh picked up a small round grotesque that was so weathered it was little more than a squat lump of stone and heaved it back into the mass of creatures. It struck a gargoyle, and both shattered. He winced with the sound, but he also realized that they could be destroyed. Pressing his hands against his ears, he squinted at the broken creature, his Awakened sight taking in every detail. The stone creatures were invulnerable to steel and magic . . . but then he noted that the stone was weathered and fragile. What destroyed stone?

. . . There was a flash of memory . . . except it wasn't his memory . . . of an ancient city, walls crumbling, pulverized to dust . . .

"I've got an idea," he shouted.

"Make it a good one," Saint-Germain called. "Is it magic?"

"It's basic chemistry." Josh looked at Saint-Germain. "Francis, how hot can you make your fire?"

"Very hot."

"Sophie, how cold a wind can you create?"

"Very cold," she said, nodding. She suddenly knew what

451

her brother was suggesting: she'd done the same experiment in chemistry class.

"Do it now," Josh shouted.

A carved dragon with a chipped bat's wing lurched forward. Saint-Germain unleashed the full force of his Fire magic against the creature's head, bathing it in flame, baking it cherry red. And then Sophie let loose a puff of arctic air.

The dragon's head cracked and exploded into dust.

"Hot and cold," Josh shouted, "hot and cold."

"Expansion and contraction," Nicholas said with a shaky laugh. He looked up to where Dee's head was just visible over the edge of the roof. "One of the basic principles of alchemy."

Saint-Germain bathed a boar galloping toward them in scalding heat, and Sophie washed icy air over it. Its legs snapped off.

"Hotter!" Josh shouted. "It needs to be hotter. And yours need to be colder," he said to his sister.

"I'll try," she whispered. Her eyes were already leaden with exhaustion. "I don't know how much more I can do." She looked at her brother. "Help me," she said. "Let me draw on your strength."

Josh stood behind Sophie and placed both hands on her shoulders. Silver and gold auras sparked alight, mixing, entwining. Realizing what they were doing, Joan immediately gripped her husband's shoulders and both their auras—red and silver—crackled around them. When Saint-Germain shot a plume of fire over the approaching gargoyles, it was white-hot, strong enough to start melting the stones even before subarctic freezing winds and icy fog rolled from Sophie's hands. Saint-Germain turned in a slow circle, and Sophie followed him. First stone cracked, ancient brick exploded, and rock melted beneath the intense heat, but when the icy winds followed, the effect was dramatic. The hot stone statues exploded and split apart, shattering into gritty, stinging dust. The first row fell, and then the next and the next, until a wall of shattered and cracked stone built up in a circle around the trapped humans.

And when Saint-Germain and Joan slumped, Sophie and Josh continued, blasting icy air over the few remaining creatures. Because the gargoyles had spent centuries as water spouts, the stone was soft and porous. Using her brother's energy to boost her powers, Sophie froze the moisture trapped within the stone and the creatures shattered.

"The two that are one," Nicholas Flamel whispered, crouching exhausted on the cobblestones. He looked at Sophie and Josh, their auras blazing wildly about them, silver and gold intermixed, traces of ancient armor visible against their skin. Their power was incredible—and seemingly inexhaustible. He knew that power like this could control, reshape or even destroy the world.

And as the last monstrous gargoyle exploded to dust and the twins' auras faded away, the Alchemyst found himself wondering for the first time if Awakening them had been the correct decision.

✧　✧　✧

On top of Notre Dame, Dee and Machiavelli watched as Flamel and the others picked their way through the smoking piles of masonry, heading in the direction of the bridge.

"We are in so much trouble," Machiavelli said through gritted teeth. The arrow had disappeared from his thigh, but his leg was still numb.

"We?" Dee said lightly. "This, all this, is entirely your fault, Niccolò. Or at least, that's what my report will say. And you know what will happen then, don't you?"

Machiavelli straightened and stood, leaning against the stonework, favoring his injured leg. "My report will differ."

"No one will believe you," Dee said confidently, turning away. "Everyone knows you are the master of lies."

Machiavelli reached into his pocket and pulled out a small digital tape recorder. "Well then, it's lucky I have everything you said on tape." He tapped the recorder. "Voice activated. It recorded every word you spoke to me."

Dee stopped. He slowly turned to face the Italian and looked at the slender tape recorder. "Every word?" he asked.

"Every word." Machiavelli said grimly. "I think the Elders will believe my report."

Dee stared at the Italian for a heartbeat before nodding. "What do you want?"

Machiavelli nodded at the devastation below. His smile was terrifying. "Look at what the twins can do . . . and they're barely Awakened, and not even fully trained."

"What are you suggesting?" Dee asked.

"Between us, you and I have access to extraordinary resources. Working together—rather than against one another—

we should be able to find the twins, capture them and train them."

"Train them!"

Machiavelli's eyes started to glitter. "They are the twins of legend. 'The two that are one, the one that is all.' Once they've mastered all the elemental magics, they will be unstoppable." His smile turned feral. "Whoever controls them controls the world."

The Magician turned to squint across the square to where Flamel was just visible through the pall of dust and grit. "You think the Alchemyst knows this?"

Machiavelli's laugh was bitter. "Of course he knows. Why else do you think he's training them!"

MONDAY. *4th June*

CHAPTER FIFTY-FIVE

At precisely 12:13, the Eurostar train pulled out of Gare du Nord station and began the two-hour-twenty-minute journey into London's St. Pancras International Station.

Nicholas Flamel sat facing Sophie and Josh across a table in Business Premier Class. Saint-Germain had bought the tickets using an untraceable credit card and had supplied them with French passports that came complete with photographs that looked nothing like the twins, while Nicholas's passport photograph was that of a young man with a full head of jet-black hair. "Tell them you've aged a lot in the past few years," Saint-Germain said with a grin. Joan of Arc had spent the morning shopping and had presented Sophie and Josh each with a backpack filled with clothes and toiletries. When Josh had opened his, he'd discovered the small laptop Saint-Germain had given him the day before. Was it only yesterday? It seemed so long ago.

Nicholas spread out the newspapers as the train left the station and pulled on a pair of cheap reading glasses he'd bought at a drugstore. He held up *Le Monde* so that the twins could see the front page; it carried a picture of the devastation caused by Nidhogg.

"It says here," Nicholas read slowly, "that a section of the catacombs collapsed." He turned the page. There was a half-page picture of piles of shattered stone in the roped-off square before Notre Dame Cathedral. " 'Experts are claiming that the collapse and disintegration of some of Paris's most famous gargoyles and grotesques was caused by acid rain that weakened the structures. The two events are unconnected,' " he read, and closed the paper.

"So you were right," Sophie said, exhaustion etched onto her face even though she'd slept for nearly ten hours. "Dee and Machiavelli have managed to cover it up." She looked out the window as the train click-clacked across a maze of interconnecting lines. "A monster walked through Paris yesterday, gargoyles climbed down off a building . . . and yet there's nothing in the papers. It's like it never happened."

"But it did happen," Flamel said seriously. "And you learned the Magic of Fire and Josh's powers were Awakened. And yesterday you discovered just how powerful the two of you are together."

"And Scathach died," Josh said bitterly.

The blank look of surprise on Flamel's face confused and annoyed Josh. He looked at his sister, then back at Nicholas. "Scatty," he said angrily. "Remember her? She was drowned in the Seine."

460

"Drowned?" Flamel smiled, and the new lines at the corners of his eyes and across his forehead deepened. "She's a vampire, Josh," he said gently. "She doesn't need to breathe air. I'll bet she was mad, though; she hates getting wet," he added. "Poor Dagon: he didn't stand a chance." He sank back into the comfortable seat and closed his eyes. "We've one brief stop to make outside London, then we'll use the map of the ley lines to get back to San Francisco, and Perenelle."

"Why are we going to England?" Josh asked.

"We're going to see the oldest immortal human in the world," the Alchemyst said. "I'm going to try and persuade him to train you both in the Magic of Water."

"Who is it?" Josh asked, reaching for his laptop. The first-class carriages had a wireless network.

"Gilgamesh the King."

End of Book Two

The Catacombs of Paris that Sophie and Josh explore really exist, as does the extraordinary sewer system, which comes, as Machiavelli observes, complete with street signs. Although Paris receives millions of visitors a year, many are unaware of the vast network of tunnels below the city.

Officially, they are called *"les carrières de Paris,"* the quarries of Paris, but they are commonly called the catacombs, and they are one of the wonders of the city. The sights the twins encounter in the catacombs—the walls of bones, the spectacular arrangements of skulls—are open to the public. They date to the eighteenth century, when all the bodies and bones in the overflowing Cimetière des Innocents were exhumed and transported to the limestone tunnels and caverns. More bodies from other cemeteries followed, and it is now estimated that there are as many as seven million bodies in this bizarre graveyard. No one knows who created the extraordinary and artistic arrangements of bones; perhaps a workman wanted to fashion a monument to the dead who would no longer have tombstones to mark their graves. The walls, made entirely of human bones, many inset with a pattern of skulls, are suitably eerie and, in some cases, have been lit for dramatic effect.

The Romans were probably the first to quarry limestone from the ground to build what would become Lutetia, the earliest Roman settlement on the Ile de la Cité. Where Notre Dame Cathedral now stands, there was once a monument to the Roman god Jupiter. From about the tenth century onward, limestone was extensively mined from the quarries to create the city walls and to build Notre Dame and the original Louvre palace. The catacombs have long been used for storage by smugglers and have provided shelter for many homeless. More recently, both the German army and the French Resistance had bases in the tunnels during World War II. In this century, illegal art galleries and even a movie theater have been found deep underground by the cataflics, the police unit who patrol underground.

Officially, the catacombs are called the Ossuary of Denfert Rochereau, and the entrance is directly across from the Denfert Rochereau Metro station. Only a small section is open to the public; the tunnels are treacherous, narrow, and prone to flooding and are riddled with potholes and wells.

And are the ideal hiding place for a Sleeping God.

A special preview of

☿ ☽ ♏ ⊕ ♃ ♓ THE ▽ ♀ ☽ ♏ ❀ SORCERESS

The Secrets of the Immortal
Nicholas Flamel

BOOK 3

MONDAY. *4th June*

CHAPTER ONE

"I think I see them."

The young man in the green parka standing directly beneath the huge circular clock in St. Pancras station took the phone away from his ear and checked a blurred jpeg on the rectangular screen. The English Magician had sent the image a couple of hours ago: date-stamped June 04, 11.59.00, its colors washed and faded, the grainy picture looked like it had been taken by an overhead security camera. It showed an older man with short gray hair, accompanied by two fair teens, climbing onto a train.

Rising up on his toes, the young man scanned the station for the trio he'd briefly glimpsed. For a moment he thought he'd lost them in the milling crowd, but even if he had, they wouldn't get far; one of his sisters was downstairs, and another was on the street outside, watching the entrance.

Now, where had the old man and the teenagers gone?

Narrow pinched nostrils flared as he sorted through the countless scents in the station. He identified and dismissed the mixed stink of too many humani, the myriad perfumes and deodorants, the gels and pastes, the greasy odor of fried food from the station's restaurants, the richer aroma of coffee, and the metallic oily tang of the train engines and carriages. Nostrils opened unnaturally wide as he closed his eyes and tilted his head back. The odors he was seeking were older, wilder, unnatural. . . .

There!

Mint: just the merest suggestion.

Orange: no more than the vaguest hint.

Vanilla: little more than a trace.

Hidden behind small rectangular sunglasses, his blue-black pupils dilated. He sniffed the air, tracing the gossamer threads of scent through the vast train station. He had them now!

The older man from the image on his phone was striding down the station concourse directly toward him. He was wearing black jeans and a scuffed leather jacket and carried a small overnight case in his left hand. And just as in the picture taken earlier, he was followed by two blond teenagers alike enough to be brother and sister. The boy was taller than the girl, and they both wore backpacks.

The young man snapped a quick picture with his cell phone camera and sent it to Dr. John Dee. Although he had nothing but contempt for the English Magician, there was no point in making an enemy of him. Dee was the agent of one of the more senior and certainly the most dangerous of all the Dark Elders.

Pulling the hood of his green parka over his head, the young man turned away as the trio drew near him, and dialed his sister, who was waiting downstairs. "It's definitely Flamel and the twins," he murmured into the phone, speaking the ancient language that had eventually become Gaelic. "They're heading in your direction. We'll take them when they get onto Euston Road."

Snapping his phone shut, the young man in the hooded parka set off after the Alchemyst and the American twins. He moved easily through the early-afternoon crowd, looking like just another teenager, anonymous and unnoticed in his sloppy jeans, scuffed sneakers and overlarge coat, his head and face concealed by a hood, eyes invisible behind the dark sunglasses.

Despite his appearance, however, the young man had never been remotely human. He and his sisters had first come to this land when it was still joined to the European main-land, and for generations they had been worshipped as gods. He bitterly resented being ordered around by Dee—who was, after all, nothing more than a humani. But the English Magician had promised the hooded boy a delectable prize: Nicholas Flamel, the legendary Alchemyst. Dee's instructions were clear; the boy and his sisters could have Flamel, but the twins must not be touched. The boy's lips twisted. His sisters would easily capture the twins, while he would have the honor of killing Flamel. A coal black tongue darted out of the corner of his mouth to lick his lips at the thought. They would feast off the Alchemyst for weeks. And, of course, they would keep the tastiest morsels for Mother.

Nicholas Flamel slowed, allowing Sophie and Josh to catch up with him. Forcing a smile, he pointed to the thirty-foot-tall bronze statue of a couple embracing beneath the clock. "It's called *The Meeting Place*," he said loudly, and then added in a whisper, "We're being followed." Still smiling, he leaned into Josh and murmured, "Don't even think about turning around."

"Who?" Sophie asked.

"What?" Josh said tightly. He was feeling nauseous and dizzy; his newly Awakened senses were overwhelmed by the scents and sounds of the train station. A throbbing headache pulsed at the base of his skull, and the light was so bright he wished he had a pair of sunglasses.

"Yes—'What?' is the better question," Nicholas said grimly. He raised a finger to point to the clock, as if he were talking about it. "I'm not sure what's here," he admitted. "Something ancient. I felt it the moment we stepped off the train."

"Felt it?" Josh asked, disoriented, and getting more confused by the second. He hadn't felt this sick since he'd got heatstroke in the Mojave Desert.

"A tingle, like an itch. My aura reacted to the aura of whoever—whatever—is here. When you have a little more control of your own auras, you'll be able to feel the same."

Tilting her head back, as if she were admiring the metal-

and-glass latticework ceiling, Sophie slowly turned. Crowds swirled around them. Most seemed to be locals—commuters—though there were plenty of tourists, many stopping to have their pictures taken in front of *The Meeting Place* statue or with the huge clock in the background. No one seemed to be paying her and her companions any particular attention.

"What will we do?" Josh asked. He was starting to feel panicked. "I can boost Sophie's powers," he babbled, "just like I did in Paris—"

"No," Flamel snapped, gripping Josh's arm with iron fingers. "From now on, you can only use your powers as an absolute last resort. As soon as you activate your aura, you will alert every Elder, Next Generation and immortal within a ten-mile radius to your presence. And here, in England, just about every immortal you encounter is allied with the Dark Elders. Also, in this land, it could awaken others, creatures best left sleeping."

"But you said we're being followed," Sophie protested. "That means Dee already knows we're here."

Flamel urged the twins to the left, away from the statue, hurrying them toward the exit. "I would imagine there are watchers in every airport, seaport and railway station across Europe. Although Dee might have suspected that we'd head to London; the instant either of you activates your aura, he'll know for certain."

"And what will he do then?" Josh asked, turning to look at Flamel. In the harsh overhead lights, the new lines on the Alchemyst's forehead and around his eyes were sharp.

Flamel shrugged. "Who knows what he is capable of

doing. He is desperate, and desperate men do terrible things. Remember, he was on top of Notre Dame. He was prepared to destroy the ancient building just to stop you . . . prepared to kill you to prevent you leaving Paris."

Josh shook his head, confused. "But that's what I don't understand—I thought he wanted us alive."

Flamel sighed. "Dee is a necromancer. It is a foul and horrible art that involves artificially activating a dead body's aura and bringing that body back to life."

An icy coldness washed over Josh at the thought. "You're saying he would have killed us and brought us back to life?"

"Yes. As a last resort." Flamel reached out and squeezed the boy's shoulder gently. "Believe me, it is a terrible existence, the merest shadow of life. And remember, Dee saw what you did, so he now has some inkling of your powers. If there were any doubts in his mind that you are the twins of legend, they have vanished. He *has* to have you. He needs you." The Alchemyst poked Josh in the chest. Paper rustled. Beneath his T-shirt, in a cloth bag hanging around his neck, Josh carried the two pages he'd torn from the Codex. "And above all else, he needs those pages."

The group followed the signs for the Euston Road exit, and were swept along by a crowd of commuters heading in the same direction. "I thought you said there would be someone to meet us," Sophie said, looking around.

"Saint-Germain told me he'd try and contact an old friend," Flamel muttered. "Maybe he couldn't get in touch."

They stepped out of the ornate redbrick train station onto

Euston Road and stopped in surprise. When they'd left Paris just over two and a half hours ago, the skies had been cloudless, the temperature already creeping into the seventies, but in London it felt at least ten degrees cooler and it was raining hard. The wind whipping down the road was cold enough to make the twins shiver. They turned and ducked back into the shelter of the station.

And that was when Sophie saw him.

"A boy in a green parka, with the hood pulled up," she said suddenly, turning to Nicholas and concentrating fiercely on his pale eyes. She knew that if she looked away, she would involuntarily glance at the young man who had been hurrying after them. She could still see him from the corner of her eye. He was loitering close to a pillar, staring at the cell phone in his hand, fiddling with it. There was something wrong about the way he was standing. Something unnatural. And she thought she caught the faintest scent of spoiled meat on the air. Her nose wrinkled. Closing her eyes, she concentrated on the odor. "It smells like something rotten, like roadkill."

The smile on the Alchemyst's face grew strained. "Wearing a hood? So, that's who's been following us." The twins heard the slightest tremor in his voice.

"Except he's not a boy, is he?" Sophie asked.

Nicholas shook his head. "Not even close."

Josh took a deep breath. "Well then, do you want me to tell you that there are now two more people wearing green hooded parkas, and they're both heading this way?"

473

"Three?" Flamel whispered in horror. "We've got to go." Grabbing the twins' arms, he pulled them out into the sleeting rain, turned to the right and dragged them down the street.

The rain was so cold it took Josh's breath away. Pellets of hard water stung his face. Finally, Flamel pulled both twins into an alley, out of the downpour. Josh stood catching his breath. He brushed his hair back out of his eyes and looked at the Alchemyst. "Who are they?" he demanded.

"The Hooded Ones," the Alchemyst said bitterly. "Dee must be desperate, and more powerful than I thought if he can command them. They are the Genii Cucullati."

"Great," Josh said. "That tells me everything I need to know." He looked at his sister. "Have you ever heard . . . ," he began, and then stopped, seeing the expression on her face. "You have!"

Sophie shivered as the Witch of Endor's memories flickered at the edges of her consciousness. She felt something sour at the back of her throat, and her stomach twisted in disgust. The Witch of Endor had known the Genii Cucullati—and she had loathed them. Sophie turned to her brother and explained. "Flesh eaters."

Have you read them all?

BOOK 1 – THE ALCHEMYST

The truth: Nicholas Flamel was born in Paris on September 28, 1330. Nearly 700 years later, he is acknowledged as the greatest Alchemyst of his day. It is said that he discovered the secret of eternal life. The records show that he died in 1418. But his tomb is empty.

The legend: Nicholas Flamel lives. But only because he has been making the elixir of life for centuries. The secret of eternal life is hidden within the book he protects – the Book of Abraham the Mage. It's the most powerful book that has ever existed. In the wrong hands, it will destroy the world. That's exactly what Dr John Dee plans to do when he steals it. Humankind won't know what's happening until it's too late. And if the prophecy is right, Sophie and Josh Newman are the only ones with the power to save the world as we know it.

BOOK 3 – THE SORCERESS

Without the Codex, Nicholas Flamel has lost the means to create the Elixir of Life, which makes him immortal and he grows weaker with each passing day. Perenelle is trapped in Alcatraz and Scatty has gone missing, leaving the group without protection. Josh and Sophie have fled to London with Nicholas, looking for help. The twins need to learn the Magic of Water. That means they need to find Gilgamesh the King and he is said to be quite, quite insane . . .

BOOK 4 – THE NECROMANCER

Arriving back in San Francisco, Josh and Sophie are both more confused than ever about their future. Neither of them has mastered the magic they'll need to protect themselves from the Dark Elders, they've lost Scatty and they're still being pursued by Dr John Dee. Most disturbing of all, however, is that now they must ask themselves, can they trust Nicholas Flamel? Can they trust anyone?

BOOK 5 – THE WARLOCK

Josh and Sophie Newman, the twins of prophecy, have been divided and the end is finally beginning. With most of their allies – Scatty, Joan of Arc, Saint Germain, and others all occupied elsewhere, Sophie is on her own with the ever-weakening Nicholas and Perenelle Flamel. She must find an immortal to teach her Earth Magic. The surprise is that she will find her teacher in the most ordinary of places . . .

The Catacombs of Paris that Sophie and Josh explore really exist, as does the extraordinary sewer system, which comes, as Machiavelli observes, complete with street signs. Although Paris receives millions of visitors a year, many are unaware of the vast network of tunnels below the city.

Officially, they are called *"les carrières de Paris,"* the quarries of Paris, but they are commonly called the catacombs, and they are one of the wonders of the city. The sights the twins encounter in the catacombs—the walls of bones, the spectacular arrangements of skulls—are open to the public. They date to the eighteenth century, when all the bodies and bones in the overflowing Cimetière des Innocents were exhumed and transported to the limestone tunnels and caverns. More bodies from other cemeteries followed, and it is now estimated that there are as many as seven million bodies in this bizarre graveyard. No one knows who created the extraordinary and artistic arrangements of bones; perhaps a workman wanted to fashion a monument to the dead who would no longer have tombstones to mark their graves. The walls, made entirely of human bones, many inset with a pattern of skulls, are suitably eerie and, in some cases, have been lit for dramatic effect.

The Romans were probably the first to quarry limestone from the ground to build what would become Lutetia, the earliest Roman settlement on the Ile de la Cité. Where Notre Dame Cathedral now stands, there was once a monument to the Roman god Jupiter. From about the tenth century onward, limestone was extensively mined from the quarries to create the city walls and to build Notre Dame and the original Louvre palace. The catacombs have long been used for storage by smugglers and have provided shelter for many homeless. More recently, both the German army and the French Resistance had bases in the tunnels during World War II. In this century, illegal art galleries and even a movie theater have been found deep underground by the cataflics, the police unit who patrol underground.

Officially, the catacombs are called the Ossuary of Denfert Rochereau, and the entrance is directly across from the Denfert Rochereau Metro station. Only a small section is open to the public; the tunnels are treacherous, narrow, and prone to flooding and are riddled with potholes and wells.

And are the ideal hiding place for a Sleeping God.

Acknowledgements

The list grows ever longer, but *The Magician* would not have happened without the support of so many people . . .

Krista Marino, Beverly Horowitz, Jocelyn Lange and Christine Labov at Delacorte Press, without whose help, patience, perseverance . . .

Barry Krost at BKM and Frank Weimann at the Literary Group, for continued support and advice . . .

A particular mention must go to:

Libby Lavella, who gave Perenelle a voice . . .

Sarah Baczewski, who gives the best notes . . .

Jeromy Robert, who created the image . . .

Michael Carroll, who reads it first and last . . .

And finally there are:

Claudette, Brooks, Robin, Mitch, Chris, Elaine, David, Judith, Trista, Cappy, Andrea, Ron and, of course, Ahmet, for everything else!

Now, I know I've forgotten someone. . . .

About Michael Scott

Irish-born Michael Scott began writing over twenty-five years ago, and is one of Ireland's most successful and prolific authors, with over one hundred titles to his credit, spanning a variety of genres, including Fantasy, Science Fiction and Folklore. He writes for both adults and young adults and is published in thirty-eight countries, in over twenty languages.

The first five books in Michael Scott's six part epic fantasy series, *The Secrets Of The Immortal Nicholas Flamel* have all been *New York Times* bestsellers, and the sixth book, The Enchantress, will be published in May 2012.

Michael Scott is considered one of the authorities on the folklore of the Celtic lands. His collections, *Irish Folk & Fairy Tales*, *Irish Myths & Legends* and *Irish Ghosts & Hauntings* have remained continuously in print for the past twenty years and are now included amongst the definitive and most-quoted works on the subject.

The Irish Times hailed him as "the King of Fantasy in these Isles." Praised for his "unparalleled contribution to children's literature," by the Guide to Children's Books, Michael Scott was the Writer in Residence during Dublin's tenure as European City of Culture in 1991, and was featured in the 2006 edition of Who's Who in Ireland as one of the "1000 most significant Irish."

For more information on Michael Scott,
please visit his website at: **www.dillonscott.com**.

HE HOLDS THE SECRET THAT CAN END THE WORLD...

Nicholas Flamel was born in Paris in 1330.
Legend has it that the Alchemyst discovered the secret
of eternal life – and that his tomb lies empty.

The legend is true . . .

Nicholas and his wife Perenelle have survived for almost seven
centuries, thanks to the elixir of life. Their secret lies within the pages
of a powerful book, the book of Abraham the Mage - a secret that
they must protect at all costs. In the wrong hands, the
book would destroy the world.

As Dr John Dee well knows. Desperate for ultimate power,
Dee and the Dark Elders will hunt for the book at all costs – and
humanity won't know what has hit it until it's too late.

Only two people have the power to stop Dee – the mythical twins
of legend. Nicholas and Perenelle must find them before Dee – and
suddenly, the lives of fifteen-year-old Josh and Sophie Newman
are thrown into a whirlwind of dark magic and danger.

DARKNESS APPROACHES...

*P*aris has fallen: John Dee's magic has reduced the city to a smoking heap of rubble and ash but his mission to find the Newman twins has failed. Josh and Sophie still have the missing pages of the book of Abraham the Mage and the Dark Elders need these for the Final Summoning which will herald the destruction of the human race.

NICHOLAS FLAMEL knows he must protect Josh and Sophie but he grows older and weaker every day. His only hope is the power of Clarent – twin sword to Excalibur. But Clarent's power comes at great cost – it is almost impossible to wield the blade without its evil seeping into the soul . . .

What price must be paid to protect the twins
and defeat the Dark Elders?

TRUST NO ONE...

Josh and Sophie Newman have finally made it home – but San Francisco is no longer a safe haven. They have not yet mastered the magic they desperately need for protection against the Dark Elders, and Dr John Dee is still hunting them down. Worse still, they are no longer sure if they can trust **NICHOLAS FLAMEL** – or anyone.

Perenelle has escaped from Alcatraz, but she was not the only powerful weapon hidden on the island – an army of monsters is about to be unleashed on San Francisco. With their powers weakening by the hour, the Flamels know that this battle may kill them both.

Having failed to retrieve the missing pages of the Codex for the Elders, Dee is now an outlaw. But he has a plan – to raise the Mother of the Gods from the dead. To achieve this, he must train a necromancer. And the twins of legend will make the perfect pupils . . .